I0581913

# BRODY

## The LaRouge Triplets

ELLIE MASTERS

JEM Publishing

Copyright © 2021 Ellie Masters
*BRODY*
*THE LAROUGE TRIPLETS*
All rights reserved.

This copy is intended for the original purchaser of this print book ONLY. No part of this print book may be reproduced, scanned, transmitted, or distributed in any printed, mechanical, or electronic form without prior written permission from Ellie Masters or JEM Publishing except in the case of brief quotations embodied in critical articles or reviews. This book is licensed for your personal enjoyment only. Please do not participate in or encourage piracy of copyrighted materials in violation of the author's rights. This book may not be re-sold or given away to other people. If you would like to share this book with another person, please purchase an additional copy for each person you share it with. If you are reading this book and did not purchase it, or it was not purchased for your use only, then you should return it to the seller and purchase your own copy. Thank you for respecting the author's work.

Image/art disclaimer: Licensed material is being used for illustrative purposes only. Any person depicted in the licensed material is a model.

Editor: Erin Toland

Proofreader: Roxane Leblanc

Interior Design/Formatting: Ellie Masters

Published in the United States of America

*JEM Publishing*

This is a work of fiction. While reference might be made to actual historical events or existing locations, the names, characters, businesses, places, and incidents are either the product of the author's imagination or are used fictitiously, and any resemblance to actual persons, living or dead, business establishments, events, or locales is entirely coincidental.

ISBN: 978-1-952625-94-7

 Created with Vellum

# Dedication

*This book is dedicated to my one and only—my amazing and wonderful husband.*

# Books by Ellie Masters

The LIGHTER SIDE

Ellie Masters is the lighter side of the Jet & Ellie Masters writing duo! You will find Contemporary Romance, Military Romance, Romantic Suspense, Billionaire Romance, and Rock Star Romance in Ellie's Works.

***YOU CAN FIND ELLIE'S BOOKS HERE:***
***ELLIEMASTERS.COM/BOOKS***

### Military Romance

### Guardian Hostage Rescue Specialists

*Rescuing Melissa*

(Get a FREE copy of Rescuing Melissa

when you join Ellie's Newsletter)

### Alpha Team

*Rescuing Zoe*

*Rescuing Moira*

*Rescuing Eve*

*Rescuing Lily*

*Rescuing Jinx*

*Rescuing Maria*

### Bravo Team

*Rescuing Angie*

*Rescuing Isabelle*

*Rescuing Carmen*

*Rescuing Rosalie*

*Rescuing Kaye*

*Cara's Protector*

*Rescuing Barbi*

### Charlie Team

*Rescuing Rebel*

*Rescuing Stitch*

### Military Romance

### Guardian Personal Protection Specialists

*Sybil's Protector*

*Lyra's Protector*

### The One I Want Series

### (Small Town, Military Heroes)

### By Jet & Ellie Masters

EACH BOOK IN THIS SERIES CAN BE READ AS A STANDALONE AND IS ABOUT A DIFFERENT COUPLE WITH AN HEA.

*Saving Abby*

*Saving Ariel*

*Saving Brie*

*Saving Cate*

*Saving Dani*

*Saving Jen*

### Rockstar Romance

### The Angel Fire Rock Romance Series

EACH BOOK IN THIS SERIES CAN BE READ AS A STANDALONE AND IS ABOUT A DIFFERENT COUPLE WITH AN HEA. IT IS RECOMMENDED THEY ARE READ IN ORDER.

*Ashes to New (prequel)*

*Heart's Insanity (book 1)*

*Heart's Desire (book 2)*

*Heart's Collide (book 3)*

*Hearts Divided (book 4)*

*Hearts Entwined (book5)*

*Forest's FALL (book 6)*

*Hearts The Last Beat (book7)*

### *The LaRouge Triplets*

*Asher*

*Brody*

*Cage*

### *Billionaire Romance*

### *Billionaire Boys Club*

*Hawke*

*Richard*

### *Contemporary Romance*

*Cocky Captain*

### *Romantic Suspense*

EACH BOOK IS A STANDALONE NOVEL.

*The Starling*

*~AND~*

### **Science Fiction**

*Ellie Masters writing as L.A. Warren*

*Vendel Rising: a Science Fiction Serialized Novel*

# Grab the First Book in The Guardian Hostage Rescue Specialists Series for Free

https://elliemasters.com/RescuingMelissa

ONE

## Brody

A FIVE-INCH STILETTO WHIZZES PAST MY EAR. THROWN WITH surprising aim, I barely dodge the flying projectile before it strikes the wall behind me. It hits hard, leaving a mark. A smirk tugs at the corner of my lips.

"Nice shot." I finish tying my tie and tug at my cufflinks.

"I missed." The leggy blonde reaches for the matching shoe.

"Gold star for effort, babe, and honorable mention for aim. Doesn't change anything. Time to go." I hook a thumb toward the door.

"You're really kicking me out?"

"Yes."

The matching shoe follows, but this time I snatch it out of the air. Damn, but I'm going to miss Whatever-her-name-is. With legs that go for miles and creamy thighs a man could lose himself in, she entertained me for hours, but I'm ready to call it a night.

"You heard me…" I close the distance between us. Her eyes grow wide and her pupils dilate. I might be done, but she's turned the fuck on. I hand her back her shoes, knowing she'll likely throw them at me again before we're through. Too damn predictable.

"Baby…" Her pert little mouth, so skillful at swallowing me whole, opens on a breathy moan. She's moments from either giving me a piece of her mind or throwing whatever self-respect she has left out the door to beg for one more fuck. I'm shameless enough to consider it.

"Uh-uh." I point to the door again.

"You can't be serious?" She leans back and sprawls on the bed. Tits in the air, she arches her back. Her toned legs part to reveal a glistening pussy which is still swollen from when I was buried balls deep inside of it. "Tell me you don't want more of this, baby?"

"I don't. We're done, hun." I no longer care what she has to offer. She's joined the ranks of all the other meaningless women passing through my bed. Another forgettable face. Another unmemorable fuck. I've had my fill, and I'm ready to move on.

Her lower lip trembles, and I brace for the avalanche of emotions that always comes next. "We had fun, didn't we?"

"Yeah, sweetie, we had fun." I gesture toward the door again. How many times is she going to make me ask? I don't have the patience for this shit.

"You're really kicking me out?" Her eyes narrow as it sinks in.

She thinks I'm playing some game.

The thing is, I'm not.

"You had fun. I had fun. Time to quit while you're ahead, don't you think?"

Her brows tug together. She wants to argue, but she won't win. I'm the man who fucks. I never date. My reputation precedes me, and even though women know it, they still flock to me. Each one believes she'll tame me. Thing is, I don't need to be tamed. As for why they keep coming, I think it's for the prestige of bagging the unattainable.

They use me as much as I use them. There's no guilt. Sometimes regret, but no guilt.

I gesture toward the door again. "We had a good time, don't ruin it." I lean against the wall, casually kicking back while my gaze takes a final leisurely stroll down her body.

Luscious lips. Perky tits. Neatly shaved mound. Legs that go on forever and wrapped tight around me as I sought oblivion inside her sensuous heat. She's gorgeous. A perfect ten. And she's one hell of a good fuck. But that's all she is. That's all any of them are.

What the fuck is her name?

She cocks her head and realizes the problem I'm having. The girl is smart.

"For the love of God." She props her hand on her hip and aches her back, displaying those luscious tits to advantage. "Brody La Rouge, you don't remember my name, do you?"

I remember her father's name. Charles Brimble is an investment banker my equity investment firm occasionally does business with. We run in the same social circles. His stunning daughter has been away at college and only just returned to the Bay Area. No longer a child, she's gorgeous and only now dipping her toes in the social waters. I'm the shark that bit first and I fucking swallowed her whole.

"Brandy?" I'm ninety percent confident that's somewhere in the ballpark.

"It's Candice, you fucking asshole."

Okay, I'm way off base.

She looks at her high heels and gives a shake of her head. "But damn if you don't fuck like a goddamn stallion. You sure you're done, because…"

"We're done." I took her every way a man can: pussy, mouth, and finished with her tight little ass. Candice Brimble is an adventurous lover, just kinky enough to keep it interesting. I like that.

"You're a fucking jerk. You know that, don't you?"

"You knew that going in." I fuck without regret, without promises, and always with an expiration date. "Now, it's getting late, and I'm sure your daddy is wondering where his darling angel went. Do you need me to call you a car?" I hitch a thumb over my shoulder, pointing again to the door.

"So, this is it?"

"I never promised anything other than a good time."

I'm very clear about my rules, but somehow these women think they're the one with the magic pussy that will turn this into something it isn't.

Her mouth works silently as she tries to find something to say that will tempt me to keep her. "I'm pretty damn sure I rocked your world. You know you want me to stay." She cups her breasts and offers them to me with an exaggerated pout. She's a good lay but doesn't come close to rocking my world.

"You're a damn good fuck—Candice. You like it rough with a bit of kink on the side. Two things which suit me just fine. Don't ruin this by making a scene."

I don't date. I fuck, and I move on.

"I could stay." She practically purrs. "I'll do whatever you want—be whoever you want. I'll beg for you." If I let her stay, I'm pretty sure she'll do whatever I want. The thing is, I'm bored. Another couple of orgasms aren't enough to entice me.

"It's late and I'm tired."

Rule number three: no sleeping over.

When it comes to sex, rules keep things clean.

I lead. They follow. And rule number three states that they never spend the night. That's a level of intimacy I don't want and I never break that rule.

Never.

Her arm rears back and I give a shake of my head. "You don't want to do that, sweetheart. Do I need to restate the rules?"

Her attention shifts to the stiletto in her hand, then back to me. The muscles in her arm twitch. I brace, but she knows she's lost. Tears well up in her eyes.

Here it comes. The drama llama arrives right on schedule.

"Your rules suck." She peeks up at me through her lashes, but now that I've had her, I'm immune to her charms. "Nobody says you can't break them." She slides off the bed to kneel at my feet. Still peeking up at me through her lashes, she reaches for the zipper of my pants. "I seem to remember you liked my mouth—Sir." Ah shit, she's really pushing things.

That's something that only got me off with one girl, a girl I ruined. With Candice, it makes my stomach turn. I grip her wrist and yank her to her feet.

"Get dressed, and get out. This is your last warning, or I'll drag your ass out the door just as you are." It's not an idle threat. I've done it before.

"You wouldn't dare?"

"Have I ever lied to you about what I will or won't do?"

A tiny gasp escapes her as she realizes what I'm going to do. As I turn the doorknob, Candice grabs her dress out of my hand and slips it over her head. Balancing on one foot, she slides on a strappy heel.

"What about a goodbye kiss? Don't I at least get that?"

"Thank you for a lovely evening." She'll get no goodbye kiss from me. I extend my hand and leave it at that.

"You really suck, you know that?"

"I believe you're the one that sucks, and I enjoyed it very much."

"Bastard." She storms out in a huff.

No doubt, the rumor mill will be churning by morning. Candice might think her words will harm me, but they'll only build up the mystique surrounding me even more. I'll have scores of women knocking down my door for their moment to see if the rumors are true.

I love women, but they're too damned predictable. I take bets on when Candice will call on me again. She is a good fuck, and I might just take her for another spin, if I get bored enough.

With a sigh, I close the door and yank my tie free. Don't know what I was thinking when I tightened it down. My fingers go to the buttons of my Oxford shirt and my clothes fall to the floor as I strip naked and head to the shower. The sudden need to wash all trace of Candice Brimble from my body overwhelms me.

Water sluices down my body as I remove all evidence of her. I can't help the disappointment flowing through me. Women are entirely too predictable. Their motivations unerringly the same. They all want to be the one to snag the 'Bad Boy Billionaire.'

Not that I've reached that esteemed status yet, but by the end of the year, that's an exclusive club I'll finally join. Which is why I'm particular about the women I invite into my bed *and* why I have rules.

That scene with Candice is one I've played a hundred times. The truth is none of them care about me. The zeros lining my bank account draw them in. I know what I bring to the equation. The question is, what do they bring? They definitely don't see the real me. Only one girl ever did, and she hates my guts.

I wash myself clean and close my eyes. If only I could find a woman who sees beyond my bank account and the stories I wish were more exaggerated than the truth. I glance down at my cock and vent a frustrated sigh at the ruby-red lipstick left behind.

Candice definitely excelled in that department. For a moment, I think I might get hard again. There's certainly enough frustration running around inside of me to rub another one out, but no matter how I try, my flaccid cock refuses to cooperate. Candice simply isn't masturbatory material. Already, I'm forgetting her face. The shower ends with frustration. It's been a long day and I'm tired.

I didn't lie about that.

I turn off the water and dry myself with a towel. Returning to the bedroom, I notice Candice's black, lacy thong on the foot of the bed. There had once been a time when I collected such trophies, evidence of my prowess, but I'm beyond such things now. I pick up the thong and drop it unceremoniously into the waste bin.

Lying back on the bed, I stretch out and wish myself to sleep. My frustration has been building for weeks. Fucking doesn't seem to be doing the trick in relieving it.

Tomorrow, I'll push my body to exhaustion. It's been too long since one of my marathon runs. Too long since I've been home. Time for a drive into wine country and a visit with my mom.

I draw the cover up over my naked body and send my mother a text.

**Me: Coming home for the weekend. Hoping for your famous pancakes.**
**Mom: Staying the night?**
**Me: Just the day. Need to clear my head.**
**Mom: You work too hard.**
**Me: Is Cage home?**
**Mom: Out on assignment.**
**Me: Then I get his pancakes.**

**Mom: Only if you stay through Sunday.**
**Me: !!!?**
**Mom: I've got a date tomorrow.**
**Me: ????**
**Mom: Yes, a date.**
**Me: Don't do anything I wouldn't do.**
**Mom: Hush!!! You're not too big that I won't swat**
**that ass.**

I laugh at that comment because it's true. Abbie La Rouge takes no shit from her boys.

**Me: No need for a switch. Be safe. XOXO**
**Mom: You're insufferable. Love you, son.**
**Me: Looking forward to pancakes.**

I don't ask about Asher. He runs La Rouge Vineyards and rarely leaves home. I wish Cage was home. I feel the need for some La Rouge triplet shenanigans, but Asher alone will do. Feeling better, I roll over and call it a night.

# TWO

# Grace

—————

At twenty-five, the weight of the world should not sit on my shoulders, but it is, and I'm one straw away from breaking the proverbial camel's back. Yes, I'm aware the weight of the whole world is not, in fact, on my shoulders. I'm allowed to be a bit melodramatic.

The thing is, I'm fighting a losing battle. I see it. I feel it. I just don't know how to accept it.

Mom didn't teach her only child to give up, and while I may lose the vineyards that have been in our family for generations, I refuse to do it while she's still with me. I can't let her die with the added heartbreak my failure brings.

I scrub at my dry eyes and blink away the sting. For the past three hours, I've stared at the computer screen. The numbers don't lie, and they tell the same story no matter how I mess with them. Atwood Estates is in the red, like deep in the red with little chance for recovery.

Three months.

I'm three months from losing everything and I can't afford to fail. Not with Mother's medical bills piling up. Not with a crew of twenty depending on me to meet payroll, and definitely not with the work I need to do to bring in this year's harvest, make next year's wine, and bring in the sales we need to keep the doors open.

No harvest and we're dead. That's my line in the sand. So, I have to meet payroll. There is no alternative.

I glance at the list of banks I've compiled and cross off the last one. We're too deep in debt to be worth the risk of a standard loan. Not that I've exhausted all my possibilities. There are four equity investors who might be willing to pull us out of this shitshow, but that comes at a price. Four names on a very short list.

Five if I'm desperate, like really, really desperate.

I'll do pretty much anything to avoid calling the fifth name on my list.

Brody La Rouge is the devil incarnate, and everybody knows what happens to people who make deals with the devil. I rub at my eyes and lean back with a sigh. The timer on my phone goes off and I push away from the desk.

Mom has faith in me. My business degree says I should be able to do this, but the books don't lie.

I head to the kitchen and pour hot tea for myself and a mug of steaming hot coffee for Mom. Placing both on a tray, I carefully dispense Mother's morning pills. The pile grows with each visit to the doctor. Although that will change when they put her on hospice. I press my fist to my chest as pain rips through me. Tears well in my eyes and I hastily brush them away. I've cried enough in the past three years to last a lifetime. Besides, tears don't change the fact that Mom is dying.

At her last doctor's visit, I saw the truth in her doctor's eyes. We're nearing the end. He prescribed more pills for the unrelenting pain caused by the cancer spreading through her body. There are antibiotics for this current bout of pneumonia, steroid pills she hates because they make her crazy, and vitamin supplements that may or may not be doing anything to boost her immunity. There are so many pills for so many things.

And what are the pills doing?

They heal nothing. All they're doing is letting her die at a slower pace. Not that I wish to hasten her death, but watching her waste away isn't any easier.

I fix a quick breakfast: eggs over-medium, fresh-cut fruit, toast with butter, and a small glass of orange juice. I carry the tray into the guest bedroom. We moved her down here a few months ago when she was no longer able to navigate the stairs. She wants me to move into the master suite, but that feels all kinds of wrong. Like if I move in there, I admit this is the end.

I'm not ready for that.

"Good morning!" Despite the fatigue dragging me down, I inject cheer into my voice for her sake. I'm not the one dying, which means I need to be strong for her.

"Morning." Mom shifts in her bed with a wince.

"Scale of one to ten?" It's become our morning ritual. If her pain is severe enough, I can give her more pills.

"It's a rough morning, luv."

"I need a number, Mom."

"Seven? Eight?" She's a fighter and tough as nails. Seven means nine, and eight?

"Let me grab another…"

"No more pills, sweetie. They make my head foggy." She pats the bed beside her. "Sit with me for a minute."

"Of course." I place the tray with her coffee and all the pills on the bedside table. Gingerly, I cradle my tea while I dip the tea bag in the steaming water. "Did you sleep at all?"

"Sleep's overrated." She swallows her first pill, one of the pain pills, and grimaces as it goes down.

"You need to rest."

"For what?" She sighs and swallows another pill.

"It's going to be a pretty day. Do you want me to move you to the porch?"

I watch her closely. She laboriously drags her gaze from the bed across the room to where a pair of French doors open onto an expansive porch. The weather in Napa is mild year-round, and we're having an exceptional run of blue skies and perfect temperatures. The fresh air will do her good, but the defeat in her expression says enough.

"Or, I can open the curtains? Let the light spill in? Open the windows for the breeze?" Mother loves the songbirds which frequent her garden.

"That sounds lovely." She leans her head back on her pillow with a soft sigh.

We sit in silence while she gathers her strength. My tea grows cold and I set it aside to pull back the long drapes and open the windows. The fresh morning air blows into the room, bringing with it the fragrant aroma of her rose garden and the chirping of the birds playing in the birdbath outside.

Mom sits back and closes her eyes. The pain pills are kicking in. I get her to take the last five pills before she's too drowsy to do so herself. Then I sit with her, holding her hand until she drifts off.

Only then do I let a tear fall.

Once she's asleep, I take the tray to the kitchen and clean up. She didn't eat any of the food. She's wasting away before my eyes and there's nothing I can do to stop it. The overhead bell gives a jingle and I glance up from cleaning the dishes.

"Hey, cupcake!" Uncle Mark waltzes in and gives me a quick hug and a peck on the cheek. "How is she today?"

"Sleeping."

"Did she take her pills?"

"I made sure."

"Did she eat?" He glances at the tray with the uneaten food.

Mom and Uncle Mark are stepbrother and sister but closer than most siblings. I never knew my grandparents. They died when Mom was twenty-one and Mark only sixteen. Mom inherited the land from her mother, got guardianship of her younger brother, and split the winery their parents built together 60/40 with Mark once he turned twenty-one. They've co-managed Atwood Estates ever since. Now, Mark and I co-manage the business. Mom sold me the land, keeping it in her family, for a dollar rather than risking it getting tied up in probate. I'd rather see her well, but it is what it is.

"No, but you're welcome to it, although the eggs are cold and the fruit is warm."

"You should eat." He prods at me. "You're skin and bones."

"I'm good. If you want it, please take it. I'm just going to throw it away."

"If you insist." He heads to the fridge to grab the ketchup bottle. I hold back a groan as he buries the lukewarm eggs in ketchup.

"That's so disgusting." My nose wrinkles.

"It's the only way to eat eggs." He digs in while I finish the dishes. "What's on the agenda today?"

"You tell me?"

My uncle manages the vineyard. He knows everything about the wine business and is slowly teaching me what I need to know. Since Mom got sick, he stepped up to let me focus on Mom's medical appointments and hospitalizations as her cancer progressed.

"You look tired." He pauses with his fork lifted halfway to his mouth. "Not sleeping again?"

"I was going over the books."

"Ah, and that frown is concerning."

"I don't get how we're losing money."

"This is always a lean time of the year. We'll get through. We always do. Once the harvest is done, the grapes pressed, and next year's product is set up, you'll see. Fall brings in the bulk of our orders, not to mention the tourists pick up."

"Our production is down. Sales are down. Our advance orders are down, and I'm afraid we won't make payroll. I know sales will pick up, but I don't know how we'll manage the gap."

"It's been rough with your mom's illness, but I'm sure we can figure something out. Want me to look at the books with you? We can see where we can cut expenses."

"That would be great."

I can't do this without him.

"Don't worry, cupcake." He scoops up the last of the eggs and winks at me. "We'll find a way to make it through."

"Other than laying off half our workers, I don't see how. I've got an appointment with the bank on Saturday to see if we can get an extension. If they call in our debts…"

"They won't. I'll take a look at the books after I check in on your mother."

"I appreciate that." Maybe he'll see something I don't.

Failure weighs me down. In one year, I'll have run the family business into the ground. It survived fire, pestilence, and drought, but I'm the one who will lose it all.

I'm missing something. Production has been steadily decreasing over the past several years. Not that I know anything about production, but something feels off. Mark finishes what's probably his second breakfast and places the dirty dishes in the sink.

"I'm going to check in on Lucy then we'll take a look at those books."

"Okay, but she's resting."

"I won't wake her. I just…" He hangs his head. "It's hard seeing her like this."

I get it. They're close, always have been. I've never seen a pair of siblings closer than my uncle and my mother. He kisses my cheek and goes to check on Mom. I finish the dishes and wonder how I'm going to keep Atwood Estates afloat. My list of equity investors rolls through my head. It'll mean bringing an outside partner into our family business. I don't like that, but desperate times call for desperate measures.

There are precious few family-run wineries left in Napa. Corporations have come in, gobbling up all the land or leasing the vineyards from those unwilling to sell the land.

Small wineries close. Big corporate wins.

After I take care of the dishes, I head back to the study, which has become my new office. I pull up the spreadsheets and stare at them. I peer at the screen, hoping this time I'll see something new that might help. Unfortunately, there's too much red peppering the screen.

I open up the past few years, looking at profit and loss, inventory, stock, and sales. Maybe if I go back far enough, something will jump out at me. I'm good with numbers, but these books are a total mess.

"Hey, cupcake." Uncle Mark comes up behind me and places his hands on my shoulders. I give a little groan as his fingers dig into the tight muscles of my shoulders.

"That feels good." I lean back and surrender to the power of his hands as he works out the knots. He's worked the fields his entire life and has the muscles to prove it.

"Whatcha looking at?"

"Last five years." I gesture toward the screen with its myriad of open files. "I'm just trying to make sense of it all. Profits have been steadily decreasing and I'm trying to figure out why."

"We have highs and lows."

"Why aren't you worried?"

"Because you're smart and talented. I can tell you this past year hasn't been the best, what with the drought. Production is down and that transfers directly to our bottom line."

"What I don't understand is how other costs seem to be rising."

"Welcome to the world of small business." He peeks over my shoulder and glances at the list of equity investors I scrawled on a piece of scrap paper. "What's that?"

I turn my attention to the list of five names, one of which I scratched through last night. I lift the paper for him to see better.

"Equity investors." I worry my lower lip, nibbling at it with my teeth. "Back-up plan."

"Equity investors?" His fingers stop their magical massage. "What do we need them for?"

"If the bank denies me, they might float the cash we need."

"Sounds too good to be true."

"Well, nothing's free. In general, they ask for percent ownership of the company and profits until their equity investment pays out. We'll lose some of our profit, a bit of control, but we won't lose the business." I don't tell him that they often come into the company they're bailing out and make major changes, all in the name of protecting their investment, of course.

"I don't like it. I hate to see you struggle. This was never what you wanted. I wish you'd let me buy you out."

"I'll figure something out." I reach for his hand and give it a light pat. "I'm lucky to have you."

"I know you had other dreams. Your mother's illness changed a lot of things for you. My offer stands. Just say the word."

"I can't let you risk your savings. We'll figure this out. You and me, we're a team now."

"That's right. We're a team." He gives me a squeeze from behind.

"You know—" I turn the computer off, "I've been staring at this for far too long. How about taking me out and showing me how all this works?"

"Sounds like a deal. We can get to the books later." Mark sounds frustrated.

So am I, but staring at the computer isn't helping. I need fresh air and, hopefully, a fresh outlook if I'm going to save this place.

THREE

## Brody

I take off early Saturday morning to make the hour-long trek from the city to La Rouge Vineyards, which nestles up against the hills of Napa Valley.

Clear skies form a blue dome overhead; that deep California blue I've never seen anywhere else. Golden hills stretch out before me rolling inland where they'll bunch together to form the foothills of the Rockies. People not used to the Bay Area see dried, crisped grass, but for those of us who live here, we know those hills turn verdant green in springtime. It's going to be an amazing day for a run.

I'm hoping to get in thirty or forty miles.

When I run, I run.

It's something I've always done; my form of meditation. There's something about pushing the body and the mind to their limits that settles me. I need the challenge, the solitude of a long run, to quiet my thoughts. Most people train for a year to run a marathon. I run one every week. Once a month, I'll do a hundred-miler and burn through exhaustion, punishing my body until it sings with accomplishment or gives up in defeat.

It's a mental game I play with myself.

Once a year, I take part in an ultra-marathon somewhere in the world. It gives me a chance to travel and forces me to keep my brutal training regimen going. Usually, I wake early each day and do something short, five or seven miles. Just enough to get the blood in my body pumping. I will often also take an hour after work to get in more miles a few times a week—short six- to nine-mile jaunts.

After that, I hit the clubs, meeting up with my boss, who's also my best friend, to let off steam and find willing female flesh to lose myself in for the night.

The drive inland is exquisite. I take the top down on my Porsche and let the wind run through my hair. When I pull up to Mom's little cottage, it's a surprise she's not there, especially knowing I was coming. I don't know who this new beau in her life might be, but they'd better not be doing the sleepover thing. At least, not until I can check out whoever caught her eye.

The key is under the rock I painted for her when I was five. I let myself in and place my duffle on the bed of the spare bedroom. A quick change and I'm in my running gear. I head to the kitchen to leave her a note. A thirty-miler sounds like the perfect distraction for my troubled mind. When I hit the kitchen, I find a note Mom left me.

*B-child,*
*Settle in.*
*Will be back before noon—maybe.*
*Love ya,*
*Mom.*

Short and sweet, she doesn't waste words. I scribble a reply telling her I'll be out for a couple of hours on a run. Asher and Cage think I'm crazy with these runs, but it's the perfect way to zone out. I fill the small water bottles that go around my running belt and head out.

Crisp California air welcomes me. I grew up running these roads and know the perfect loop that will challenge my body and reset my mind. I set off, feet pounding the pavement, lungs chugging, heart pumping. My arms swing and my stride lengthens as my body warms up.

I keep to the back roads that remain unpaved. Tourist traffic has only grown over the years, making running on the roads dangerous. Not that I mind. I prefer running on dirt over asphalt.

My run takes me along La Rouge property. I'll make a full circuit of our family's lands by the time I'm done; then I'll head up the forest trail Asher uses for his side business. We have about a score of horses and offer trail rides for eager tourists looking for something other than yet another wine tasting.

The first five miles pass in a blur. The next five, I barely process. My mind zones out, and I'm all about the physical needs keeping my body in motion. Vines cover nearly all the land in the valley, stretching as far as the eye can see.

La Rouge is a moderate player in the local wine scene. We're too small to be corporate. Too big to be considered family owned, even though we are. Our land does well. Asher knows how to get the most from his grapes.

I run past the property lines of two more wineries before making my first turn. I keep to the dirt roads the farming equipment uses and enter the property of Atwood Estates. Unlike La Rouge, it's one of the smaller wineries in town. Like La Rouge, it's family owned, and like always, guilt stabs through me. I'll never forget what I did to Grace Atwood.

My stride lengthens as I get my second wind. Atwood Estate's crop looks good. Surprising, considering how most vineyards struggle with the drought, but I see why. They invested in supplemental irrigation. Drip lines in addition to standard delivery options. Lucy

Atwood is a savvy businesswoman and good friends with my mother. Some might say best friends.

Unlike others who abhor competition, I enjoy seeing their success. Not many of the small vineyards can say the same. Every year, the giants gobble up more and more of the smaller operations.

Nearing the end of their property lines, a cloud of dirt churns up behind a tractor meandering down the dirt road. It pulls to a stop and two people climb down. The diesel engine chugs along, idling, and my attention shifts to the people who climbed down. I squint against the sun. The man sees me and lifts a hand in the air.

"Hey, Asher, out for a run?"

I slow and wave back.

"Hey, Mark, nice to see you, and it's Brody, not Asher."

The curse of being an identical triplet is there's twice the confusion. I get confused with not just Asher but Cage as well. It makes for interesting times, and we definitely take advantage, playing pranks and blaming them on each other. Here, in Napa, I'm mostly confused with Asher. Cage is the absent brother, out traveling the world and making a name for himself with the award-winning photos he takes. The dude is seriously talented.

"Ah, Brody. It's been some time." Mark walks toward me, hand extended in greeting. We shake while my eye shifts to the woman he's with.

Her back is to me and she stiffens when Mark mentions my name. Normally, I wouldn't notice, but she's bending over, and I can't help but admire her heart-shaped ass. The flare of her hips, and all her sexy curves, send my mind straight to the gutter.

"A few months, I'd say." I try to place the woman, certain I've seen her before. "Your vines look healthy." His vines aren't just healthy, they're thriving.

"We're hoping for a record harvest."

The woman turns around. My heart skips a beat when Grace's gaze collides with mine. I can barely breathe as she takes me in.

Does she feel this same pull?

Does she remember me?

The desire to touch her grows stronger with each breath. My fingers itch to skim across her golden skin, to twine in her long, auburn curls, and to see if her lips taste the same as I remember, sweet and innocent, pure and perfectly mine.

I feel like a kid again, experiencing my first crush.

Only Grace wasn't my first crush. She wasn't even the first girl I slept with. No, Grace is something else entirely. She's my first and only mistake, my biggest regret, and now she's back.

It's been years…

I can't help myself. I take half a step before stopping dead in my tracks.

The look on her face radiates pure hatred.

Our past is complicated and that look is well deserved.

She was a gawky freshman, new to high school. I was a senior, sitting at the top of the high school hierarchy. She and I didn't run in the same circles, and I never would have noticed her except she landed a spot on the varsity cheer squad.

The most astonishing girl I'd come across, she was easy to talk to, easy to open up with. She made me laugh and was a lot of fun to be around. She listened well, never once going on and on with vapid conversation about makeup and fashion, like her peers. She knew how to share the quiet and I liked that. I felt comfortable around her.

We connected over the strangest things, and she always had a way of making me see the good in the world. Whenever something brought me down, Grace turned it around and showed me things from a different perspective. She taught me how to be less judgmental of others, and I always admired the purity of her spirit.

Grace Atwood was everything I wanted in a girl and more. Back then, she was all arms and legs, not fully grown into her body, and most definitely lacking the feminine curves she currently rocks. Despite her awkwardness, the girl could move. She flipped that tight body of hers, running circles around the other girls, and while gangly and gawky off the field, she was on fire during her dance and cheer routines. In private, she rocked my world, and for most of my senior year we secretly dated. Hell, we did far more than that. We delved deep, experimenting with things we barely understood. Her sweet submission melded perfectly with my darker desires. We explored so many delicious things. Candice on her knees has nothing on Grace. When Grace went to her knees before me, it was like a sucker punch to the gut along with the headiest thrill I've ever experienced. She was my first experience with that kind of thing, as I was for her. For the two of us, we found our rhythm, and it was the most amazing thing in the world. At least, until I ruined it. Ruined her.

Many of the senior boys stared at her more than we should, which made the other girls jealous. Especially the senior girls who didn't like the upstart freshman who turned their boyfriends' heads. But Grace knew nothing about any of that. She liked everyone and didn't have an evil bone in her body. Not to mention, she only had eyes for me.

But that was Grace.

Even as an awkward girl, she had the ability to turn our heads. Nothing about her was fake. I sensed she was special, and damn if she didn't turn out to be spectacular. *My sweet little sub, I'm so damn sorry.*

She looks nothing like that awkward kid now. Time has been kind to Grace Atwood; a diamond in the rough, that's what she is—the ugly duckling with a heart of gold turned into a graceful swan. All that hidden beauty needed only a bit more time to fully develop. It's been more than ten years since I last saw her, and I feel like a love-struck teen, gawking at her with my mouth open. My body certainly acts the teenage fool. My cock takes notice, growing stiffer by the second. It remembers her. Hungers for her. I cup my hands over my groin.

My biggest regret, she's the innocent I ruined. Too young and too stupid to know what I was doing, I not only broke her heart, I stomped on it in front of the entire school. I humiliated her and walked away with a grin on my face, proud of my conquest and mindless of the destruction I left behind. All that mattered to me, at the time, was my reputation and making a name for myself outside of being one of the La Rouge triplets. It worked.

People talked about Brody The Heartbreaker for months.

I regret all of it.

About to say something, hoping time healed her wounds, she tears her gaze from mine. Grace pivots, kicking up a cloud of dust, and marches away without a backward glance.

Mark, oblivious to the entire exchange, rambles on about his hopes for this year's crop. I deserve her dismissal for the pain I caused, but damn if I don't wish I could go back in time and erase what I did. I'd do anything for a second chance with her.

FOUR

# Grace

---

Seeing Brody La Rouge brings back savage memories from high school, horror stories of the young, innocent, and stupid girl I once was. I thought I moved past all that trauma. Evidently, I haven't, and it doesn't help that Brody looks even more incredible than I remember.

That signature smirk still fills his face. His body, hewn by hard work, steals my breath. Those verdant-green eyes mesmerize me. That perfectly mussed-up hair makes me want to drag my fingers through it as he kisses me senseless. Those incredibly broad shoulders that taper down to a washboard midsection make me want to wrap my arms around him and do nothing other than breathe him in and remember how I had once been happy in his arms.

Damn, but he still holds incredible power over me, even after all these years. I hate him most for that. I yearn to hear that tone in his voice, the one which never failed to flip that switch between us. The one that turned us from innocent boy and girl into something carnal and eager, delicious and forbidden. I squeeze my thighs together and squirm as heat licks between my legs. I hate how my body responds to him. I hate the loss of control.

*Never again, Brody La Rouge. Never again.*

His skintight running outfit highlights each ridge and valley of his washboard abs and draws my eye like the love-struck teen I once was. I hate it, but I shamelessly take the plunge as my gaze moves past his trim waist to linger on the bulge nestled between his powerful thighs.

Like he did in high school, Brody La Rouge renders me speechless. I'm not prepared for the flood of emotions washing through me. A torrent of mixed signals swirling in chaotic dissonance; intense attraction followed by even more vehement hatred. It leaves me dizzy and spinning.

I know his story. I lived through a rather insignificant piece of it.

Insignificant to him.

The world to me.

I remember all the girls who threw themselves at him. The girls he took behind the bleachers, behind the gym, and those infamous La Rouge triplet parties I only ever attended once.

I wasn't the one who drew his eye, at least not at first. His reputation made me cautious, and I kept to my side of the rigid high school social hierarchy as long as I could.

But then I stumbled. And I fell. I fell head over heels for Brody La Rouge.

I bet little has changed for him. He's probably still taking advantage of gorgeous women either too stupid or too frivolous to care about the monster he can be. Desperate hopefuls, they probably believe they'll be the one to snag the un-snaggable. They don't know the truth lurking beneath the surface.

Brody La Rouge is a monster.

I suppress a groan as my eyes continue to wander. I tell myself to stop, but I can't help it.

The years have been kind to him. He's taller than I remember, putting on another couple of inches after high school. He has the same rugged good looks, although they've been refined by the years. He packed on muscle and is trim and fabulous, and every woman's dream. There's more, something unrefined when I knew him, but firmly in place now. Power swirls around him, dangerous, mesmerizing power, and it calls out to me to bend before him and take that magical plunge.

I remember him being a runner, always competing in the long-distance trail events. Looks like that hasn't changed either. I guess little about him has changed, except he's more attractive than I remember, more devastating than before, more—Brody fucking La Rouge.

I hate how he still affects me. I'd like to think I moved beyond my high school crush, but evidently, I haven't. My mind spins with questions.

Does he recognize me?

Does he think about me?

Is he making the same comparisons?

How do I stack up against the gangly teen he knew? I'd like to think I make some impact, but the truth is I meant nothing to him back then and mean nothing to him now.

He was a major player back then, a straight-A asshole for sure. I thought the world of Brody La Rouge until he showed me what an asshole he could be.

I know why women are attracted to him, but after I had my look under the hood, there isn't much to be impressed by. I'll tell any sane woman with half a brain to run and to run fast.

I desperately pray he doesn't remember me, especially since I filled out an application for equity investment from his firm. Although, the chance of my application crossing his desk is zero to none. Evidently, he's pretty high up in the hierarchy of Sterling

Enterprises. I checked. He's the fucking CFO of a multi-billion dollar company.

No surprise. Brody always rises to the top of everything.

After the bank refused to extend our loan, the first thing I did after coming home was to frantically fill out equity investment applications, at least until Uncle Mark asked if I wanted to take a look at our operation. There's so much to learn.

As I stand here looking at Brody, all I see is the boy who destroyed me.

For now, I give him my back. If I'm lucky, our paths will never cross again. Looking at Sterling Enterprise's client list, we're small fish, probably not worth a nibble.

Still, there's a tiny voice inside of me that hopes, but do I really want to be anywhere near Brody La Rouge?

This is why I don't think of the past.

The shame and humiliation from my past bubble to the surface, and I choke on the sob trying to escape my throat. After all these years, Brody still elicits strong, visceral reactions from me.

Attraction. Shame. Desperate love. Intense anger.

Hatred.

My emotions follow an all too familiar path. I'd been an eager freshman who saw my vision of the future me, the woman I wanted to be. I signed up for the debate team—even though I was a freshman. I joined Future Business Leaders of America—even though I was a freshman. I tried out for, and made, the varsity cheer squad because it would look good on my application to Stanford—even though I was a freshman.

That was my downfall.

I should never have joined cheer, but I was obsessive about checking all the boxes and needed something that wasn't totally nerdy to round out my college application.

And I was good. I'd been enrolled in some form of dance or gymnastics since I was three. I had all the moves, could do all the tricks. Making the varsity team as a freshman had me walking on cloud nine. Little did I know it would be the worst decision of my life.

All because of Brody La Rouge.

Like all the girls at school, the La Rouge triplets fascinated me. They were on the football team. I watched them during practice, swooning over them with the rest of the girls. For some reason, my eye gravitated toward Brody, the middle triplet. There was just something about him I couldn't resist. An irresistible pull. An undeniable attraction. A crazy need to be with him.

Where others often confused the three triplets, I could always distinguish Brody from Asher and Cage. There was just something about him that entranced me. I swooned and smiled like all the other girls, but he was a senior, and I was a lowly freshman. In his world, I didn't exist, except when it came to football. The cheer squad practiced on the sidelines while the players hit the field. I got to watch him every day after school, and my fascination grew.

Then he destroyed me.

With that thought, I walk away. Some memories are best left in the past and I certainly don't need him in my life. As soon as I get home, I'm going to pull my application for equity investment from his company.

FIVE

## Brody

After I get Mark to stop talking, I return to my run. Seeing Grace does something to me. My guts twist in knots as my last year in high school runs on a nonstop loop inside my head.

So different from all the other girls, I liked spending time with Grace. She made me feel normal, relaxed, like I could let all the pretense fall away. I was myself around her in a way I couldn't be around any of the other girls. With them, there was this pressure to live up to my reputation, which I did admirably, but Grace never cared about any of that. I took her sweetness, her kindness, and consideration, and I turned it inside out. I destroyed her in the process.

And why?

I'm not proud of who I was. Hell, I'm still that same guy. I stumble and come to a halt as the realization kicks in. I'm still the same rotten bastard I was at seventeen.

Well, shit, if that doesn't sting.

If I hadn't been such a self-centered prick, who could I be now?

It's an unsettling question.

Instead of going the full thirty miles, I take a shortcut and head back to La Rouge Vineyards. The need to talk to my brother overcomes me.

Half an hour later, I jog up our drive.

The new barn seems to be going up without a hitch. It burned down not too long ago, victim of arson and an attempt on Asher's life; his and Evelyn's. The arsonist is still in the wind, running for his life. If any of us get a hold of him before the cops do, there won't be anything left to prosecute, let alone lock up in jail.

I pull to a stop between the barn and the family home. A large covered porch wraps all the way around it. I grew up on that porch; first as a kid sleeping outside with my brothers telling ghost stories and chasing fireflies, later as a preteen shooting the shit about stupid stuff. High school turned that porch into make-out central. The barn, the one that burned, is where we each became a man, although not at the same time.

It was a race to see which of us would lose our virginity first. Asher looked to be the one to close the deal first, but when he came to us bragging about his first time, Cage let it slip that he'd been first. That left me as the only virgin of the three of us. I took care of that immediately. The sad thing is I don't remember who it was.

The door to the new barn stands open, much like its predecessor. The weather's far too perfect out here to keep it shut. The new barn is a good size larger than the previous one. Curious, I head over to investigate.

Looks like Asher's increased the number of stalls and upgraded the dirt floor to stone. The tack room is easily twice as big as before, and he's got something that looks like a classroom set to the side with wooden benches and an old-fashioned chalkboard. High ceilings keep the air circulating, and if it gets too hot, industrial fans high overhead churn the air to keep it flowing.

I check in on our horses. Knight, Spirit, and Chesty come to the front of their stalls snorting hello. I don't get to ride Spirit as much as I'd like, but I have a feeling he's okay with that.

Evelyn seems to have adopted him as her own horse in my absence. I give them each a rub and move on. Asher's added a dozen new stalls, but they stand empty. I'll need to ask him about that. A noise at the far end draws my attention. Knowing what we used to do in the barn growing up, I call out to make my presence known. No need to be walking into something I have no business seeing.

"Hello!" I cup my hands over my mouth and shout.

"Who's that?" A lilting female voice answers. Asher's fiancée, Evelyn Thornton, peeks out from one of the stalls. It takes her a minute as she gives me a good hard look. "Nope. Not a clue. Which one are you?"

Poor Evie had a very interesting introduction to me and Cage. With no idea Asher was the eldest of identical triplets, the morning after her first night at La Rouge, she got handsy and shoved her hands down my pants. I remember the deep scarlet of her cheeks when she realized her hands were on the wrong man's junk.

She then understood Asher had an identical sibling and made her second mistake, thinking we were twins. I may, or may not, have had a bit of fun and sent her out here, when the old barn was still standing, knowing full well Cage was inside. He didn't get his junk felt up like me, but Evie certainly felt the rest of him up. To be honest, Asher is one hell of a lucky man. He wasn't happy with either of us, but we didn't care. As for poor Evie, she took it in stride. That's when we knew she was a keeper.

"I'm the one you got handsy with, luv." I toss her a bone, although I could make her sweat. The thing is, I like Evie. She's cool, and I totally love that she still can't tell Cage and me apart. She can pick Asher out of the three of us, we've tried to fool her, but she knows her man.

"Nice to see you, Brody. How's it hanging?" Evie rolls right on past the fact she didn't know which triplet, apart from her fiancé, I am.

I glance down at my running shorts, which allow absolutely nothing to hang left or right. Everything is nicely tucked up. A smirk turns up the corner of my lips.

"Wanna cop a feel and check me out? Will that help?"

"As if…" She opens the stall door and dusts her hands off on her jeans. "I'm sure there are plenty of ladies willing to feel you up. You don't need me taking the plunge."

"Well, you're one of the few who knows the answer to a very important question."

"And what would that be?"

"Who's got the better package."

"Now, you see, that's unfair."

"Unfair?"

"Seeing how I never felt up your brother, I can't rightly judge who's got the better package."

"I would think you know every inch of my brother's cock."

"I do at that." The corners of her mouth tilt up. "I meant Cage, and do you really want to know what I think?" Her pert lips lift in an impish grin. "I remember feeling something quite limp…"

"You wound me." I press my hand over my heart. "I'd offer a hug, but I'm all sweaty."

"Air hug." She spreads her arms wide and gives a little beat of her arms. "So, what brings you out here? It certainly wasn't to discuss your unimpressive dick size. Did we know you were coming out?"

"Just needed some fresh air. I'm staying with Mom. Didn't want to interfere in your little love nest. And my package is quite impressive —as you should know, considering we're identical triplets."

"Is there ever a moment when you're not thinking about sex?"

"Is there ever a moment Asher doesn't think about sex?"

"Touché. But really, this is your home. You're welcome anytime. You don't have to ask, and you don't have to stay with Abbie if you don't want to." She emphasizes the point.

"And what if the two of you…" I make a rude gesture.

"Why do you think he built the barn as big as he did?" She spins in a circle, taking it all in. "It's the perfect place to have tons of fun with a bit of rope, and you know…" She gives a mischievous wink. This is what I love about Evelyn. Not only can she take our shit, but she can dish it right out.

"I didn't realize it was going to be so much bigger?"

"Are we talking about the barn, or…"

"The barn, wise ass."

"Well, I'm expanding the trail riding business. Taking it over actually. Asher's interested in expanding operations with the winery, but with that and firefighting, he doesn't have the time for it. I'm also offering horse boarding and riding lessons for kids. I heard about this group that uses horses as therapy animals for kids with disabilities and children on the spectrum. We have so much; it feels good to give a little back."

That's an understatement if I ever heard one. Evelyn is an heiress, or was. I guess she's no longer an heiress considering she lost her entire family in a tragic accident. All that inheritance is hers now, and her net worth is in the nine-figure range. The girl is loaded, not that you'd know it.

"Is Asher around?"

"Should be." She glances at her watch. "Or actually, he might be out with George." George is our foreman, responsible for the operations of the vineyard.

"You know where they might be?"

"Not a clue. I can call if you want."

"Nah. I'm going to head in and take a shower, throw on some clean clothes. Mom's supposed to be making pancakes."

"You sure about that?" She props her hand on her hip. "I have a feeling Abbie's not going to make it, so while you're inside, you might as well make yourself useful and whip us up some food."

"Me?"

"You can cook, can't you?" She flashes a wicked grin, knowing full well that Mom taught all three of her boys to take care of themselves in every way. We just choose not to and let her mother us when we come to visit. "I know you're good at whipping up bacon in the pan."

Evelyn's famous groping session occurred in the kitchen. I was making breakfast for everyone, frying bacon actually.

"Do you want bacon?"

"I'd love some. You know where everything is. I'll call Asher and let him know you're here."

I head inside, plucking a few choice tomatoes off the vine, and head to my room to shower and change. Much like Cage, I never fully moved out. In fact, the only person who moved out of the family home is our mother.

After Dad died, she said the house held too many memories. We built her the tiny cottage at the edge of our property, nestled right up against forest lands. She moved out, but the three of us kept everything the same.

We often complain of the triplet curse, but the triplet bond ties us together. We'll always be inseparable. My thoughts turn to Grace Atwood and I can't help but wonder if she's thinking about me. Although why I would think that makes no sense. She's more likely to plot my murder than anything else, but still, I wonder if it's not too late to make up for the sins of the past.

SIX

## Grace

———————

I think about Brody for the rest of the afternoon. If Sterling Enterprises accepts my proposal, I'll be one step too close to the man who destroyed me. I vowed to pull back my application from his firm, but I can't do it. My finger hovers over the button that will withdraw my application, and I sit there wanting to yank it, but I can't afford to be petty.

'*Grudges do more damage to the person holding them than the one they're directed at.*' Those are my mother's words, and I should listen to her wisdom.

I'm bigger than this.

What happened to me is in the past and has no part in my future. Besides, if that capital is what keeps Atwood Estates from going under, I'll take it. My feelings mean nothing when it comes to the livelihood of our workers, and I owe it to them to explore every avenue before admitting defeat.

The alarm on my phone goes off. It's time for Mom's afternoon pills.

I head to the kitchen and pull down all the bottles with all the pills. Mom's had a good day. She was able to rest without the unrelenting pain waking her up. In addition to a glass of juice, I load the tray down with fresh-cut fruit, a handful of pills, and three tiny chocolate bars; whatever I can do to entice her to eat.

She doesn't answer my knock. I give it a second, then head inside. It's bright and airy in her room. The gauze curtains billow in the light breeze blowing through the windows, and a shaft of sunlight spills through the open French doors. The chirps of birds tickle my ears as they frolic in the birdbath outside her window. I try to do as much as I can to make her last days as peaceful as possible.

Not really asleep, her rest is fitful, but it is rest. I take what I can get, focus on the positives.

Mom taught me that.

I'd love to let her enjoy drifting in the moment, but I learned the hard way not to let her miss a scheduled dose of pain medications. I did that, accidentally, one too many times. If I can keep her levels even, she manages the pain. Skip even one dose, and the pain magnifies. Fives turn to tens, and we have a hell of a time beating back the pain to simmer at a seven or eight.

It's been weeks since her pain's been a five. She sits around seven and eight constantly, although I think she's lying to me. After setting down the tray, I sit beside her and take her hand in mine. The skin's nearly translucent with thin, blue veins easily seen. There's the bruising from the IV they placed last week. There's always a bruise marring her delicate flesh. Like the rest of her body, the veins in her hand are fragile and tend to 'blow.' That's what the nurses call it when her IV fails. Her hand is cold, limp, and weak. I'm holding onto the shell of the woman I've loved my entire life.

I hate cancer. I hate everything about it.

"Mom…" I thread my fingers with hers. "You need to take your pills."

She doesn't respond and there's that hitch in my throat. It lasts a second before I realize she's still with me. I hate that sinking feeling when my stomach drops and my breath catches. I've had months, a little more than a year, to prepare myself. Every time I think I'm ready to accept the inevitable, a moment like this comes along.

And I know.

I'll never be ready to say goodbye.

She stirs and takes a breath. "Cupcake?" Her eyes open and a smile curves her lips. "I was dreaming about you." A tear rolls down my cheek at the nickname. She and my uncle are the only ones who call me that.

It's well deserved and comes from the Great Cupcake Massacre. I was five at the time, precocious and determined to be as grown-up as possible. Mom signed up to bake six dozen cupcakes for the church's 4th of July picnic. She included me in everything, and I helped stir the batter, pour the milk into the mix, and set out the tiny paper cups to load up with batter. There wasn't much else I could help with, but I worked hard to do what I could. My reward for being such a good worker was the coveted prize of the very first cupcake that came out of the oven. To this day, I remember the mouth-watering aroma of the batter baking and Mom's smile as she pulled the first batch out of the oven. I remember her setting the hot tray on the counter and telling me not to touch it.

Which I did.

How could I not?

Of course, I burned my fingers and we had to deal with that. Meanwhile, my reward, that hot, delicious cupcake, grew cold.

I cried.

I cried because my fingers hurt. I cried because my cupcake was ruined. I cried when my mom tried to make it all better by allowing me to put the icing on my cold cupcake all by myself, like a grown-up.

Which I did and made a terrible mess of my cupcake, myself, the counter, and the floor when I dropped my cupcake and watched it tumble to land upside down.

I bawled my eyes out.

Mom soothed me.

I felt so bad. We weren't going to make the picnic.

She never yelled at me, just finished icing the cupcakes, and then loaded them with great care into these big plastic cupcake containers. She replaced my cupcake with the very last one, placing extra icing on top for such a well-behaved kid. I ate it while she set me in front of the TV and took a shower to get ready for the picnic.

The cupcake was amazing, like they always were, and my five-year-old brain wanted just one more. Of course, the three tubs of cupcakes were up on the counter, but I knew how to push a chair close so I could climb up. I dragged the chair to the counter, climbed up, then stared at three containers of neatly stacked cupcakes. I only wanted one more.

Just one.

A smile fills my face as I remember Mom's scream when she came back to the kitchen. I had tipped all three of the tubs onto the floor and sat in the middle of the entire mess with a half-eaten cupcake shoved in my mouth. She could've yelled. She could've punished me for ruining all the cupcakes, but my mom is a great mom.

She looked at the chaos, surveyed the destruction, then gave a shake of her head and sat down beside me right in the middle of the mess. She reached across me to grab one of the few intact cupcakes left on the floor.

"Well, I guess you really like cupcakes." I'll never forget her smile.

I giggled and finished off my half-eaten cupcake. It's one of my fondest memories. She always knew how to turn something bad into something wonderful.

It's a lesson I'll never forget.

"The birds sung me to sleep." Mom grips my hand and draws me from my memory.

"Did they?" I try to focus on the present, but my memories of her are too beautiful. I miss her already.

"Such a pretty song they sing."

"I'm glad you got some rest." It's hard to drag myself from the past, but I do. She needs me now more than ever.

"Me too." She shifts in bed all by herself, and I barely hold back a gasp of surprise. Today really is a good day. I can't remember the last time she moved without help.

"I brought juice." I lift the glass and wait for her to respond.

"That sounds wonderful." She struggles; maybe she's not all that strong after all. I hate the way the cancer saps her strength.

"Here, let me help you."

With the difficulties she's having drinking from a cup, I place a straw in her drink. I hold it for her until she can wrap her lips around the small tube. Her cheeks suck in, and I breathe a sigh of relief as I watch the calories go down her throat.

When we moved her out of the upstairs master suite and into the guest bedroom on the ground floor, we did it knowing what the future held. Uncle Mark and I removed all the furniture to open up the space and rented one of those adjustable hospital beds. I settle her into a better position, then place the remote in her hands. I try really hard to let her do as much as she can for herself.

Her frail finger presses the button to elevate the head of the bed, and she slowly transitions from lying flat to sitting semi-upright. Once the bed stops moving, I take the bed remote, and leave it where she can reach it.

"What's your number?"

"Seven." Her hand shakes as she brings the straw to her mouth. She's lying, but that's okay. I'll play along. Out of her line of sight, I add another pill to the pile. The juice in the cup sloshes.

I want to help with her drink, but hold off. I've learned never to fill her glass more than three-quarters full. Surprisingly, none of it spills on her when she finally takes a sip.

"Let me…" I take the glass from her and exchange it with three pills. Two are pain pills. When she places them in her mouth, I give her the glass back. We do this several times until all the pills are gone and she finishes the last sip. "I cut some fruit for you. Do you want some?"

She presses a hand to her belly and I know she doesn't feel like eating. Her eyes close and she takes a breath, but then she opens her eyes and tries to smile.

"I'll try a little."

Her answer breaks my heart. She's too sick and fatigued to eat the most basic things but will try for my sake.

"Grape, strawberry, or melon?" I can probably encourage her to eat one bite, maybe two.

"Melon." She opens her mouth and lets me feed her, as another piece inside of me crumbles.

"The doctor mentioned a protein drink. It's supposed to taste good and has all the nutrients you need." It's high in protein, high in calories, and I need her to eat. She's wasting away to nothing in front of me.

"Have you ever tried those?" Her mouth twists with distaste.

"No."

"When you find one you can stomach, I'll try it, until then…" She pats my hand as she slowly chews the melon. It's a good day because I get her to eat five more bites.

"How are you doing, cupcake? Hanging in there?" She's not asking about me, but rather about how I'm managing the winery.

"Things are okay."

"Okay? That doesn't sound okay."

I take in a deep breath. This is something I hoped to avoid discussing with my mother, but I can't lie to her. I never could, not as a kid, never as a teen, and I won't start now.

"Things are tight right now."

"Tight?" She rallies a bit of strength and shifts her position in bed. "What does that mean?"

I go into a discussion of lagging grape production from the vines, how our water costs escalated due to the drought. I talk while she listens because I know she's too weak to carry on a real conversation, but her illness has not stolen her mind. She takes in everything I say and reaches out to touch my thigh to get me to stop spewing facts and figures.

"You talked to the bank?"

"I did, but they extended us once already and refused another extension."

"That's okay. There are things you can do. Other avenues to explore."

"I sent out proposals to equity investors."

"That's what I would've done." She nods, and I bask in her praise. It means so much to me that she approves of my decisions. I can't help but sit a little straighter under her praise. "Be mindful of the terms. You have to be careful. They'll want a share of the profits, but don't let them come in and take over. This is your business, not theirs."

I hate how she says it's my business and not hers. We don't talk about her death, but we certainly dance around it. It seems we do that more and more with each passing day.

"Uncle Mark wants to buy me out."

"Don't let him do that. He's got a big heart, but I don't want him losing his life's savings." She leaves unsaid that her savings is depleted. The only thing she gave me is this vineyard and the land it sits on. It's why I can't fail. "You'll find a solution, love. I have faith in you."

The burst of words saps the last of her strength, and she sinks into herself. Either that, or the pain pills finally kick in. She drifts off in the middle of our conversation and I sit with her until she falls completely asleep. Only then do I get up and leave.

My mother has faith in me, which means I *will* find a way to save the winery. If that means making a deal with the devil, then so be it.

SEVEN

# Grace

___________

I SPEND THE REST OF THE WEEKEND WITH UNCLE MARK. ON Monday, it's past dusk by the time I come in from the fields. I spend nearly every day with him trying to learn the business of making wine. I'm a business major, not a farmer, and most definitely not a vintner.

I'm way over my head when it comes to running a winery.

The accounts I understand. Numbers are my happy place. Soil pH, pesticides, root grafting, and a million other things make my head spin. I'm lucky to have Uncle Mark. After washing the dishes, I load up a tray for Mom and head to her room.

"Hey there." I keep my voice low, not wanting to spook her. "I brought dinner."

It's peanut butter and jelly. Not the best meal, but peanut butter is packed with calories. It's my secret weapon.

"Hey, cupcake. How was your day?"

"Great. Uncle Mark is showing me how everything works."

"I'm glad he's helping you out." She pats the bed beside her. "You cut the crusts off?" Her smile is weak but present. Anything I can do to make things easier for her, I do without question.

"I could cut it into a star."

Her laughter, soft and weak, makes my heart sing. When I was growing up, she not only cut off the crusts but cut my sandwiches into different shapes. Stars were my favorite.

"No need for that, but thank you." She lifts her hand and I place the sandwich in her shaky grip. She takes a bite. I call that a win. I settle back and enjoy spending time with her. In between bites, I offer a smorgasbord of pain pills and other things the doctor prescribed. "Have you heard anything?" She speaks with her mouth full and I cock my head.

"Excuse me?"

"From the investment companies?" She does this, picks up conversations from before. I'm always chasing her, trying to keep up.

"It's only Monday. I sent everything on Saturday and those kinds of places don't work on the weekend."

"I'm sure something will come through." Her confidence is something I wish I shared.

"Me too."

"Who did you send stuff out to?"

I rattle off the five equity investment firms, leaving Sterling Enterprises for last. I don't know why.

"What is that last one?" Her head tilts to the side.

"Sterling Enterprises."

"Thought that's what you said."

"Why?"

"Nothing, cupcake." She points to her cellphone. "Can you hand me my phone?"

I hand her the phone and sit back.

I tell her about all the things Uncle Mark is teaching me and how interesting it is. She asks questions about our workers, people who are more like family than employees. She cares deeply about them and is as concerned about their future as I am. We talk for nearly an hour, the longest conversation I've had with her in weeks, but slowly the fatigue settles in. I pick up her dishes and load them on the tray. When I get up, she stirs.

"Cupcake?"

"Yes, Mom?"

"Abbie La Rouge will be stopping by this afternoon. If I'm sleeping, please wake me."

"You sure?"

"Yes, I want to talk to her."

"Okay?"

"Please don't meddle."

"Why would you say that?"

"I mention Sterling Enterprises, and all of a sudden, Abbie is stopping by?"

"Cupcake, one thing about business is you need to take advantage of the connections you have. I just want to talk with her. You never know where the right word whispered in the right ear might land."

"I wish you wouldn't."

"And why not?"

"The proposals are sound. Our business plan is solid. I'm sure one of the other firms will step up."

"A little push won't hurt."

"But I don't want to be obligated to accept a charity offer. I'm going to take whichever offer is the best for Atwood Estates. Not the one you push along because you know the CFO's mom."

"He hurt you, cupcake, but that was a long time ago. This is business. Accepting a little help isn't admitting defeat."

I know this, but I don't want that help coming from Brody La Rouge, especially if it's only because of a plea from his mother to help out an old friend. I don't accept charity, and I won't accept any kind of pity money from Brody La Rouge.

Right around three, Abbie La Rouge descends on our house like a hurricane. She knocks, then walks right on in as she calls out my name. "Grace, you around?"

I pop my head out from the kitchen. I'm baking cupcakes. It's something I do to relieve stress. "In the kitchen." I'd tell her to come on in, but Abbie is already peeking her head inside my kitchen.

"Whatcha making?" Her nose lifts and her eyes close as she takes in a deep breath. "Smells like heaven, luv."

"Cupcakes." I pull a steaming pan from the oven. "Want some?"

"Oh, I never turn down cupcakes. Is that Lucy's recipe?"

"You bet." I pull off the heavy oven mitten and set it on the counter. "As soon as those cool down, it'll be time for icing."

"I'll definitely take you up on that. Do you need any help?" Abbie's jade-green eyes simmer with warmth. She and my mother grew up together and are closer than sisters. She's one of the few constants in my life, despite what happened between her son and me.

"I've got it, but thanks."

"What about otherwise?"

"Otherwise?"

"Yes, dear." Her gaze softens as she closes the distance. Stretching out her hands, she grasps mine and gives a light squeeze. "How are *you* holding up? I worry about you."

"I'm doing okay. Taking it day by day. Keeping busy. Learning the ropes for when…" My voice catches and I swallow the lump in my throat.

Saying the words makes it seem real. Not that I'm in denial, but I try not to think about my mother's imminent death. I have a feeling we're closing in on the end. No matter how much I prepare—have prepared—I'm not ready.

"I'm here if you need me. Even when you don't think you do. You should stop by my place next weekend. I'll make my famous pancakes."

"I'd love to, but I can't leave Mom."

"It's only breakfast, and I'll make enough for you to bring back. You need to remember to take care of yourself as well as Lucy."

"Thanks." I grab the bowl with the chocolate frosting and give it a good beating. It really just gives me something to do to keep the tears from falling.

"Is Lucy up?" Abbie's eyes take in everything. I'm not hiding anything from her.

"She's not, but she asked me to wake her when you came around."

"That's very sweet. I promise I won't be long." Abbie glances around the kitchen. "Is there anything I can bring her? A cupcake, maybe?"

"She'd like that, although they're still hot. The frosting will probably melt right off."

"If that's the worst disaster of the day, it's nothing. Let me help you." Abbie rolls up her sleeves and gets to work beside me.

I made enough for dozens of cupcakes. The need to do something special for our workers fills me with restless energy. Abbie takes the cupcakes from the baking pan and sets them on a rack to cool. Then she doles out fresh paper cups into the pan while I whisk the batter.

We work in silence for a time, until the next batch is loaded in the oven, then she hands me a plate with three of the cooling cupcakes on it.

"How about we make these super messy?" Abbie knows how I earned my nickname, although she never uses it.

"Sounds wonderful." We make the ugliest cupcakes on the planet and set them back on the plate. It's the first time I've smiled all day. With our work done, Abbie takes the plate.

"Now, let's see how many of these I can get Lucy to eat." She spins her finger in the air, pointing up at the end with a flourish.

I grin like a little kid as I lick frosting off my fingers. The icing warms on the cupcakes and is already starting to slide off and make a mess.

"Come." I don't know why, but I whisper like a co-conspirator. We sneak toward the guest room with smiles on our faces. Abbie follows me into my mother's room and pulls up a chair beside Mom's bed. I sit beside my mother and gently shake her awake.

"Mom, Abbie is here." It takes a moment for her to rouse. That familiar sinking sensation in my gut makes me nearly sick to my stomach, but my mother stirs, and I know it's not yet time.

"Cupcake?"

"Actually…" A smile fills my face.

"We brought cupcakes!" Abbie sets the cupcakes down with a flourish so Mom can see.

Mom's eyes widen and spark with amusement.

"Those are the ugliest cupcakes I've ever seen," she says. "But, they smell amazing."

"Do you want some?" Abbie lifts one off the plate and takes a bite. Icing falls onto her shirt and smears across her chin. "Oh my! These are the messiest cupcakes in the world." She turns to me. "Honey, do you mind getting me a wet washcloth. I think I'm going to need it."

It's official.

I love Abbie La Rouge.

Like, I love her to death.

She did that on purpose, but only because she knew Mom wouldn't be able to eat the cupcakes without getting horribly messy. As I retreat into the bathroom, the sound of their laughter puts a spring into my step. It's been a long time since I've heard my mother laugh.

I give them a moment, not wanting to intrude. Abbie comes by every week on Sunday and sometimes on Wednesday after church. She spends time with my mom while I take a breather from the oppressiveness of it all.

Or at least, I like to think I can take a breather.

The truth is I'm suffocating. I return with the wet washcloth. Abbie tells Mom all about her new beau, some judge or lawyer, who's been sweet on her for years.

"I need to take the next batch of cupcakes out of the oven." I pat Abbie on the back. "I'll be back in a bit." A quick glance at Mom and I see she's putting on a brave face. The easiest things tire her these days, such as a simple conversation with a lifetime friend.

I leave them alone and pull out the next batch of cupcakes. After icing the first batch and starting the third, I head back to Mom's room. It's time to politely let Abbie know her visit needs to come to an end. I cup two pain pills in my hand and carry a glass of milk.

Milk or orange juice, I try to bring something either high in sugar or high in fat to my mother. She needs all the nutrition she can get.

Not really sure why, I hover at the door, eavesdropping like a loser.

"You think he might help?" My mother's thin, reedy voice makes me cringe.

"He will, or I'll swat his ass." Abbie is as free with her smiles as she is with her laughter. "My boy might be pushing thirty, but he's not too big for me to yank down his britches and give him a good swatting."

"Thanks. Something's not right with the business, and I don't know what it is. She needs this place to succeed. It's the only thing I have to give her. I'd like to think what little there is of her inheritance isn't a huge burden."

"I'm driving into the city to see the B-child tonight. We'll have a chat and I'm sure he'll do what he can to help out."

"You think he will, considering…"

"That boy's made many mistakes in his life, but his heart is good. Grace is the only girl who ever really got to know the real Brody. Don't worry about your Grace. I'm going to watch out for her like she's my own. I swore to you I would, and I keep my promises. I always wanted a little girl to spoil, but with three obnoxious boys, my hands were filled from day one."

"Thanks, it means a lot to me."

I knock on the door, feeling guilty for eavesdropping and invading their privacy.

"Come in. No need to be knocking in your own house." Abbie wipes at the chocolate smear on her shirt and stands. "Lord, but I need to get going. I've got a long drive into the city."

"It was nice having you." I glance at my mom and the smile on her face. She barely lifts her wrist when Abbie bends down to give her a hug and kiss her cheek.

"I'll swing around tomorrow and see how things are going." Abbie glances at me and smiles.

I don't know why, or how, but that smile means the world to me. It makes me feel less alone in the world, and hell if I don't need a little of that right now.

"Thanks, Abbie." My mom sinks into the mattress, overwhelmed with fatigue.

Abbie grabs the empty plate and follows me into the kitchen. She glances around and her eyes widen. "You've been busy. What are you going to do with all these cupcakes? Feed an army?"

"Just wanted to give the workers something special."

"You have a true heart. Now, do you think there's any way I can snag a few to take with me?"

"Take as many as you want." I grab a plastic container and watch her put four of my cupcakes inside. Surely, she's not intending on eating them all herself?

"If it's okay with you, I might stop by a little more frequently. I don't want to get in the way, but…"

I understand. We all know we're approaching the end.

"Mom would love that."

"You're a wonderful daughter and an amazing woman. Never forget that. And never accept less than perfect in anything, or from anyone. You deserve perfect." Abbie cups my cheek and stares at me for a long moment. "Do you hear me? You deserve nothing but perfect."

I wave goodbye and lean against the doorframe with a sigh. If only there were someone perfect out there for someone like me.

EIGHT

## Brody

---

"Hey, Brody, got a few more for you." Hawke Sterling, CEO of Sterling Enterprises and my best friend, drops a stack of folders on my desk.

"Seriously? I thought I said no more?" I push the stack away, hoping it will fall in the trash.

"You totally love this shit." Hawke puts his hand on the stack, stopping my trash dump. "There's a diamond in the rough here, I'm sure of it. Besides, you live for this kind of shit." He taps the papers. "Get that brain of yours to work and find our next great investment."

Hawke's convinced I'm some genius when it comes to money and finding what he calls 'the diamond in the rough.' I have an eye. I'll give him that, but it really comes down to hard work and determination. I'm the numbers guy of Sterling Enterprises. Hawke Sterling is the CEO while I'm the CFO and somehow the unofficial head of acquisitions.

I started out in that department when Hawke first hired me. Now, I work as the Chief Financial Officer and dabble in acquisitions;

emphasis on dabble. He sends me the files our acquisitions department passes on because Hawke believes in my superpower to identify a true gem.

Our partnership has been lucrative for us both. We're the undeniable power duo in the San Francisco Bay Area when it comes to venture capital and equity investing. I squeeze the bridge of my nose and lean back. He pushes the stack of folders back toward me.

"Take a look." He flashes his megawatt smile, knowing full well how cheesy it makes him look.

"Fine." I grab the stack and place it on top of a nearly identical stack of folders to my right.

I feel undeserving of all the accolades he showers upon me. All I do is find companies struggling with short term cash flow issues. I look at their books, make a few tweaks to their operations, and our equity investment grows as we receive a portion of the profits for the term of our contract.

Fortunately for me, my choices have been incredibly successful.

"Who are you doing tonight?" Hawke looks at me expectantly.

"Ha-ha, very funny. I'm not doing anyone. My mother's driving in from Napa and I'm taking her to the ballet." Once a month, Abbie La Rouge uses me as her excuse to spend a night in the city. Ballet is simply the cherry on top.

She and Dad used to head into the city once a month to watch whatever the current production was. After Dad passed, I stepped up and surprised her with tickets to the first showing of The Nutcracker for the winter season. It became a thing between us, and we rarely miss a date.

"Okay, can't compete with your mother. Tell Abbie I say hello."

"Will do."

"And please take a look at those tonight." He points to the folders. "I'd like to interview any hopefuls and close out on a contract by the end of this week."

"Why the rush?"

"No rush, but you'll understand when you look at them. Their need is great, and the opportunity for us to step in is small but maybe great. There's one you might find interesting. Maybe you could get Asher's eyes on it."

"Why?"

"It's a vineyard. Oh, and don't forget Friday night."

"What's Friday night?" Shit, did I forget something? I glance at my calendar.

"Our kickoff party?" He shakes his head. "For the VR startup? Quinn's company."

"Ah, yes." That's his wife's startup, and it's a big deal, worth billions.

"It's black-tie." He points at my neck and the open collar. My tie is somewhere on the floor. Me and ties have a complicated relationship.

They're required in my line of work, and I hate them.

"Bring someone interesting." Hawke ignores my audible groan. "You know, not your usual type. This is a different kind of crowd. Young. Whiz kids. Clueless about money. Blind to wealth. Super smart. Your usual arm candy will leave them slack-jawed and hard all evening long. Find someone they can relate to."

"I'll be there." As to who I'll take? I might have to go through the list and see who's the least pissed off at me, or who might be interested in a second round. Despite my reputation, I do double-dip from time to time. I have no idea who I want to endure a black-tie event with. Hawke leaves me to work.

A glance at my watch reveals it's just after four. No kicking off early tonight. Mother won't arrive until closer to seven. The ballet begins at eight, which leaves me with a couple of hours to kill. I text her and tell her to park her car at my building. We'll walk from here and enjoy a stroll through the city.

I survey my office, as I sometimes do. I'm thankful to my dad for raising me with a solid work ethic. He helped my mom raise troublesome triplets, and we certainly gave them a run for their money. Never once did he allow us to slack off or accept less than our best. It shows too.

Asher is the CEO of our family-run winery. On the side, he's a volunteer firefighter and not just a run of the mill kind of firefighter. My eldest brother is part of an elite helitack woodland crew who rappels into woodland fires in the most rugged terrains to fight forest fires and save lives. He thinks nothing of risking his life to save others.

I'm the CFO of our family business, although Asher pretty much runs everything. I just keep the books looking pretty, make sure we pay our taxes on time, and make payroll each month. My job with Sterling Enterprises is my real job.

Cage is a world-class photographer. He travels the world taking photos in some of the most austere places on Earth; they'll steal your breath. He's been featured in countless magazines and his career continues to astound me. His photos are amazeballs. Fucking brilliant.

We're all highly successful, driven men leaving our mark on the world. A deep sense of gratitude fills me for the values our parents instilled in us. The values which find me sitting in an expansive office overlooking the San Francisco skyline through floor-to-ceiling windows.

I could've hired an interior designer to design my office, but I did this myself, setting the right tone of prestige, success, and wealth for the clients who come to Sterling Enterprises asking for an equity investment to breathe new life into their failing dreams.

When Hawke first hired me, I thought the tiny office they crammed me into was the height of success. I had a desk, a fern I killed within three months, and half a window. A dividing wall cut the small window in half, but I thought I scored it big. I wasn't shoved into the maze of cubicle desks in the center of the office. I was a kid right out of college with a business degree and a resume that looked better than it should, and I thought I had made it in the world.

Dad passed just after college. Asher, Cage, and I stepped up to take over La Rouge Vineyards. Asher, as the eldest, took over as CEO. I had the business degree and stepped in as CFO, and Cage had his degree in marketing. He used every trick in the book to make La Rouge a success.

I thought my dreams would end there, mired in taking over the family vineyard, but Asher had a unique flair for the business. It quickly became clear to both me and Cage that he didn't need us. I might feel guilty about leaving Asher to run everything, but he loves being in charge and is damn good at making wine.

I hate to even think it but my father's death directly led to Hawke hiring the green, untried hopeful that I was at the time onto his acquisitions' team. Having CFO of La Rouge Vineyards, an established winery with an awesome track record on my resume, said something. Hawke took a chance on me.

It was all work and no play those first few years with Hawke. I had a lot to prove and couldn't afford to fail. But I turned a profit for Hawke in my first quarter. It wasn't much, barely a blip in the grand scheme of things, but it was enough to get his interest. I doubled down, worked harder, and the next quarter that blip turned into my first six-figure deal. Still not much in the grand scheme of things, but for my first six months on the job, Hawke took notice.

I flip open the first proposal and peruse the contents. Nothing strikes me at first glance. I dig a little deeper, looking to see how Sterling

Enterprises can turn around a flagging photo business. After a quick ten-minute read, I decide against them, but jot down a few notes for the rejection letter.

They aren't maximizing their online presence and are losing sales as a result. If we stepped in, we could turn the business around, but for the time investment, it's not worth it to Sterling Enterprises. I add a few minor equity firms to my notes for the company to check out.

Hawke used to raise an eyebrow at the comments I left to those we rejected. He didn't understand sending business elsewhere, but I can't in good conscience leave them to flounder when I see opportunities for improvement.

We may not help turn their business around, but sometimes all people need is a little coaching to get things back on course. I do the same for the second and third folders Hawke left behind.

Mother texts me she's about forty-five minutes out. Traffic headed into the city is nothing like that flowing out at rush hour. It's one of the reasons I only make it home about one weekend a month. At this time of the day, it can take well over three hours to get to Fairfield and another hour to get to our vineyard in Napa. Fortunately, Mom's drive is just a little over an hour. I'd worry about it, but I know she's probably listening to one of her steamy audiobooks in the car.

With under an hour left, I open the last folder. My heart catches in my throat when I see Grace Atwood's name at the top of the next equity investment proposal.

NINE

## Brody

___________

I slam the folder shut and take a few breaths. For some reason, my heart hammers in my chest, and my palms begin to sweat. I open the folder again and press my fingers over her name. I've made mistakes in my past, some bigger than others, but the mistake I made with Grace was an epic, colossal fuck-up.

I was cruel, heartless, and an all-around asshole. There are few things in life I'm not proud of. In general, I'm a good person: thoughtful, considerate, the man my parents hoped to raise.

With Grace, I became something else.

I need to change that, and I have one very good idea how. After jotting down a few notes, I send a message to my assistant to set up an appointment with Grace Atwood for the morning.

I don't understand how her vineyard is so deep in the red, but with my business acumen and Asher's expertise in running a successful winery, we can turn things around. Hawke will definitely give me side-eyes for accepting the proposal. It's a massive risk, but I honestly don't care.

This is personal.

Less than half an hour later, Mom texts she's pulling up in the garage. I head down to meet her and greet her with a kiss.

"How're you doing?"

"Fabulous. And you?" Her eyes twinkle and her smile beams.

"You going to tell me about your date, or are we going to dance around it all evening?"

My visit to Napa, specifically to see her, resulted in nothing more than lunch with Evie and Asher. Our mother turned into a major no-show. Asher and I were ready to mount a manhunt, only to be sidelined by Evie. She told us to stand down. To my amazement, that's exactly what Asher and I did. I pried Evie for information, but she remained tight-lipped.

Mom's keeping something from us. Not that it matters. For the next three hours, Abbie La Rouge is all mine.

"So…" I hold open the door to the parking garage and grin as she shuffles past me.

"So, what?" Her grin is flirtatious and unflappable. Mom never gives away the good stuff. We have to dig.

"So, where were you?"

"You need to be more specific."

"I came to visit you and you weren't there."

"Oh, you mean this past weekend? Honey, you really need to be more specific."

"Don't play with me. Who is he?"

"Who is who?" She gives a little smirk.

"You're not going to tell me, are you?"

"No. Now don't meddle in my affairs." Her bony finger pokes against my sternum. Abbie La Rouge is one fierce woman.

"Fine. But you can't hide him forever."

"I'm not hiding anyone. Do you tell me about all your conquests?"

"So you admit he's a conquest."

"He's no such thing."

"But, you just said…"

"I was talking about you. Now, sweetie, when are you going to settle down?" She reaches for my arm and settles her hand in the crook of my arm.

"I don't want to settle down. I'm perfectly happy…"

"You're not happy. I see it and feel it in here." She presses her hand against her chest. "You're spinning your wheels, wasting time on women you know don't matter, because you're afraid of commitment. Why is that?" The look she gives me is one of true pain. "Didn't your dad and I teach you anything?"

"Mom…" I grit my teeth and close my eyes for a second. This is not the conversation I want to have with my mom.

"Don't Mom me. When the right one comes along, you need to grab her by the horns and wrestle her to the ground."

"That's really not how it works."

"Oh, you know what I mean. Women want to know the man they're with is worthy of their love. They need to feel sheltered, protected, loved…"

"You mean suffocated and oppressed? Sorry, but those are antiquated notions."

"Those antiquated notions are precisely why you spin a new girl through your bed every night."

"We are not discussing my love life."

"You're right, because there's no 'love' to discuss. You fuck women to soothe this emptiness within you. When are you going to get your head out of your ass and figure shit out?" Mom only swears when she's making a point.

"I'm totally not having this conversation with my mother."

"You most certainly are. I read the press. Skim the articles. I keep up with all of you."

"Then focus that shit on Asher or Cage. I'm doing just fine over here."

"Don't lie to your Mamma."

"Mamma?" I chuckle. "Since when do we live in the south, Mother?"

"Pish-posh, you know what I mean."

"I know you're putting your nose in my business when I should be putting mine in yours."

"We're not talking about me."

"Who's the new beau? Who's the man who stole you from me all weekend?"

"Like that's a bad thing?" She yanks her hand from my arm and sulks beside me. "You should be happy I found someone who tickles my fancy."

"As long as it's just your fancy he's tickling."

"Stop." Mom halts in her tracks, which causes a commotion considering the line of ballet goers trailing behind us. They split and flow past us as we stare at each other. Like always, I'm the one to give in first.

"Fine!"

"Good." She makes a show of taking my arm and resting her hand in the crook of my elbow again. "Now, speaking of old friends…"

This is how my mother works around to a problem. I listen with half an ear while I navigate us the few blocks to the ballet. My senses are on high alert. San Francisco is not a gentle town. With all the homeless and beggars on the street, I do my best to shield her as I can.

Only after we make it to the theater do I take a breath. We won't be walking back to the garage. Not at ten in the evening. We walk up the stairs, joining an ever-growing throng of eager theater hopefuls. I present our tickets, and we're permitted inside.

With plenty of time to spare, I take her to the bar and order drinks. I keep a reserved box, one I share with Hawke. Most nights, he doesn't fill his seats, leaving me and Mom in peace. Tonight is one such night.

The performance is magical. Brilliant actually. The dancers are on pointe, literally and figuratively. Their performance captivates me, but only because I imagine Grace dancing before me. With my thoughts wrapped up in Grace, I find myself wholly unprepared for Mom's comment.

"So about Grace…"

It takes a second for my heart to start beating again.

"Excuse me?"

"Let's just say a little bird told me something might be coming your way. I told her not to worry. That 'my boy' would make things right. Are you going to make your mother a liar?" I stare at her. Mom's a lot of things, but emotional blackmail? It's way beyond her, or so I thought.

"I'm sorry. I don't know what you're talking about."

"No doubt, you do." She sniffs and rolls her eyes. "I'm just saying sometimes the universe throws you a bone."

"Mom."

"Take the bone. Don't miss. Catch the damn thing."

"I have no idea what you're talking about." I know exactly what she's talking about.

"Be the man I know you can be. Do the right thing."

"And what exactly is that?"

"You're a smart man, honey. Figure it out. In the meantime, call us a car. It's late, and I'm tired. I'm assuming your guest bedroom is free?"

"It's always free."

No one spends the night.

Ever.

TEN

# Grace

_____________

"ARE YOU SURE ABOUT THIS?" MARK PACES IN THE KITCHEN. HE tugs in a deep breath and lets it out on a slow exhale.

"I know, but desperate times…" I can only shrug. Desperate times leave desperate people to do questionable things, like accept an appointment with the devil. My gut tangles in knots. "I'm worried too." I lay my hand on his arm. "But there really is no alternative."

"That's not true. I have my savings."

"Mom doesn't want you to dip into your savings." Mom's terrified Mark will blow through his retirement. With her medical bills, her entire savings is gone. I inject confidence in my voice. "This is going to work."

"I guess it's best to investigate all our options." He doesn't look convinced and shoves his hands deep in his pockets.

"I agree." I give him a hug. "We're going to make this work."

We're small fry when it comes to Sterling Enterprise's usual clients, which is the only thing that makes this whole thing bearable. Hopefully, our case is assigned to some lowly functionary in

Acquisitions. My goal is to get in and get out without any accidental encounters with the company's CFO.

"It's just…" Mark drags the toe of his shoe in an arc across the kitchen floor. "Our loans have always come from banks before, with terms I understand. I'm concerned about what we might have to agree to. The loss of control bothers me."

"I'm worried about that too, but if they take us on, it'll be because they think we're viable." I look through my purse to find my phone. "It's not like we're signing Atwood Estates away. That's not how this works. They're not looking to take over, and I'll retain controlling interest."

"Then, how does this benefit them?"

"We give them a portion of our profits…" *To be determined by them.* "In exchange, we allow them to make an assessment of our business plan and formulate suggestions that we're contractually obligated to implement."

This is the one part I'm in complete agreement with Uncle Mark. The thing is, we're beggars.

"Can you check the traffic? I'm going to change."

"Again?" He stops his back and forth pacing to look at me. "Didn't you change just a bit ago?"

"This blouse is too frilly." It's too damn feminine.

I race up the stairs and head to my bedroom for yet another last-minute wardrobe change. I want to look professional, put together. Not too casual. Not too sexy. Not too much of anything really. Professional and boring is the look I'm going for, something that will leave me feeling comfortable and confident.

I hope my confidence is enough to ease Mark's worries. Equity investing is one of the subjects I excelled at in business school. I'm comfortable with the process and know what to expect. Poor Mark is not, and I get his concern.

Panic lingers at the fringes of my mind because this really is our last shot. I've yet to hear back from the other equity investors, and time is slipping through my fingers. I hide my feelings of inadequacy and fear from my uncle. He doesn't need that burden added to his already overwhelming concerns. I lock up my insecurities and shove them way back in my mind, where I'll deal with them later.

There are other things I need to prepare for, like a confrontation with Brody—if it occurs.

My gut says to give him a piece of my mind and tell him exactly what I think of the trail of broken hearts littering his past. My head says that's the worst possible thing I can do, considering I came to his company asking for help.

Honestly, like many things, I overthink it.

My heart wants revenge, but Mom's words run through my mind. *'Revenge only hurts the one who seeks it. Don't let revenge turn you into a hater. You don't need that ugliness in your life.'*

Her words are sound, but damn if I don't want a little revenge.

I know Brody La Rouge. Women find him irresistible. At one time, that included me. I'd like to think things are different now that I'm more mature, that somehow the years between high school and now give me a better perspective, but I remember that undeniable pull when I saw him last weekend. It overwhelmed me.

Am I really ready to face him?

A little voice inside my head tells me it would be fun to mess with him. He's a womanizer who always gets the girl but never keeps her. How can I turn that to my advantage?

I give a shake of my head. These are precisely the kinds of thoughts I should avoid, but damn if I can't help myself.

The thing is, I'm way over my head with a man like Brody. I've done some digging since reading the email requesting a meeting. Bad Boy Brody, known womanizer, is evidently the catch of the century. He's one of the few, unattainable, still eligible bachelors, wandering around the Bay Area, and his pockets are deep and growing by the second.

I dug up other things, like him being a workaholic with an unusual flair for investing in failing companies and turning them into exceptionally profitable business ventures. His determination and drive make all that possible. Not much seems to have changed from the Brody I knew in high school.

He was always driven to succeed—pushed in many ways to separate himself from his brothers. They were the undeniable power trio at school. Three identical triplets, insanely hot, incredibly talented in sports, and at the top of the class in academics. The La Rouge brothers were gods back then.

I suppose they still are.

CEO of La Rouge Vineyards, Asher La Rouge is not only making a name for himself in the local wine scene, he's also a bona fide hero. Numerous articles speak to his heroics as an elite member of a helitack crew. I didn't even know what that was until I looked it up.

Cage La Rouge is a highly sought after nature photographer. His photos are stunning. I lost over an hour last night perusing his work online.

Then there's Brody, the brother with the Midas touch. He's carving out an empire in the business world. Everything he touches turns to gold. I can't help but hope some of that rubs off on Atwood Estates. We need a little bit of good luck to turn our way.

Which brings my revenge plotting to a screeching halt.

Nothing can jeopardize what's truly important. My wounded pride means nothing when stacked against the livelihood of our workers, not to mention my uncle's future. Atwood Estates has been his bread and butter for his entire life. If it wasn't in such a mess, I'd consider his offer to buy me out, but there's no way I'd do that to him. He could lose everything.

Sterling Enterprises comes with a stellar reputation in equity investments. I remind myself what's important and shove all that other shit way back in the back of my head.

"Cupcake, you need to hurry up," Uncle Mark calls out from downstairs. "Traffic is going to be heavy, and we can't be late."

"On my way." I change out of the fifth blouse and throw it on the bed with all the other discarded candidates. The mirror catches my eye and I turn away from it in a huff. If I tone down my appearance, there will be no chance of Brody taking an interest. Not that he would, and why do I care?

I don't answer that.

We'll be nothing more than two people who once knew each other, and there's where I plan on leaving things.

I examine my reflection one last time, taking in the light foundation that smooths out my skin tone. I avoid blush. My goal is to minimize my appearance and become as plain as possible. I sweep my fingers through my hair and decide to put it up for the meeting. There's no time now, but I can pull it back into a tight bun in the car while Mark navigates the roads and heavy traffic.

I line my eyes and put on mascara, but no eyeshadow to make my eyes pop. I'm going for clean, simple, and serious. With Mark encouraging me to hurry up, I fly downstairs and strap into the passenger seat of his car. We head out of Napa and merge onto I-80, where we come to a crawl stuck in the tail end of the morning commute.

Nearly three hours later, we pull up outside an impressive building. It takes a moment to park, but then Mark and I stand on the sidewalk staring at the gorgeous structure. All steel and glass, everything about it screams wealth.

"Wow." My head tilts back as I try to take it all in.

"That's an understatement." My uncle stands beside me and reaches out to take my hand in his. "You ready for this, cupcake?"

"I thought I was." I gulp and shift my attention to take in his troubled gaze. "They certainly know how to impress." I feel incredibly small and insignificant.

"Impress? This thing screams money."

I agree with him there. From the ornate façade to the elegant lobby, this place is intimidating, even more so because of who waits for me inside.

Mark and I work our way across the expansive lobby. The interior of the building is hollow. A grand atrium takes up the entire center.

I can't help but stop dead in the middle and let my head hang back. It has to be thirty, forty, or more stories tall. Bridges span the open space far ahead, causeways connecting one side to the other, and in some places, one floor to another. It's a beautiful interconnected spider web of architectural genius.

Until now, I didn't understand exactly how successful Brody was in the fascinating world of venture capital and equity investments.

"It's now or never." I glance over at Mark and bite my lower lip. Nervous doesn't begin to describe my current state. I'm terrified of coming face to face with Brody. Although, there's a good chance we've been assigned to a lowly functionary.

"Let's do this, cupcake." Mark takes my arm and guides me through the atrium lobby to a bank of elevators waiting on the other side. We walk past massive ficus trees, perfectly trimmed, that tower over our heads. A miniature stream flows between the gaps in the stone floors and spills out into a meandering pond filled with sparkling koi of every color. A food dispenser stands to the side. For a quarter, visitors and guests can feed the fish.

I take in a deep breath, realizing how remarkably clean the air smells in here. There's even a slight breeze that ruffles my hair. I don't want to think about what it takes to keep all this running.

Mark and I gawk like a pair of tourists as we make our way to the elevators. Steel and glass, like everything else, we'll have an impressive view of the atrium as we ascend to the fortieth floor.

The elevator dings and we file inside, just the two of us. I go to the back of the elevator and press my hands against the glass, then spin around at the sound of Mark's ragged breathing.

"Oh, no." I rush to him and put a hand on his back. He faces the steel doors, huddling against them. "I forgot about your fear of heights."

"It's okay. My eyes are closed and it'll be over soon."

I glance over my shoulder, a little bummed to be missing the ride up the elevator, but I stay by Mark's side. We're in this together.

The elevator ride is quick and comes to a near motionless stop. The doors slide open and Mark exits the elevator in a rush. He tugs at his tie as he places a palm against the far wall. Head down, he takes a few breaths to calm himself.

Fortunately, the walkway is broad. I give Mark the wall while I settle in beside him, a buffer between him, the banister, and the forty-story plunge to the atrium. I want to lean over the railing and peer down to the lobby far below, but I hold back that urge.

"It's right around the corner." Despite its size, the building is exceptionally easy to navigate. "Looks like we're in the wrong business."

"No kidding," he says. "These equity investors don't seem to be doing too poorly."

They're definitely not at that. I have a feeling they're raking in the dough hand over hand. Once again, I'm reminded of how small Atwood Estates must seem to these people.

I take a deep breath, fortifying myself for whatever comes next. We'll either walk out of here with the funding we need to turn our business around, or we'll walk out with our tails tucked between our legs as we contemplate bankruptcy.

We head to a set of massive doors marked with Sterling Enterprises on the outside. A receptionist looks up from a desk that spans the length of the welcoming interior lobby.

"Welcome to Sterling Enterprises." Her smile is soft. Her teeth bleached white. Not a hair is out of place. "Mr. and Miss Atwood, you're a few minutes early. I'm happy to meet you. My name is Katy. May I get you something to drink?"

I hold back my surprise that she knows our names, but then that would be something an executive assistant might do.

"Um, no, thank you." My mouth is parched, but I'm afraid my hand will shake and I'll pour whatever she offers all over my blouse.

"I'd like some water, please." Mark covers his mouth and coughs. He's still recovering from his fear of heights.

"Excellent. If you'll follow me, I can take you to the conference room where you'll be having your meeting with Mr. La Rouge."

"Excuse me?" I stop in my tracks, nearly tripping over my feet. "Our meeting is with Mr. La Rouge? I thought…"

"Yes, he specifically requested to meet with you. I'm sorry, but I thought you knew?"

I knew there was a very small, minuscule, highly unlikely chance. I take a look at my reflection in the highly-polished marble walls and am thankful I opted for professional and plain.

"This way, please." Katy ignores my comment as if it's commonplace for us to be meeting with the CFO of Sterling Enterprises. Then it hits me. Fortieth floor, the executive level. I missed all the signs.

With my heart racing, I fall in behind Katy and my uncle.

"How was the drive into the city?" Her lilting voice, and cheery disposition, is perfect for soothing anxious clients.

"Not as bad as I thought." Mark tugs at his collar.

Katy guides us deeper into the executive suite of Sterling Enterprises, exchanging small talk with my uncle. I trail behind and try not to gawk. The hallway she leads us down is wide enough to swallow our home. Impressive doesn't come close to describing this place.

She turns a corner and presses a metal plate on the wall. Twin glass doors to a conference room slowly swing inward.

"Here we are. If you'll just make yourselves comfortable, I'll tell Mr. La Rouge you're here. Like I said, you're a few minutes early, and he's with another client but will be with you shortly. I'll get that water for you, Mr. Atwood. Is there anything else?" She turns to me with an expectant expression.

"Where are your restrooms?" I'm fighting a sudden urge to hurl. Not to mention, the nearly three-hour drive, with no pit stop, has taxed my bladder.

"Right next door. If you'll follow me." Katy does a mini-pirouette and spins around. Her overly enthusiastic voice is meant to welcome visitors, but it's getting on my nerves. She shows me to the lady's room and gives a little flap of her hand. "Have a great meeting!"

With those words of encouragement, she leaves me to refresh myself. I assume she's off to get Mark's water. Since we're early, I don't rush and take a long moment to stare at my reflection after washing my hands.

"You've got this." I say it again, firmer, with more oomph. "You've got this." I check my hair and tame the flyaways; then it's time to head back and wait for Brody La Rouge to make his appearance.

On the way back, doubt creeps back in. I have no idea what I'm thinking, and I'm no longer sure why I'm even here. The fear and doubt I've been struggling to contain comes back with a vengeance. There's a pit in my stomach and that queasy sensation returns.

This whole thing is crazy. I'm crazy. Brody La Rouge runs an empire of wealth I can't comprehend, and I'm here to beg for help. How desperate does that make me sound? Certainly, not like some kid he used to know who's talking herself out of a silly revenge plot.

What's his interest in Atwood Estates? We're such a small operation. Any time and investment his company makes in us will probably cost them more in lost revenue from the time invested alone. My hands shake and my palms are slick with sweat. I hastily rub them on the seams of my skirt and swallow down the lump in my throat. Whatever optimism I shared with Mark is gone.

When I return, Mark is seated at the large conference table. A tray with a pitcher of ice water and three glasses sits in the middle of the table. He looks out of place, shoulders slumped, features sagging, worry lines furrowing his brow. He looks up when I enter and smiles weakly at me.

"Have you ever seen a table this big?" His smile turns up into a grin.

I hold back a laugh because the table is massive, and to be honest, more than a bit pompous. It sits twelve on each side. Mark chose to sit right in the middle with his back to the floor-to-ceiling windows. As the only person sitting at the table, he looks like a little kid.

A massive chair sits at the head; a throne for a king—a Midas Mogul.

"It's crazy, freakin' huge." I place a hand over my mouth and giggle. I can't help it. "You'd think they'd put the two of us in a broom closet instead of this place." A laugh escapes me as I start to lose it. Totally not professional, I imagine all manner of boardroom shenanigans that might happen on a table this big. "Do you think they use it as a Slip-n-Slide for the office Christmas party?" I move to the head of the table and glance down its length. Perfectly smooth, it would be great for a bunch of drunk adults to have a little fun.

I imagine Brody standing at the head of the table and other thoughts enter my head: filthy, dirty, naughty thoughts. I'm so involved in the fantasy that I don't notice the sudden change in Mark's demeanor. Instead, the atmosphere suddenly shifts, moving from my light-hearted comments to tense and anticipatory.

I feel the heat of Brody's gaze lick along my back as the fine hairs at my nape suddenly lift. With a glance at him, I tumble into Brody's turbulent gaze.

ELEVEN

## Brody

Light, free, entirely unscripted, her laughter draws me to the room. Grace Atwood mesmerizes me with the way she stands at the head of the conference table with an impish grin on her face. I wish I knew what she was thinking because I'd love to be the reason for that much joy.

She's here. She's really here.

So close.

So fucking close.

She leans forward, splays her palms on the polished wood, and my mind turns the whole scene filthy. Maybe it's not joy that I want to put on her face, but carnal ecstasy instead?

Absolutely, fucking filthy.

Thoughts of stripping her bare and grabbing hold of her hips make me instantly hard. It's been a long time since something like this happened. I feel like I'm sixteen again, an eager little horndog with zero control. I'm actually a bit light-headed and sway on my feet.

I thought I was prepared. I thought this would be no big deal, meeting with her in person, but the whole situation slams into me with the weight of a sledgehammer, stealing my breath. I take a moment to recover—to get a hold of myself—and casually reach down to adjust my erection.

I fucking ache for her.

My teeth slam together as I tell myself to get a grip, but it's only with great difficulty that I shove the overly-eager teenage horndog back where he belongs. Fuck, but I want to do terrible things to Grace Atwood.

When was the last time a woman stopped me in my tracks like this?

*Never.*

Phenomenal doesn't begin to describe the vision before me. Her head tilts down, making it so I can't see her face clearly. Not that I need to. Every delicate feature is indelibly imprinted on my mind and seared into my soul.

I ruined her and walked away, yet she's the one I never forgot. She's the mistake I wish I could erase. I'd been such a goddamn fool back then with far too much to prove, a reputation to uphold, and... Shit. I was such a fucking jerk.

It feels wrong watching her like this, like I'm a peeping Tom. I stand tall and push the metal plate that opens the doors to the conference room. They swing open, whisper-quiet. Mark Atwood notices me first. His eyes light up in recognition as he stands to greet me.

We don't technically know each other.

He only knows me through Asher and La Rouge Winery. Everyone in town is familiar with the infamous La Rouge triplets, which means they often feel like they know us better than they do. I play along. Doing otherwise serves no purpose, but my attention fixes on Grace.

Like she did in the dusty field the other day, her entire body stiffens. I watch, with more than casual interest, as she schools her features to an impassive expression. Her gaze collides with mine, tunnels right into me, and leaves me staggering. It's like the world shifts on its axis, leaving me reeling in place. I approach the table and grasp one of the chairs to cover my sudden uneasiness.

Her long hair is pulled up into a severe bun. It tightens her facial features, lending a hard edge to her expression. Or maybe, that's simply how she feels about me. The desire to yank her hair free and let it run through my fingers overwhelms me. Her complexion is flawless and I love how her makeup isn't overdone.

How many women have passed through my bed made up to the nines?

It's like they're afraid to reveal their face to the real world. Grace isn't like that. Her makeup is light, minimal, elegant, and sophisticated. It doesn't obscure her face. Instead, it highlights her natural beauty.

She's confident in her own skin, not needing to sculpt and rearrange her features to meet unattainable standards for female esthetics. I love how her true beauty shines through.

Once again, that strange magnetism pulls at me. I don't understand it, and I'm hesitant to break free. If I allow that to happen, I might lose her forever. No way in hell will I sever our inexplicable connection.

I decide right then to have her, but how? And where? Most importantly, when?

"It's nice to see you again." I make my way around the conference table, moving away from Grace to greet her uncle first.

I feel a need to delay my reintroduction to her for as long as possible. At least until I can decide the how, where, and when. Those are three of the most pressing questions of my day.

"Thank you for meeting with us." Mark Atwood's handshake is firm and calloused by good honest work.

"It's my pleasure, of course. When I saw your proposal cross my desk, it grabbed my interest." I shift around Mark and close the distance between Grace and myself. My heart hammers and my pulse thrums, humming as my blood races past my ears. "And, Grace, it's nice to see you again."

I stretch out my hand and she gives it a wary eye. It may be my imagination, but I swear her hands shake as she rubs them along the seam of her skirt. She surprises me by not taking my hand. Instead, she pulls out my chair at the head of the table and sits down like she owns the place.

*Well played, Grace Atwood. Very well played.*

"Thank you for taking the time to see us." She glances at her nails, then looks up at me.

A range of expressions flicker across her face, far too quick to follow. Seething hatred comes first, followed by irritation—not at me, however—then resignation finally settles. I don't understand any of it.

She settles in my chair. It being far too big for her small frame, swallows her whole. "I'm a little surprised. I wouldn't think Atwood Estates would merit the eyes of Sterling Enterprise's CFO. I hope we're not bothering you."

She takes in a deep breath and lets it out. The soft, breathy sound snags the attention of my dick. I need to sit before it draws unnecessary attention to itself. I take the chair beside her and motion for Mark to join us at the head of the table.

"You could never bother me, and of course, I'd take the time to see you. It's not often I get a chance to see someone from high school."

"Oh, that's right," Mark's voice rises with excitement. "Grace, why didn't you remind me that the two of you went to school together?"

"It was nothing," she says dismissively. "I was a freshman and he was a senior. We barely interacted." Her brows pinch together with the lie.

She and I did a whole hell of a lot more than interact. We got to know each other intimately, in more ways than one. She gave me her virginity. Or maybe I stole it. And we explored things we probably shouldn't have, playing a very adult game of transferring control. It was as exciting then as now. How easy would it be to slip back into that special place where she becomes the center of my universe; mine to cherish, to protect, and control?

That familiar rush of adrenaline surges through me. It's been a long time since I've unleashed that part of myself, but we're not in that same place anymore. I tamp down my need to travel back down that road with extreme difficulty.

"It's been how long?" I settle back in my seat, too entranced by her beauty to discuss business.

"A lifetime, I suppose." She gives a shrug like she couldn't care less.

All I can think about is taking her in my arms and placing my lips against her delicate mouth. Sweet Jesus, but I still remember how sinfully sweet she tastes. My reaction to Grace is not normal. It borders on obsessive, and I don't understand it. This isn't like me.

Walking away from women is what I do best. I walked away from her, a dick move, but I did it.

But this carnal need to take? To claim? To control? It's not me, or rather it's no longer me. I've never felt that need to dominate any other woman. It must be some residual from before. That's my only explanation, but why then does it feel so different?

My desire to touch her grows with each passing second.

I shift in my seat and pull a remote from the breast pocket of my suit. We're a green industry, practicing a paperless business model as much as possible. I turn on the wall screen at the far end of the room. It opens directly onto an image of the proposal Grace Atwood sent this weekend.

"I'd like to go over our vision here at Sterling Enterprises. We invest in people, not businesses. Of course, there needs to be an adequate return on our investment, but everything ultimately comes down to the people involved. I also believe in fate and serendipity. This grabbed my eye."

"How's that?" Mark Atwood, who appears oblivious to the nonverbal interaction between me and his niece, fixes his attention on the screen.

My attention, however, is entirely focused on Grace. Her bristly response to our little reunion is no surprise. There's a lot of ground to cover; things which need to be settled, forgiveness which needs to be asked and hopefully granted, but that's not something we'll accomplish in a board room. Oh no, not at all, but I finally have an answer to where and when.

"I find it an odd alignment of fate and circumstance that I happen to be running past your vineyard on the same day my company gets a proposal for equity investing from Atwood Estates. Add in the personal connection I have with Grace and the fact my brother operates La Rouge Vineyards, there are too many coincidences to ignore. There was no possible way I couldn't handle this case personally." I stare at Grace. Her stiff posture doesn't budge, and I swear she's erecting shields as we talk.

"Well, we certainly appreciate it. Don't we, Grace?" Mark fills in the gap with aimless conversation.

"Have you read my proposal?" Her tone is bristly, bordering on snappish.

There it is, the test.

I'm well prepared but find myself a little surprised. I made a mistake in thinking Mark was in charge.

*Grace Atwood, you fascinate me.*

"I have."

"And?" She wants to rush our meeting. Her arms cross over her chest and she pushes back from the table.

I can tell she hates being in this position, although I don't understand. We have hundreds of companies coming to us each year. I think of us as dream catchers. We catch failing dreams and breathe new life into them. It's a win-win for everyone involved.

We hold each other's gazes, neither speaking, with her challenge hovering in the air between us. Handling some of her residual hostility toward me is a given, but this seems more than simple hostility.

Although, she has every reason to hate me.

She breaks her gaze first and her head tilts down to examine her cuticles. Her fingers twist as she takes in a breath and then another. When she finally looks up, it's as if she's a different person. Gone is her vulnerability. The rawness of her emotion disappears. In their place, she fronts an impassive mask.

"Mr. La Rouge, thank you for taking the time out of your day to look at our proposal. No doubt we're much smaller than most companies you deal with, but I believe we're a sound investment. If you think we'd be a good match for Sterling Enterprises, I would be thrilled to discuss conditions and terms with one of your associates."

Ouch, her professionalism hurts. And what's with this Mr. La Rouge crap?

"The first step will be to develop a solid understanding of your current operation. The financials you sent are extensive and perfect from that standpoint, but I'll still need to dig through them. We'll discuss that more at length."

We, means me.

I'll take great pleasure in discussing her financials in private. I continue on, laying out our standard terms.

"Generally, I hire out expert consultants to look over the business, but in this case, I think having my brother take a look is sufficient. He not only knows your business model but is intimately familiar with the local business environment. Asher is well-connected and well suited to assist."

"And what about terms?" Her eyes narrow.

"Our terms are standard for every partner we take and are non-negotiable. I'll have my assistant send over the documents by the middle of the week. As for financials, I see you have loan payments. We'll need to understand the terms of that loan. We can be somewhat creative with refinancing and restructuring."

"Restructuring?" Mark shifts in his seat. "What does that mean? You don't mean cutting our workers, because if that's the case..." He turns red in the face.

"Nothing like that." I hold out a steadying hand. "Very rarely do we look at laying off employees. We will, however, do a deep dive into the benefits packages, wages, salaries, and hours. You may be surprised, but it's not uncommon that one of our suggestions is to increase the workforce rather than reduce it. Lean is not always the best way to go."

"That's good to hear." He exchanges a relieved look with Grace. I sense the whole idea of equity investing doesn't sit well with him.

"As for our recommendations, they come in three forms. We're not here to take over your company, but we protect our interests. Our goal is to see you succeed. The more profitable Atwood Estates becomes, the better for the both of us."

"Explain what you mean by your recommendations?" Grace's attention shifts to her uncle. I sense her statement is more for his benefit than hers. I need to improve my background knowledge regarding Grace. She's not reacting at all, almost as if none of what I'm saying comes as a surprise.

That's interesting, because this next bit is usually the biggest hiccup.

"First-tier recommendations are non-negotiable. You're contractually obligated to implement those changes." Like I expect, Mark bristles at this comment. He takes his cue from Grace, who responds with a reassuring nod. "Second-tier are suggestions. Meaning, we strongly recommend them, but you are free to discuss and modify them as you see fit. We expect all of the Tier 2 recommendations to be implemented, but how that's done is ultimately up to you. Tier 3 recommendations are modifications that are left to your discretion. You have the freedom to adopt them, modify them, or disregard them. I would challenge you to take a serious look and consider any recommendations we offer, however, before discarding them. We have a strong track record at turning things around. If you haven't already, I have a list of clients you may wish to speak with regarding the process."

"My uncle would probably like that. I think that will help settle some of his concerns." She leans forward and presses the pad of her forefinger on the burnished wood. "Mr. La Rouge, excuse me if this is silly, but am I to understand Sterling Enterprises is taking on Atwood Estates as a client?"

"Grace…" I lean forward, placing myself closer to her. "This may be business, but call me Brody. We're friends."

"We *were* friends." The way she grinds out the words says she's not pleased at all. "That's not what we are now." Sharp and cutting, she draws a line in the sand. "It's best we keep this strictly professional."

I'm not okay with that. I didn't get where I am by turning away from a challenge. I ignore her comment and continue as if I didn't hear it.

"I'll personally be taking Atwood Estates on as a client. I have a vested interest in seeing you succeed."

My statement is vague and open to interpretation any number of ways. I intend to find my way back into her life, and I'm not above pressuring her. She's wired to respond to my commands—at least, there was a time when that was true—and I'm hopeful her need to acquiesce to my demands remains. I'm desperately hopeful. If not, I'm prepared to beg.

Her uncle takes what I said for the promise that Sterling Enterprises will take Atwood Estates on as a client. Grace, who's far more savvy than I appreciate, hears the subtext I imply. She doesn't like it one bit. I may find myself on my knees.

"I don't want to waste your time. I'm sure anyone in your acquisition's department can handle our case." Grace crosses her arms and legs, completely closing herself off to me. Any thoughts of pressuring her to do as I want go right out the window. She's not the same girl I knew.

"Nevertheless, you're stuck with me." I make a show of looking at my watch. "Now, I think a celebratory lunch is in order. Katy has booked us a table at one of my favorite restaurants."

I make sure to set Grace up so that it's impossible for her to refuse. She's dying to get away from me, which makes me all the more eager to keep her with me.

"We really don't want…" Her cheeks turn pink with indignation.

"It's already arranged. Over lunch, we can discuss when would be a good time for me to come around and see Atwood Estates in person."

"Wow, this is really great." Hesitant, Mark seems to warm up to the entire idea. He's going to be my biggest ally in my quest to reacquaint myself with Grace Atwood.

I turn off the computer screen and push away from the table. The business portion of this meeting is over. Now, it's personal.

"Shall we?"

The fire in Grace's eyes makes me smirk. I outmaneuvered her, and she's not happy about it.

*Bring your best game, Grace Atwood, because I always get what I want. And I want you.*

# TWELVE

## Grace

————————



Lunch? With Brody?

This is my worst nightmare. And he's taking a 'vested' interest in this project?

*Not so subtle on the subtext there, dude. I know exactly what you're doing.*

Bastard's trying to worm his way into my life, make me lower my shields, and then what? Swoop in and destroy me like he did a decade ago?

*Not happening Brody La Rouge. Not happening at all.*

But it's a lunch meeting. With his personal oversight of our project, there will more than likely be others. I must find a way to deal with him in a social setting, and while there's no way to avoid that, I'm not going to make things easy on him. I'll do what I must to get Atwood Estates out of the red and back in the black, but that's it. After this damn lunch, there will be very limited interactions.

He didn't like me calling him Mr. La Rouge. I file that away for future ammunition. For now, until the ink is signed, I'll play his little game. Thankfully, Mark is with me, which means there's a buffer between us during lunch. Mark is a talker. I'll lean on him to carry the conversation.

"After you." Brody gestures toward the door.

My lips press together and I stand. If I concentrate on keeping my lips closed, then maybe I won't slip and say something stupid that will ruin this whole thing. I head toward the doors, then pause for Mark to catch up. Brody looks at me expectantly, waiting for something. Not sure what that might be, I take Mark's arm and give a little squeeze. Despite having to deal with Brody, I'm excited. This is exactly what we need: a quick infusion of cash, outside eyes on our business; there's nothing about this that isn't good.

All in all, this is exactly what we need. I'll be able to breathe a little easier after today. That deserves a little celebration.

It's just lunch and I can fake it through that.

Brody lifts his hand toward the small of my back. My entire body bristles and I shift position, placing Mark firmly between me and Brody. His head cocks to the side and a smirk tilts the corner of his mouth. It makes him even more devilishly handsome, the bastard.

"Where to?" Mark glances out the doors. His gaze lands on the vast open area of the atrium and his muscles lock up.

"Actually, not very far." Brody guides us through the double doors and glances up. "We're having lunch on the top floor. The view is spectacular."

"Um…" Mark's hesitation is clear.

"The top floor?" My attention shifts from Mark to Brody. "Heights aren't really my kind of thing. Maybe we can forgo lunch and arrange that meeting for you to take a look at Atwood Estates?"

Brody's lids narrow. He knows I'm an absolute sucker for heights. In high school, I was the smallest and lightest of the cheer squad, which meant I was always the one at the top of our pyramids and often the one sailing through the air. Not to mention, there's our secret spot where I dangled my feet over a hundred-foot drop, but Brody's smart. He'll figure it out.

"There are tables that are not near the edge. It's a simple matter to change. Besides, it's a long way back to Napa. I'd hate for you to endure the drive on an empty stomach."

I'd prefer driving on an empty stomach to dealing with rush hour traffic out of the city. Unfortunately, Mark nods his head.

"That sounds perfect." Initially worried over accepting equity investment, he's in high spirits.

I suppose we both feel a weight lifting off our shoulders, but can't he sense the subtext here? I loathe Brody La Rouge. My goal is to minimize interaction, not increase it.

"Perfect. We'll take the elevator up. They're expecting us."

No doubt. I have a feeling they bend over backward for the CFO of Sterling Enterprises. My grip on Mark's arm tightens.

"Ouch! You're going to put bruises on me, squeezing that hard." Mark, unfortunately, lacks subtly.

"Sorry." I let my grip relax but continue to use Mark as a shield. He's the barrier I'll keep between Brody and myself.

A flash of adrenaline surges through my body. I refuse to acknowledge what it means. It's been forever and an age since I've experienced such an intense rush. Actually, I only ever experienced it once before—eleven years to be exact.

My focus shifts to Brody as he guides us toward the elevator. It zones in on his lips, those pillowy soft, sinful lips that deliver wicked pleasure. What would it feel like to have those lips on me now? And what about the rest? That heady transference of power is something I've sought from other men, but never achieved again. Not like it was with Brody. With him, it was effortless. Intoxicating. Absolutely amazing. A shiver runs down my spine. *Get a fucking grip.* It's like I'm fifteen again.

We head up in the glass elevator. Brody stands with his back to the glass, a confused expression on his face as Mark huddles facing the door. I stand a bit sideways to him. I've yet to release Mark's arm.

Brody's gaze shifts from Mark to me and back to Mark again. He rocks back on his heels and clears his throat. Then his magnetic gaze captures mine. Steely green, I forgot how mesmerizing his eyes can be. He pins me in place, communicating without words, as the elevator rises to the top of the building. He wants me. No, there's more to it than that. I sense his promise and the demand wrapped inside of it. He wants what we once shared. I feel his dominance unfurling. He's got something up his sleeve.

*That's okay, Brody La Rouge. Bring it on. You won't hurt me again.*

"Welcome, Mr. La Rouge, your table is waiting." A pretty hostess in a black dress with a brass nameplate marked *Brandi* in elegant scrollwork greets us. Her entire expression lights up as if there were nowhere else she'd rather be than here, serving us.

Not us, but rather Brody La Rouge.

The restaurant is fabulous. Capped in glass, the ceiling allows natural light into the room. The deep blue sky opens up the space. I bet this place is amazing at night, a perfect, cozy date place for couples looking for romance.

The walls are glass as well. White linen table service makes an impression. The tables are set well apart, ensuring privacy. It's quiet, with soft instrumental music playing through nearly invisible speakers tucked into the walls. Delicious aromas tickle my nose, and my mouth waters in anticipation. I press a hand over my belly, praying my stomach doesn't choose this moment to rumble loudly. It would too, and prove Brody right.

I'm hungry.

Mark hesitates as Brandi leads us inside, but he relaxes when she seats us in a secluded alcove situated on the interior of the restaurant. It's a small, semicircular booth. I step back, trying to get

Mark to slide into the center of the booth, leaving me to sit on the edge as far from Brody as possible. The corner of Brody's mouth ticks up, and he gives an amused shake of his head. His hair shifts in front of his eyes and he gives a practiced flip to clear his vision. My stomach does a little squeeze, remembering how much I loved that little mannerism.

"Miss, where are your restrooms?" Mark pulls away from me and looks at the hostess expectantly.

"If you'll follow me, sir. I'll show you." She heads off, taking Mark with her.

Not to be dissuaded, I sit at the edge of the booth while Brody folds his long, lean body into the other side across from me. I ignore him and grab my napkin. Head down, I wonder how long I can avoid talking to Brody and measure that up against how fast it will take for Mark to return to the table.

"It's really nice to see you, Grace." Brody's smooth voice whispers across my skin, lifting the fine hairs and sending electrical shockwaves shooting through my body. Damn, if he doesn't have the perfect voice. "It's been a long time. I look forward to reconnecting with you."

"I appreciate you taking on Atwood Estates as a client." I keep my reply efficient, sincere, and professional. "But you and I will not be reconnecting."

"I see." He leans back and unbuttons his jacket. "We're playing it this way."

"That's correct. Don't confuse this with anything else. I'm here on business, nothing more."

"Why is that, Grace?" He leans forward as my name slips past his lips. He elongates the soft-c in my name, something he always did when we were younger. It was something he did when he stood over me. When I let him—I give a sharp shake of my head and push all those thoughts out of the way. "It really is a pleasure to see you."

"It's certainly no pleasure for me." I gasp as the words spill out of my mouth completely unfiltered.

"Perhaps that's something we can discuss later?"

"I don't think so."

"We'll see about that. Nevertheless, it's nice to see you. How have you been? What have you been up to?"

"I'm not here to reconnect over a past I'd rather forget. You were nothing more than a silly girl's fantasy. A mistake I'd rather not repeat. This is purely professional."

"You sure about that? Because that's not the vibe I'm getting."

"Vibe?" I laugh. "There is no vibe. I don't know what you're talking about."

"You feel it. I know you do." He grasps at the air, fingers plucking at the invisible strings which connect us. I feel each and every vibration.

"No idea what you're talking about." I glance up and make a show of looking for Mark.

"He's not going to be rushing back to the table." Brody leans back.

"You don't know my uncle." I cock my head, confident about Mark's eagerness to know everything. "He won't want to miss a second of this."

"Perhaps not, but I know Brandi. She's an excellent hostess with very specific instructions to give us a moment alone."

"Excuse me?" I give a start and bump my knee on the table. The glasses clink as the table shakes.

"I wanted a moment alone." Brody settles the table. His broad hands splay across the fine white linen. My gaze flicks to those hands, muscles hewn out of granite. Shit, even his hands are sexy, and those fingers. I remember the things he could do with those fingers. I bite my lower lip and force my gaze away. "We have personal things to discuss."

"No. We don't."

"You don't believe that. The air crackles between us, stronger now than it was in high school. You feel it, Grace. I know you do."

"There is no crackling air. No vibrations stirring it. You mean nothing to me, and I'm sorry if that's a blow to your ego, but it is what it is. As far as *reconnecting*, I have no interest in spending any time alone with you." I lean back and close myself off, crossing my arms over my chest. I make a show of crossing my legs as well, but this time without making the table jump. "What happened before was a huge mistake. I never should've let you—"

"And yet, you did. What we had was special, as for what we did when we were together, I'll never believe that was a mistake. I'm intensely interested in getting reacquainted with you."

"Is that how this works? You take on my company, bail us out, and you somehow think I owe you something? What exactly did you think was going to happen? That I would eagerly go to my knees for you, grateful for the bailout?" I uncross my arms and press my forefinger on the table, making a point, and taking a stand. "This is a professional relationship. That's it. If you need a woman on her knees, you can pay for that shit."

The muscles of his jaw tic, but Brody doesn't lose his cool. He takes a moment and collects himself before responding. He slowly taps his finger on the table. For some reason, I can't draw my eye away from it.

*Tap. Tap. Tap.*

"First things first, Grace Atwood, Sterling Enterprises is not bailing out Atwood Estates. We don't engage in charity like that. We're investing in an opportunity we believe will benefit us both. Our professional relationship will be exactly that—professional. As far as owing me something, I admit there's something I want, but I would never force you to do anything like that. You know me better than that."

"Do I? As far as whatever you want, my answer is no." He can't argue with that.

"I haven't told you what I want yet."

"Doesn't matter. Whatever you want, outside of our professional arrangement, is a hard no as far as I'm concerned."

"Don't you want to know what it is first?"

"Frankly, I don't give a damn." I fold my napkin and toss it on the table. "I'm not interested in anything other than the future of my company. What you want outside of that is irrelevant to me."

"If that were true, your face wouldn't be flushed right now, and your breaths wouldn't be so rapid and shallow." His gaze drops to my chest and I know exactly what he sees beneath the thin fabric of my blouse.

I may know what I want, but that doesn't mean my body isn't reacting to the overwhelming presence of the boy I once loved who is now a grown man with more sexual potency than I've ever experienced. I ignore the tingling in my body and cover my overly eager nipples with my hair.

He, of course, takes all of that in. "I mean something to you all right, and we're going to deal with it."

"There's nothing to discuss."

"That's not how I see it. Our past…"

"Means nothing. Like it never occurred. Look, you may not be able to separate business and pleasure, but I can. You've seen our proposal, and no doubt investigated us, you know I'm not in a position to walk away, but you will not use my past against me. I'm not that love-struck little freshman anymore, and I'm not interested in playing games. I'm not interested in you at all. Whatever you think I want, you're wrong. Whatever you want, isn't my concern. As for the flushing in my face, that's called indignation."

"And there it is." He gives a nod, like he won this round.

"There it is, what? What are you talking about?"

"Your anger. That's what I want to talk about."

"No." No way in hell is that happening.

"No?"

"Yeah, that's what I said. You do know what the word means, don't you? Or are you still the same self-absorbed asshole who thinks you're God's gift to women?"

"I see." He leans back and taps the top of the table. "You want to keep this all business. We can do that, but your idea of business and my idea of business are a bit different."

"No doubt."

"You're accompanying me to a social event this Friday."

*Hell to the no.*

"What part of this conversation are you not understanding?"

"Consider this your first Tier 1 requirement."

"That's not a Tier 1 request. You can't demand something like that."

"It's business."

"No, it's you throwing your weight around. If it's business, take Mark. I'm sure he'll look amazing draped over your arm."

"I'm thinking about draping you over my knee right now." It's his turn for his face to flush red. I'm getting under his skin, and I like it. In fact, I like it entirely too much. He knows it too. Heat rises in my face as I remember why he knows. The over the knee thing is my kryptonite.

Was. It *was* my kryptonite.

*Keep it together, Grace. Don't let him in!*

"That's exactly the kind of comment that's unprofessional, Mr. La Rouge."

"Oh, get over yourself, Grace. You have issues with me. That's obvious. If we're going to work together and turn Atwood Estates around, you'll have to be able to carry on a civil conversation with me. If not, then maybe a turn over my knee is exactly what you need." He looks at me expectantly, judging my reaction. I keep my impassive expression firmly fixed to my face. But his words do the trick. I'm horribly, and terribly, turned on.

We stare at each other for a long moment. I'm not the only one breathing fast. I also remember I'm not the only one who enjoyed being bent over his knee. He recovers first but shifts in his seat. I've made him uncomfortable. I don't know why, but that brings a smile to my face.

"As for this Friday," he continues, "it's a charity event where I'll introduce you to vendors you need to make contact with. I'm talking about all the best chefs at the most exclusive restaurants in California. It's a Tier 1 requirement. You'll be there. It's black-tie formal, and you'll be pleasant and excited to be there with me. You and I are officially a team."

"We're officially nothing." Doesn't he get it?

"We're partners, with a contract to prove it. Tier 1, Grace. You can't refuse."

"And the fact it's a social event has no bearing on any of it? You're not using this to take advantage of the situation?"

"I would never take advantage of you."

"That's a lie. You'd do anything to stroke your ego."

"Look—" He reaches across the table, but I'm not interested in his touch. I draw back. *Never again.* "About that…"

"Back away, Brody La Rouge. I want nothing to do with you in a social, personal, or—whatever, capacity." I wave my hand, frustrated I can't find the proper word. "I don't make the same mistake twice."

"Nevertheless," he grits his teeth, "you will be there."

Mark returns to the table, and before I realize what's happening, Brody scoots around the booth, opening up a spot for Mark to sit. He places himself right next to me. His thigh touches mine and heat licks up my leg to settle with a throbbing ache where I don't want it.

*Dammit, Brody La Rouge. Well played. Fucking well played.*

THIRTEEN

# Brody

___

Lunch is nothing short of torture. Grace is not happy with me sitting beside her, not that I let it deter me. I remember what she was like: opinionated to the nines. She digs in to defend her position, which is fine by me. I'm determined to break through her walls or wear her down. Once I get her to where she's open to listening, we'll talk. Until then, game on.

"This Friday?" Mark looks at Grace. "A benefit?"

"Raising money for a good cause is the perfect venue to showcase Atwood Estate's new exclusive vintage," I explain my tactic to Mark while pressing my thigh against Grace's leg. She moved over once already, but there's nowhere else for her to go unless she falls out of the booth. There's nothing subtle about my attack, and as far as I'm concerned, it's a no-holds-barred war we wage.

I want her, and that's the end of it.

The begging and apologizing will come later. I owe her that much. I actually owe her a hell of a lot more, but I can't get there until I deal with the barriers she erects between us now.

"But we don't have a 'new exclusive vintage.'" Poor Mark uses air quotes. He keeps checking with Grace, taking his lead from her.

"Mark's right about that." Grace shifts, twisting slightly away from me. "How are we supposed to make that materialize out of thin air?"

"It's called creating demand for a limited product. As you stated in your proposal, you have limited stock on hand to sell."

"Correct?" She's hesitant but listening.

"First, we stop all future sales."

"We need those sales if we're going to avoid going bankrupt. We're counting on that revenue…"

I hold up a hand to reassure them.

"Scarcity is your greatest commodity right now. Step one is repackaging and rebranding. Atwood Estates is a small, family-run winery catering to the astute purveyor of fine wine. That's your selling point. We'll work on a snappier tagline, but that's your vision statement. You're not going to compete against the big corporate wineries with their cheap, store-bought wines. Do that and fail. We fulfill whatever orders you currently have and stop any new orders. Temporarily, at least, until the rebranding is complete. We're going to market Atwood Estates as an exclusive commodity. Impossible to get unless you're on a very select list. In fact, we'll make it a waiting list. People must apply, and be approved, before they may set up accounts to be exclusive vendors. Before you know it, you'll have people lining up to be a part of the new VIP club. That's our goal."

"I'm a little uncomfortable with this." Mark leans back and takes a sip from his iced tea. "This really works?"

"Only if we drive up demand." I glance at Grace. "This is where Friday comes in play." She thinks it's all about me getting her alone —which in many ways it is—but I'm a shrewd businessman. I already know how we're going to save her company. "The benefit is for childhood cancer, which is great, but irrelevant as far as we're concerned. The theme is the Culinary Masters of California. All the top chefs will be in attendance. We're going to take what you have now, and I'm assuming it passes basic quality standards…"

"Our wine is exemplary." Mark puffs out his chest.

Of course, I already know this. I spent all Saturday night and Sunday trying out their product. Asher thought I was nuts, but he tasted and approved the wine. It's good. Top shelf, in fact.

"We offer each of the attending chefs one bottle as a gift, and then we pair your wine with their dishes at the event and offer that to the guests. That gets your brand in the faces of not only the chefs but the movers and shakers of the area. We donate another couple of bottles for the auction. People love exclusive. While there, I'll make introductions to those who can benefit you the most. We'll establish exclusive agreements with those in attendance. Grace is there to seal the deal."

"And what about Mark?" Grace once again shifts away from me, but there's no place for her to go.

I rest my hand on her thigh and watch her reaction. All she's given me is cold and distant. I need a sign I'm not wrong about the attraction smoldering between us. I'll push, but only so far. There are lines I won't cross.

The muscles of her thigh tense. She reaches down. Her delicate fingers wrap around mine, and there's the slightest hesitation the moment our hands connect. Since I'm specifically watching for it, the catch in her breathing is unmistakable. She wants to hate me and hold the sins of my past over my head, but our connection is still there. It's frayed and singed but not completely severed.

"Unfortunately, the tickets I have for the event are only for two." I turn my hand over, and our palms press against each other for the briefest second before I release her and remove my hand from her leg. "It has to be Grace."

The breath she takes falters and is full of the chemistry sizzling between us. I just have to coax the rest of that energy out and let it grow from there. I shift away, placing space between our legs. It's time to let up on the pressure and give her some breathing room.

"You have to go." Mark gives a nod. "Besides, I'm not really the black-tie kind of guy. You can totally pull off the exclusive angle."

Grace nibbles on her lower lip. Another subtle play of emotions moves across her face. She finally gives the slightest shake of her head as she comes to a decision.

"Fine. Friday it is. I don't know what I have to wear, but I'm sure I can come up with something. Send me the details, and I'll meet you there."

"No need for that. I'll be in Napa on Friday visiting my brother. In fact, that's a good time for him to take a look at what you've got. We'll meet in the morning and go over everything. Mark, if it's okay with you, I'll have you show Asher around while Grace and I go over the books. We'll break for lunch, then I'll pick you up around four in the afternoon. It'll be a beautiful drive into the city." At least two hours where I'll have her all to myself. I'm already thinking about that drive and how to use it to my advantage.

"I wouldn't want to put you out." Her resistance remains, but some of it fades.

"Nonsense. I have to drive back anyway. My mother's promised to introduce me to her new boyfriend. I'm very eager to meet him." That's a total lie, but I'll make it work. If I give Grace any wiggle room, she'll find a way to worm her way free of me. That can't happen.

Mark slowly comes around, warming up to the entire process. There's something about him. I'd say it's simple discomfort from being forced into a process he doesn't understand, but I feel like something else lurks below the surface.

Lunch is done, and I can no longer draw out my time with Grace. I hate leaving her and try to think up another excuse to get her to stay. I convince myself I only need five more minutes of her time. The thing is, I'll never get enough. I send a note to Katy and pay the bill.

"Before you leave, if you would walk back with me to my office. My assistant is preparing the background documents for you. They state our general terms. By close of business tomorrow, we'll send over the official contracts for you to sign, but this way you'll have a chance to look at our boilerplate. Any questions, just call." I give Grace my business card, then lean in. "That's my personal line. Call me for anything."

She takes the card and puts it inside her purse. I practically jump for joy because I expected her to rip it to shreds.

We head back to my office, and I smile inwardly at Mark's fear of heights. Grace walks beside him, shielding him from the openness of the atrium while I hang back and admire the curves of her figure.

The open atrium design was my idea. I love having the gardens down below and personally designed the series of waterfalls and meandering streams. Hawke added the koi to the ponds because he loves the flashes of color. Most days, that's where I go for lunch, brown-bagging it like a kid.

It's the simple things in life which matter.

We head to my office to wait while Katy gathers the boilerplate of our standard contract. She can send it by email, and will, but I needed an excuse to keep Grace with me for a little bit longer.

Despite what Grace said earlier, she walks right up to the floor-to-ceiling windows to stare out over the city. We've got the best view of the bay and Golden Gate bridge. Mark takes a seat on one of my couches, staying as far from the windows as possible.

I leave him there and move to stand beside Grace. We're close, closer than strangers would stand. I very subtly invade her space. It's a statement. She can't deny my interest. If she moves away, she admits I'm making her uncomfortable. If she stays, she acquiesces to my display of dominance.

"It's really good to see you again." I keep my voice low, too soft for Mark to hear. This is a private conversation between the two of us.

She doesn't look at me but continues to stare straight ahead.

"I've missed you." I shift slightly closer, feeling the electric charge between us building. We've got impressive chemistry. It's been forever and a day since a woman's elicited such a strong reaction from me. With Grace, I can only describe it as carnal, animalistic, and raw.

"I don't see how that's possible." She gives a dismissive sniff and tilts her nose up.

The long, graceful curve of her neck entrances me. My fingers curl as I resist the urge to grab her and lay a trail of kisses down her neck. Just as I get ready to respond to that comment, she shifts half a step away from me. Her tone hardens, turning brittle and fills with long-simmering pain.

"You've never cared about anyone but yourself. It's impossible for you to *miss* me when you're the one who walked away. As for missing me, that's a total lie, and frankly more than a little insulting. You not only turned your back on me…" Her voice hitches and trails off. "You destroyed me…"

"Grace…" I reach out, but she shrugs away. I let my arm drop to my side, defeated, because she's right. She's right about everything. I bend my head. "I'm not proud of many things in my past. That includes what I did to you."

"Don't worry about it. It's ancient history, and I've moved on. If you think I've been pining away for you for over a decade, think again. You simply didn't mean that much to me. I got over you and moved on. Present circumstances excluded, I'd be happy if I never saw you again."

"You don't mean that."

"Don't I?" Her brow arches in challenge.

Movement in my peripheral vision draws my attention. Mark stands and moves away from the couch.

"Hey, can you tell me where the facilities are? It's going to be a long drive back, and well, you know."

"Down the hall, take a right, and fourth door on the left." I send him the wrong way, but only because I need time alone with Grace. I've lost her, and a weird sensation runs through me. A low noise rumbles in the back of my throat and Grace's entire body stiffens beside me.

Unable to stop myself, the thought of losing her is too much. She's mine. That's all there is to it. I made a mistake when I was young, but there's no way in hell I'm squandering this second chance. If my words don't convince her, I know one thing that will.

The moment Mark leaves, I spin her until she faces me. Her hands fly to my chest, but before she can push me away, I silence her with a kiss. My lips crash down on hers, and I take what I've been aching for since the moment she walked back into my life. Her shuddering exhale makes my entire body come alive.

That's not rejection. It's something else entirely.

Our problem is all the bad memories festering between us. I'm here to sweep those aside and prove my point. There's still something between us, something we must explore. I lean back, pulling away as a test.

Instead of ending my kiss, she follows me.

That's it. It's all I need.

I splay my hand across the small of her back and tug her tight against me as I capture her mouth with mine. Dragging my tongue against hers, my other hand curls around her neck. I tilt her head to deepen the kiss and feast on her mouth.

She tastes sweeter than I remember and I can't get enough. I focus on her mouth, licking and sucking, as I remind her exactly how good we are together.

She breathes out. The sound of her soft surrender accelerates my heart. I move my lips from her mouth and kiss up along her jawline until I reach her ear. That's where I pause and regain control over my ragged breathing.

"You feel this. I know you do, and I'm here to tell you I won't let you run from this. We're going to talk about what happened and clear the air, but this is something we're going to explore."

"Please." Her fingers curl in my shirt. "Don't do this."

"Run if that's what you need. Push me away if you have to, but I'm here. I've found you again, and I'm not letting you go. Didn't you hear what I said about fate? You were put in my path for a reason."

She resists my affection but doesn't force me away. I kiss along her neck, reaching the soft hollow near her collar bone, nuzzling as I go. I'm hard. I'm fucking desperate and achingly hard. I pull back and gaze deep into her eyes.

"This isn't something you're going to walk away from. Accept it, or fight it, if you must, but we already know how this will turn out."

Her brows bunch together, then her attention shifts to the window. "I'm not the same person you knew." Sorrow fills her voice. "I don't want to go down this road again."

"Grace…"

"We're not doing this." Her fingers bunch in my shirt, and she pushes me away.

"You felt that. I know you did. You fucking melted for me." That kiss proves everything I know.

"All that proves is that you're still the best kisser in town, but I'm not interested in being one of many, and I'm definitely not interested in a one-and-done kind of fling. That's not who I am. It's not what I want."

She's telling me that's exactly the kind of man I am. Unfortunately, every word she speaks is true. I don't keep women around, but none of them affected me in the way Grace does. This is different. As far as a one-and-done kind of thing, there's no way I'll be satisfied with one night.

No way am I leaving things like this.

I take her in my arms and reclaim her mouth. She opens for me. It's such a natural reaction it sends a thrill through me. My fingers dig into her waist as our tongues slide together. There's no tentative exploration of a first kiss. We've been here before. We know what we'll find.

There's still something between us.

My kiss doesn't remain soft and gentle. I attack her mouth, pushing her. My teeth graze her lips, nipping as I remind her who's in charge. Her fingers wrap around my neck. The shock of her reaction, her willingness, stops me only for the span of a heartbeat.

I abandon nipping at her lips and reclaim her mouth. Our lips meld together as our bodies press close. Her breaths quicken, as do mine. I plunge my tongue deeper, reacquainting myself with her mouth.

Deeper.

Hungrier.

Mine.

Every cell in my body reacts as a tingling sensation rushes through me.

But we don't have much time. I break off the kiss earlier than I'd like and lick my wet lips. Her taste lingers on my tongue, and I love it. I want more of it.

"You can't deny that."

She touches her mouth, tracing her thick, swollen lips. It's crazy how my chest tightens as I wait for her to respond.

"No, but I can deny you. I hope you got what you needed because that's the last kiss I'll give you."

"That's not the last one I'll take."

Her eyes widen at that comment, and she takes a step back, placing distance between us. "I'm not the same girl you remember. I'm not stupid, or naïve. I know what you are."

"I never lied to you about what I am. If you want me to stop, you know what to do. Say the word, and everything ends." I stare at her, challenging her to utter the one word that will end us. It's not a simple 'No.' That word has no meaning between us. Or rather, it didn't back when there was an us. Things might be different now.

She shakes me to my core when her lips part. I tense, waiting for her to strike the killing blow. Instead, the door opens, and Mark enters. We break apart.

"Hey, sorry it took so long. I took a wrong turn and got lost." My assistant wanders in behind him. "Katy sent all the files to my email. I guess you can start looking through them on the ride home." He rattles on, oblivious to the tension swirling between me and Grace. "We should get going, or traffic's going to be insane." He rocks back on his heels and looks expectantly at Grace.

My attention shifts back to Grace. Her lips clamp tight.

"Thank you for lunch." Her gaze flicks to Mark and then back to me. "We'll go over the contract and get back to you."

"No doubt." I place my hand on her upper arm and give it a light squeeze. "I look forward to seeing you Friday. It's one word. That's all it takes to end this forever."

She doesn't answer but gives a pointed glare where I grip her arm. I release her, and she moves away. Absently rubbing at her arm, she heads to the door.

"It was nice to meet with you, Brody." Mark advances and shakes my hand. "I look forward to showing you around Atwood Estates."

"I'm sure the pleasure will be all mine."

She didn't say it. Once they leave, I can't help but smile.

Grace is mine.

# FOURTEEN

## Grace

SWEET HELL, WHEN BRODY BROKE THAT KISS, I LICKED MY SWOLLEN, throbbing lips and felt the world shift beneath my feet. My head reels and I stagger beneath the weight of memories—memories of a young, innocent, and stupid love that he destroyed.

But then he had to go and challenge me, demanding the one word that would end everything. I thought I was beyond all that. It was something silly we played with in high school when we thought we were mature and sophisticated, but something happened when he offered me a way to stop this.

I should've said it, but I couldn't. I didn't want to give him the satisfaction of knowing he got under my skin. That's what would've happened. There's only one reason to say it, and that's to make everything stop. But I didn't.

I can't.

I'm too weak. What's far worse is that tiny glimmer of hope buried so deep I didn't know it was still there.

"Are you feeling okay?" Mark's head cants sideways. We're in the elevator with the glass walls and he's hyperventilating. He practically hugs the elevator door.

"I'm fine." Butterflies riot in my belly. I still reel from that kiss.

"You don't look fine. You look like you're going to be sick."

"It's nothing." *Understatement of the century.* "It's been a stressful day. I expected a meeting, but a contract? I feel like we've been given a gift, and we didn't have to plead our case. Honestly, I thought we'd have to work harder."

"Like he said, I guess it's fate."

Fate? Can that be true? It sure seems like some greater force is at work. Although, knowing how closely I'll be working with Brody in the near future, I'm wondering why I didn't say the word. By not saying it, I practically give tacit approval for—well, for whatever comes next.

Although, I know the answer to my question. While a part of me wants revenge on Brody La Rouge, I can't ignore that small voice in my head that whispers '*What if?*'

"Do you think this is the end of our worries?" He taps the steel door of the elevator and glances up at the numbers counting down from forty to the lobby level. The bell dings with each floor we pass while his anxiety rises.

"Nothing's ever certain, but I'm hopeful. They bring a lot to the table, strategies we can't take advantage of by ourselves."

"Like what exactly?"

"Restructuring our debt for one thing." I look out at the expansive atrium and feel the wealth dripping down the walls. Brody's company is more than capable of paying off our debt and internalizing it within its financials. We'll still pay for it down the line, but not having to serve that debt will free up the capital we need for establishing our new image and rebranding our entire business.

I'd love to work for a company this size. The magnitude of it is staggering. The challenges are hard enough to stimulate my eager mind. This is the kind of place I always saw myself working at, a company where I could move and shake the world. Not once did I see myself managing a small, family-run business, and a struggling one at that.

But fate doesn't care what I want. It does its own damn thing, like cross my path with Brody again. As far as Atwood Estates goes, we're in bed with Sterling Enterprises. The only question remaining is whether that will remain figurative or if I allow it to become literal.

There's no doubt what Brody wants. *Who* he wants. He's obsessive enough to get it, driven enough to go after it—it being me in this scenario.

As for me?

I'm at war with the voices in my head, and the pain in my heart remains a jagged ache. The problem I face is that I'm foolish enough to give in to my most secret desire. If I convince myself one night with him will be enough, that's all it will take to fall. But this is where I need to be strong.

Resolute.

I place my hand between Mark's shoulder blades, providing support as the elevator escorts us to the lobby.

"How do you feel?" I rub at the tight muscles of his neck. "You seem okay with things?"

I'm happy to see some of his concerns ease up a bit. While I know this is the only way to save Atwood Estates, I want him to be on board with the changes. We're a team, and I don't want him to feel like I'm changing everything around without taking his thoughts into consideration.

"You asked me to trust you, and that's what I'm doing. You're the one with the MBA."

"There's something to be said for real-world experience."

"Perhaps, but those who are the freshest out of the gate are the ones full of so much knowledge they forget to fear. They're the ones with enough faith to jump and have the guts to know when to take that leap. They've yet to be tempered by experience, burdened by fear. You're not hesitant."

"I'm not sure about that."

"Trust me, cupcake, you're fearless."

The elevator comes to a halt. The moment the doors open wide, he makes his escape. He takes a deep breath and cranes his neck to look back up from where we came.

"I really hate heights." A whole-body shudder shakes him. Then he grins because he knows it's a foolish fear. I get it, though. Fear isn't rational.

Look at me. My head knows Brody isn't a threat. My fear says otherwise, nearly paralyzing me in the process.

"If I'd known what this place looked like, I wouldn't have asked you to come." I spin in a slow circle taking in the beauty of the building. Whoever designed this atrium is a person who misses the outdoors. "But I'm really glad you did. You're my rock."

"I'm glad I did as well. I have a better understanding of what to expect with this whole process. I'm hopeful, I suppose, but I've always had faith in you. I knew you wouldn't propose it if it didn't make the best sense for us, but I've been around the block a time or two. I fear change." He gives a soft laugh. "But you didn't hesitate. Circumstances demanded you step up, and you did just that—fearlessly."

"I don't know about all of that. Most days, I feel like I'm drowning. In class, everything was abstract. It was just an assignment. If you fucked it up, all you got was a bad grade. I can't do that with Atwood Estates."

"And what is your gut saying?"

"This is what we need."

"Then we go with your gut and all your fresh ideas. I did like the tier system he mentioned. It makes it feel like we're not giving up all control." He clasps my hand. "We'll turn this place around, you and me. You with your business sense and me with my knowledge of operations."

"Yeah."

Except my business sense is untried, and his knowledge hasn't been enough to keep us afloat.

I cringe. Blaming Mark is unfair. He's not at fault for the drought that starved our vines, and my mom is the one who's been in charge of the business side of things. I feel better about our chances of turning things around.

I lift my fingers to my lips.

They're puffy, swollen, and still aching from Brody's kiss. Other parts of me throb in response.

Next time I see Brody, we're going to lay down some ground rules. Atwood Estates is my livelihood. I don't have time for anything else.

There are consequences if things go wrong. Consequences which matter more than a silly girl's reputation or a silly girl's fantasies.

The drive home is not as bad as I think it'll be. We don't escape rush hour traffic, but we're at the leading edge of the great bulge of commuters fleeing the city.

And it's a gorgeous, sunny day.

We roll down our windows once we're off the interstate and let the aromas of California wine country carry us home. It's not too long before we pull up the drive outside Mom's house.

"I'm going to tell Mom how things went." I want to jump out of the car the moment Mark brings us to a stop, but he grabs my hand and gives it a squeeze.

"Let's tell her together."

"Abbie's here." I'm happy to see Abbie La Rouge's car parked outside.

"I noticed she's been coming around more often."

"Yeah, I think she knows there's not much time."

"Unfortunately, that's true. Lucy deserves to be surrounded by those she loves, and Abbie's always been a dear friend."

His statement is true. Abbie promised she'd come by and check on Mom while we were gone and would be here to give Mom her afternoon pills in case we didn't make it back in time. Traffic is always unpredictable.

Abbie's light and airy voice carries on the wind, and I stop in my tracks. Mark pulls up short as I point toward the porch. He stops and tilts his head.

*She's outside?* He mouths the words, and I hold my hand over my heart as I fight the tears.

It's been weeks since Mom felt good enough to move from her bed to the rocking chair outside her room. Abbie has a miraculous touch. Mark and I march up the steps leading to the large, wraparound porch. We head around the corner and stare at what's surely a miracle.

Mom sits in her chair with blankets piled on top of her lap. Abbie sits beside her, and they giggle like little girls. Abbie holds a book in her hands, a well-worn book with frayed edges, dog-eared pages, and a broken spine from frequent re-reads.

I know that book very well. It's what I once shared with Brody.

FIFTEEN

## Grace

I SEE THE ICONIC COVER WITH THE GRAY TIE, BUT MARK'S oblivious. When they hear us, their laughter cuts off. Abbie hides the book, tucking it behind her back, and smiles brightly at us.

"How did it go?" She clasps her hands in her lap and looks expectantly at me.

Before I can answer, Mark opens his mouth and spills the beans about Sterling Enterprises.

"They're taking us on."

"You're kidding!" Abbie gives a little clap and reaches over to grasp my mom's arm. "Did you hear that, Lucy!"

My mom turns toward me. There's a weak smile on her face, and her movements are slow, but her eyes brighten and brim with tears. I don't remember her being that pale.

"I knew you could do it." She lifts her hand and her fingers tremble as they beckon for us to join her. "Tell me everything!"

I drag another rocker to sit beside Mom and recount our meeting with Brody. Every now and again, my gaze shifts to the book Abbie is doing a poor job of hiding, and my heart skips a beat.

"I'm going to grab a celebratory bottle of wine." Mark rocks back on his heels. "Abbie, will you join us?"

"Absolutely!" Her bright eyes dance with joy. "This is such good news."

That may be true, but I can't help but feeling I'm in way over my head. Mark departs, leaving the three of us alone.

"So, Brody is coming home two weekends in a row?" Abbie's eyes sparkle. "This is a wonderful treat. He's never done that for me." Her attention shifts to me. "You must be special."

"I don't know about special, but I'm excited. This gives us the breathing space we need to get our feet back under us. And he has some really exciting ideas."

I don't know how much Abbie La Rouge knows about what happened between me and her son when we were in high school, but she's more attentive than people give her credit for.

"Honey," Abbie leans back and rocks in her chair, "to bring Brody out of the city on a Friday is pretty damn special. For him to drive out here, then back for whatever this Gala event is, and make yet another trip out here?" She gives another shake of her head. "I'm going to have to thank you for this magic trick."

"I don't know how thankful you're going to be."

"Why's that?" Her brows tug together.

"He said something about checking out your new boyfriend? He said it tongue-in-cheek, but I feel like you deserve fair warning."

"Oh, girl, thanks for the heads up. You and I are going to get along really well." She rubs her hands together like she's looking to stir up a bit of trouble. "How much fun do you want to have with my son?"

Her comment takes me off guard because my mind heads straight to the gutter and toward fifty shades of fun, but I don't think that's what she's talking about. In fact, I know it's not.

*So why did your mind go there so quickly?*

Because, I'm hopeless, and despite everything, I still harbor a crush on my very first love. That's not something any girl really recovers from.

Brody La Rouge.

First crush.

First love.

First broken heart.

He checks all the boxes. He might still check some of the boxes. Brody was, and continues to be, my worst mistake.

I must be a sucker for punishment because I had a chance to stop him in his tracks and did nothing. Instead, I gave him the green light to proceed. If there's one thing I know about Brody La Rouge, he's a man who goes after, and gets, what he wants.

Only he doesn't know I'm not the same, impressionable girl he used to know. I'm older, wiser, and carry a decade's old grudge.

*Bring it on, Brody. Bring it on.*

"Tell me about this boyfriend he seems to want to interrogate?"

"Well…" She drops her voice to a whisper. "It's Judge Simon. I've known him forever. He's been entirely respectful toward me since…" Her voice hitches. Abbie grows misty-eyed, remembering her late husband. She dabs at her eyes, glances up toward the sky, and continues. "The thing is, I haven't told the boys about him, not that they don't know. My boys are nosey and more than a little overprotective of their mom. I don't need that whole meet and greet Mom's new boyfriend thing to complicate things. They think to devise a way to work around me, but I'm going to remind them who's boss."

"I love that so much." I grin, thinking how Abbie might deal with her meddling triplets. "Sign me up. I'm more than willing to be your co-conspirator."

"I love that about you." She taps Mom's arm. "I'm so happy you brought Grace home." She points at me. "As for my troublesome boys, you keep your ear to the ground. If you hear Brody mention anything, you let me know."

"I can definitely do that." I turn my attention to my mother. "Brody's having Asher stop by on Friday. He's bringing Asher in as a corporate expert." My gaze shifts back to Abbie. "If you want, we can have a bit of fun…"

Abbie leans back. "It's a shame Cage is out on assignment. It's been a hot minute since they've all been home. Although the three of them together can be challenging."

My mom laughs. She follows every word of our conversation, but it's hard for her to jump in. It's taking all her strength to sit with us as it is.

I glance at my watch, noticing it's nearly dinnertime, and turn to Abbie.

"If you don't have dinner plans with your beau, I'm making spaghetti with meatballs. Mark's probably stuck in the cellar trying to figure out which wine to pair it with, but I know he'd love to have you stay." I take my mom's hand in mine and weave our fingers together. "He's actually more excited than I thought he'd be. I'm so worried I'm pushing him—taking over too much too soon."

"Cupcake…" She pauses to cough and then retches from trying to cough. I wait for her to collect herself. "He loves this place more than he'll ever admit. He's got an eye for making wine, but not for numbers. I'm glad the two of you are working together." It's only a few sentences, but it's enough to steal her breath. Mom leans back with a sigh and closes her eyes.

Abbie watches everything. She reaches over to grasp my mom's other hand. "Feeling tired, Lucy? Have I overstayed my welcome yet?"

"I'd love for you to stay." My mom's words come out slow, tremulous, but stronger than I expect. It's incredible the way she feeds off Abbie's energy. I wish I could bottle some of that up to dispense throughout the day. Not one time during our conversation does she wince or grimace in pain.

If I had three wishes, I'd spend them all on my mom.

"It's settled then." I point to the book Abbie's been hiding. "I'll leave the two of you out here to finish that chapter you're reading."

"You saw that?" Abbie's face reddens.

"Thankfully, poor Mark did not. It's one of my favorite books, by the way. The spicy scenes are the ones with the double dog-eared pages."

"What did any of us do before this book?" Abbie shakes her head and reaches for the novel. "And we already figured out who dog-eared the pages, luv."

Before my face turns scarlet, I make my excuses. I've got dinner to cook and other things to consider.

It feels good having company—normal. It's been far too long since we've had a normal day.

But it comes at a cost, wearing Mom out. I miss *normal*. After dinner, Abbie helps me put Mom to bed, then she starts washing dishes.

"How was it seeing Brody today?"

I tense, not sure how to respond. In high school, I never hung out at the La Rouge's. As far as I know, she knows nothing about the history I share with her middle son.

"He was very nice. Seemed genuinely interested in helping us out. I certainly didn't expect something like that from someone in his position. To be honest, it was a little intimidating."

"That's nice to hear, but not really what I was asking about."

"I'm confused."

"Luv, my boys are no angels. The honest truth is they're hellions. I'd like to think I brought them up right, but there's only so much a mom can do. My boys made a lot of mistakes growing up, but they're turning into better men. When I found out Brody was taking on Atwood Estates…"

"Wait, you knew?"

"Hunny, there's little I don't know. He talked to Asher about it, who spoke to his darling Evie about it, who whispered in my ear, and of course, there was your mom."

"Mom?" That's no surprise.

"I know things were messy between the two of you in high school." Abbie's expression softens.

"Abbie—"

"Let me finish." She turns her attention back to the pot she's scrubbing, while I aimlessly dry the same plate again. "Let me tell you a few things I know about my son. Brody never takes on a client unless there's a killing to be made. He's done well for himself, exceptionally well, and I'm a very proud mama. He's kind and generous with his wealth. But he's driven. He's a lot like his daddy, a man who went after what he wants. So when I see him taking on a client of your scale, there's more involved. Since it's not about money, that leaves only one thing."

"What's that?"

"Sweetie, it's about a girl. And it's not too hard to put two and two together."

"I don't know what to say."

"I'm not asking you to say anything, just listen. Right now, we're just two women having a conversation. When a man changes his routine, there's a reason behind it—a motivating factor. I don't know what he's up to, except there's something going on in that head of his. I'm not going to tell you what to do—I'd never presume —but I will say this…"

I'm not sure I want to hear whatever she has to say, but Abbie is a woman who speaks her mind.

"Whatever happened between you two is years in the past. You've grown. He's grown. Maybe there's a chance you grow back toward each other. Maybe this is his way of reaching out to make up for what happened between the two of you. Maybe the gulf between you has grown too wide to overcome. No one can really say, but no matter which one it might be, don't be hasty."

"Hasty?"

"Yes, luv. Don't discard him out of hand, but don't run back into his arms either. Both of those are mistakes, and you're a smart girl—a brilliant young woman. If he wants you, make him work for it. Make him make amends for the past, but don't hold the past over his head. You're not the same person you were, and neither is he."

"I don't really know what to say."

"I know my boy, and I have a feeling I know what he's up to, but like I told you, he's no angel. Brody has a history with women, not a good one. Don't let his reputation make up your mind, and don't let your experience in high school dictate your future. Don't let it ruin something that might be exactly what you need. When the right woman comes along, Brody's not going to know what hit him. All that's to say is that you don't owe him anything, but he's sure bending over backward and breaking his rules for you. Don't dismiss him out of hand. And if you need any help putting him in his place…" She places her hand on my arm. "I know exactly how to do that. I've done it his whole life. Men like to think they're in charge, but they're really lost without a good woman telling them what to do. I've held that crown for far too long. It's time to hand over the reins, if you get my drift?"

No doubt about whether Abbie La Rouge is in my corner. My only question is which corner is she in? The one where I walk away, or the one where I stay?

For whatever reason, Abbie's little talk helps. I don't feel alone anymore, and I know she's got my back. Which is funny knowing she's his mother and not mine.

As far as Brody's concerned, bring it on.

And boy does he bring it. After my talk with Abbie, or rather her talk with me, I can't get Brody out of my head. I toss and turn all night, until exhaustion pulls me under. When I wake in the morning, the havoc he wrecked on my sleep is evident all around me.

My bed's a mess. My pillows lay in scattered heaps all over the floor. I have no memory of flinging them off the bed. My sheets twist around my legs, and my head spins. I know one thing with absolute certainty.

I'm in trouble when it comes to Brody La Rouge.

# SIXTEEN

# Brody

It's been two long days since Grace Atwood left my office. Three days since I kissed her and pushed something I shouldn't have pushed. The five-knuckle-hustle's been giving my arm a workout as my fantasies run wild. A madman morning and night, and a few times in between, I can't stop thinking about her—obsessing about her. For the first time, in a very long time, I appreciate the perks of a corner office with a private bathroom.

My fantasies regarding Grace are positively sinful and over the top. This is the first time I've felt anything so raw and powerful when it comes to a woman. Sure, I date them. I fuck them. I relieve the physical need stirring within me, but this obsession? It's all-consuming.

I punch my pillow, groaning with frustration. My brain is on an endless loop, thinking about her lips, the way she tasted, the way she felt in my arms. When I close my eyes, my skin tightens with traitorous thoughts. I imagine kissing her, slowly, deeply, thoroughly. She moans with pleasure as I kiss her, hold her close, and remove her clothes.

I've tried to bury this raw energy by working my body to exhaustion. I've tried to smooth it over through meditation. But it's all to no avail. I'm constantly hard and aching. My heart pounds relentlessly, sending scorching currents of heat throughout my body. I'm an anxious, nervous, and frazzled mess.

In my life, I take what women shamelessly offer. If sex means nothing to them, then it sure as shit means nothing to me. But with Grace, it's different. We share a common history; a bond along with a common pain. I want to make up for that and erase the pain I caused her. I want to make her life easier, shoulder her burdens. I don't know what this is, but I need to make up for what I did.

I don't like the man I've become. I'm ashamed of myself, and for the first time, I'm relieved my father is gone. He would be disappointed by the man I've become, but with Grace, I can be something better. I know it.

These are the thoughts which ghost through my mind as Thursday morning rolls around.

I know I shouldn't, but I'm unable to stop myself. The need to see her again is too great. I wait until nine before dialing her number.

"Hello?" Soft and seductive, her voice is dick-twitching magic. That one word sends a riot of sensation flooding my system.

I'm instantly hard and it takes a breath before I remember I'm the one who called her.

"Grace." My reply is short, clipped, and wanting. I cringe and hope she doesn't hear the strain in my voice.

"Brody." Her reply is a shock to my system, like she breathes life into my soul, but it's short. Clipped. Hesitant.

"I need to see you." I'm not against laying it out there. I want her to know I've been thinking about her.

"I don't think that's such a good idea." Her hesitation isn't unexpected, but I'm prepared to work for what I want.

I need time alone with her to figure out what the hell is happening inside my head. I don't obsess over women—like never. It's not a part of my makeup, but I obsess over her.

"Why not?"

"Because we're business partners, and we need to keep things professional. I don't think it's a good idea for us to see each other outside of that."

"That's shit and you know it. After that kiss…"

"I wish you hadn't kissed me. It complicates things."

"Doesn't have to complicate anything."

"Do you kiss all your clients?"

"No."

"Then it complicates things."

"I also don't sleep with any of my clients, but we both know where this is going to end. I'm coming over."

"Brody…" Her breathy voice tells me I'm on track, a bit too pushy, but on track.

"If you can swear you haven't been thinking about that kiss, I'll hang up, and this is the last you'll hear about it. I haven't stopped thinking about you, and I'm pretty sure I've been on your mind. You felt our energy. No way to deny it. You melted in my arms, Grace. Don't deny it. Why do you think that is? Why can't I turn off the thoughts in my head?"

"I don't know."

"Have you?"

"Have I what?"

"Have you been thinking about me?"

"Of course I have. The things Sterling Enterprises can do for Atwood Estates are incredible. I'm not going to lie, but it's the answer to my prayers." Her tone is totally not what I want to hear.

Where's the desperation? Her need for me?

"That's not what I meant, and you know it." My voice deepens and becomes more demanding. It's a natural flow between us, and I know she'll respond. I grind my molars, frustrated with her response. "When you lie down at night, do you think of me? Do you ache for me? We were pretty good once…"

"That was a long time ago."

"That's not an answer."

"Brody, please."

"I haven't stopped thinking about you, or that kiss, and I know you haven't as well."

"I'm not doing this." Her voice hitches. "I haven't thought about you."

"You're lying." I'm not against pushing her. "There was a time when you'd never lie to me."

"There was a time when I thought you could never hurt me. It goes both ways. You ruined what we had together, and you can't step in and pick up where we left off because I may, or may not, have kissed you back. It doesn't work like that."

"And why not?"

"Because we're different people now. Not to mention, it's unfair to me."

"If you think I'm going to walk away, you're wrong. What I did was reprehensible. It was me being a selfish, arrogant ass, more concerned about my image and reputation than my feelings for the girl I loved. I can't change what I did, but I'll make it up to you. You're my number one priority."

"My company is my top priority."

"As it should be, but what about us?"

"There is no us."

"Tell me you haven't thought about that kiss and I'll hang up right now."

"Brody…" Her breathy reply tells me all I need to know.

"Say it," I demand an answer.

"Fine." Her irritation shows in the warbling of her voice. "I've thought about the kiss. So what?"

"I need to see you."

"We shouldn't…"

*We…* My heart leaps for joy at her use of that word. She may not realize it, but she opened the door. It may only be a tiny crack, but I can deal with that.

"We shouldn't do a lot of things, but that doesn't mean they're not going to happen. I have a lot to make up for. I can't explain what I'm feeling, except I need to see you. I need to see you today."

"I don't know about that." Again, she fails to give me a hard no. Hope is my friend.

"I only need an answer to one thing." My fingers cramp with the death grip I hold on the phone.

"What's that?"

"When I get to your door, are you going to turn me away?"

"That's not fair."

"Fair has nothing to do with this. I know what I want, the only question is, do you? Do you want me? Will you give me a chance to make up for what I did?"

"I can't…"

"Tell me you don't want to see me."

"I…" She tries to say it but can't.

"That's what I thought. I'll be there at two."

There's a long pause on the other end of the line. My fingers clench, waiting for her to answer. A breathy sigh sounds through the cellphone.

"I'll be here." Resignation fills her voice. "But we need to talk. First, promise me we'll talk. Don't try to confuse me with…"

"With what?"

"You damn well know what I mean. Just don't."

I like her choice of words. First means something else will follow.

"Deal, but Grace…"

"Yeah?"

"After we talk…"

"Please don't say it."

I've got so much shit to wade through with Grace, but I'm hopeful. She wants to talk before anything else happens, but until we work out the restless energy surging between us, neither one of us is going to be in the right frame of mind to talk about the past.

I know exactly how to take care of that problem.

"Expect to be gone the rest of the day. We're going for a ride, and we'll talk on the way up." No need to finish that thought. We had a secret hangout up in the hills. It's a vigorous six-mile hike on foot but much easier on the back of a horse. She knows exactly where I'm taking her.

"Brody…"

"Yes?"

"Don't make me regret this."

"I won't, baby. I promise."

A quick glance through my schedule and I call my assistant, Katy, to rearrange my afternoon meetings. I also have her cancel my clients for the morning. I won't be coming back tonight. I plan to be busy reconnecting with Grace.

We end the call and I race around like a madman packing my bags. It takes longer than it should, but only because I have to pack my tuxedo for the charity event on Friday. I pack for the entire weekend. Once I get my hands on Grace, I'm never letting go.

SEVENTEEN

# Brody

By some miracle, I make it to La Rouge Vineyards by noon. My hope that my nosey brother won't be home is dashed the moment I walk inside the newly constructed barn. Asher looks up from inside the tack room where he's working on a saddle.

"What the fuck are you doing here?"

"Nice to see you too, ass-wipe." I don't answer him, choosing instead to head down to where my horse is stabled. Asher watches as I say hi to Spirit. "Hey, boy, want to stretch your legs?"

"A ride?" Asher's brows pinch together. "You do know it's Thursday?"

"So?"

"So, the last time you came home in the middle of the week was—well, never. So, what's up?"

"Nothing. Just letting Spirit out to stretch his legs." I move over to Cage's mare.

"Then why are you nuzzling Chesty?"

"Because." I grit my teeth. No way am I getting out of here before settling Asher's curiosity. "I'm taking both horses."

"Again, where are you taking them, and who will be joining you?" Asher abandons whatever he is working on and comes to stand beside me. While I say hello to Chesty, Asher nuzzles Spirit. "Need any help saddling up?"

We grew up with horses. I can saddle them in my sleep, but I give a nod. It's the best way I can think of to keep Asher's questions to a minimum.

We lead the horses to the front of the barn and tie their leads while we grab their saddles. Asher works beside me in silence, saddling Chesty, while I tighten and snug the saddle down on Spirit.

"You can spill now or talk later. One way or another, you're going to tell me. Might as well get it over with."

"Don't want to talk about it."

"That's okay because you're an open book. Besides…" He taps his temple. "My triplet sense is pinging like a motherfucker." He pauses and his lips press together. "Not that you're going to listen, but do you really think this is the right thing to do?"

"Depends what the *right thing* is." Chances of Asher knowing what I'm up to by our inexplicable triplet connection are about ninety-nine percent in his favor. We've always had an uncanny ability to intuit what the other's up to.

"Well, let me throw this out there and you tell me if I'm warm, cold, or lava hot."

"That's stupid." It's a dumb kid's game we used to play growing up.

"First off, it's Thursday, and you're here instead of in the city. That means something drew you here. Since the only new thing in your life that has anything to do with Napa is your new client, Atwood Estates, and Grace just happens to…"

"That's enough." As I suspected, he's lava hot. Hit that one right on the head, but then I could never keep secrets from my brothers.

"I haven't even begun to peel back these layers." He grins like a goddamn fool.

"Stop it." I want to punch that smug expression off his face.

"So, Grace…" Asher rocks back on his heels. "You're really going after her? Think that's wise?"

"I'm warning you…"

"I'm just curious as to why you're chasing one of the few, if not only, women in the world with a valid reason to hate you. I should get you my gun so you can defend yourself when she takes a shot at you."

"Shut your mouth." My growl intensifies.

"Right, Grace Atwood it is. You're here, saddling up, not one but two horses, to presumably take Grace on a ride. There's only one place you'd take her."

"You're really getting on my nerves."

"Trail ride it is." Asher flashes a snarky grin. His intuition is scary accurate. "I have only one question."

"Fine. I'll bite."

"What the fuck are you thinking?" Asher steps back and stares at me. "The two of you were close in high school. Freakishly close, but after you so spectacularly fucked things up, I have to wonder what you're thinking."

"That was a long time ago."

"And you think time heals all wounds?" He laughs. "Brother, you know shit about women. They hold grudges for a lifetime."

"And you're some expert?"

"I'm the only one who's engaged. I'd say that makes me an expert, considering I'm the only one capable of keeping a chick around for longer than one night."

"We're done talking about Grace."

"At least you admit we're 'talking' about her." He makes finger quotes like he's all badass.

"Ass…"

"Hole." Asher finishes the expletive. "You've got balls. I'll give you that. Something pretty fucking amazing must've happened when you saw her to think you have a snowball's chance in hell of making things right with her."

"I do."

"Shit no, you don't."

"And why not?"

"Because, you fucking bastard, you fucked her, took her virginity, and then you blabbed to everyone about your kinky games. That video—it made you look like a king, but what it did to her…" He looks around. "You sure it's wise to be alone with her up in the hills?"

"I know what I did, but there's no way to go back and rewrite history. Besides, there was a lot more to it than just that. Grace is different."

"Right, but she's the one who got hurt, probably because she thought you'd never use her like that."

"I didn't use her."

"You sure about that?" He crosses his arms. "Look, I was there. We were total asses in high school, always bragging about who bagged which chick first. We kept a damn scorecard, or did you forget about that?"

"I didn't forget about that."

"Girls fought to get their names on that list, everyone but poor, innocent Grace who thought you were being nice to her because you cared. She thought you'd protect her. When she realized what she really meant…"

"She meant the world to me."

"Could've fooled me."

"Just because I didn't tell you and Cage all about her doesn't mean shit. She was the one girl that was cool. We clicked. It was different with her than with the other girls. I kept that from you because it was special."

"Then why did you share that video with the whole school?"

"That was an accident." It's my greatest regret.

"That's not how you acted."

"Because I was an idiot!"

Asher takes a step back at my shout. He holds up his hands. "Dude, you never said it was an accident. That's not how you played it."

"It was an accident. A total, stupid, dumb accident. But instead of owning up to it, I soaked up the attention."

"Why?"

"Because I was a selfish prick back then. You weren't much different. Eighteen, lord of the school, with a reputation to maintain, and it was more important what people thought about me than what it did to her. Besides, I was graduating in less than a month. There was no way what Grace and I shared could stand the long-distance thing. She had all of high school ahead of her. I didn't see a future… It was easier to walk away."

"Fuck, you really screwed that up. Does she know?"

"Know what?"

"That it was an accident?"

"Nobody knows."

"You never told her?" His eyes practically bug out of his head.

"No." I hang my head in shame.

"Oh shit." He shakes his head. "I don't think you can bounce back from that."

"I'm going to do everything in my power to do just that."

"Why?"

"Because… Grace is special. When I saw her, the earth moved beneath my feet. I know I fucked up, and I know I've got a lot to apologize for, but I'm not letting her go."

Asher scuffs the floor with the toe of his boot. "Well, good luck with that. If it were me, I'd shoot you."

"Gee, thanks."

"You better be prepared to beg." Asher hands me Chesty's reins and walks away while shaking his head. "Of all the bone-headed things…"

His words follow me all the way over to Atwood Estates.

EIGHTEEN

## Grace

_________

TRUE TO HIS WORD, AT TWO SHARP, BRODY COMES RIDING UP THE lane. The jangle of tack and bridle, along with the clomping of hooves, catches my attention. I rush to peek outside.

My heart leaps to my throat the moment I see him astride his horse. All hard angles and chiseled muscles, masculinity rolls off his confident frame. His searing gaze cuts toward the window where I peek out at him.

Immediately, his eyes pinch as he captures and holds me in a possessive gaze. Worn jeans, a black and green shirt, and a hat which shades his glowing, green eyes, his presence penetrates my senses and ravages my determination to remain unaffected by him. I feel his eyes burning me as they lick across my skin. A smug expression fixes on his face.

Bastard knows he affects me. Heading to the back of the house, I check in really quick with Mom.

"He's here." No idea why I'm breathless, but I am.

My chest squeezes as past pain rushes through me. Why do I think this time will be any different from before? There's no reason to believe it won't be, but I made a decision not to let the past define me, to cripple me.

I face Brody with my eyes wide open. I know what kind of boy he was—what kind of man he is now—I'm not fooling myself about him or what he wants with me.

But I want to see—or need to know—for myself. What do I want?

"Brody La Rouge?" Mom turns her head to me with a worried frown.

"Yeah. How do I look?" I dressed for the trail in jeans, a plain t-shirt, and my boots are waiting for me on the porch. As far as dates go, this is super casual.

"You look fine." She leans her head back and sighs. "I worry about him hurting you again."

Today is a good day. Her voice is stronger, not as tremulous, but she worries about me going out with Brody—on a date.

I think this is a date. Maybe I assumed it was, and it's not? Hell, I hate the insecurity raging within me.

I upped the dosage on her pain medication after Abbie shared with me how much better Mom felt with an extra dose. I called Mom's doctor and discussed the change. He agreed, saying it was more important to keep Mom comfortable than worry about the sedating effects. We discussed formally moving her to hospice. That's something I need to deal with next week.

"I know what I'm getting myself into, and it's just an afternoon trail ride."

It's that, or something far more dangerous, but I'm guarding my heart and protecting myself from turning this into something it's not.

Pain stabs me in the chest as I dispense two of her pills onto a plate. Her water glass is full, just like she likes it, and she's engrossed in reading a book—or rather, listening to an audiobook. She's no longer strong enough to hold her e-reader, but thankfully there are amazing audiobooks that take her away and keep her mind off the pain.

"Just—promise you'll be careful?"

"I will. Promise you'll take your pills?" I'm her daughter, treating her as if she's a recalcitrant child who won't take her medicine.

"I worry about you, cupcake."

"Don't. I'll be fine."

"I thought Brody was coming tomorrow."

"He is—this isn't a business call."

"That boy broke your heart, luv; are you really sure this makes sense?"

"It doesn't make any sense."

"Then, why?"

"Because…" I sit on the edge of her bed and take her hand in mine. "I guess I want to see what he has to say? I never had a chance to confront him about what he did. Maybe, I need closure?"

"He was your first love and your greatest heartbreak. We took you out of that school after what happened."

"I know." I breathe out a sigh. "I know, but it was something Abbie said to me."

"What's that?"

"She said, *don't let the mistakes I made at fifteen ruin the rest of my life.* Or something along those lines."

"She's a dear friend, but still… I'm the one that held you while you fell apart."

"You were always there for me, Mom."

"I always will be." She removes her hand from mine and covers her heart. "You'll carry me in your heart when I'm gone. All I ask is that you guard your heart. Don't repeat the mistakes of your past."

"I'll be careful, Mom. I promise."

A knock on the front door gives me a start.

"That's him."

She gives a solemn nod. "Guard your heart."

"I will." I lean over and give her a kiss on the cheek.

I'll guard my heart, but I'm done shutting myself off from love. Not that I'm interested in pursuing anything with Brody, but I need to move on from the damage he caused.

For the longest time, I thought I could do that on my own, but I can't. I need to confront him before I can bury that part of my past.

I make a quick stop in the kitchen to pick up my backpack. Knowing how men think, or don't, I prepared for an afternoon ride up in the hills. Nothing fancy—I don't want to give Brody any wrong ideas—but I packed cheese, crackers, dried salami, some grapes, and sliced apples. I kept the cores for the horses. I also opened a bottle of Atwood Estates' best wine and repackaged it for the ride. Glass doesn't transport well on horseback.

I take a deep, shaky breath before opening the door and remind myself what I want.

Closure.

Only when I open the door, Brody's dazzling green gaze sweeps me off my feet. I stare, taking in his undeniable presence, and any thoughts of protecting my heart go out the proverbial window.

The cold, hard truth is I never got over my first love. I swallow thickly with that realization and try to repair my defensive shields.

Although, why I try is a mystery to me.

"You look absolutely stunning." His wide smile, perfect teeth, and those kissable dimples steal my breath. Brody wings up an eyebrow as he takes me in. His expression makes him look younger, playful, intoxicating, and dangerous. His presence overwhelms me and steals my breath.

Dressed for the trail, a weathered, brown cowboy hat sits atop his head and completes his devastating look. With effort, I close my gaping mouth.

"Th-thank you." My recovery is piss poor. I've underestimated my opposition.

It's much easier to wage war on Brody La Rouge when he's not standing in front of me. He glances at my shoes, and the corner of his mouth ticks up.

"I thought I taught you better." I hate how his scolding tone sends a lick of heat between my legs. I grip the frame of the door and try not to let my legs buckle.

Brody taught me everything I know about horses and riding. Although, at the time, we always rode on his horse double. A sturdy pair of boots was an absolute requirement. Next to that, jeans or other long pants. I learned the hard way when I went riding with him in cutoffs. I nursed that rash for over a week.

I glance around his massive frame and take in a gorgeous Arabian and broad-chested, chestnut mare.

"Which one is yours?"

He points to the Arabian. "Spirit's mine. You're riding Chesty, Cage's horse. She's got a great mind for the trail and is exceptionally mild-mannered."

"It's been a bit since I've ridden."

It's been well over a decade. The last time I rode a horse, I sat behind Brody as we snuck up to our favorite spot—the place he's taking me today.

"Chesty will take good care of you, but it'd be better if you had boots."

"Oh, I have some. They're on the porch." I heft my backpack on my shoulder and wait for Brody to move out of the way. "I don't wear them indoors."

"How's your mom doing?" He glances over my shoulder.

"It's a good day. Thank you for asking."

"I feel like I should stop in and say hello."

"That's probably not a good idea."

"Why?"

"You're the boy who broke her daughter's heart, and she's not happy I'm headed out on a date with you."

"It's confirmed then." His entire face beams as his grin stretches ear to ear.

"What's confirmed?"

"This is officially a date."

"I shouldn't have said it like that. This isn't a date." I look down and kick at the doorsill.

Brody places his finger under my chin and forces me to look into his mesmerizing eyes.

"This is most definitely a date, Miss Grace Atwood." He steps close, invading my personal space, and leans down until he hovers kissably close.

# NINETEEN

## Grace

_____________

MY ENTIRE BODY MELTS BENEATH THE PROMISE OF A KISS, BUT I shake off the unsettling feeling.

"You promised you'd behave."

"Promises are meant to be broken." Brody's tone is deep, heated, and determined. He loops his fingers under the shoulder strap of my backpack and places it on the floor. Then he closes the distance and presses his lips against mine.

My senses ignite as awareness of him tingles throughout my body. Every point of contact arouses me, from the firmness of his lips, to his fingers reaching around to graze along the back of my neck, to the way the heat of his breath spins my brain. Brody takes what he wants and desire races through my veins.

He breaks the kiss far too soon and brushes the back of his knuckles against my cheek. It's a feather-light touch that sends shivers down my spine.

"I promised we'd talk, and we will, but don't hate me for needing this first."

He returns to my lips and bathes me in a shuddering exhale. His entire body is tense, rigid, and barely restrained. He kisses my lips, forcing my mouth to open beneath his assault. He attacks, nipping at my mouth, and sweeps his tongue inside to tangle with mine.

Brody is a man who leads and a man who takes. As for me, I barely hold on. A shudder rips through him, and I realize I may not be the only one barely holding on.

His arousal, palpable and undeniable, charges the air between us, shortens his breaths, and sends my pulse spiking. There's no denying I want this as much as him, but I pull back.

"Brody…"

He cups my jaw and places the pad of his thumb over my lips, where he sweeps it back and forth, feather-light but devastating. Tingles of sensation rush through me, unlike anything I've felt before—scratch that. I've felt this before, over a decade ago. The memory makes me uncomfortable, and I doubt the wisdom behind this entire afternoon.

"We both want this, but if you're worried about my restraint, I'm capable of holding back. I can stop before this goes too far."

"Can you?" I'm too nervous to stop anything. I know I'll cave. With Brody, I know nothing about restraint. I place my hand on his bicep and pull his thumb away from my mouth. His muscles bunch beneath my fingers.

"I can, although I don't want to." His husky tone sweeps over me.

"We need to talk before this goes that far."

"You're all I've thought about." He grips my waist and yanks me against him, bringing his mouth back down on mine.

The air electrifies and sizzles, crackling through my whole body as the brush of his tongue sends shockwaves coursing through me. Every cell in my body takes notice. My lips tingle as our mouths meld together, and my knees weaken with the collision of our breaths.

His hands roam as he deepens the kiss. The movement of his jaw as he kisses me is restrained, slow, determined. When he licks along the seam of my lips, it's a request, likely the only one I'll receive, and I can't help myself.

I give in.

In the next breath, he parts my lips and kisses me, taking control of our past and sealing our future.

My resistance, as always, melts beneath the dominating power of his desire. All I can do is hold on as memories of what it felt like to surrender to him course through me. His hands slide up and down my back. One hand lifts to grasp my neck where he tilts my head to deepen the kiss.

"If you don't want this, say no." His voice slides over me, silky and full of desire. A voice which lowers my defenses and allows bad decisions to gain strength.

I can't. My treacherous body betrays me. I lift on tiptoe, practically climbing his towering frame, and hook my arms around his neck. Threading my fingers into the hair at his nape, this is the farthest thing from *No* a girl can get.

He digs his fingers against my back, crushing me against him. My hands slip down to his shoulders, where I grab hold and revel in the feel of our bodies pressed tight together.

He backs me against the doorframe and lifts me, wrapping my legs around his hips while leaning against me. I straddle his muscular waist as fantasies tumble in my head. Brody's full, pillowy lips wrench untethered groans from my mouth. My blood heats with the shocking sensations he pulls from my body. His firm lips never waver, taking and claiming as he reacquaints himself with my mouth.

We kiss for what feels like an eternity, making up for lost time. He sucks and licks and eats at my mouth like a man starved of sustenance. The intensity of his kiss expresses his desire and states his intent. With Brody, words were always optional in moments like this.

"Fuck, Grace, but you taste like coming home." Deep, sultry tones infuse his breath and lick along my skin, sending shivers racing along my nerves. His hands roam from my waist down to my ass, where he cups my butt and tugs me hard against the firmness of his erection tenting his jeans. "Do you feel what you do to me? How hard I am for you?" He nibbles at my mouth, teasing, playing. Pulling at my bottom lip, he bites down hard for a split second before kissing me again. He knows my reaction to pain, how it weakens my knees and holds me on the edge. "You taste like heaven. Like life itself."

Mercy, but the heat of his mouth, and the velvety press of his lips on mine, spin my brain. I miss this, his all-consuming passion. The honesty of his desire expressed in the heat of his mouth is something I crave.

I want this. I need it.

A barrage of sensations bursts within me, but one in particular coils below my waist and aches between my legs.

Brody's breathing slows. His hands return to my waist, where he lifts me and settles me back on my feet, severing our connection. He tears his mouth away from mine, panting.

"You're going to be the death of me, Grace Atwood. You make me burn and set fire to my body. I can't keep my hands off you. I shouldn't have…" His forehead presses against mine as he sags against me. Propping his hand on the doorframe over my head, he pulls away and stares down at me. "This, I swear, no matter what happened between us, who better to put the pieces of your heart back together than the boy who broke it in the first place?"

"Brody…"

His finger presses over my lips.

"I lost the most precious thing I ever had. I'm giving you notice that I'm taking it back."

My entire body thrums with the passion of that kiss, the loss of his body pressed against mine, and the undeniable conflict his words evoke.

His palms slide up my arms and wrap around my shoulders. He pulls me into his embrace and tucks my head beneath his chin.

"I suppose it's time we have that talk because if this kiss continues much longer, I'll strip you and bury myself in that sweet pussy of yours long before you're ready to beg me for it."

Spirit whinnies and snorts as he shakes his head. His long mane ripples in an undulating wave down his neck. His rear foot stomps at the dry, baked ground, and he stamps with impatience.

Brody gives a low chuckle.

"Cock-blocked by a horse. I guess that'll have to wait until we get to Lookout Rock." He steps back and glances at the porch. Suddenly somewhat uncertain, he rubs at the back of his neck. "Where are these boots of yours?"

I stare at him, shocked, surprised, and blown away by what he said. I straighten and roll my shoulders back. Brody laid out the gauntlet. If I continue, I give tacit agreement for whatever happens. Am I ready to have sex with him again? I curl in my lower lip and bite it with my teeth. Virile. Masculine. Brody is a gorgeous and potent male who steals any good sense I may have left.

"Don't break your promise, Brody. Don't break my heart again."

"I promise." He spies my boots and retrieves them.

While I put my boots on, he takes my backpack and secures it behind his saddle on Spirit. He walks Chesty over to the porch, giving me a hand as I swing up and into the saddle. As I settle in, he stares at me in brooding silence.

"What's wrong?" My hand grips the pommel of the saddle as hesitation runs through me.

"I can't believe you're here, that's all. And thank you." He presses his fingers to his chest, and his eyes close for a moment before he steps around Chesty to mount Spirit. "You ready?"

"As I'll ever be." I want to ask what he's thankful for but decide not to press. Brody isn't a man who bares his emotions. It feels wrong to press. I don't want to scare him off, but I need Brody to be open and raw with me.

With the lingering heat of our kiss cooling off, we head down the lane and toward the trailhead where our individual properties abut one another. Brody leads. Chesty proves she's a gentle creature, carrying my inexperienced ass up the meandering trail. It doesn't take long before we transition from grass and rocks to scrub and brush as we climb.

Brody doesn't speak, keeping his own counsel, as I focus in on the wide expanse of his back and the way his broad shoulders taper down to a narrow waist. That's where my gaze settles, watching his sculpted ass as it shifts in the saddle with each of Spirit's steps.

A beautiful day, there's hardly a cloud in the sky, leaving deep blue overhead. A light breeze takes away the heat, leaving me comfortable in my jeans and heavy boots. I opted for a light t-shirt, knowing the trail would be dusty, and if it gets cold, a light jacket is tucked into the bottom of my pack.

Before long, trees takeover from the scrub oaks, towering over us and close out the sky. We continue on in silence, twisting up the trail. Through breaks in the trees, I watch the floor of the valley drop. Spirit crests a rise, and the trees fall away as we reach the ridge with an unobstructed view of the valley.

"How're you doing?" Brody twists in his saddle.

"It's gorgeous up here." I take in a deep breath, filling my lungs with the smells of pine, soil, and the musky loam. "I forgot how beautiful it is."

How secluded.

"It sure is." His gaze doesn't waver from me and heat rises in my cheeks.

"It's been forever since I've been up here."

When I was a kid, these hills, and the forest lands, were my second home. I loved hiking, often alone, but mostly when Brody joined me. Nobody knew about our hikes. We didn't hang out together at school; me the lowly freshman and him lord of the school. I never attended any of the infamous parties he and his brothers put on at their home. We didn't keep our friendship a secret, but as our friendship turned into something deeper, we kept that bit all to ourselves.

Not too far up this trail, Brody took my virginity, with exquisite tenderness, but he also introduced me to the thrill which came from handing over power and submitting to his will. I knelt before him for the first time up here. And I said yes. My breath catches with the memories.

Good and bad, it all happened here.

TWENTY

## Brody

It's official. I've found heaven and hell. Not too bad for an afternoon's work.

Heaven in Grace's arms and hell upon Spirit's back. My rigid arousal doesn't abate after that kiss and gives me fits the first mile of our ride as I shift back and forth in the saddle.

Kissing Grace is different from kissing other women. With other women, I kiss as a necessary step toward fucking them. With Grace, I want to kiss her *more than* I want to fuck her. What the hell does that mean?

I take off my hat and run my fingers through my hair. Her lips tasted so damn good, and it took all my will to release them—to let go of her.

Instead of removing her clothes—which would have been the next logical step—all I could think about was kissing her again. As if taking off her clothes would've been a crime because it deprived me of her mouth. I slip my tongue between my lips and hold back a groan as the lingering essence of her teases my taste buds. The way our tongues tangled together was nothing short of magnificent.

Hot, wet, and welcoming, three words I usually reserve for pussy, describe how it feels to kiss Grace. That kiss should've ended in a bed with me buried balls deep inside of her hot body. Instead, I mustered enough restraint to end the kiss and let her go.

I believe that qualifies me for sainthood.

I suffer the aftereffects now because my body reels from the heady sensation of holding her in my arms. I need more of that.

Grace.

In my arms.

Only she's not in my arms. Grace is frustratingly behind me, riding Cage's horse. Don't know why I didn't have us ride double on Spirit, except I thought it would make things easier on my horse not to carry the extra burden. I regret that decision now.

I turn my attention back to the trail. This place holds special memories for me—for both of us. When I came here with Grace, I wasn't one of the infamous La Rouge triplets, but rather just me, Brody. I found it easier to breathe when she was around. Easier to find my true self. I relaxed and enjoyed hanging out with my best girl.

Then I fucked that up.

"We're almost there," I call out, although I'm sure she remembers.

"I forgot how beautiful this trail is." Her breathy voice reaches out to me, wraps around me, and takes my breath away. This feels like a dream, having her with me, and I don't for the life of me know why I ever thought I could walk away and leave her behind. I'd been such a goddamn fool.

Soon, our ride will end. Our special spot isn't that far ahead. I pull Spirit to a halt and dismount. Grace watches; her shimmering gaze follows my every move. I hitch Spirit's reins to a low-lying branch and pretend I don't notice the way she looks at me.

We're in sync with each other because she waits for me to help her down. Grace is more than capable of getting out of the saddle on her own, but she senses my tension spiking. She knows I need to help her down. When we first started coming up here, it was just to sneak away. Later, as friends turned into something else, things shifted between us. Power flowed differently.

We aren't those same kids, but that itching returns; that need to take control rises within me.

I say nothing as I come to Chesty and take the reins from Grace. The look we exchange changes things. She bites her lower lip, and I hold back a groan.

"Come." I spread my arms and wait. Already I feel the change within me.

Grace places her hands on my shoulders. Stepping in the stirrup, she swings her other leg around. I grab her by the waist and gently lower her to the ground. We say nothing as she leans against Chesty's flank and stares up at me with tempestuous eyes filled with far too much doubt.

I grip the back of her neck and trap her between myself and the horse, taking control. Sweeping her hair aside, I press my lips just behind her ear and breathe in the light floral scent of her shampoo. Her breaths accelerate, as does the beating of my heart. She reaches up to grip the saddle, and I envision her eyes closing as she takes in a deep breath.

"Turn around." Low and throaty, I issue the first command.

Grace spins around, and I kiss along her neck, nibbling and licking until her entire body trembles. I move her hair to the side and kiss up along the other side of her neck until I suck the softness of her ear into my mouth. Using my teeth, I bite down gently as my breaths accelerate, and all reason flees.

My body brackets hers, closing her in between myself and Chesty. Grace moans and arches against me. Her ass presses against the tightness in my jeans, brushing my cock and bringing a groan to my mouth.

Fuck it. I lose all restraint.

I wrap my hand around her waist and spin her around until she faces me. I tug her tight, and before she can react, my lips crash down on hers, claiming her mouth.

Chesty stomps the ground and snorts as I devour Grace's mouth. I expect more hesitation, but Grace reaches between us and cups my cheeks. She lifts on tiptoe and kisses me back.

I nearly lose it when she practically forces her tongue down my throat. Didn't think I'd be the one slowing us down, but if we don't stop soon, there will be only one way this ends. I kiss her back, reclaiming control, as I remove her hands from my face and place them on my hips.

I never want to end this kiss. I want to taste her forever, but I made a promise. Severing our connection, I take a step back. Puffy and swollen, her lips glisten with moisture.

"Let me tie Chesty up; then we'll go to our spot." We're supposed to talk. Hell, if that's what I want to do after that kiss…

Grace nibbles at her lower lip and shoves her hands in the back pockets of her jeans. Her attention never wavers as I secure Chesty to the same low limb I tied Spirit to. Spirit already grazes at the fresh grass near his hooves. Chesty follows before I'm done.

Our special rock is a short distance off the path, something unnoticed by those who hike these trails. It's something we discovered together and made ours.

"Come." I take her hand and lead her into the brush, holding branches out of her way as she slips under my arm.

She continues to worry her lower lip with her teeth, driving me crazy. I can't stop looking at her mouth and nearly trip over numerous rocks and roots along our path.

The thick brush finally opens as we step out onto a massive rock ledge. Late afternoon, half the valley lies in shadow. Behind us, the sun sinks toward the horizon. We still have several hours until sunset, more than enough time to talk, or fuck. With the heat spiking between us, it's more than likely we'll fuck and forget about talking.

"I forgot how incredible the view is from up here." Fearlessly, Grace walks right up to the edge.

The ledge juts out from the ridge and leads to a hundred-foot drop. The view is spectacular, but that's because I'm looking at her ass.

She sits and dangles her feet over the edge. It used to anger me when she did that. My need to protect her at all costs consumed me, but she always insisted on sitting at the edge.

But that's Grace.

She's fearless.

I join her, and our thighs touch as we kick our heels against the rock.

"It feels good being here with you." I nudge her with my shoulder.

"How often do you come here?" Soft, inquisitive, her question reveals some of her fear. She wants to know if I've ever brought another girl up here, but she won't ask outright. Nevertheless, her question takes me by surprise.

I never come up here.

"The last time I was here was with you." I take her hand in mine, threading our fingers together.

Her body stills and she gazes out over the valley.

"That's a shame. It's too beautiful to be forgotten."

"I never forgot you."

"Is that so?" She pulls her hand free and leans back. Her head tilts to the sky as she closes her eyes. "Why?"

"Why, what?"

"Why didn't you come back here?"

"It didn't feel right, like it was a betrayal coming here alone."

"The betrayal was sharing that video and destroying my reputation. Not coming here without me. You really hurt me." She makes a fist and rubs the spot over her heart. Her voice drops to an agonized whisper. "You ruined me."

"I never meant…"

"The teasing, the bullying—the name calling—it got so bad Mom pulled me from school. She homeschooled me the rest of my way through high school."

"I'm sorry."

"When you wouldn't talk to me afterward, it hurt the most. It was worse than when you shared that video because I realized the truth."

"Grace…"

"No, let me finish." She shifts away. "You used me until I was no longer *of use* to you. Once you got what you wanted, you moved on and left me behind. You never talked to me after that party. I thought you were going to make it better somehow and tell the whole school that I was your girlfriend. That would've eased some of the ridicule. Instead, I became nothing more than one of the many girls you slept with. Nothing special. Nothing important. How do you do something like that to someone you claim to care about?"

"I don't have a good answer." I hang my head in shame. "Not that it matters now, but the truth is that I was trying to delete that video. My finger slipped, and it got sent to the team chat instead. I should've stood up for you, protected you, but I froze. I'm not proud of what I did. I reacted like a self-centered prick, too worried about what people would think about me. It was easier not to tell people the truth." I close my eyes and take in a deep breath. "The thing about it is that it was easier to eat up the attention than to tell everyone what really happened. I didn't want them to know how I felt. I wish I had something better to say, but I don't. I'm not proud of how I handled that."

"And why did you act that way? Were you ashamed that one of the famous La Rouge triplets reached so far below himself that he was going steady with a freshman?" Her words are harsh and sting, but they're true.

"Back then, what people thought of me meant the world to me. I didn't want to tell anyone I was in love with you."

"Right, because that would've messed with your reputation. You were a self-centered, self-absorbed prick."

"I know."

"I kept waiting for you to stand up for me and tell everyone to stop slut-shaming me. But you never said a word and let the rumors grow. I became the fifty-shades of slut, the freshman who loved to be dominated during sex. The girl who knelt and begged for your dick. I never felt so ashamed. You protected your reputation while destroying mine."

"I'm not proud of that."

"And you never said a word to me after that party. You never even looked at me. That's what hurt the most. You were supposed to protect me, but when I needed you, you disappeared. It was like I ceased to exist to the great Brody La Rouge. You discarded me like yesterday's trash, and for the longest time, that's how I felt. You made me feel filthy for letting you do those things to me. Instead of feeling special and cherished, I was ashamed."

"You're my greatest regret, my biggest failure. I can't go back in time and change anything. I apologize for putting you through hell, and I can't believe you don't hate me, but you don't. We still have the same insane chemistry together."

"I don't hate you because I'm a grown-ass adult. I had eleven years to work through what you did to me. By the time I went to college, it no longer mattered. Nobody there knew me. Nobody knew about my shame. Like most things, time took care of my feelings, smoothing the raw, rough edges until only lingering memories remained. I was happy you were out of my life and planned on moving far away from here after graduation, just to make sure our paths never crossed. Unfortunately, life got in the way."

She pulls a lock of hair over her shoulder and plays with it, absently twining it around her finger. Her gaze never lifts. Not once does she look me in the eye. Grace bares her soul, and all I can do is sit here and take it like a man. Each word is a strike against my heart, but the truth is I deserve each devastating lash.

"I'm sorry." I take her hand in mine. "I'm not that same person. Give me a chance to show you."

"Yet, nothing's really changed." She lifts her heavy gaze. Sadness lingers in her expression, laced with hopelessness.

"Why would you say that?"

"Brody, we were never short on chemistry. The air sizzles when we're close. You make me weak. Weak in the knees, weak in the heart, and weak in the head. I shouldn't have let you kiss me, but I couldn't say no. I've never been able to say no to you. I don't like that about myself."

"But you're here. I thought it was because you wanted to talk and try this out again?"

"I'm here, even though I know this is a mistake." She stares out across the valley, and her expression shifts. It fills with regret and sorrow. "When you called this morning and told me you were coming, I got excited. Giddy. I responded to the way you spoke to me like I always have. It's instinctual when I'm with you. This odd power you have over me is scary as shit. I let you get into my head and let my mind spin with fantasies. Somehow, I believe this time will be different. This time, you won't break my heart. But I can't trust my heart with you. Not again. You didn't protect me then, and I have no reason to think now will be any different."

"This is different. I'm different." I feel her slipping away, and it terrifies me.

"Are you?" She pulls her legs up and folds them in front of her. "I googled you, the great Brody La Rouge, the most eligible bachelor in the country. Rich. Powerful. Every woman's wet dream. And I read what they say about you, how you never have the same woman on your arm twice. That nobody's been able to snag your attention for more than an evening. And here I am. Spending the day with you, returning to our spot, thinking everything's changed, when really nothing's changed at all."

She shakes her head and folds her hands into her lap. "When it comes down to it, why should I think you won't walk away again after you get what you want? I don't know why I'm here, except it's impossible to deny you. That kind of power is unfair, but there you have it. I'm yours for the taking."

Her chin dips and her gaze casts down, defeated. She hates her lack of control. Every word she speaks is the truth. I feel the weight of that responsibility, the power I hold over her, and I hate it.

I loathe it.

This isn't what I want with Grace. I don't want to be the man she can't say no to. I want to be the one she says yes to; to know, she chooses me because I'm who she wants. How the hell do I recover from this?

"I don't know what to say. You're right. My reputation is no different now than it was then, but I'm not the one with the power here." *You have the power to destroy me.*

She sniffs and rolls her shoulders back. "I guess… I wanted to know how it felt to be with you, one last time, but that's not fair to you. It's not fair to me." She draws her knees to her chest and looks everywhere but at me.

"Grace…"

"Mark offered to buy out my interest in Atwood Estates. He's got just under two million in savings. It's enough to cover our debts. Mom doesn't want him to put his savings at risk. I don't want that either, but I'm considering it." She finally looks me in the eye. "I don't think it's a good idea for us to be in business together. I'm obviously incapable of telling you no, and there's no way I'll survive being used a second time. God knows I'm willing. I let you come over today, get me on a horse, and bring me to this spot where only one thing will happen. And I very much want to feel what it's like to be in your arms again." She wipes at her eyes. "I'm such a goddamn fool."

Each word slams into me with the weight of my past mistakes, stealing my breath and knocking me down. Everything she says is true.

Asher warned me. He said she'd take a shot at me. He meant it as a joke and offered me his gun for protection. The volley she lobbed, however, is far more damaging than a simple bullet. Her words rip and tear through me, shredding my heart into thousands of pieces.

I say nothing because there's no defense for my actions. I thought I could apologize and that would be it. I expected forgiveness for my mistakes. Instead, I tuck my chin to my chest and let each and every word tear through my heart. Asher's right.

There's no recovering from this.

# Grace

---

AN UNEASY SILENCE DESCENDS BETWEEN US. MY WORDS HAVE AN effect on Brody. I feel it in the tension girding his frame. His jaw bunches. His eyelids twitch. His fingers flex and curl.

"I'm not here to take anything from you." He finally breaks the silence.

"I shouldn't have said all of that."

Guilt washes through me. I unloaded a shit-ton of grief. I didn't mean to be so direct, but it feels good to unburden myself from the past. I've kept all that poison locked up since it happened. My mother may have held me while I cried, but I never told her why it hurt as much as it did. She wouldn't understand.

Brody is the only one who can.

"Don't ever be afraid to tell me how you feel," he says. "Especially now."

"Why?"

"Because, I need to know. I need to know when I fuck up and when I'm being an ass. I need to know when I'm making you happy, or making you cry. I don't want you to hide your feelings from me, even when they paint me in the worst possible light. I have a confession to make."

"What's that?"

"Even though you have every reason to hate me, I'm glad you're here. Not because all I can think about is kissing you, and I have to be honest…" He huffs a laugh. "I really want to fuck you—but I can't."

I shift to a more comfortable position. No denying it, I want the same. A small voice inside my head says if I can have one final moment with him, I'll find my way free of this power he holds over me.

"Why not?"

"I don't want a quick and easy fuck. That's never what I wanted with you. It's not what I want now." He scoots back from the edge and stands. Holding a hand out to me, he speaks with his heart. "I want a forever with you. To do that, I have to regain your trust. You may think it's funny, but I really do believe in fate. There's a reason I ran across you the other day, no pun intended. If I'd known you were back in town, I would've run straight to your house and begged your forgiveness. Instead, you came to me, or I came across you. Either way, I need you to make me a promise."

"What kind of promise?"

"Promise you won't make any decisions regarding Sterling Enterprises and Atwood Estates, at least not today. Most definitely not in the heat of whatever this is. We still have our assessment to complete. Let me do that, and if you still want to proceed, I'll assign your account to someone else. It's a great deal for Atwood Estates, and it would be a crime to turn it down because of personal issues between us. We can keep business separate from this."

"Can we?"

"I will. I'll step aside from your business, but I have every intention of proving I'm worth your trust."

I take his hand, and he pulls me into his arms. There's no kissing. It's nothing more than a simple embrace. Only there's nothing simple about Brody holding me in his arms.

"How do you feel about dinner at my place?" The corner of his mouth ticks up with a boyish grin. For a split second, I see the teen I fell in love with.

"I really should get back to my mom." The unfortunate truth is I can't leave her alone for too long.

"Is there any way I can convince you to hang with me tonight?"

*Hang?*

Such an innocuous, innocent word. It takes me back a decade, and I want what we had then. Even now, I want it.

"I suppose I can ask Mark to sit with her…"

"Yes, do that." His eyes brighten. "We'll cook up something special. Um, do you mind if Asher and Evie are there?"

"Who's Evie?"

"Asher's fiancée."

"Asher's engaged?"

"To a great girl."

"That's funny."

"Why?"

"Who would've thought any of the La Rouge triplets would settle down?"

"Miracles happen." He glances at my left hand, and his gaze lingers for longer than it should. "You never know what the future holds, Miss Grace Atwood."

The future isn't something I think a whole lot about. In fact, it's more of the present I lament.

No sex with Brody means no working him out of my system, but as we meander back down the trail on horseback, I wonder if that's what I want at all. The desire to trust him stirs within me. Our chemistry is undeniable, explosive, and crazy insane. Our past is ugly and complicated, although laced with some of the best memories of my life.

As far as my future?

That's hard to say.

Once we're back into clear reception, I call Mark and ask if he can look in on Mom. He says yes, enthusiastically, and another realization runs through me. Have I been keeping him away from his sister? Mom's time left with us is limited, counted in months, if not weeks. I do everything for her. Have I inadvertently pushed Mark away? I hope not and resolve to be better at making time for him to spend with her, both alone and with me. After Mom's gone, it'll just be the two of us, and I don't want any regrets.

I'm blessed we share such a tight bond.

Instead of taking me home, Brody guides the horses to La Rouge Vineyards. Nervous energy spikes through me. I've only been here once before. That night changed my life, but I try to focus on the positives.

La Rouge is much like Atwood Estates, only bigger. Atwood Estates is a small, family winery. La Rouge is also family run, but they have a much larger operation. The differences are subtle but distinct. Mechanization for one thing. Irrigation is another major difference. Their vines sit heavy with grapes as the harvest nears. I want to see their processing facilities but don't want to appear too nosey.

My gut says Atwood Estates should be doing much better, but I don't have the knowledge or experience to back that up, and I'm cautious in the questions I aim at Mark. He needs to know I trust him, and those kinds of questions don't help with that. I want to ask the hard, intrusive questions about crop yield, production, wages, and all the rest.

The ground below the horses' hooves levels off, and I pull myself from troubled thoughts. We meander onto La Rouge property, and I can't help but gape.

"Wow!" The barn Brody leads me toward is massive. I expect something much smaller, but he takes me to a commercial-sized facility. Then I remember the La Rouge brothers operate a trail riding side business, but I thought they kept those horses in the pasture neighboring the barn.

The door to the massive structure stands open. Brody takes us inside, then dismounts. I practically salivate watching the way his muscles bunch and flex. Brody in a suit is a force to be reckoned with, but Brody dressed down in faded blue jeans and that green and black shirt of his is drool worthy.

Like I did on the trail, I wait for him to help me down. He doesn't ask me to wait; I simply sit in the saddle and wait until he helps me down.

"How'd it go, bro?" A voice, which sounds nearly identical to Brody, calls out from inside the barn. "Did she feed you your balls?" Asher exits one of the stalls carrying a shovel and slams to a halt. Identical to Brody in every way, the only thing distinguishing them is the color of their shirts. Asher wears red and black, whereas Brody dons green and black. "Um—hello there." The corner of his mouth tugs up in a smirk.

"Asher, do you remember Grace?" Brody shakes his head as he helps me out of the saddle.

"Hi, Grace." Asher removes the cowboy hat from his head and holds it close to his chest. "I take it you didn't disembowel, dismember, or otherwise rip my brother a new one?" He tucks his chin.

"I did not."

"It's been a long time, and it's really nice to see you again. This is an unexpected pleasure." His intonation rises in a question directed at Brody instead of me. "This is a pleasure, right, bro?"

"Grace is joining us for dinner." Brody keeps a hand on my hip, tugging me close. "Despite your hopes, I arrive home bowels intact and balls attached. No disemboweling, dismembering, or ass ripping."

"Sorry, Grace. It was just a joke." Asher smirks. "It really is nice to see you again."

While Brody and I talked up a storm in high school, I can count on my fingers the number of times Asher and I engaged in conversation.

"It's nice to see you too." I glance at Brody, concerned. "I'm sorry to drop in unannounced. I thought Brody might have let you know ahead of time. If it's an inconvenience…"

"No inconvenience." Brody gathers the horses' reins in hand. "Asher is thrilled to have company. Besides…" He flashes me a wink. "We can talk about his visit to Atwood Estates tomorrow."

"Mixing business with pleasure?" Asher shakes his head. "Sorry, Grace, my brother has no manners at all."

"If it really is a bother, I can go."

Dealing with Brody challenges me all on its own. Add Asher into the mix and it's twice as intimidating. Not to mention, Asher knows my history. He, along with the rest of the school, got an eyeful of me on that video. It may be years in the past, but if I'm thinking about it, I'm sure Asher is too. He and Brody obviously talked about me. Enough that he figured I'd read Brody the riot act. My cheeks heat thinking about what must be going through Asher's mind when he looks at me.

"It's no bother at all. In fact, why don't you head inside? Evie is pulling chicken out to roast on the grill." Asher watches his brother lead Spirit and Chesty over to the tack room.

Go into a stranger's home unannounced? So not my comfort zone, but that feels less threatening than staying out here with Asher and Brody, two of the infamous trio in one place.

"Grace, he's totally pulling your leg. I texted him from the trail. He and Evie are thrilled to have us. I'll take care of the horses while you clean up."

I look between them, not sure who's telling the truth. Known for their antics, the La Rouge triplets are notorious for the pranks they pull. Instead of hanging out in the barn with the two of them, I decide I'm better off seeking out female companionship.

"I'll just head to the house." I back out of the barn, keeping my eyes on them the whole time.

"Smart move." Asher winks, then he grabs Chesty's reins and slugs his brother in the arm. "What the hell happened?"

Leaving them to it, I march across the gravel drive and climb the stairs, which lead to a massive, covered porch. There's no doorbell, just a screen door. I pound on the doorjamb and listen for a response. When I hear nothing, I debate what to do next. Do I hang out on the porch or barge in?

Not comfortable hanging outside by myself, I shift foot to foot like an idiot. Fortunately, a voice calls out from inside.

"Hello? Grace? Come on in, girl. I'd come to the door but my hands are full."

Hesitant, it takes a second to get over my awkwardness. I open the door and step inside La Rouge triplet central.

TWENTY-TWO

# Grace

"Hello?" It's uncomfortable walking into Brody's house.

"Follow my voice. It's a big house. I'm in the kitchen, elbow-deep in batter. Head to the right, through the great room, past the library, and you'll find me."

Gorgeous doesn't begin to describe the house Brody grew up in. Stone walls, wooden floors, and massive beams overhead, I feel like I'm in a rustic cabin on steroids.

There's a gravitas which hangs over the decor, the weight of history; a family joined through the generations. Family portraits decorate the walls, images of La Rouge families march backward in time. Smiles fill their faces, and I instantly feel welcomed and at home. I can't help but wrap my arms around myself and soak it all in.

I don't come from a big family. My grandparents died when I was little. My father was absent, chasing a life without a wife and kid weighing him down. Mark never married. It's just me, Mom, and my uncle. I don't have brothers, sisters, aunts, uncles, and smiling grandparents. I feel the love filling the space and stop for a moment and imagine what that must be like.

The sound of a mixer draws me through the great room, past the library, and I wind up in a magnificent kitchen where a cloud of flour puffs in the air and makes a huge mess.

"Shit, shit, shit!" A woman slaps at the power button of the blender and looks up at me with a sigh. Flour dusts her face and settles in her auburn hair. "You'd think I could figure out how this works."

"You're supposed to add the flour in gradually. Let it mix slowly into the dough."

She flashes a smile and beams. Radiant, welcoming, I feel like I've known her my entire life.

"You must be Grace." She wipes at her forehead, smearing the flour.

"And you must be Evie."

"That's me." She drags a kitchen towel over her face. Tenacious as all get out, the flour sticks to her skin. "Evelyn Thornton, otherwise known as Evie, and the better half of Triplet Number One."

"You smudged the flour on your forehead. It doesn't really wipe away like that." I try my best not to laugh. "You have to wash it off."

She grabs for a washcloth.

"Oh, not like that. That'll just gum everything up."

"Well, it's all over me. I'm open to suggestions."

"What are you trying to make?"

"Would you believe sugar cookies?" Her lips twist in a wry smile. "Cooking is not my strength, but I'm determined to figure it out."

"I can help if you want."

"That would be great." She looks around at the mess of flour dusting the counter, cupboards, and her clothes. "Is that in helping me clean up or in helping with the dough?"

"Both. I'm actually pretty handy in the kitchen."

"Well, get in here. I'm not above putting a guest to work." She turns to the sink and wets a cloth to dab at her face. "Asher told me Brody was bringing a girl over, and I got this crazy idea in my head to make cookies to go with dinner, and well—you see how that's going." Her eyes sparkle with mischief. "And if you're up for a little prank, I can most definitely use some help."

"You really didn't have to go to all this effort, and prank? Tell me more."

She walks over and clasps my hands in hers.

"My motto in life is to overcome and conquer. If I don't know how to do something, I take that as a personal challenge to master it. So, I'm going to learn how to do this—eventually. In the meantime, another one of my mottos is nothing is fair in love and war."

"I think you mean, *All is fair in love and war.*"

"You'd think that." She raises her forefinger as if making a point. "You'd be wrong. These boys love to prank, and I've been dying for a way to pay Brody back."

"Pay him back?"

"You don't know what he did to me?"

"Until a few minutes ago, I didn't know you existed. And congratulations, by the way, Brody told me you and Asher are engaged."

"We are, and since you're going to be hanging around, you and I need to consolidate forces and form a united front, as it were. Are you with me?"

"Just tell me what to do."

Evie makes me laugh. Her energy is infectious, and I love that she's willing to go head-to-head with the brothers. I remember the pranks they played on everyone and anyone. Well, anyone but me. Asher and Cage didn't know about Brody and me.

"Not sure what you're thinking, but sign me up. As for the cookies, cooking isn't hard. I can teach you everything you need to know."

"That's awesome. You know how people have green or black thumbs when it comes to plants?"

"Yeah?"

"Well, I have the scorched thumb, or burnt thumb, when it comes to cooking. I can survive in the wilderness with nothing but my wits and a pocketknife, but throw me in a kitchen, and I'm a hopeless mess. I'm the person that burns water. In my defense, I always had a cook who made everything."

"A pocket knife?" I raise my eyebrows, not believing her boast. A cook? That's a question for later. Who has a cook growing up?

"No lie." Her grin is infectious. "I used to not know how to open a pocket knife without slicing my thumb off, but the world throws obstacles in our way. I'm an accomplished solo hiker now, but don't mention that to Asher. He seems to think it's too dangerous for me to hike alone."

"You hike alone? Wow."

"Well, not since Asher rescued me."

"Wait. He did what?"

"That's a story for another time. I'll tell you all about it after we deal with this mess."

"Well, I'd say the best reaction right now is to abandon the cookies. Take a shower before you gum up your hair any more than you already have."

"I wanted to make something special." She winks at me. "You know, like a La Rouge triplet special."

I take a long, hard look at her. She's feisty, fire with a hint of spice. Growing up, I always wanted a little brother or sister, but that wasn't in the cards. I imagine Evie and I could be close friends.

"I like you."

"Likewise."

"Kitchens and cooking are kind of my jam. Get yourself cleaned up, but don't take too long. If you leave me with the *Trips*, I'll stab you."

"The *Trips*?"

"It's what everyone used to call them in high school. *The La Rouge Trips*."

"I like that." She wipes her hand on a dishtowel and sets it down. "One thing I learned on the trail is how to take the quickest shower on earth. I'll be back in less than ten minutes."

"I'm going to hold you to that promise."

Evie's entire face lights up. "It's good to have female companionship around here. Asher's a hoot, but when he and his brothers get together, I run for the hills and hide. With the two of us to balance out the two of them, I feel like we may have a fighting chance."

"A fighting chance?"

"Yes. Those boys are pranksters, and I'm always on the butt end of their jokes. It's time to turn the tables on them. As for those cookies —if you really are some kitchen whiz—is there any way to, I don't know, make two batches?"

"What are you thinking?"

"I don't know, like one that's super awesome. You and I will chow down on those, but the *Trips* will get the nasty batch."

"Nasty?"

"Yeah, is that something you can do? Like super salty, super hot? Super disgusting, but look like the good stuff?" Evie grins ear to ear. "Come on, you've got to help a girl out. Especially after what Brody did to me."

"What did he do?"

"He didn't tell you?"

"No."

"That boy—that cocksure ass—is a piece of shit." She winks at me. "Not to get too personal too quick, but ask him about it when you get a moment, and I apologize up-front. I didn't know it was him and not Asher. Now, what about those cookies?"

"Oh, that's easy." I've got this. I know exactly what to do, and I'm dying to find out what the hell Brody did to Evie.

While she leaves to clean up, I acquaint myself with the kitchen, clean up the mess, and roll my sleeves up. Fucking with Brody and his brother might be just the thing I need to get out of my head and stop thinking about all the rest of the stuff that is keeping us apart.

And the kitchen really is my happy place.

Asher said nothing about cookies. Somewhere around here, Evie's supposed to be getting chicken ready. After mixing two batches of cookie dough, I find the chicken—still in its wrapper—nearly thawed in the fridge. With no idea what Evie's plans were for dinner, I take it upon myself to raid the fridge.

Uncle Mark says I'm a magician who can pull a ten-course meal out of an empty fridge. I don't disappoint. After raiding the fridge and liquor cabinet, I decide on a bourbon glaze for the chicken, veggies, and garlic bread alongside two—nearly identical—batches of cookies, and a salad.

Evie returns, takes in a long, deep inhale, and gives me a long, hard look.

"I'm grabbing wine. Any preference?"

"Surprise me."

After all the emotions I spilled on the trail, this feels good.

Natural.

Normal.

For the first time in over a year, I breathe.

I breathe because I can.

The only thing I need to accomplish is making dinner, and I do that with skill and finesse. It's the only thing in my life that's not a complete mess.

What does that say about me?

# TWENTY-THREE

# Brody

Asher takes Chesty and leads her into the barn while I follow with Spirit.

"All your appendages appear intact." Asher takes me in from the tips of my boots to the top of my hat with a smirk that says I'm full of shit. "Not too shabby for a wealthy businessman with the ethics of a devil."

"Ass—"

"Hole." He finishes my sentence, enunciating loudly. "We both have them, but only you are one."

"Don't be a dick. And as for business, my ethics are beyond reproach."

"Wasn't talking about your business ethics. I was talking about your moral ethics, or rather the way you keep your dick wet with fresh, willing pussy night after night. Grace isn't your typical fling. What the hell are you doing? You're going to hurt her when you toss her aside again. That's a major asshole-dick move."

"I have no intention of tossing her aside."

"Come on. It's what you do. Brody La Rouge, Billionaire Bachelor. Untouchable. Untamable. Every single woman is dying to get a piece of you. Or better yet, dig in her claws and ride you for all you're worth."

"She's not like those women." I tense as something shifts inside of me. Those words carry the weight of truth with them.

"And how is she different?"

"The women I date are more of a pass-the-time-and-scratch-an-itch kind of thing. Grace is different."

"Again, *how* is she different?"

"I don't know, just feels different. She always was different from any of the chicks I dated in high school."

"Dated?" His brow wings up in challenge. "I don't remember you *dating* anyone in high school. Hanging out and fucking, maybe, but you never went *steady* with any chick. Never have."

"I was with Grace."

He arches a brow. "We always wondered about that slowdown of yours, but you bounced back pretty damn quick after…"

"I know. I was a fucking putz back then."

Asher's right. It's been my motto nearly my entire life, but it doesn't matter what he says.

"This feels different."

"So you keep saying, but I bet you find some way to fuck this up. Don't you think you did enough damage for one lifetime? If you're not serious, you need to walk away while you still can. Before you hurt her again."

I cringe because while my intentions are good, Asher's right. My reputation speaks to a major fuckup looming in my future, but I refuse to let old habits ruin whatever is happening between me and Grace.

"I'm not going to fuck this up." If I say it enough times, maybe the universe will manifest my desire and make it true. Lord knows I can use a little help. Although, why leave it to fate? "I want her. And I'm going to make her mine."

"Why?" Asher's not sure if I'm full of shit or telling the truth. He should support me, but it seems as if he's more in Grace's corner than mine. I don't like the way he keeps pressuring me about Grace and my intentions.

"For the first time in my life, I see a future with her in it."

"Whoa, that's big."

"I know." I glance toward the main house. "Is this how you felt with Evie?"

"Pretty much. The moment I saw her, it felt like getting struck by lightning. I couldn't walk away. The need to be with her overwhelmed me. To protect her became the only thing I cared about."

"I walked away from Grace."

"And did major damage as a result."

"I wish I could take it all back. Go back in time. Erase that damage." I rub at the back of my neck and stare at the rafters. A decade ago, my feelings for Grace terrified me. Perhaps that's why I did what I did?

"Unfortunately, you gotta deal with what you did." Asher levels a stare at me that says *It's time to step up and deal with the shit you caused.*

I give a shake of my head because I really made a mess of this. I was young, bold, blessed with good looks, impeccable charm, a stellar physique, but completely lacking humility. I preened like a fucking cock, strutting my stuff to all my classmates, playing up my reputation until it reached near legendary proportions. The fact I used Grace, and destroyed her, meant nothing to me.

All that mattered to me—was me.

"I was such an ass back then." I glance at the house. Regret surges through me knowing I hurt the woman inside.

"We all were self-absorbed assholes." Asher claps me on the shoulder. He's right about that. We aren't called the 'infamous La Rouge triplets' without reason.

"Any advice?"

"Beg." Asher tosses his head back and laughs. "Be humble. Listen to her. Don't let things be about you. Put her needs first. Isn't that what a good Dom does?"

"You're having a lot of fun with this, and that's what a good man does." I don't deserve a title like that, not after what I did to the one who was supposed to be under my care. I fucked that up fifty ways to shitville.

"Heck yeah, I'm glad not to be the one in the hot seat for once. I got my girl. Once again, I'm first. Now, I'm just waiting for you and Cage to pull your heads out of your asses and fall in line."

"Asshole."

"Just stating the obvious."

"You know what you do to assholes who are first?"

"What?" He turns his back to me.

"You rub their smug noses in it." I tackle him, forcing him down on the floor. He sprawls face-first on the straw, and I rub his nose in it.

"Asshole." He reaches up behind him, trying to grab at my shirt.

Matched in every way imaginable—we're identical genetic copies of the same fertilized egg—he's admittedly the stronger of the two of us. I'm more of an endurance enthusiast, forcing my body to weather the grueling demands of ultra-marathons. Asher works the land. His body is hewn from hard, honest labor. He's got more bulk and brute strength than me. It doesn't take long for him to toss me from his back.

We roll around on the straw, swinging, punching, laughing like the best friends we are. We finally roll to a stop, chests heaving and gasping for breath.

The tension I've been holding eases. Knots release in my shoulders as reality sets in. I can fix things with Grace. Convincing her I won't turn my back on her becomes my top priority.

"I need to fix this."

"Don't."

"Huh?"

"Don't feel like you gotta fix shit. Your job is to listen to what she says. She's not looking for you to fix anything in her life. Do that, and it'll be the biggest mistake you make. Listen to her and you'll be amazed by what happens."

"I don't know how to be passive like that. I'm a doer. I make shit happen."

"You can't *make* anything happen in this case. All you can do is show her that she's the most important thing in your life. Support her and prove to her how this time is different. You're different. Words mean shit. Actions are what really count."

I'm happy to have Asher in my corner, but I don't know if I believe him. My shitty history with Grace is my mess to straighten. Problems demand solutions.

One way, or another, I'll prove I'm worthy of Grace's trust. My heart refuses to abandon its goal, and while it rattles with reckless abandon inside my chest, I think about how I'm going to convince Grace I'm the only man worthy of her love.

"What the heck is going on here?" Our mother's voice snaps our heads up. "Why are the two of you covered in straw? Are you fighting again?"

"We're not fighting," Asher speaks first. "Just carrying on a conversation."

"With your fists?" Mom shakes her head. "Or do we talk now by rolling around on the ground?" She clicks her tongue at us and I suddenly feel like I'm seven again. Asher too. He dusts off his jeans and ducks his head, refusing to look her in the eye.

"We really should be getting inside." Asher grabs his hat and dusts it free of dirt and straw. I glance around, find where we kicked my hat into the corner, and retrieve it as well.

Asher and I are spitting images of each other, with the exception of our shirts. Otherwise, the triplet curse struck again; same boots, trousers, and hats.

"You think they're talking about us?" I slap my hat on the side of my trousers and glance toward the house.

"Not us, but they're definitely talking about you."

"Asshole."

"Who is *them*?" Mom looks between the two of us, demanding an answer.

"Evie and Grace," Asher answers before I can stop him.

It's a bad idea letting Mom anywhere near Grace. She'll mother me and dig for information I'm not ready to provide.

"Grace is here? Lucy's Grace?" Her mouth curves into a not-so-innocent smile. "I just came from visiting Lucy." Mom's already got Evie firmly in her corner. I don't need her working that weird magic on Grace—at least not until I have a better idea where Grace and I stand.

"Come on, let's head inside." I tug at Asher's sleeve, the message implicit. I need him on my side.

"We weren't expecting you for dinner." Asher reaches Mom first and gives her a kiss on the cheek.

"I was just stopping by. I have something to give Evie, but if you're having dinner…"

This feels like the worst first date in history. Not that Grace and I are on a date, but still. I can handle Asher and Evie. They're known quantities. Throw Mom in the mix and anything can happen.

"We always have room for one more." Asher beams, and I want to throat punch him.

My small and intimate dinner is turning into something quite different; a family affair.

I'm totally fucked.

We make our way toward our family home, crossing the distance from the new barn with our long strides. La Rouge Vineyards, and its associated buildings, are nothing short of spectacular. Growing up, we never suffered for money, but that didn't stop our father from teaching us about the value of hard work.

Asher, Cage, and I were put to work by the time we were seven, laboring beside our workers during the harvest. We started by hauling empty bins to the vines for the workers to fill with grapes. The following year, our father taught us how to hand-select the grapes and cut them from the vines. Our empty bins turned to burdens as we labored beside our father and his men in the field.

By the time we were ten, Dad had us fixing broken trellises that support the vines. He taught us how to train the vines, giving every plant the room it needed to produce the best grapes. At twelve, we dug the post holes that supported the trellises.

He kept our young bodies fit, exhausted, and mostly out of trouble by burning up the excess energy of three young boys who bucked authority at every turn. We earned our livelihood by blood, sweat, tears, and good honest work. Because of that, the family business thrived, and our family reaped the benefits.

The family home bears testament to the hard work of our forefathers. Built out of river rock and high Sierra timber, it's withstood the test of time. The extensive master suite takes up the entire west end, and the eastern side is where I grew up with my brothers. Three separate bedrooms protrude off a central living space where we made a mess of things as we grew into men.

Asher now lives in the master suite. Mom moved out to the small cottage we built for her after Dad died. Cage and I still keep our things in our rooms, never quite managing to fully move out. Cage has no real home. He heads out on assignment for months at a time, then returns home until he's sent out to another part of the world. I keep my things here as an anchor because this place keeps me grounded.

People who don't know me believe I keep a pricey penthouse in the city. The truth is I manage a small, top floor, two bedroom unit. It's modestly decorated, nearly spartan, and I never bring women home, always taking them to a penthouse suite in my favorite hotel.

Why not, when I have money to spare?

"Brody?" Mom calls out, pulling me from my thoughts.

"Yes, Ma'am?"

"I asked you a question."

"Sorry, what was it?"

"Got your head in the clouds, I see." Her motherly look speaks volumes. "I asked if you minded if I join you?"

"Of course, I don't mind." That's a total lie. Sharing Grace with Asher and Evie is one thing; inviting Mom into the mix makes this a whole lot less spontaneous and much more complicated.

"Then it's settled. I'll see you inside after you wash up." And just like that, Mom downgraded us from men to boys.

"Yes, Ma'am." Asher hangs his head but smirks at her motherly command. He's thinking exactly what I am. "Come on, best we hurry up. Don't want to leave the women alone for too long."

"Right back at you." I launch myself up the porch steps, taking them two at a time, and race to wash my hands and face—just like

Mom so politely asked. By the time I make it to the kitchen, Grace stands with Mom and Evie. They take one look at me and smiles fill their faces.

Guilty smiles. The back of my neck tingles because I'm pretty damn sure they were talking about me.

TWENTY-FOUR

# Brody

---


"What's going on?" I look at each of them, demanding an answer.

"Nothing, just talking." Evie shrugs. "You know, a little girl time."

"A little girl time, my ass. You're up to something." I glance around the kitchen. Nothing seems out of the ordinary, except for the dozens of cookies cooling on the counter. "Who baked the cookies?" My attention shifts between Evie and Grace. I've tasted Evie's cooking, and it leaves much to be desired. Not that I would say that out loud, but a little advance warning isn't a bad idea. "Evie, did you make these?"

Evie stands beside Grace and holds a knife loaded with frosting. About half a dozen sloppily iced cookies sit on a tray in front of her. Grace stands right beside her with well over a dozen perfectly frosted cookies. Grace picks up an unfrosted cookie from a cooling rack and slathers frosting on top of it.

"Want one before dinner?" Grace takes a bite of the cookie and closes her eyes. "Mmm, so good." Making a show of licking her lips, then sucking her finger into her mouth, Grace turns my blood from heated to a raging boil.

I'm forced to take a step toward the kitchen island to hide the effect she has on me.

"Oh, sweetie," Evie bats her lashes at me. "Brody won't want to ruin supper. If you let him taste one of your amazing cookies, he'll eat the whole lot." She takes an unfrosted cookie off the cooling rack and nibbles on it. Her eyes light up and she pops the rest of the cookie into her mouth. "Oh my, that's delicious." Evie's eyes close as she savors the cookie.

My focus shifts between Grace and my mother, who perches at the end of the kitchen island on a sturdy high-top chair. Something feels off, but I can't put my finger on it. Evie continues icing her disastrous cookies like nothing out of the ordinary is going on.

"I'll wait." The delicious aroma of something mouthwatering comes from the oven. I shift over to the oven and take a peek inside. "Evie? You cooked this?"

Evie ices another cookie. "Grace put that together. This girl is a whiz in the kitchen."

A faint blush fills Grace's face. I ache to go to her and feather kisses all over her beautiful face. She catches my hungry gaze and sucks in a breath.

"It's not much. One of my mother's recipes, bourbon-glazed chicken." She turns from me to my mother. "Abbie, I was going to fix a salad to go with the chicken. Do you mind getting that started while I fry up some bacon?"

"Oh, let Brody do that." Evie looks me dead in the eye. "He's really good at frying bacon in the pan. Aren't you?" Her reference to how I first met her draws a warning growl from deep in my throat.

"Careful…" I say.

"Why?" Her innocent doe-eyes are anything but innocent. "Maybe you can get Grace to give you a hand?"

"What have you two been talking about?" Mom bats her eyes like she doesn't know.

"Nothing." The impish grin on Evie's face says otherwise. Mom chuckles while Grace looks at me with an innocent, doe-eyed expression.

"I can help out, if you need a *hand*." Grace's gaze cuts to Evie and they burst out laughing.

"I take it you told her how we met?"

"Definitely." Evie makes a mess of the poor cookie she's icing.

Grace tries to keep from laughing, but she can't help herself.

"Ha-ha, not funny."

"Nobody is getting handsy with anyone while I'm in this house," Mom speaks up, putting her foot down. "You'll have to wait until I leave for those kinds of shenanigans."

"Mom!" I don't mean to shout, but Mom surprises me sometimes when she lays it out there like that.

"What? You think I don't know what you boys get up to when I'm not around?" She looks down her nose at me, letting me know I'm no innocent.

"We're not having this conversation." I pull out a stool and try to get comfortable.

"What conversation?" Asher joins us and steps right into things.

"I was just telling Grace she should give Brody a hand with the bacon."

"Never gonna live that one down, bro." Asher chuckles and slaps me on the back.

"Hey, I was an innocent victim. You're the one with the fiancée who can't keep her hands off my junk."

"There's absolutely nothing innocent about you." Asher's attention shifts to the cookies. "Mmm, cookies." He reaches for one, but Evie slaps his hand.

"No cookies until after dinner. Our guest made those and dinner as well."

"I thought we were grilling?" Asher looks between Evie and Grace. "How did you have time to make cookies and dinner? We didn't leave you alone for that long."

"Just handy in the kitchen, I guess." Grace shrugs and exchanges another look with Evie.

The girls giggle. To be honest, coming here for dinner isn't my best play. Instead of close and intimate, Grace is getting an up-close and personal look at the inner workings of the La Rouge family. All we need now is for Cage to randomly show up to complete this epic fail of a date.

"Oh my lord, something smells amazing." Cage wanders into the kitchen. His clothes are rumpled. A scruffy beard dusts his chin, and he looks tired and gaunt.

"What the hell?" I spin and gape, not believing my eyes.

"Look what the cat dragged in." Asher greets Cage, drawing him into a hug and slapping his back. "You're looking a little rough around the edges, bro." Asher cants his head and takes in Cage's appearance.

"Cage!" Evie screeches with joy and practically flies around the kitchen counter and into Cage's outstretched arms.

"How's my future sister-in-law doing?" He wraps Evie in a hug and holds her until Asher yanks her out of his arms.

"Hands off my girl," Asher growls at Cage, but it's all in fun.

Cage moves on to our mother, folding her into a hug. "And how's my best girl?"

"You made it." Mom gives him a kiss on the cheek, then holds him at arms' length. "You lost weight."

"Nothing that your amazing pancakes can't fix." He looks up at me, then his gaze slides over to Grace. Recognition sparks in his eyes, and he wings up an eyebrow with a question I'll answer later.

"Grace Atwood, this is a nice surprise. You look amazing."

"Hi, Cage." Grace gives a little wave of her fingers, looking lost amidst my entire family.

I finally buck up and go to her. So much for playing things casual. I wrap an arm around her waist and tug her to my side. "Grace and I are…" I glance down at her, not really sure what it is that we are. "We're working together."

Cage's lips quirk up in a knowing grin. "Is that what we're calling it these days?"

"Manners." Mom pinches Cage's arm. "We're thrilled to have Grace over, and she cooked for us, although I don't know if there's enough for everyone." She glances at Grace, and the two women exchange something in that look.

"Oh, we'll have plenty. I tend to overcook. Let me whip up some veggies and throw some bread in the oven. If y'all want to catch up, you've got about half an hour before dinner's done." Grace pushes away from me but keeps a hand on my arm.

"Come on boys…" Mom shoos Asher and Cage out of the kitchen. Evie follows them out into the great room, leaving me alone with Grace.

"Hey, I'm not really sure what happened, but it was never my intention to subject you to a family dinner. We can escape all this madness. Just say the word and I'll make our excuses."

"Your family is fun. I like Evie, and there's no way I'm leaving her to finish up in here."

"Tell me what you need help with…" I glance around the kitchen, not really knowing how I can help. Unlike when Evie cooks, everything is perfectly clean. I'm not sure how that's possible.

"You don't have to stay here with me. Don't you want to catch up with Cage?"

"I can catch up with him anytime. I want to spend time with you."

"Odd as it sounds, cooking is my happy place, and after our talk, I don't mind a bit of silence."

Silence? I think she means space. Asher told me to listen; this sounds like a good time to take his advice.

"Well, let me apologize in advance for whatever mayhem my brothers create. Are you sure you don't want help?"

"A bit of peace and quiet is what I need right now. I really am good, and it's not going to take but a second to prep some veggies."

Not sure if I believe her, I sense she's being as open and honest as she can. Grace bared herself to me up on the ridge. I sense her fragility and understand she needs space to regroup.

"I'm going to go in for a second, but I'll be back in a bit to help. I hate that my invitation to dinner turned into you cooking for my whole family."

"Honestly, it's my pleasure. It feels good to be doing something normal. If I was uncomfortable, I'd tell you."

"You promise?"

"Absolutely." Her soft smile slides over me with truth and conviction. She may not realize it, but she's softening toward me, seeing me in a different light. I'm good with that, the more she can see of this side of me, the better.

# TWENTY-FIVE

# Grace

WHILE IT MAY BE WEIRD—ME COOKING FOR BRODY'S FAMILY—I love that they leave me to it. I get a chance to mull over my thoughts. Besides, I love cooking. It's been far too long since I lost myself to the soothing tasks of creating something mouthwateringly delicious.

I open a bottle of La Rouge wine. Not sure if I should've asked beforehand, it doesn't occur to me until the cork's out and I've poured a generous glass.

From the boisterous conversation trickling in from the great room, I take that it's been a bit since Cage has been home. Which is good, they're occupied, and it gives me a reason to get a little fancy. After a little digging through the fridge, I get bread baking and julienne some green beans. As I fry up some bacon on the stove, I try to imagine Evie coming up behind Brody. If something like that happened to me, I would've died, and I certainly would never show my face around here again. Evie seems like a pretty amazing woman. Given time, I bet we'd make great friends.

While I asked Abbie to help with the salad, she abandoned me. She's having fun with all three of her boys in the other room. Cage is telling some tall tale about his last assignment as I finish my first glass of wine. Bits and pieces of their conversation drift to my ears. They're a tight-knit family, warm and loving.

Evie comes in while I'm pouring my second glass.

"You want some?" I pull out a wineglass before she answers.

"Which bottle did you pick?" She sits across the kitchen island and leans on her elbows while I pour her a glass.

"The first one I saw?" I give a soft laugh. "I'm usually much more of a connoisseur, but I saw the bottle in the fridge and figured a glass, or two, couldn't hurt." I slide her glass across the counter and lift mine. "To boisterous boys?"

"To the *Trips!* And to new friends." She lifts her glass and toasts me. She surveys the kitchen and her eyes widen as she takes in everything I have going on. "How do you do it?"

"Do what?"

"The kitchen? It's practically spotless."

"I clean as I go."

"Well, I'd like to apologize for putting you to work, but it looks like you're creating a culinary masterpiece, so I'm going to be totally selfish and sit here and watch. I'll do the dishes afterward."

"I don't know about a culinary masterpiece. I picked something simple."

"Well, your simple smells delicious." She sniffs the air and tilts her head back. "Can I hire you out?"

"I wish. I love to cook, but I don't get much of a chance these days."

"Why's that?"

"Running a failing family business and my mom barely eats anymore. The chemo destroyed her taste buds and her appetite isn't there."

"I'm really sorry about your mom. Asher mentioned she was sick, and of course, Abbie filled me in on the rest. Not that we've been talking behind your back or anything, but…"

"No, I get it. You're curious about the girl Brody brought home."

"Evidently, you're the first."

"I don't know about that."

"No, it's the truth. Asher and Abbie both mentioned it."

"I meant it more as Brody and I really aren't a thing. His company is investing in mine. This is more of a business thing. We're not dating."

"You sure about that?" Evie makes a sweeping gesture around the kitchen. "Does Brody know that, because bringing you to his house for dinner is a big deal? Like *huge*." She stretches her arms out wide for emphasis.

"I thought this was Asher's house?"

"It's the *Trips* house." She winks at me. "I like that word. But really, Asher may live here, but Brody and Cage consider it home. I think it'll always be home base for the three of them."

"Are you okay with that? After you're married, won't that be intrusive? Having them here all the time?" I take a sip of wine and let the citrusy flavors coat my tongue. "This is really good."

"It's one of their award-winning vintages."

"Was I not supposed to open the wine?" A pang of guilt runs through me.

"Grace, you made us dinner. I think a bottle of wine, or two, is more than fair compensation. And as for the *Trips* bothering me, it never really occurred to me. Those three are tight. Like freakishly tight. They call it the triplet curse; I call it supernatural. I envision a very crowded house in my future with lots of nieces and nephews running around and new sisters to commiserate with. If you're thinking about joining this family on a permanent basis, be forewarned. That's not even a tenth of how boisterous it can get." She points toward the great room where Brody, Asher, and Cage practically shout at the top of their lungs.

The look she gives me makes me feel funny inside, like I'm supposed to be one of those new sisters. But I'm not. I'm so far from that, it's laughable. I ignore that part of our conversation and focus on something safe.

"I remember that from high school. Not too many people could tell them apart. It was a superpower of theirs."

"I forgot. You knew them in high school." She leans forward eagerly. "What was that like?"

"Honestly, I only knew Brody. I was a freshman. They were seniors. Our paths rarely crossed, except on the football field."

"Huh?"

"I made the varsity cheer squad as a freshman. Best and worst decision of my life. Brody and I were friends, close friends, but I never really talked to Asher or Cage." I can't keep my mouth from twisting on the bad memories.

"I sense a story there."

"A long story and not a good one. Brody and I didn't part as friends."

"And now? If you're going into business with him, how does that factor into things? Not to mention, you look pretty darn close for people who didn't part as friends."

"It's complicated."

"He seems acutely interested in you. I just assumed you were dating by the possessive vibe he's throwing."

"That's why it's complicated."

Over the next half hour, I tell Evie everything there is to know about Brody, our history, our reunion, and how it's all a complicated mess. She's easy to talk to, like a sister, and listens to my woes with rapt attention. She helps with a bit of slicing and dicing for the salad, but I see why her kitchen skills are lacking. She nearly cuts off several of her fingertips before I rescue the mangled produce and relieve her of the knife.

We share stories, swapping tales of how we met our respective *Trips*.

"He rescued you from a forest fire?" I stare at her for a long moment, mouth gaping. "I don't know what I would've done."

"You already know this, but if you put your mind to it, you can accomplish anything. A little over a year ago, I would've laughed if you told me I'd be an accomplished solo backpacker who worked my way across the country alone. I was a spoiled brat who never lifted a finger for anything, and honestly, didn't know how to take care of myself. But life intervened. It places obstacles in your path to see what you'll do. I decided to learn how to be self-sufficient. That began with a hike in the woods."

"I never thought I'd be the owner of a winery. I've been learning a ton."

"What did you want to do?"

"Actually," I glance toward the noisy *Trips*, "work at the kind of company Brody works at. It was my dream before Mom got sick."

"What was?" Brody's deep voice sends a chill down my spine as he strolls into the kitchen. "How's it going? Are we being exceptionally rude leaving you alone?"

"I'm going to go listen to Cage's tall tales and give you two a moment alone." Evie scoots off her stool. After topping off her wine, she winks at me and leaves Brody and me alone.

"We don't need a moment..." But she's already striding away.

"Thanks, Evie," Brody calls out. "We'll let you know when dinner's ready. You think you can handle them for a bit?"

"Not a problem." She takes a sip and makes her exit.

A chill works its way down my spine, followed by a wave of blistering heat as Brody closes the distance. He wraps me in his arms.

"I'm really sorry about this." He draws me tight against his body. "Forgive me?"

"It's my pleasure, and to be honest, it feels good to let myself go in the kitchen. I miss it."

"It smells amazing." He kisses my forehead. "Put me to work. Let me help out so I don't feel like a total loser bringing my girlfriend home to cook for my family."

*Girlfriend?*

"Um…" I take a quick inventory of all the dishes and where they are as far as being done. "Where do you guys usually eat? Is it casual; sitting in front of the television kind of thing, or more formal, like a sit down in the dining room thing?" My cooking works with either of those options, from casual to classically elegant.

"Actually, I was thinking outside in the garden. It's too beautiful not to enjoy the outdoors, if that works for whatever you're cooking up?"

"I've got everything handled in here, but if you could get the table set, that would help." Honestly, he's more in the way than any help to me at this point. I've got everything timed perfectly to finish together.

"Asher! Cage!" Brody shouts toward the other room. "Set the table outside. Dinner will be done in…" He glances at me with a question on his face.

"Fifteen minutes." I don't know why I whisper, but I do.

"Fifteen minutes!" His bellow makes the air vibrate.

Cage and Asher stride into the kitchen. It takes a moment, watching them walk in, because all I see are two exact replicas of Brody. They're identical, not only in looks, but mannerisms as well.

Or nearly identical.

I can easily pick Brody out from his brothers, but if asked which one is Cage and which is Asher, I'm lost.

Without any prompting from me, they pull flatware from drawers and dishes from cupboards. Abbie wanders in behind them and pauses at the door. Her eyes mist up as she takes in all the commotion. When she notices me watching her, she places a hand over her heart and smiles.

Abbie wrangles her sons into setting the table. Evie joins them to help get everything set up, while Brody stands by my side, holding me in his arms. That's when I realize why Abbie's eyes misted over. She looked in on her kitchen with her boys and two of the girls that might someday make her family complete.

Whoa! Where did that thought come from? Brody and I are not dating, and we're certainly not looking toward a future together. From the way he stays right beside me, I wonder how much of what Evie said is true.

Together, we get dinner from the kitchen to a table set up outside in the garden. Brody keeps one hand on me as we head back and forth, either holding my hand, resting it on my hip, or when he gently places the broad expanse of his palm across my lower back. He's with me until we settle down to eat with his family.

After I describe each of the dishes, dinner goes off without a hitch. Brody and his brothers rave about my cooking, and I can't help but soak in their praise. There are few opportunities in my life to relax.

I didn't lie about cooking being my happy place. Since Mom got sick, I struggle to make anything she'll eat. Whipping up a real meal isn't easy when cooking for one. I never go to this trouble for myself.

"This is the best food I've had in months," Cage announces to the table. "Damn, you're a good cook. If Brody doesn't want you, I'll gladly…"

"Grace is mine." Brody's warning growl takes me by surprise. Actually, it stops all conversation. I wiggle beside him and wait for anyone to fill in the heavy silence.

"Well, I'll be." Cage shoves a spoonful of the scalloped potatoes into his mouth and grins like a fool. "You got bit."

"Anyone need a drink refill?" Asher pours the last of the fourth bottle of La Rouge's prized wine into Evie's glass. She's a bit tipsy and smiles like a fool when he leans down to kiss her.

"I do." Abbie stands and clears her plate. "Anyone else done? I know Evie and Grace made some amazing cookies for dessert."

Cage looks up as he shovels another mouthful of food into his mouth. "Don't you dare clear this table. There's still tons of food left."

That's not true. The *Trips* devoured nearly everything. The chicken is gone. The salad demolished. There are two lonely green beans left in their dish, but Cage reaches for that bowl when Abbie threatens to take it inside.

"Here, I'll help." I scoot back and freeze at Brody's harsh glare.

"You made us dinner. No way in hell are you doing the dishes." He snaps his fingers and points at his brothers. Cage clears the last of the food and looks around for scraps. "Come on, let's go for a walk while they clean all this up." From the way Brody practically drags me away from the table, he's a man on a mission.

That mission involves taking me far out of eyesight from his family. We wander out into the fields, coming to the base of a towering oak. He grabs me by the hips and leans back against the broad trunk.

"Kiss me." His voice slides over me, ushering in shivers as it licks along my skin.

## TWENTY-SIX

## Grace

———————

Brody's magnificent green eyes, half-hooded and framed by dark lashes, smolder with desire. His pupils dilate and my breath hitches. The way he positions us, him backed against the tree, me cradled in his arms, gives me the power to do as I desire. Fierce dominance blazes in his eyes, an unwavering acknowledgment that he can quickly turn the tables on me, but there's something else there as well.

He wants to know if I want this; if I'll initiate instead of him. An anguished expression steals across his face when I hesitate, a look of loss I can't describe.

As I take all this in, my attention focuses on his mouth. On the full, pillowed lips, which drive me insane. On lips capable of wrenching the most base, most desperate, screams from my throat. Lips that chase, claim, and devastate. They're dangerous and seductive. Which makes it hard to remain focused on what my head tries to tell me.

*You can't trust Brody La Rouge.*

No doubt about that. He says things have changed, but words are easy and cheap. They cost nothing and fail to carry the weight of commitment and action. If I kiss him, he'll dominate and destroy me. He'll draw forth screams of unadulterated pleasure—from me. It's not an *if* statement, but rather an absolute certainty.

My desire for Brody goes without question. My need to surrender— indisputable. My head tries to govern my next steps, but in this, I will fail.

I'll fail because I'm desperately, and hopelessly, in love with Brody La Rouge. Even though I know he'll hurt me, even though I know this is a bad decision. I can't stop myself from leaning against his hard frame. I can't stop my hand from lifting to thread my fingers through his dark hair.

"It's not safe to kiss you."

His low growl excites me, sending a lick of pleasure to my core.

"You know what I want."

I do, and I know he wants nothing more than to take from me. He's holding back, resisting his urges, while waiting for me to catch up. Only he doesn't know I'm already there. I never fell out of love with Brody La Rouge. That is why he's so dangerous.

While our gazes collide, his talented fingers knead along my spine, working out kinks I didn't know were there. Each press of his fingers sends ripples of heat shooting through my body.

He claims an unfair advantage as my muscles melt beneath those magical fingers. His touch exceeds any other touch set upon my body, wrecking my ability to think as his fingers travel up and down my spine.

The devil incarnate, he lays siege to my senses, making it impossible to think and remember why I need to be careful around him. His hands move outward, fingers digging into my heated muscles, as he divides and conquers and stakes his claim.

"Tell me you want this. Tell me you'll say yes." His touch is everywhere at once, gliding from my back to my shoulders, dipping down to my waist, and wrapping around the flare of my hips. He forces my aching muscles to surrender beneath his touch. Each caress builds on the last, commanding nerves to surrender, skin to heat, and teaching my body to crave more of his devilish touch.

He knows how to touch me. How to stroke me. How to push my limits. Most importantly, he knows how to destroy me.

I'm at a disadvantage, and yet he places me in a position of power. This kiss won't happen unless I make it happen. He's waiting for me to give in to the desire swirling between us.

He knows exactly how to touch me. How much pressure to use. Which spots along my spine will make me sigh. The power he wields is beyond intense. It's excruciating. Tantalizing. Seductive and captivating.

My body heats as his fingers continue their wicked dance, stroking along my back, sending tendrils of sensation shooting to my core.

"Brody…" I barely recognize my own voice.

He grasps my chin between his thumb and forefinger, lifting my face to meet his steely gaze.

"Kiss me, Grace." Low, guttural, fully aroused, and one hundred percent male, his command causes a shift within me.

"I can't." If I do, then it's an admission I want this. That I want him. I'm not ready to acknowledge this truth. Not yet. I harbor resentment and pain, and—holy hell, I need him to stop that maddening swirl of his thumb over my lower lip.

"Kiss me." He repeats the command and presses the pad of his thumb between my lips.

When he glances at me, our gazes collide, and I clamp my teeth down on my lower lip.

"I'm barely holding on, luv. If you don't kiss me, I'll spin you around and take what I want. But I'm warning you…" A low growl emanates from his throat. "What I want doesn't end with a kiss. If you're not ready to feel me sliding inside of you, either walk away or kiss me now."

"Kissing generally leads to the sliding in and out kind of thing."

"I'm not against that."

"What about your family?"

"Why do you think I brought you out here?"

"I don't think I'm ready for that."

"The kissing or sliding in and out thing?"

I blow out a breath and lean against him, enjoying the way his arms slide around me and hold me up.

"The you and me thing." I look up at him. "I'm not interested in a one-night stand. If that's all this is, we should probably stop right now."

"Is that what you think this is?"

"Isn't it?"

"Not for me."

"I hear the words, but…" My blood heats where he touches me. Tremors of sensation spread from there.

"I get it. Words are only so good, but that's okay. I have all the time in the world to show you I mean what I say." His grip on my waist tightens.

All the time?

I gaze into his arresting face and tumble into the powerful glint in his eyes. If I let myself fall too far, serious ruin will be my fate. I thought I could work Brody out of my system if I slept with him. Now I know that will only make things worse. We've only kissed, yet every nerve in my body thrums with need as he leans down to whisper in my ear.

"You're mine. I don't think you understand what that means, but I'll show you." Strong and powerful, that's a promise I can't ignore.

His lips wrap around my earlobe, and he sucks it into his mouth. Hot, wet, and devastating, my toes curl, and heat licks between my legs where it settles into a needy, insistent throbbing. He lifts one hand to tangle in my hair, twisting, pulling, fingers pressing against my scalp.

When did the trembling start?

It's hard to say, except his lips abandon my ear and kiss and suckle their way down the curve of my neck. His expert tongue licks a torturous path while I burn beneath the quickening of his exhales. I'm right there with him, breathless and on my way to losing control of any higher brain functions I might have once possessed.

Another moan escapes my lips as he licks and nuzzles my collarbone. They're just lips, yet I feel ravished in the best possible way.

"Brody…" I don't know what it is I mean to say, whether to encourage or discourage, except this isn't something I want to stop. As his lips drag against my skin, he groans against me, building desire and dragging me toward a breathless surrender. He reaches the tip of my shoulder and pauses. Brody's body stills as he simply breathes. How wrong would it be to give in to this carnal craving he draws from my body?

*Don't answer that.*

If I give in, if I fall, I know what waits for me at the bottom of that maddening plunge. Pleasure might surge through me for a blissful moment, but that fall will break me. Every skilled touch is a reminder of what happened the last time I gave in to what he wanted.

Those memories don't match the skillful adoration he showers upon me now, but that pain lingers in the corners of my mind. I wish I could take a chance, fall over the edge and plunge into the maddening abyss of pleasure he promises, but I uncover a last-ditch reservoir of strength and pull back.

"I can't do this."

He regards me with that sweeping gaze of his. Too easily, I forget the impressive figure he cuts. His hawkish glare cuts into me, measuring and assessing as his lips tense and draw tight together.

"Perhaps not today, then, but I'm not going anywhere." The heat of his passion rushes through me as those smoldering green eyes of his capture me and bind me.

I accomplish the nearly impossible feat of drawing air into my lungs as my head spins with the promise those words create.

"Why?"

"Why, what?"

"Why now?" Tears swarm in my eyes, and I fight back the hot pinpricks, daring them to fall and betray me to this uncompromising man.

"Because I'm not a self-centered asshole anymore. I walked away because it was easy. I stayed away because that was easy too. I convinced myself it was better for us both, when it was simply easier on me. After so many years, I figured you moved on." He leans his head against the trunk of the tree. "But you're here now, and I have a second chance; a chance to be the kind of man you deserve and to make up for the pain I caused. I intend to work on it and earn your trust." He takes my hand and traces out the lines on my palm as his expression grows distant.

"It's all a bit much to take in. I don't know what's real and what's not real."

"Every word I've spoken is the truth. I haven't tried to hide from what I did. I didn't sugarcoat or downplay what happened, but soon, you'll feel the truth, and you'll know."

"What? What will I know?"

"That you can't escape this."

"I don't even know what *this* is."

"It's you and me forging a future together."

A future?

He kicks off from the tree. "We should probably get back. I'm sure Asher is dying to taste your fabulous cookies. At least, if Cage hasn't devoured them all by now." His expression softens, but all I feel is the raw, sexual energy heating the air between us. I shouldn't have stopped him.

Why didn't I take that kiss?

## TWENTY-SEVEN

## Grace

I don't mean to be a downer."

Brody takes both my hands in his and leans in real close. The raw potency of his masculinity floods my senses, making me regret my words. It would be too easy to take that kiss and damn the consequences.

"I'm going to show you what you're worth. Come."

A sigh escapes me as he leads me back inside. His brothers stand side by side at the sink, doing the dishes, while Evie and Abbie look on with impish grins. When they see me, Evie winks.

"Didn't expect the two of you back so soon." Evie reveals the cookies we made earlier, well-guarded by her and Brody's mom. "These boys tried to sneak cookies."

"You better not have." Brody releases my hand and walks up behind his brothers at the sink. He taps each of them upside the head. "My girl made those; that means I've got dibs."

"And we gotta wait while you're out back swapping spit?" Cage flicks soapsuds at Brody. "Dude, bros before…"

"Don't say it." Brody's tone of voice drops a register, turning deep, possessive, and protective.

"Oh, I wasn't going to say hoes."

"You just said it." Brody takes a jab at Cage, but his brother twists away.

"Jeez, climb down off that high horse." Cage turns to me and gives a semi-bow. It looks funny on him, and I can't help but smile. "I would never disrespect Grace or Miss Evie, and I most definitely wouldn't in front of Mom."

"Darn straight." Abbie rises to her feet and props her hands on her hips. "I didn't raise you to disrespect women."

"But he said bro's before…" Brody twists, complaining to his mom.

"I know what I said, ass-wipe." Cage turns back to the dishes. "Like I said, someone's done got bit."

My eyes pinch, wondering what that means. I join Abbie and Evie by the cookies and whisper. "Bit?"

"By the love bug." Evie places her hand on my arm and whispers back. "They're giving Brody grief."

"Oh." I suddenly feel stupid, not getting the reference, but my mind is a little distracted after my conversation with Brody.

"You ready to let them try out your cookies?" Evie gives a little friendly jab to my ribs.

"Did you tell Abbie which ones to avoid?" I glance at Abbie.

"She sure did." Abbie rubs her palms together. "Let's do this."

We marked the two batches of cookies. The good batch is on the bottom of the stack. The doctored batch, made with too much salt, too much baking soda, and sprinkled with more than a few touches of cayenne pepper, are on the top. We discreetly marked six of the good batch and placed them on top of the pile.

"We'd better let them try these out before an all-out brawl starts." While we talk, Brody and Cage grabbed towels. They twisted the ends and snapped each other on the ass. Asher grabs a towel, but when I clear my throat, they suddenly stop.

"Guys, if you're done, we're ready for dessert." I gesture to Evie. "Go ahead. Girls go first."

Evie picks out two of the good cookies from the top of the stack and takes a bite out of one. Her eyes close as she gives a moan of appreciation. I pivot and offer Abbie the cookies. She makes a show of deciding which cookies to take but finally grabs two of the good ones. Her boys look on, and I swear they're salivating. I could walk over and offer them the cookies, but I don't want them to accidentally take the last two good ones on top. Instead, I carry the tray to the kitchen table. After I put it down, I take my cookies.

Abbie bites into hers and takes a seat at the table. "Darling, these are amazing, mouthwatering." She pops the rest of the cookie in her mouth and makes a show of enjoying it.

"Thank you."

Evie joins me at the table. She's nearly finished with her second cookie. She makes a show of snatching a third and fourth cookie from the bottom of the pile.

"Oh my, so good." Evie closes her eyes. "Like an orgasm, but in my mouth."

"Evie!" I blush at her comment.

"Hey, we want some." Asher strides over to the table, but not before Brody grabs his shirt and hauls Asher back.

"My girl. I go first."

"So good." Evie giggles and ducks her head as she licks her fingers. She's a bit too obvious, but Brody and his brothers don't seem to pick up on it.

"You sure Grace made these?" Cage stands back, looking suspicious. "Cause if Evie did…"

"Hey!" Evie says. "You won't eat my cookies?"

"I make it a point to never eat anything you cook." Cage gestures in my direction. "Brody's girl is amazing. I'll eat her cookies, but I've tasted too many of your disasters."

"You're an ass, Cage La Rouge." Evie's face reddens with anger, but it's fast and fleeting.

The insults aren't real and lack any sting. I hang back a little and chew at my lower lip. These brothers accept Evie into their midst and treat her more like a little sister than an outsider. I've never had that, and if I'm being completely honest, I'm a bit jealous.

"Come on, boys." Abbie silences the *Trips*. "Stop bickering."

I pick up the tray and offer it to Brody first. He stands closest to me, but I feel like I owe him some loyalty. Not enough to keep him from picking up what are probably the worst cookies ever made, I maintain solidarity with the females as we unite against all the raging testosterone in the room.

Brody takes three cookies. Asher waits his turn and scoops several into his hand.

"You promise she didn't bake these?" Finally, Cage, whose eyes narrow with suspicion, takes one.

"Promise. You only want one?" I urge him to take more.

Evie, Abbie, and I have a bet going on. I bet they will each take a bite and spit it out. Abbie claims her boys will eat everything I give them, not wanting to hurt my feelings. Evie says they'll eat all the cookies, but Brody will figure it out. If she keeps grinning the way she is right now, there's no way they won't figure it out. Evie has no poker face.

I set the tray down and take a seat.

Abbie holds up a hand as Cage tries to take a bite, halting him in his tracks. Asher and Brody also wait.

"Boys, Grace has been so very kind to not only cook an amazing dinner but also treat us to her homemade cookies. I think we owe her some gratitude."

"Thanks, Grace." Cage comes over to me and tugs me into a hug. "You're a keeper for sure."

"Yeah, thanks." As soon as Cage releases me, Asher gives me a kiss on the cheek. His gaze turns toward Brody. "Really loved dinner. Looking forward to more." Brody issues a low growl when Asher doesn't immediately release me, making Asher laugh. "Bastard's getting damn possessive." Asher puts his cookie in his mouth. He takes one bite. His eyes widen, and his brows tug together. Asher chews and swallows with a gulp.

At the table, Evie takes another bite of her third cookie while Abbie finishes off her second. They overplay it, and I give a little shake of my head.

"Hun, these really are amazing." Abbie pulls another cookie out from the bottom of the pile.

"Absolutely amazing," Evie agrees.

Cage takes a bite, and his eyes nearly bug out of his head. He hacks and coughs but manages to swallow the bite. Brody looks at his brothers, eyes shifting left then right as their expressions twist with distaste. Brody tugs my arm and pulls me tight to his side. He leans down and whispers while his grip tightens.

"Hun, what did you do?"

"Me?" I flutter my lashes while I give my most innocent expression. I take a bite of my cookie and make a show of how good it tastes.

Brody looks at the half-eaten cookie in my hand and the two in his. He lifts his cookies to his nose and sniffs, then grabs my hand with the cookie in it and smells that as well. He very carefully nibbles on his cookie. Immediately, his nose crinkles.

Before I can do anything, he snatches the half-eaten cookie out of my hand and takes a tiny bite of it as well. Meanwhile, Asher and Cage stoically bite and swallow their cookies.

"Well?" Evie offers Asher and Cage more cookies. "What do you think? Can't eat just one, right?"

"Did Evie put you up to this?" Brody stays by my side and whispers as he holds me tight against him.

"Don't know what you're talking about," I whisper back.

He discreetly places his cookies on the counter and takes a bite of mine. It takes a second for his eyes to close as the buttery treat melts in his mouth. My baked goods are a thousand times better than anything I made for dinner. Baking is my superpower.

"Best damn cookie I've ever tasted." Brody's grip around my waist tightens. "What do you think, guys?"

Asher and Cage glance up. Their mouths twist as they struggle to swallow the foul salty-peppery mix with the added bonus of far too much baking powder.

"It's something." Asher manages to speak while Cage stares at the rest of his cookie. I can practically see the gears turning in his head.

"What the fuck is this?" Cage's eyes narrow to thin slits as his attention shifts to Evie.

Evie innocently takes another cookie from the bottom of the tray. It has to be her fourth or fifth, not that I'm counting, and pops the whole cookie into her mouth. She closes her eyes as if she's found bliss.

"So delicious."

Cage glances at his second, untouched, cookie.

"They pranked us." Asher points to Brody, who shoves the last of my cookie into his mouth. "Were you in on this?"

"In on what?" Brody licks his fingers, making a smacking sound. "Best damn cookie on the planet."

"Not cool, bro. You gotta stand with your brothers. Can't let the chicks win." Cage's eyes narrow. He looks at his cookie then shifts his attention to the stack of cookies on the table.

Abbie leans back in her chair, arms loosely folded over her chest; a smile lingers in her eyes as she takes us all in. I want to know what she sees; what vision swirls in her head. To be honest, I want more of this in my life; this feeling of belonging and being a part of something greater than myself. Having family I can lean on and turn to when things feel down.

Not that Uncle Mark isn't amazing, but we don't share this unbreakable bond.

Cage and Asher stomp over to the table. They look at each other, then attack the stack of cookies, breaking each cookie in half before moving onto the next. The frosting disguises the flecks of cayenne pepper in the dough, but not when the cookies are broken in half.

Asher finally reaches one of the good cookies and gives a shout when he notices the difference.

"Here!" He shoves one of the halves toward Cage, then bites into the other piece. Immediately, he closes his eyes as the cookie melts in his mouth. "Holy fucking shit, but that's good." When he opens his eyes, his attention lands on Evie. "I'm not putting this on Grace. You did this." Evie giggles, then gasps as Asher reaches for her. Their scuffle is short-lived, with Evie losing as he flings her over his shoulder. He grabs a few more cookies in his free hand, then heads for the door. "Excuse us."

"Where is he taking her?" I keep my voice low as Asher marches out with Evie kicking and screaming but not really putting up much of a fight.

"My guess is the barn."

"The barn?"

"It's where the rope is."

"Why would he need…" I glance into Brody's smoldering gaze and decide that's a question I don't want an answer to, at least not just yet. It shouldn't surprise me Asher and Brody share the same desire for dominance during sex.

"These are fucking amazing!" Cage occupies Evie's vacant seat. He demolishes the pile of cookies, breaking each one open to keep or discard.

Abbie chuckles, mirth filling her face, as Cage goes to town.

"How are you feeling?" Brody nuzzles my neck. "Ready to get out of here?" Before I can answer, Brody makes an announcement to the room. "I'm taking my girl home. Catch you on the flip side."

"Thanks for dinner, and watch your back." Cage points toward me. "We will get even."

Abbie tucks me into her embrace. "Dinner was lovely, hun. I really appreciated it. Maybe I can repay the favor and have you over for my famous pancakes?"

"Pancakes!" Cage gives a shout. "I should come home more often."

"They're not for you, silly boy." Abbie shakes her head and makes a tutting sound.

"Maybe not, but I'll still be there, chowing down. What time?"

"Grace needs to take a raincheck," Brody speaks for me and takes my hand in his. The pad of his thumb rubs circles over the back of my hand. It's a promise of sorts, although I'm not sure what kind.

"Why's that?"

"We're working tomorrow, going over Atwood Estates' assets and operations. The pancakes are all yours, bro."

"Yes!" Cage gives a pump of his arm and eats another cookie.

I estimate they won't last another ten minutes.

"Abbie, I'd love to try out your pancakes, but maybe another time, and Cage?"

"Yeah?" He looks up.

"You've got icing on your face." He rubs at his face and grins. "There's also another dozen hidden in the pantry." I felt bad ruining an entire batch of cookies for Evie's little prank and baked extra.

"Ah, thanks. You're off the hook." Cage gets up and heads to the pantry. "I'm just going to take these to my room." He gives a false yawn. "I'm going to leave you lovebirds to do your thing."

"Well, yes." Abbie nods. "It's time for me to be heading home. Thanks again for a wonderful dinner. I hope this isn't the last we see of you around here." She reaches up to cup Brody's cheek. "Don't mess this up. I like Grace."

TWENTY-EIGHT

# Brody

*DON'T MESS THIS UP. I LIKE GRACE.*

Mom certainly doesn't mess around. At least, I agree. I like Grace too. I like her a lot. All I have to do now is figure out how to fix a decade's old disaster of a mistake.

*Actions, not words.*

Asher's words of wisdom sound in my head. Somehow, I have to show Grace I mean what I say. But how? And how do I not fuck things up when all I want is to slip inside of her hot body and drive her crazy with pleasure?

I could force the issue. If I push, she'll cave, but Grace is leery of sex with me. Considering my reputation, never sleeping with the same girl twice, and after what I did to Grace, that would be epic mistake number two. I'm hard and aroused thinking back to my time with Grace. The way her body surrendered to my will isn't something I'll ever forget. I want more of that. I need to have *that* in my life.

Instead of giving in to my base desires, I take Grace home and leave her without a kiss goodnight. Kissing is too dangerous. She's right.

Kissing leads to the sliding in and out thing. I fantasize about that all night long while getting busy with the five-knuckle-hustle. Right now, my hand is the only relief my poor cock will see.

As agreed, Asher and I show up at her house just after nine the next morning. Grace begged off pancakes with Mom, and I understand why when I see the half-eaten plates in the sink.

I forget her mother battles a disease she'll eventually lose. Too caught up in my own head, I forget about the struggles Grace faces. Which is the perfect lead-in as to how I can best show her I mean what I say. That starts by taking interest in her life rather than obsessing over her body.

Asher and I stand in her living room while she closes the door to what I assume is her mother's sick room.

"Mark will be here soon." Her warm smile tells me everything I need to know. Although a bit hesitant, she's excited to see me. "Please make yourself comfortable while I clean up breakfast."

I turn to Asher and we communicate without words. He pulls out his phone and gives it a little shake. While he settles on the couch, I join Grace in the kitchen. She hand washes the dishes. Before she can say anything, I grab a clean dishtowel and slide in beside her, pulling dishes off the drying rack.

"You don't have to…"

"You're right. I don't have to. I want to."

"Thanks." Her gaze drops beneath the fluttering of her lashes. It's cute seeing her like this, gracious and knocked a little off her feet. *That's okay, Grace; I intend on sweeping you off those feet. Better hold on tight.*

We work in companionable silence until the dishes are done. A few minutes later, the bell over the backdoor rings, and her uncle enters.

"Brody or Asher?" Mark Atwood's eyes pinch with the question.

"Brody." I dry off my hands and greet him with a firm handshake. "My brother's in the other room."

Grace finishes the last of the dishes while I head into the living room with Mark on my heels. He and Asher exchange pleasantries while we wait for Grace to join us. When she does, I shift into business mode.

"Great. Thanks for making time to meet with us, and thank you for returning the documents to our office. Sterling Enterprises has agreed to take on Atwood Estates as a client, but there is a bit of background information we need before moving forward. I don't anticipate we'll need more than a few days. As mentioned, Asher is here as a subject matter expert. He'll work with Mark to assess the state of operations. I want to remind you that we're here as partners and have no intention of taking over, but some of our recommendations will be required. This part of the process usually takes a couple of weeks, but I anticipate we'll be done in a week. At that time, we'll give you our tiered recommendations. Up and until that point, either party may opt-out of this agreement. We finalize everything after you accept our tiered recommendations. Any questions before we start?"

"Maybe guidance on what I should be showing your brother?" Mark shifts from foot to foot, uneasy with the process. I don't blame him. I'd be uncomfortable if outsiders were poking their noses in my business, but we have a responsibility to complete our due diligence when taking on any new client.

"It's easy with me," Asher answers. "We can start with a tour, and then I'll guide you from there." Asher's smile is easy and meant to make Mark more comfortable with the whole process. "I have a confession to make."

"What's that?" Mark asks.

"Your chardonnay is one of my favorites. I have a case in my basement."

"You do?" Mark's eyes round in surprise.

"I do. I'm really interested in your process. How about we get to it and leave these two to the boring numbers?"

"Sounds like a plan." Mark ushers Asher out the back way leaving Grace and me suddenly alone.

"I feel like we just got ditched." Grace twists to watch them leave.

"They don't know the joy of numbers." I rock back on my heels and debate whether I should touch her. Except if I touch her, I'll want to hold her. If I hold her, I'll want to kiss her, and kissing leads to the sliding in and out thing. So I stand like an idiot and wait for her to make the next move.

"So how does this work, exactly? You have our P&L numbers."

"I like to look at the raw numbers as well as the profit and loss ledgers. You know how it can be. Numbers have a rhythm to them. Too many times, I find something unexpected in the numbers."

"Is that a bad thing?" She holds her hands in front of her and twists her fingers nervously.

"Not usually. Oftentimes, it's a goldmine. There are far too many ways to waste money. That's what we're here for, to tighten up the ship, patch any holes, and optimize the shit out of Atwood Estates."

"I really am thankful for this opportunity. When I forget to tell you that, just know I mean it."

"I'm happy to be here, but you know I have ulterior motives."

"I know." She ducks her head. "But maybe we can focus on business?"

"Agreed. I'll shelve that for now. We have a job to do and a business to save. And don't forget about our date."

"Our date?"

"To the gala tonight. Please tell me you didn't forget."

"Oh, no. I'm ready for that. Actually, I asked Mark to set out our best wine. I didn't know how many bottles you wanted to take."

"We'll go over that after we look over the numbers. Do you have an office?"

"Yes, it's right this way."

And just like that, I lose three hours of the day. I love this part of taking on a new client, the discovery process. It's interesting to see how people structure their business. More often than not, simple tweaks result in huge improvements. The problem is Grace's accounting and overall structure of the business turns out to be top-notch. She has a flair for organization and structure.

As we share a simple lunch of ham and cheese sandwiches, I resist the temptation to sweep her into my arms and have my way with her. All day, her light fragrance tickles my senses. I've been a veritable saint keeping my urges in check. It's time to dig a little deeper and get to know her better.

"How long have you been managing the business?"

"Just after Mom got real sick. It was the month after graduation."

"Was this your dream then, stepping up to run the family business?"

"Not at all, but…" She shrugs and her smile slips. I make a mental note to find out more. What dreams did she not follow? I sense this is a situation she found herself in rather than the dream job she hoped for.

We finish lunch in silence, and I check in with Asher. While I speak with him, Grace puts our dishes in the sink.

"Hey," Asher answers on the first ring.

"How's it going?"

"Pretty good. They've got a sweet operation going. Great quality. Impeccable inspection records. Love their processing, and Mark and I are currently picking out the best wines for tonight."

"I think Grace said she already did that." I lower the phone from my ear. "Didn't you say you picked out the wine already?"

"Mark did. He put a couple cases in my trunk. Why?"

"Asher says he's sampling right now."

"Sampling?" She gives a soft laugh. "More like goofing off."

"Don't forget you're working for me today, brother. Don't get too happy sampling the wine."

"No worries, but take the wine I picked. Mark told me what he gave Grace, and to be honest, it's not one of their top-tier offerings. Not really sure why he would do that, but regardless, I've got four cases for you to take with you."

"Great. Thanks. We'll compare notes later."

"Sounds good. Talk at ya' later." Asher hangs up, and I turn to admire Grace's slim figure as she puts everything away. My mouth goes dry, and my heart speeds up. The woman is simply amazing, and she tastes like sin.

"You're staring." She stops and glances at me.

"Can't help it."

She affects me. Already, my breathing's erratic and raw; sexual need heats my blood. This hands-off routine isn't going to last much longer. I need to get my hands on her hot body and pull forth sounds of pleasure from us both. The long length of my arousal strains the zipper of my trousers, making me swallow down the potency of my need.

"Ready to get back to it?" she asks.

"I am, but we need to cut out no later than two. I need to be back here by four or we're going to be late."

"I'm nervous about tonight. You never told me how many cases to bring."

"Asher is swapping out the cases Mark gave you. I guess Mark didn't understand what we're doing tonight."

"I'm not surprised. Mark isn't big on giving away stuff for free, especially our more expensive wines."

"Sometimes, the best way to make money is to give a token away for free. Are you nervous about that tonight? Or is it that you're going with me?"

"Both, honestly. I'm a little more comfortable after today with you. I thought it would be stressful, or that you'd be pushy about… Well, you know. But it's been an easy day. Thank you for that. As for chatting up famous chefs? I'm not really a people person."

"You're great with people. You don't see what I see. Wrap that amazing body in a dress men will go crazy over, and you won't have to worry about anything. Besides, I'll prep you on the drive in. Do you think that would help?"

"That would be great. I never really know what to say, and selling my product to strangers… I'd just like to give them the bottle and say, 'It's good, trust me.'"

"That's certainly the easy way out. While you get ready, think about what it is Atwood Estates has to offer. Why they want to join your exclusive club. Remember, we're drumming up interest in a select club. They have to join it to get access to your top wines."

"When you say it, it doesn't sound corny. When I say it, I feel like a fool."

I draw her close and give her the lightest feathery kiss on her forehead. Anything more would undo me. Behaving like a real gentleman, instead of the scoundrel I am, is more challenging than expected.

"You're going to do great." I release her and take a few steps back. "I'll be back in a bit to pick you up. I'm really looking forward to spending time with you tonight."

TWENTY-NINE

# Grace

______

It takes less than two hours to shower, dress, and show off my dress to Mom. I take a leisurely spin near the foot of her bed.

"You look like a vision of loveliness." Mom pats the side of the bed. She looks tired and weaker than this morning. More pale. Every day is a gift. I remind myself of this often.

"What's wrong?" I take a seat beside her and hold her hand.

"Are you okay?" Her eyes pinch. There's more she wants to say—to ask—but breathing alone saps her strength.

"I'm good."

"You sure? Brody…" She takes a breath, and I wait, not willing to rush whatever it is she wants to say. "He's—being—decent?"

"More than decent." I give a vigorous nod. "I thought things would be really awkward, working with him." I say the things I know she wants to hear, and I answer the questions she's too weak to ask. "Spending that much time with the boy who broke my heart worried me too, but he's been good. Very professional. Decent."

"Has he…" She runs out of steam and closes her eyes.

"He kissed me."

Her eyes flicker open.

"I'm being careful."

She arches a brow, expressing her doubt through expression alone.

"He's an attractive man, more so than he ever was in high school. He says things are different now." The corner of my mouth draws up. "There's always been something between us, a magnetic force pulling us together, but I'm keeping my head on my shoulders, and he's keeping his hands to himself."

Her left eyebrow wings up again. She doesn't believe me.

"He's a *really* attractive man. I'm not pretending there's not something there. It feels different this time." She gives me another look. "No, I'm serious. It really feels different." Almost like I can trust his intentions.

The doorbell rings and I squeeze her hand.

"That's him. Do you want to see him?"

She gives a shake of her head. Mom's not as willing to forgive Brody for the pain he caused me. I get it. The month after the whole sex tape incident was more than bad. It was my worst nightmare, but even more so for her. There was no way she could protect me, or shield me, from the way my life blew apart. All she could do was help me pick up the pieces afterward.

The bell rings again.

"Okay, I gotta go." I check her bedside table and count out the assortment of pills. "You need to take your pain pills in an hour. Please don't forget. Uncle Mark is going to check in with you before he leaves for the day, and Abbie said she'd come by later tonight to keep you company. I probably won't be back until well after midnight, but if you need anything…"

"I'll call." She taps the back of my hand. "Be safe, love."

"I will." I lean down and kiss her forehead, then head to the living room where I grab the small clutch purse that matches my red silk dress. With a deep breath, I open the door.

Brody faces away from me. With his back to me, my gaze sweeps over a body hardened to steel. The corded muscles of his neck sweep down to broad, sloping shoulders. Beneath that black tux, he's all chiseled torso and ridged muscle created for the sole purpose of driving women crazy. Trim waist, tight ass, and well-muscled legs, I take in the full force of his presence and nearly shatter.

I shouldn't stare at his ass, but it's tight beneath his tailored slacks, firm and hard enough to bounce a quarter off if I were ever so bold to try. It makes me wonder about other parts of his anatomy that may, or may not, be hard and firm as well.

Brody has a way of changing my mind about the things I know are good for me, like staying the hell away from thoughts that go—there.

He spins around with a smile that slips to surprise. His mouth gapes as he takes in the slinky red dress I dug out from the dregs of my closet. Emerald fire lights his eyes as smoldering desire blows out his pupils.

"Holy shit, you're breathtaking."

My stomach sinks beneath his lusty gaze, as if it's telling me whatever battle I might wage is already lost. I'm completely at his mercy, head over heels, drunk with the need to be taken by him. The air between us crackles. Sparks of energy fly, sending heat licking along my nerves where it tunnels deep to warm my core.

His eyes widen and his nostrils flare. Brody drinks me in, and as he does, the emerald blaze in his eyes sets me on fire. The raw expression of his passion is a potent force. I'm not prepared to resist it. Heat rushes through me, penetrating my body with devastating force. That fire takes over every cell of my body as Brody delves deep into my core and settles in. He makes himself comfortable there.

"Hi." That's the extent of my vocabulary right now.

Brody in a tux is a force I'm powerless to resist. The man oozes sensuality and power, masculinity and domination. He promises to take and claim with heat and virility, stamina and power, fury and uncompromising demands. My thighs clench as wanton need pulses through me. I can't help it. He captivates me.

"I'm not sure if we're going to make it to the banquet." He touches the curve of my jaw and sweeps the pad of his fingers over my cheek. "I want you. Now."

My entire body shakes beneath the press of that finger. How can one digit possess such potency? Probably because it's attached to a viral male with one thought on his mind.

"We're going to be late." I dip my head and bite my lower lip.

"Traffic's light right now. We'll be fine." His thumb sweeps down my jaw and presses against my lips. He forces my lips to open while I gulp. Brody presses closer, breathing my air, as he stares so deeply into my eyes that it feels as if he wants to peel me open and climb inside. "You're stunning. Absolutely stunning." He licks his lips, tasting the words. "I want to make you mine, Grace." A growl accompanies the possession of his words.

His masculine presence and his virility are all I can think about. I feel him all over, humming through my veins, heating my blood, and depriving my brain of oxygen. I can't think. I can't look away. He entrances me with the lust simmering in that heated gaze of his.

My hands land against his chest, solid granite encased in hot skin, and a shiver sweeps through me. Beautifully built, he doesn't seem real. There's no denying that flawless definition or the sculpted precision of his features. My head tilts, slants into his touch, as if compelled. His eyes are right there, staring, simmering, smoldering with lust. Shining vividly with his need. His mouth parts and I gasp.

We share chemistry. No denying that, but this is something beyond mere chemistry. It's explosive attraction and something I can't fight.

"Brody…"

"Kiss me." There it is again, that command. He'll take if I don't give this to him, but he'll give me this one chance to decide for myself if this is what I want.

I meet his stare with one of my own, questioning, wanting, fearing what comes next, but I'm too far gone. I lift up on tiptoe and obliterate the distance between us. This may be my second worst mistake ever, but it's mine to make. I press my lips to his, kissing him.

His lips lock around mine, and his palm presses against my back. Brody lifts me to deepen the kiss, taking over. I've never been more captivated by a man before. Those mesmerizing green eyes don't help. They sweep me away as his sculpted lips devastate my mouth. The tension between us only increases as he draws back with an open-mouthed sigh.

His caressing fingers continue to glide across my face, wrapping around my neck to grab my hair at the back of my head. It's beyond arousing, the way he tugs at my hair, turning me into a quivering, moaning mess as his lips drive savagely against mine. His tongue presses and demands entrance, burrowing deep as if seeking the limits of what I'll allow. It's a hot weapon of destruction, sweeping through any defense I might have left.

Swirling, tasting, his mouth owns me as he grips my nape and hauls me against his hard body. His lips continue their plunder, softening as my resistance melts, feathering against my lips, barely touching me. My breath stutters and my nostrils flare as his potent male aroma floods my senses. He smells too good to be real. His body is too hard, unyielding, demanding, and devastating.

"You will be the death of me." He makes no effort to hide his arousal, reaching down to adjust his hardened length. "No more kissing until the end of the night. Work first." He presses the pad of his thumb against my lips. "Pleasure later."

Pleasure later.

There's no going back. This is happening between us. On the other side lies complete and utter devastation. When I fall, it will be a devastating drop on the other side, but that's okay.

All I want is one more night with Brody La Rouge.

One night to fulfill a lifetime of fantasies.

I'll deal with the aftermath later, because despite what he says, I don't trust Brody La Rouge.

We walk to his car in silence, saying nothing as he opens the door to help me inside. I buckle in while he walks around to the driver's side. Brody shifts in his seat, saying nothing as he adjusts himself in front of me, except for the smoldering look he gives me while he does. There's a promise there, and I can't help but squirm in my seat.

Conversation is minimal as we drive. It's not until we hit I-80 that Brody breaks the silence.

"Let's work on your pitch." His fingers grip the wheel: strong, confident, and in charge.

"Okay?"

He huffs a small laugh. "Relax. Asher already sent the wine. Notices went out to the chefs. It's not a cold pitch. Several of Sterling Enterprise's eager interns are already setting everything up. All you need to do is close the deal."

"I've never done anything like this."

"Here, let me show you how I would do it." Brody leans back and he takes in a deep breath. A change comes over him as he shifts into business mode. Or rather, aggressive mogul mode. He's dominating in his personal life, but even more so in the professional arena. It's no wonder he does so well, with that commanding tone, the overwhelming confidence, the desire he instills in others to follow his lead.

For the next hour, Brody coaches me on what to say, how to approach people, and ways I can maximize the impact of my pitch.

His people already reached out to the chefs, letting them know about this exclusive opportunity to partner with Atwood Estates. Sample bottles were delivered days ago, without my knowledge, to establish confidence in our brand.

I didn't even know this was being done. Evidently, after our Monday meeting, Brody made all this happen. By the time we pull up to the event space, I've been thoroughly coached and prepped. Brody's played the eager enthusiast all the way to the negative skeptic.

"You ready to kick ass?" Brody reaches over and squeezes my thigh. His touch detonates all my nerve endings, instantly waking up my body.

Explosive? Check.

Incendiary? Check

Devastating? No doubt about that.

I bite down on my lower lip and rein in my body's response to his touch. I don't know what it is, but I feel alive, electrified, and looking forward to something for the first time in a very long time. Relief floods through me. No longer worried about the consequences, I accept my decision with open arms.

"You're beautiful." Brody reaches across and brushes a lock of hair from my face. "And mine for the night." His simmering gaze sends delirious licks of pleasure sweeping through my body.

"Ready as I'll ever be." And I'm not talking about getting through this event. I'm thinking about what comes after—the collision of our bodies as we finally give in to our mutual attraction.

"Let's do this." The heated look in his eyes drugs me with dark desires, turning my craving for him into the addiction I never overcame. My pulse jumps wildly as my foolish, overly eager heart quickens.

*Yes, let's do it.*

THIRTY

# Brody

I don't know what the hell just went through Grace's head, but the air sizzles as the latent sexual energy between us sparks and ignites. The valet opens her door and helps her out while I tamp down the primitive reflex which demands I snap him in half.

No man touches my woman.

I toss him the keys as I take her in hand and tuck her against my side. She's not leaving my sight, or my side, until this evening is done.

I touch her constantly. A sweep of my thumb across the back of her hand. A bump of our shoulders as we head inside. I release her hand, but only to press my palm against the small of her back to guide her inside the event.

The heated look in her eyes matches the desire in mine. She leans into my touch and allows me to guide her around, introducing her to those people who will skyrocket her small vineyard into the next century.

Everything about her intoxicates me, from the light perfume she wears to the way the red silk of her dress hugs her curves. She's quickly turning my desire for her into a full-blown addiction. How did I ever manage to walk away from this amazing woman? It's a mystery I'll never solve.

Not that I need to.

She's mine now.

"We're leaving as soon as our work is done. I don't know if I'll be able to behave, not with you looking as sensational as you do." I bend my elbow and transfer her hand to the crook of my arm. My fingers feather along the gentle sweep of her neck and move across the graceful curve of her collarbone. I stroke her neck, her cheek, her bare arm constantly, brushing her skin. It's impossible to stop touching her. My fingers feather along her collarbone as I lean down to whisper in her ear.

"Grace…"

"Yes?"

"You're so fucking gorgeous. I can't keep my hands off you." The yearning she stirs within me frightens me and makes it nearly impossible to concentrate. Torn between overwhelming lust and needing to focus on the reason we're here, I twine my fingers in her hair and pull her to a sudden stop.

Her breath catches as she looks up at me. My fingers tighten around her nape, and I press my mouth against hers, hot, needy, possessive as all hell. I don't care that we're in a crowd; I'm staking my claim. As I drag my mouth against hers, the faintest flavor of strawberries clings to her lips. I want to rub my thumb over one of her nipples and drag my hand down to her hips. The question of whether she's wearing anything under that dress is quickly becoming the only thing I can think about.

She groans, letting me kiss her, probably longer than socially acceptable in a place like this, but I'm too far gone to care. I'm wrapped up in the decadent fusion of our mouths, the swirling of our tongues, and the melding of our breaths. But I'm not too distracted that I forget why we're here.

My goal is to focus my attention on Grace's needs rather than my own. Mine are primal and simplistic. Hers are much more complex. Asher's words rattle through my head. I want Grace with every fiber of my being, but I need to show her what she means to me. More importantly, how much I value her needs above my own. Lust aside, we've got a business to save.

"You taste like sin." I should release her, but that's not happening. This woman isn't leaving my side all evening. "Let's start working this room. Time to put Atwood Estates on the map."

Her fingers lift and press against her lips. Very slowly, her lids flutter closed, and I'm dying to know what thoughts swirl in her head. Is she thinking about me? She's definitely thinking about that kiss, but where else does her mind go?

"Let's do this." Her lids slowly lift. When she looks up at me, it's with a smile on her face, an acceptance of what this is between us. She grabs my hand and gives it a squeeze. "What's our first step?"

"Follow me."

With those words, I take her around. As usual, the event planning committee pulled out all the stops. The ballroom is decked out in the best finery. Luscious floral arrangements draw the eye with pops of color displayed against intricate greenery. I survey the room, taking everything in with a clinical eye. Round tables, covered in expensive linen, are set with crystal glasses, fancy china, and sparkling silver service.

Scented candles flicker with dancing flames. They're on the tables and distributed around the room. They add warmth and a touch of cozy to the classical elegance to achieve the perfect blend of upscale sophistication and warm intimacy. It's designed to loosen pocketbooks and let money flow to the children's cancer charity.

Overhead, crystal chandeliers bathe us in a soft luminescence while a string quartet tucked into the corner fills the air with soft, delicate notes. While tables fill the room, there is no assigned seating, but rather an assortment of smaller tables sprinkled amongst larger tables with plenty of room for eager attendees to move about. All around the periphery of the ballroom, long tables are set up with steaming dishes that fill the air with the most decadent aromas meant to make the mouth water and taste buds dance.

Chefs and their limited staff stand behind the tables offering samples of their most exclusive dishes while pairing them with small quantities of a most exclusive wine.

I secured an exclusivity contract with the organizers of this event. Only wines from Atwood Estates are being served with the food, showcased right beside the most well-known chefs. We approach the first table and Drake Demond smiles as I catch his eye.

"Brody La Rouge." He steps out from behind the table and spreads his arms wide. There's no shaking of hands with Drake. He pulls me into a massive bear hug and thumps my back.

I barely have enough time to let go of Grace, lest she get squashed in the jubilant greeting of one of my oldest friends.

"Hey, Drake, so nice to see you."

"Always good to be seen." He winks and his attention swivels to Grace, where he takes her in from head to toe. "You must be Grace, the heart and soul of Atwood Estates." He releases me and takes her hand in his. With over the top flare, he turns her hand around and brushes his lips over the top of her knuckles. "Brody told me you were stunning, and I can see he doesn't lie. It's a pleasure to meet you, and your spectacular vintage is making a splash." His voice lowers at the end as if he's the caretaker of a great secret.

Grace's breath catches, but she collects herself. "Thank you for hosting our wine. I'd love to taste your dish."

That's all the encouragement Drake needs to launch into his special dish. I lose her for what seems like forever, but really isn't more than a few minutes. Nevertheless, it's ten minutes too long. Sharing her with anyone is torture. But I make good use of my time admiring Grace. She's beautiful, stunning even. The woman is oblivious to what a striking figure she cuts. Her graceful glide draws appreciative gazes from the men in the crowd and inquisitive stares from the ladies as they try to determine how much of a threat Grace may be to their man.

From the way I hover, protecting what's mine, they get the message Grace isn't on the prowl. For the first time, in a very long time, the same goes for me.

Grace listens to Drake, rapt with attention, as he describes his award-winning dish. He picks up a bottle of her family's wine and they discuss how it's the perfect pairing for his creations. Grace didn't need all the prepping we did on the drive in. She's a natural when it comes to her family's product. Their excited conversation draws a crowd, and it's not long before I wave over one of Sterling Enterprise's summer interns to cart in more wine.

The whole time, Grace remains alert. She takes in the grandeur of the event with wide-eyes and keeps pressing her hand to her belly. I can tell she's overwhelmed, but I'm not about to put the brakes on what's happening.

Drake introduces her to one of his longtime competitors, a friendly rival, at the adjacent table. After a bit of small talk, Drake transfers Grace down the line. A smile tugs at my cheeks as the same scene repeats over and over. I don't know the chef speaking to her, but they hit it off, talking wine and food pairings. Grace slips in some of the keywords I prompted her to say, but otherwise, shines all on her own.

That chef introduces her to the next in line, and over the course of an hour, we slowly make our way around the entire ballroom.

"How are you doing?" I pull her back to me, checking in.

"This place—wow—it's spectacular. And the chefs seem to really love our wine."

"Did you have any doubt?"

"I always have doubts." She lifts up and places a soft kiss to my cheek. "Thank you for this. I'm almost out of business cards."

"I'm surprised you have any left. They seem to be flying like hotcakes."

"The chefs seem excited to add it as a specialty pairing to their menu items. I already have meetings with four of them to discuss it more in-depth." Her eyes glisten with tears. "This never would've happened without you."

The soft orchestral background music changes as the evening wears on. Couples gravitate toward the front of the ballroom where the dance floor sits.

"Come." I stretch out my hand and wait for Grace to take it. Without asking why, she takes my hand, displaying a level of trust which hits me on a gut level.

I draw her toward the dancers. The crowd tonight is a bit on the older side, mostly men and women in their fifties and sixties, some older, very few younger, wealthy executives with their spouses who've accumulated deep pockets over the years and are known to be generous donors at events such as this. As a result, the music is rather tame, somewhat sedate, and perfect for close, intimate dancing.

I lead her out into the middle of the dance floor, where she glides effortlessly beside me. As soon as we stop, the music shifts to something low and sultry. Perfect really. I take her into my arms and the world dims around me.

Every nerve in my body comes alive as my need for her flares with a rush of adrenaline so strong it nearly knocks me off my feet. My grip tightens and I tug her close. My hand travels freely up and down her back, moving to her shoulder blades, then sweeping down to the flare of her hips and over the rise of her ass. I feel every inch of her as her body seamlessly melts into me.

"I want you to spend the night with me." I close my eyes and breathe her in. "Please say yes."

# THIRTY-ONE

## Grace

_____________



WHAT'S HAPPENING TO ME?

It's as if I've lost my ever-loving mind and have no control. I should push Brody away. Instead, I burrow into his embrace as his hands, those delicious hands, stroke my back, electrifying every cell in my body and short-circuiting my brain.

Heat, lust, desire. They battle it out as if they're in a mad race for first place. Brody holds me tight as we sway in place, rocking back and forth. Music fills the ballroom with its sensual energy. This is a song for lovers. Something we will soon be again. Why? Because I tilt my face until my gaze captures the green fire burning in his eyes. I meet that desire with my own need. With our gazes locked, I give my answer.

"Yes."

His low, throaty growl sends a ripple of heat shooting through my body. Those hands of his continue to roam all over my back and dip indecently down to my hips, over my ass. His fingers dig in, pulling me against his hardness.

I nestle into his strength, overwhelmed yet eager. Everything feels surreal as if this isn't me standing in his arms. As if the press of his arousal isn't hot, needy, and throbbing between us.

He gives another appreciative groan as I decide to do some exploring of my own. Smoothing my hands over his back, I trace up the wide flare of his shoulders and dip down precariously low on his waist. We're spiraling fast and need to stop before we make a spectacle of ourselves on this dance floor.

"Grace…" His soft breath heats my cheek. "I need you now."

"Now?"

"Now." The resolute certainty in his voice should make me cautious; instead, my blood heats and my skin feels like it's on fire.

"I need you." His eyes fill with lust and desire. He slowly moves his lips toward my ear. His breath whispers across my neck. "I can't wait to sink inside of you. It's all I can think about."

"But…"

He places his mouth on mine, tender at first, but quickly becoming more insistent and demanding as he deepens the kiss. The world fades around me as I cling to him and hang on tight. Soft and gentle builds to hungry and determined. I part my lips, unable to deny him anything he wants.

With that invitation, he takes full advantage and destroys any sense of self-preservation I may have left. Hands searching, lips pressing, and tongues tangling, the combination floods my senses.

All I can do is feel.

His body presses closer as the kiss turns hard, demanding, and wildly out of control. Sensations I've never felt before roll through me. Then everything comes to a sudden, crashing halt.

I stutter and stop; then my gaze lifts as I take in the room. Hundreds of eyes look back. Most with smiles. Some with smirks. And a few of the women hurl eye-daggers directly at me, slicing and dicing their competition. Their arms cross with expressions meant to kill. I've stolen their toy.

My breath hitches.

"I think we should go." Brody's husky laugh tells me he's aware of the reactions in the room. He takes my hand in his and leads me off the dance floor as if we hadn't been shamelessly groping each other moments before.

Brody leads me out into a hallway and drags me toward the entrance.

"I'm taking you home." It's a statement, not a question, but then, I already said yes—with my words and with my body on that dance floor just now.

"Okay."

Sucking in a deep breath, I take the plunge. When I'm around Brody, my brain forgets why it's there. My brain cells fizzle and pop, overloaded with sensation and the need to do very bad things.

"I'm going to fuck you." He pulls to a stop and forces me to face him.

"I know."

"You're saying yes." Although he says it as a statement, his eyebrows arch in question.

"Yes."

He rubs at the back of his neck and shakes his head. "No second thoughts? No concerns? You do know what's going to happen. I haven't changed that much." A wolfish grin fills his face, hinting at the beast raging inside, howling to be let loose.

"I wouldn't expect anything else."

"You're killing me, Grace. Just…" He releases me. "I don't want any regrets."

"No regrets."

"You don't understand."

"What's there to understand?" We're going to have sex. It's the eventuality that's been building between us since he literally ran past me nearly a week ago.

"Afterward, I'm not letting you go. You do this, and you're mine." The finality of his words slam into me, making my mouth go dry, and ramps up the crazy banging going on inside my chest. My heart's in overdrive, racing, stuttering, panicking—wanting what he promises.

"Yours?" My brows pinch together. I don't know what that means.

To a man like Brody La Rouge, being his is a state of existence along a continuum of anywhere from 'his for the night' to 'his forever.' I'm too jaded to believe in the latter, but I'll take one night.

I accept the eventuality hurtling toward us, and I'll deal with the aftermath later. There will be fallout, but no regrets.

We leave the venue in a rush and hop in his car. Before long, we're speeding down freeways and racing through downtown streets. Brody pulls into the garage of an upscale building and whisks me into an extravagantly decorated elevator with gilded mirrors on three sides and overhead.

We stand side by side, but the moment the doors close, he's on me. Hands grope. Words fail us as we ascend to the top floor. Mouths meld. Lips crash. Brody's hips gyrate. We seal our fate by the time the elevator doors open.

Green eyes blown black with lust, Brody pulls me toward one of only two doors on this floor. There's no key. Instead, his fingers dance over a keypad until a loud beep sounds.

"Last chance." It's more of a growl than words.

I bite my lower lip and nod. I could tell him I want this, vocalize it a million times over until my voice fails, but there's no reason to waste any more time. I've waited a decade for this, although it feels more like a lifetime.

Besides, words aren't needed between us, not when we have something better. The language our bodies speak is enough. Passion simmers between us, heating to a raging inferno, fusing us together, and making us one.

Brody slows down, drawing me over the threshold slowly, deliberately, as if it means the world to him. For a second, I wonder how many times he's done this before. How many women has he welcomed into his bed? Quickly, I tamp down those damaging thoughts. I don't care about those that came before. He's mine now, at least for the night.

Once I'm in his apartment, he pulls me to him and clutches me snug against his chest. The door slams closed behind me, and the steady hammer of his heart pulses in his chest—erratic, wild, ready to unleash its ravenous fury.

On me.

I lock my hands around his powerful frame, grasping my wrist behind his back as I lean against the warmth of his chest. Slowly, I close my eyes as he sways us to a silent beat only he can hear.

I sigh. This promises to be better than any fantasy, any dream where I've ached for him. I'm in his home. Held in his arms. Soon, I'll be in his bed. Although, Brody isn't known for something as mundane as fucking in a bed.

He hooks a finger beneath my chin, lifts my face, and stares down at me for what seems like forever.

"I never want to forget this moment."

"Why?"

"Because, I finally get you back. No way am I walking away from you again. No way will I ever hurt you again. You have my heart,

Grace. It's undeniably yours." His firm lips descend as he puts his mouth on me. He tastes dark and sinful—dangerous.

His firm lips are familiar and comforting. Without hesitation, he takes, claims, and devours.

The roll of his tongue as he forces his way inside my mouth promises another intrusion to come. His tongue spears in and out, mimicking what our bodies will soon be doing instead of our mouths.

His hand glides up to my shoulder, where he hooks a finger beneath the tiny strap of my dress. He slides it down my arm as I press my thighs together.

"You look amazing in this dress, but I need to know what you're wearing under it."

"Nothing." My voice breathes out in a soft whisper, sultry, needy, deliriously turned on. A dress like this doesn't allow anything underneath it. It hugs all my curves and conforms to the softness of my body.

The dress slips down, revealing the swell of one breast.

He bites my lip, holding us together, but there's more going on. Brody isn't an easy lover. He's hard, demanding, and always takes control. Those are qualities I love, something he knows very well. He reminds me of this and takes control.

A whimper escapes me as his teeth bite down hard enough to cause pain but not to draw blood. He asserts his dominance, and I surrender to his will. This—this feels familiar, comfortable. It's a natural flow between us.

He removes his hand from my arm, but not before sweeping his finger along the swell of my breast. "I'll get to these in a moment."

His hand slides down to my leg, where he gathers the silky fabric of my dress. He lifts it to my hips, exposing me, and slides his fingers underneath. His other hand joins the first until he grips the back of my thighs. He lifts me up, off my feet, and braces my back against the door as he deepens the kiss. His fingers tease between my legs as I grasp the hair at his nape.

Skillful and determined, his fingers trace my folds, discovering how wet I am for him.

"So hot. So silky."

My entire body lights up, rioting beneath the sensual caress of his touch.

With me braced as I am, he keeps his fingers moving while his other hand reaches up to pull down the remaining strap from my shoulder. He yanks the bodice of my dress down to my waist, exposing my breasts, and places his hot, wet mouth on my bare skin.

That talented mouth seeks my nipple as his tongue reaches out to ravish the tightening nub. Sucking it deep into his hot mouth, my head falls back with a moan. My spine bows against the door as he works his fingers and mouth until I'm a gasping, quivering mess.

Brody isn't content to let me focus on one thing at a time, demanding instead to drown me in sensation as his fingers sink between my folds and my nipple is sucked into his mouth. My fingers clench, pulling at his hair. He knows how to work those fingers, sinking them deep in my pussy as moans spill from my mouth.

I love this man. I always have. And while I don't know what the future holds, it doesn't matter.

I have this.

I have now.

His gaze lifts to mine while he continues the assault on my nipple. I gasp as he bites down. Pain shoots through my body, where it morphs into delicious pleasure.

"You know your word." He speaks around my nipple, maintaining the pressure.

I roll my lower lip and bite down.

My word.

It's unoriginal, but back in high school, when we were new and experimenting with forbidden things, we picked a word for safety. Something to stop things if he went too far, or I got too scared.

"Say it." His voice threads with command as his fingers find my nipple and squeeze down like a vise. My breath hitches as the pressure increases. "We don't move forward until you do."

I release my lip and grip him tight around the waist with my thighs. This whole time his fingers are busy. Not the ones on my poor nipple, but those that thrust inside of me.

Delicious licks of pleasure heat my core and I close my eyes. I'm close. Brody's skill with his fingers has only increased through the years. The pads of his fingers drag along the sensitive wall of my pussy, stroking my g-spot with each glide out. His fingers on my nipple pinch harder, drawing a squeak from me.

"Your word…" The demand is undeniable. The pain inescapable.

My eyes fly open as his fingers clamp down.

"Red. It's red." I gasp as he releases my poor, tortured nipple.

He leans forward and brushes his lips over mine. "Next time you say that word, we stop."

One thing about Brody I'm quickly relearning is that while he may be a powerful businessman with incalculable wealth, when it comes to sex, he's raw and unpolished, a heathen, and a devil who happens to wear a tuxedo with impeccable style.

Brody tenses the moment I say the word. He draws back, both his head and those magical fingers leave me. Heat pulses between my legs as he rests his forehead against mine.

His fingers tackle his belt and tear at the button of his slacks. "I've spent every day since I ran across you imagining fucking you here, just like this." He draws the zipper down and slowly draws himself out. Reaching into his pocket, he pulls out a foil packet. With a devilish gleam in his eyes, he rips it open and quickly sheathes his turgid length.

My bare legs tremble around his hips as he notches the broad head of his cock against my pussy.

"Hold on tight because I'm going to make you scream." His gaze holds mine as he thrusts. A low, deep groan fills the room as he slides all the way in.

Pleasure floods my body, one wave building upon the next, gathering into an overwhelming haze of sensation. His lips once again find mine, and he kisses me passionately as he thrusts in and out, rocking my back against the hard door as our bodies slide together, in and out. He thrusts harder as our breaths mingle in mutual pleasure and panting groans. My hips absorb the impact of his thrusts as he fucks me into oblivion with a wild and frantic rage.

Through it all, his eyes never leave mine.

"Harder." I grip his nape and give him free rein to do as he pleases. We strain toward each other, needing to fuse our bodies.

Hands clutch. Eyes lock.

Together, he works us into a frenzy, powering up an impossible cliff, until I fall over the edge. My screams fill the air and are soon followed by his low, deep groans. His hips thrust in and out, powerfully gliding as he follows me in ecstasy.

We soar together, lost in our private world, breaths mingling, souls melding.

We fly together as one.

Getting fucked against the door is only the beginning of our evening. Slowly, Brody sets me down on the floor.

"Strip." His dominance sends a heady thrill shooting through my body. This is the man I remember, a man who doesn't just have sex, he fucks. And when Brody fucks, it's with his entire being; all senses engaged. There's nothing gentle about it. All that potent masculinity fuses fire and passion into a potent force.

I follow his commands, knowing my submission drives him heady with lust. Before long, the red silk of my dress pools in a puddle at my feet. Brody takes two steps back. His hand shakes as he rakes it through his hair.

Tousled from my fingers, he's the vision of a raw, potent male. Brody fists his cock and takes another step back. He points to the floor in front of him. His gaze darkens, turns dangerous and powerful.

"Kneel."

I don't hesitate. Each word sends a lick of pleasure shooting through my trembling body. I close the distance until my bare breasts drag against the rough starch of his shirt. With my eyes on him the entire time, I lower to my knees. Once my knees hit the floor, I rock back and settle my ass on my heels. Only then do I lower my gaze.

"Shit, Grace. Seeing you like that. The thoughts in my head aren't decent."

I say nothing, sinking into my role. Only when asked a direct question will I answer. It's been ten years, but we settle in without any awkward pauses.

Brody toes off his shoes and yanks off his jacket. He tosses it haphazardly on the floor, then tugs on his tie. The thin strip of black flutters to the floor.

His breathing deepens, growing hoarser by the second, as arousal floods his brain. He kicks everything away as he prowls in a circle around me. All hard angles, long muscled legs, he overwhelms me, makes me feel small, but not insignificant.

Right now, I'm his entire world.

Circling, he stops in front of me.

"Eyes up." His gaze lands boldly on mine. He barely moves, doesn't blink. Brody is in control. His stare isn't just a stare. It's a complicated puzzle with twists and turns I can't fathom. I'm entranced by the secrets he holds, and yet confused.

There's a promise there as well, if I can unravel it. Instead, my heart squeezes with memory and the useless organ floods my system with doubt. A thousand needles stab at my eyes as past, deeply buried pain worms its way to the surface. I won't let it cripple me or detract from this moment. With a deep, shaky breath, I look into the greenest, most damaging pair of eyes I've ever met.

His crisp white shirt gapes open, revealing the ridged definition of his well-honed physique. His fly is open and his cock juts outward, weeping for me.

I shift and meet the heat of his gaze.

"I like what I see. Once I taste you, I know I'm going to go insane. I'm going to savor you tonight, work your body until you can barely move, making you mine as you've always been meant to be. I'm going to spend my night inside of you, making you come until you can't move and scream until your throat is raw. You'll come with such violence that my cock will be the only one that matters from here on out. You're mine, Grace Atwood. Then. Now. And for all the days after. Before we start, open that mouth."

He presses the flare of his cock to my lips and I obediently take him in. His eyes close with pleasure as he slowly feeds me his cock. Holding still for a moment, his breathing settles. Once he's back in control, Brody moves.

He tastes amazing, salty with virile masculinity and potent raw desire. With a palm placed on the top of my head, Brody takes what he wants until his body tightens and shakes with his release.

Before I can swallow, he pulls out and sweeps me into his arms. Striding purposefully through his apartment, he heads to the bedroom, where he places me down and spreads my legs.

I scream when his tongue licks me down there, then my body crumbles beneath the onslaught of his fingers, tongue, and mouth.

Our night moves on from there. Brody's sexual appetite is ravenous and insatiable. He takes me on the bed and on the floor. Then bends me over the sofa where he smacks my ass and takes me roughly from behind. In the shower, he puts me to my knees again, where I make him shudder and come undone with my mouth. We sit together in the shower, me on his lap, as steam fills the room. Then he lifts my hips and lowers me down on top of him. I rock back and forth, taking my time, as I'm in no hurry for this evening to end.

We fall asleep, finally, in a mess of twisted sheets and tangled limbs. My dreams fill with forevers but are haunted by the ghosts of the past.

I awake with a start.

Something's wrong.

"Grace…" Brody's voice is groggy, drugged with sleep. "Is that your phone?" He rolls over and places a pillow over his head.

I extricate myself from the tangle of limbs and kick off the covers. It is my phone, and from the ringtone, Uncle Mark is calling.

THIRTY-TWO

# Grace

______

"Hello? Mark, what's up?" My hand shakes, but I don't know why. Something feels off.

"Grace." The tremor in Mark's voice drops the bottom out from my world. "Where are you?"

"I'm in the city. The traffic…" I stumble over a lie, but before I can make up an excuse as to why I didn't come home last night, Mark cuts me off.

"You need to come home. Now."

"What's wrong?"

"Just get here, as fast as you can. She needs you. I need you."

My hand shakes as tears fill my eyes. Uncle Mark won't say the words. He's too choked up, but it's enough. I scramble around the room, looking for my clothes, but I can't see anything.

Everything's a blur. A fist grabs my heart, squeezing hard, too hard. And what happened to the air? I gulp, unable to take a breath.

"Grace?" Brody rises out of bed. Concern edges his features. "What's wrong?"

"I-I've got to go." I race into the bathroom and stare in the mirror. I look like I've had my brains fucked out. No way am I going home looking like this. I turn on the shower and lean against the bathroom counter, panting, while the water warms.

"Grace?" Brody moves behind me and my entire body twitches as I try to shrug him off. He backs up and lifts his hands, palms out, but then his demeanor changes. "What's going on?" He takes a dominant tone with me, demanding an answer, pulling one reluctantly from my body.

But this isn't sex.

I'm not in *that* headspace right now.

My entire body convulses as I shove him away. Once I'm in the shower, the first sob wracks my body. My mother is dying, and I'm not there.

*I'm not there. I'm not there!*

I'm not there because I spent last night with Brody instead of going home like I should have.

I'm a mess, a complete, horrible, no good mess. I try to wash my body and my hair, but I can't get my limbs to work. I keep dropping everything.

Brody steps into the shower, and I seethe with resentment that he dares to invade my space.

"Go away!" I squirt shampoo into my hand, only to realize it's conditioner instead. With a shriek, I rinse it off and growl with frustration. I blindly search for the shampoo. Strong arms wrap around me, and I fight. I hiss and twist and kick at him. "Let me go," I sob.

"Not until you tell me what's going on."

*Red. Red. Red.*

The word flashes in my head, but I don't say it. I can't. I need someone to take control because I'm losing my ever-loving mind.

"I just want to go home." I slap at him, ineffectually, as he tightens his grip around my shoulders, pinning my arms inside his protective embrace.

"Stop." He pulls me back, nearly lifting me off my feet. "Take a breath and tell me what happened? Who was that on the phone?"

My mother is dying. It's a fact, one I've lived with for months, but I'm not ready for this. I won't survive her death. I still need her for so many things. My sobs turn agonized. The beginnings of soul-sundering howls build in my throat.

"Tell me," Brody's voice firms, growing stronger, more demanding.

"Mom…" A low, keening wail escapes me as I draw a knee to my chest.

Brody's grip on me doesn't falter. If not for him, I'd be huddled on the floor. I'm breaking inside, battling fear, abandonment, and loss. My vision blurs as my strength fades.

I break.

I fall apart.

"I'm here. I'm with you. And I'll get you home." Brody manhandles me until the spray of the water shoots between us. It's in his face and sprays down on my head. He's some kind of magician because he manages to wet my hair, lather in shampoo, rinse it, and wash the rest of my body clean from our amorous activities. He even conditions my hair.

Strong fingers massage my scalp and work the conditioner through to the ends. I'm a weeping, howling mess. Somehow, he manages to wash his body as well.

The water turns off and I shake, but before I know it, he wraps me in a plush cotton towel. I hold it around my body, completely useless and unable to dry myself, as he quickly combs through the tangles of my hair and secures everything in a ponytail at the base of my neck. Then his hands are on me, drying me off. Brody sweeps me off my feet and carries me to the bed.

"Stay there. I'm going to find you something to wear." His hand runs through his wet hair. He heads to the massive walk-in closet and disappears while I huddle on the bed. When he returns, he's dressed in loose-fitting jeans and a green and black shirt. "Let's get you dressed."

"In what?" All I have is the red, silky dress from last night. I'm going to go home, doing the walk of shame, in last night's dress?

No!

Another whimper escapes me.

Brody pulls me off the bed and shoves one of his shirts over my head.

"It's the best I could find." He kneels before me and feeds first one foot and then the other into a pair of black running pants. The stretchy fabric hangs loosely on my much smaller frame. "Stand up."

The only reason I find my feet is because he pulls me to them and leaves me there to wobble. Disappearing into the kitchen, he returns with two large clips. Back to his knees, he burrows under the oversized shirt and gathers the loose fabric at my waist. He places a clip on either side of my waist and draws the pants tight enough so that they won't slip down.

"No shoes, but I can carry you." He stands and his heavy gaze settles on me, full of concern and worry.

"I can walk." I sniff and wipe at my nose. "I'm sorry."

"Why?" His brows pinch together.

"For losing it."

"Grace…" He grips my shoulders. He bends until his forehead touches mine. "What did Mark say? Is your mom…" He clears his throat. "Did she pass?"

I don't really know. I've been waiting for this moment for months, and just assumed. "He said I need to get home."

"I'm driving." He dips down to get to my level. "She may just have had a turn for the worse. You may not have missed it."

*It.*

He means her death, but his words are something to latch onto. I nod and glance around his place. I feel so damn helpless.

"I don't know where anything is." I have my phone, but as far as anything else I may have had with me last night, I'm lost.

"Don't worry about anything. Your purse is on the kitchen counter, and I already put your clothes in a bag. It's time to go." He grips my hand, lending me enough strength to put one foot in front of another. I lean on him as we make our way to the elevator. When we make it to his car, I collapse as if I'm carrying the weight of the world on my shoulders.

The drive home is a blur. More tears fall. Grief hounds me. I curl into a ball and dissolve in a fit of choking sobs. The tears simply won't stop. All the while, Brody is right there with me, touching me, caressing me, digging out a tissue so I can wipe my nose.

He's simply there.

When we pull up to my house, I don't wait for the car to come to a full stop. The door opens, and I run. I fly up the stairs, practically levitating, as Brody shouts from the car to be careful in my bare feet.

I race into Mom's room and come to a sudden stop. Mark sits at the side of her bed and holds her hand. His head is bowed, and tears stream down his cheeks. His head lifts and he turns red-rimmed eyes toward me.

"Is she…" I can't say it.

I won't.

"Come." He stands and gestures to the chair he was sitting in. "It won't be long now."

"She's still alive?" Her ashen complexion is the worst I've seen. Her frail body lies limply in the bed. Her chest isn't moving. I can't see if she's breathing.

"Not for long." He grabs my shoulders and draws me in for a hug. "I tried calling you last night, but you never picked up. Abbie was here most of the night. She sat with Lucy last evening. She tried to call you too, then called me. The hospice nurse is on her way."

I grab for a tissue to blow my nose. I'm a snotty mess and stand like an idiot, too afraid to sit down.

"I don't know what to do." I look to Mark for direction, but he's too lost in his own grief. His shoulders slump and his complexion is pale, worn out. He's tired.

"Sit with her. Talk to her." He takes my hand and guides me to the chair.

"Is she in pain?"

"No. We called her hospice nurse and gave her something to ease her…" Mark's voice cracks. He shifts so I can sit and takes a step away. "I'll give you a moment to say your goodbyes." He blows his nose with a tissue and wipes at his puffy, red-streaked eyes.

"You don't have to go." If these are her last moments, she deserves to be surrounded by those who love her.

"I'm not going. I'll be in the living room. I need—I just need a moment."

"Okay." I settle myself on the stool beside my mom and take her limp hand in mine.

Tears stream down my cheeks as I think back to the last time I remember my mom as vibrant and healthy. I focus on her smile and the brightness of her expression. She was always filled with such joy.

"I'm here, Mom. I'm here." Gently, I pat the back of her hand.

Her fingers are cold and blueish-white. There's no muscle tone. I stare at her chest for several long moments, willing her to breathe. Mark said she's still with us.

Barely perceptible, her chest rises. I gasp and watch again. I breathe three times before she takes another shallow breath. When I glance at her face, there's no color to her lips. Her eyes are closed and her features slack and loose.

I shouldn't complain. This is what I wanted for her. It's what she wanted. To be able to die at home instead of inside a sterile and cold hospital room. I knew it would be hard, but I never thought it would be this unbearable, this devastating.

I hate cancer.

Her disease was horrible, heartbreaking in the way it bled away her vitality to leave only this husk of a body behind. She battled the cancer, enduring treatment after treatment, for me. To ensure I was able to complete my education before this day came.

That battle drained her finances, wiped out her savings, and put the future of Atwood Estates in jeopardy, but this is what she wanted. To fight long enough—to live long enough—for me to be in a position to take over her legacy.

"I won't fail you, Mother." I lift her hand to my mouth and kiss the back of her hand gently.

A soft sigh escapes her mouth. She hasn't moved since I arrived, but I hope she knows I'm here. I'm here in the home where we pieced together a life of happiness, just the two of us. In spite of her disease, I'd like to think her last days were good.

Her strength and determination to fight and hold on for as long as possible is something I'll never forget. Her laughter is something I'll carry with me forever. She's the bravest person I know.

"I'm going to miss you."

A presence shifts in the doorway and I glance up. Brody stands like a guard, his back to me as he faces out toward the living room. He's close, watching over me, but gives me the space I need to say my goodbyes.

"Do you want to come in?" My voice shakes, but I manage to get the words out.

"I don't want to intrude." He shifts, pivoting to face me.

"You're not."

"Is she…" Brody surprises me with the hitching in his voice.

This affects him.

"Not yet."

While the drive home passed in a blur, I'm fairly certain Brody broke every speed limit to get me here as quickly as humanly possible.

"Do you mind if I come in?" Hesitation isn't something I'm used to seeing in Brody La Rouge. I stretch out my hand, urging him to join me. I need him beside me, something to hold onto, someone to lean on.

This is harder than I thought it would be.

He crosses the room and takes my hand, then, he shifts around to stand behind me. Strong fingers dig into the knots in my shoulders. I close my eyes and feel him lending me his strength.

I take a deep breath for the first time since getting the call from Mark. My mother is going to die, but I won't be alone. I sniff and look down at my clothes.

"I'm going to change."

He shifts back to give me room to stand. "Do you mind if I stay and say a few words?"

"If you want to." I wipe at my cheeks.

Mom isn't happy Brody's back in my life. She won't be happy about what we did last night. He knows this, and I think he needs a moment to tell her he'll never hurt me again.

"I do." He sits on the stool. "I'll just keep this warm for you until you get back."

"I won't be long." As much as I love wearing Brody's clothes and being enveloped in his scent, I'm not comfortable wearing them around my mom on what is surely her last day.

Mark sits on the couch, head bowed, hands clasped together, body shaking as he holds himself together. I thought that would be me, that the months watching her health decline would've prepared me better than this.

I'm falling apart, and I think the only reason I'm keeping myself together, even as poorly as I am, is because of Brody. Things changed between us last night. I hold on to that because there's no way I'm making it through Mom's final moments alone.

# THIRTY-THREE

# Brody

—————

GRACE'S MOM'S THIN FRAME LOOKS SO SMALL AND FRAIL. IT FEELS weird being alone with her, but I'm happy to have a moment. There are things I need to say, and maybe my words will give Lucy Atwood a bit of peace.

I keep my voice low.

This is private. I'm not ready for Grace to hear what I have to say, but it's the truth. One I've known for far too long.

"I'm in love with your daughter, Mrs. Atwood. I think I always have been. I'm sorry I hurt her and ask for your forgiveness. I was young, stupid, and an idiot. I focused on things that didn't matter. Out of all those kids I tried to impress with my tall tales, wild ways, and that damaging video, which did so much harm, none of them—those kids—matter to me. The only people I talk to from back then are my brothers and your daughter."

I take her hand in mine and trace out the veins beneath her papery skin. She doesn't move or react in any way to show she knows I'm here.

"I hurt your daughter. I'm ashamed of what I did, and if I could, I'd go back and erase all the damage I did. I would make better choices. I want you to know I'm going to take care of Grace, in whatever way she'll allow. You have no reason to believe me, or trust me, but I give my word. I'll watch over your daughter." Bowing my head, I say a prayer for Grace's mother and thank her for listening to me.

A sound at the door lifts my head.

It's Mark.

I stand quickly and take a step back as he moves to the foot of the bed.

"It shouldn't be long now. Lucy will finally be at peace." Red and puffy, his eyes brim with tears. "Where's Grace?"

"She went to change."

Mark looks over his shoulder. "How are things between the two of you?"

"They're good, or at least I hope they're good. I'm making up for past mistakes."

"Grace is a good girl. Smart. She has a good head on her shoulders." He grips the footboard of the bed tight enough to turn his knuckles white. "She's destined for greater things than Atwood Estates."

"I thought this was her dream. Isn't Grace happy here?"

"That's what she says, but she always had her eye on the corporate world. I hate that she gave that up."

"I didn't know."

"I've tried to help. Offered to buy her out, but Grace is stubborn. She'll cling to this place even as it drags her under, if only to honor her mother's wish."

"Grace can be tenacious, but Atwood Estates will turn around." I speak with conviction and truth. Sterling Enterprises has turned around companies in much worse shape than Atwood Estates. "We made great contacts last night."

"We?" The muscles of his jaw bunch.

"Grace did. She was amazing. You should've seen her sell the idea of Atwood Estates' exclusivity. People love her."

"I love her." Mark looks down. His tired gaze travels up the length of the bed until he settles on his sister's tired face. "Lucy, of course, loves her, but this isn't what she wanted for her daughter."

"If Grace goes, will you run Atwood Estates yourself?"

"I've pretty much been doing that since Lucy got sick. Talk to Grace. See what you think. Encourage her to follow her heart and not to burden herself with this. Maybe you can convince her to let all of this go."

I'm not in a place to tell Grace to do anything. Everything Grace says and does, speaks counter to what Mark claims. Yes, she didn't plan on taking over Atwood Estates, and the company is teetering on the brink of bankruptcy, but we made great strides last night. Those connections will bring in the revenue stream required to turn everything around. As long as their operation keeps up with supply, within a year, or two, this place will flourish. A knock on the door ends our conversation. My mother peeks her head in.

"Hi, Brody."

"Mom." I cross the room and give my mom a kiss on the cheek.

"How is she?" Mom looks into the room, hovering at the doorway.

"Hard to say. Sleeping?"

"Good morning, Mark." Abbie forces a smile to her face.

"Abbie." His shoulders slump as he practically falls into the chair I vacated. "It's nice to see you. Do you want a moment to visit?"

"I will in a bit, but I came to make you and Grace something to eat." Mom's eyes sparkle. The answer to any calamity is a home-cooked meal, something she excels at famously.

Grace comes down the stairs. She draws my eye. It's an instinctual reaction. Dressed in denim and a long-sleeved t-shirt, she looks far more comfortable than she did wearing my clothes. Although, I prefer her in my clothes, or out of them completely.

"Oh, you poor thing." Abbie rushes over to Grace and gathers her in her arms. "How are you holding up?" Mom releases Grace. "Hold up. Never mind. Bad question."

"It's nice to see you." Grace wipes a tear from her cheek.

"It's nice to be seen. Now, you go in and sit with your mom. I'm going to take care of the two of you. I brought stuff to make my famous pancakes." Mom turns toward me. "Brody, do you mind helping me?"

Mom *never* asks any of us to help her in the kitchen. She says Asher, Cage, and I are heathens who make a mess of everything, but I get what she's doing. Grace and Mark need to have time alone with Mrs. Atwood. As much as I want to be by Grace's side, supporting her, she doesn't need me hovering while her mom dies.

"And finally discover how you make your famous pancakes?" I rock back on my heels and fail to hide my enthusiasm. "You bet."

"Honey, you're not helping with the pancakes. I'll give you a skillet for the sausage and bacon. I'm pretty sure you can't screw those up, but my pancakes are mine."

I take Grace's hands in mine, give a little squeeze, then wrap my arms around her. "If you need me, I'll be the one held hostage in the kitchen."

"You don't have to cook for us." Grace leans into my arms, almost as if she's soaking up strength. That's fine with me. I want Grace to need me. To want me. I want more of this. The two of us needing and depending on the other.

"Nonsense." My mom gives a sharp shake of her head. "You look like you can use a little bit of home-cooked love. I've got everything covered for the whole day. You don't have to worry about anything." Just like that, Mom takes over. I get roped into helping her in the kitchen while Grace and Mark sit with Lucy. A little digging and I find a skillet and get to work with the bacon.

"Stop it." Mom gives a shake of her head.

"Stop what?"

"You're going to burn the bacon if you keep staring at that door."

"I'm just worried."

"Worried about Lucy, or worried about Grace?"

"Can't it be both?"

My mother takes one good look at me and gives a sharp shake of her head. "You love her."

My attention shifts from Mrs. Atwood's room to my mom.

"Do not." Telling Mrs. Atwood how I feel about her daughter is one thing, but confessing I love Grace to my mom? I'm not ready for that.

"Hun, I've seen that love-struck look too many times. And for what it's worth, it's about damn time."

"Excuse me?"

"It's taken far too long for you to get your head out of your ass."

"Again—excuse me?"

"Oh, come on. I've watched you over the years, sleeping with all the pretty things, chasing the illusion of love while running from it at the same time. You're not like your brothers."

"Technically, I'm exactly like them."

"And yet, you're the one who feels things the deepest while pretending you've never cared for anyone your whole life. Grace bit you when you were far too young to really understand things. It scared you, and you fixed it so that you didn't have to deal with your feelings."

"You're making a lot of assumptions."

"I'm stating facts, and you know I'm right."

"I'll never admit you're right about anything."

"You don't have to. I'm your mom, therefore, I'm right. Besides, I know things, and I don't care if you believe me or not. That girl got under your skin when you were still a boy on the cusp of manhood. You've been running from her, and those pesky feelings, ever since. I'm having fun watching your arrogant, lofty, untouchable-self finally fall hard for a girl."

"I'm not falling."

I already fell. I'm absolutely and desperately in love with Grace.

"Like a brick." She flashes a grin and goes back to making her famous pancake batter, giving me her back as she hunches over the bowl. Her brows lift when I peek over her shoulder.

"No peeking!"

"I will figure it out."

She makes me smile. Mom is particular about her pancakes. She's trying to fake me out and packed the countertop with all manner of baking ingredients, most of which don't belong in pancake batter.

"Don't let that bacon burn, sweetie."

"It's not going to burn." I'm pretty damn good in the kitchen. Frying bacon is child's play, and I've never burnt bacon in my life. I turn back to the stove while Mom finishes with her batter. "Do you think Grace is happy here?"

Mark's words tumble in my thoughts. If Grace truly is unhappy, will she leave to pursue a more lucrative career elsewhere? The thought of losing her after recently finding her doesn't sit well with me. In fact, it sits quite poorly.

"Why would you ask that? Grace loves it here."

"It's just something Mark said."

"Ignore Mark. Grace is happy."

"How can you be so sure?"

"Because you're here."

"Okay, outside of my mother's hopes of me hooking up with Grace, how can you be sure?"

"Luv, you can never be sure of anything, and I'm not interested in you hooking up with Grace. I'm waiting for the white dress, the wedding, and the grandbabies."

"Grandbabies! Getting a bit ahead of yourself there."

"A mom can dream. Someday, you'll all fall in line and give me the grandbabies I deserve after having to put up with raising your obnoxious selves."

"Gee, thanks." I don't blame her for the comment. The three of us were hellions growing up.

"As far as Grace goes, don't worry. Lucy wasn't ready to take over the reins of this business when she did, but she's never regretted it. This is her life, and Grace's too. This is Grace's home, her passion."

"You sure it's not Mrs. Atwood's passion that Grace is getting stuck with?"

"Lucy would never do that to her daughter, and don't listen to Mark. That boy doesn't have a head for business. Lucy was always complaining about having to follow up behind him."

"I thought they were a great team."

"They're siblings, but stepsiblings. There's always friction between siblings, more so with stepsiblings, especially when one's the boss and the other's not. And it's nothing much, just comments here and there. Mark's been trying to get Lucy to sell out to him for years. She never would, because this place is the one thing she wanted to give to her daughter. The land has been passed down from mother to daughter for generations. Grace belongs here. Granted, it wasn't supposed to be this soon, but this place is more than a profit and loss balance sheet to them."

"Them?"

"Lucy and Grace. It's a mother-daughter thing. You wouldn't understand."

"And you do? You don't have any daughters."

"You're right; I have three very obnoxious, hard-headed boys who each need a strong woman in their life to keep them in line. I'm not going to be around forever, you know."

I wrap my arm around my mother and kiss the top of her head. "You're not allowed to leave us. At least not until you surrender your pancake recipe."

She shoves me away, laughing. "I'll make you a deal."

"A deal? You're giving me the recipe?"

"The first one who gives me grandbabies will get the recipe."

"Now you're playing dirty."

"Am I?" Her eyes twinkle, and her attention shifts to the door. "Asher and Evie are getting married soon. He's always been first you know…"

A low growl builds in the back of my throat.

"But I'm your favorite."

"My favorite will be the one who gives me grandbabies. You boys are waiting far too long to settle down and carry forward our family's name."

"You're insufferable."

"Perhaps." She lifts the finished bowl of batter. "But my pancakes are amazing. You done with the bacon?"

That's one piece of her pancake recipe I've got down. She cooks her pancakes in the bacon grease.

"They're done."

"Then step aside." My mother legit hip checks me, pushing me out of the way and shooing me out of the kitchen. I'd go in to check on Grace, but there's a knock on the front door.

When I open it, Asher and Cage grin like two damn fools. Cage's camera dangles around his neck like he's ready for a photo shoot. The triplet curse strikes again because Cage wears a black and yellow shirt identical to the black and green one I have on. We both roll our eyes while Asher grins. He's got his red and black flannel shirt on too.

"There's a rumor Mom's making pancakes." Cage rubs his palms together and lifts his nose, sniffing the air. The smell of bacon curls in the air, as does the very beginnings of Mom's famous batter becoming the best pancakes on the planet.

I step outside and close the door behind me. "She's making pancakes for Grace and Mark. Lucy's dying."

"We know." Cage bows his head. "Mom told us, but *pancakes!*"

"This is honestly the worst possible time for the two of you to crash a pancake breakfast."

"That's not really why we're here." Asher drags the toe of his boot over the wooden planks of the porch. He pulls at the back of his neck. It's a nervous habit we all share.

"Then, why are you here?" I block the door, determined not to let my obnoxious brothers inside where they will only cause mayhem, destruction, and chaos. Grace doesn't need that kind of shit right now.

Cage lifts up the camera. "Asher was telling me about rebranding Atwood Estates. I thought I'd help out, scout the property, and see if I can find a vision for this rebranding campaign."

"I was coming over anyway," Asher says. "Mark and I were supposed to go over more of the vineyard's operations today." His mouth twists at the end.

"What's wrong?"

"Nothing really, or rather nothing jumping out at me, but this place should be producing more than it is."

"You sure about that?" I lean against the door and cross my arms. Cage is trying to sidestep around me. If I don't hold him off, he'll barge right in and scoop up Mom's pancakes before anyone's the wiser.

"I want to look around. I figured since Mark's busy, I'd hang with Cage and show him around. Kill two birds as it were. He can get photos for marketing, and I can look around without Mark breathing down my neck. You gonna stay here?" His chin juts toward the door. "I take it things are going well with Grace?"

"We connected last night."

"By connected, do you mean fucked?" Cage leans against the porch railing while he fiddles with his camera. He looks up at me with his piercing gaze. We all have the same eyes, but Cage's are wilder and more unhinged, more primal than Asher's or mine. He shakes his head, disappointed in me. "Guess this means you're done with her again?"

"Don't speak about Grace like that." My fists curl, but I hold the punch. "It's not like that."

"So, one of the most eligible bachelors ever is off the market?" Cage goes back to his camera like he doesn't care what my answer might be. "Guess that makes me the last man standing."

"You're always last." Ash can't help but get a dig in.

Our ABC names aren't by chance. We were literally named according to our birth order. Asher came early, by a few weeks, hogging all Mom's attention in neonatal intensive care while Cage and I battled it out in the womb as to who would be next. I won that race, leaving Cage the youngest of the La Rouge triplets.

"Not last in everything." Cage smirks. "I beat you both out when it came to becoming a man."

"Becoming a man?" I can't help but stare. "That sounds stupid."

"Better than saying I lost my virginity first. That's too girly. And not as uncouth as saying I fucked first."

"You're the epitome of uncouth." I shoot back at him.

"Using them big words, I see." Cage dodges and fake punches my gut. "Come on, you wanna join us? Or are you going to sit around here all day?"

I glance over my shoulder, feeling like I should stay with Grace, but I don't want to be intrusive. "I'll come with, but let me tell Grace first." I point to each of them. "Stay outside. If you pilfer any of those pancakes, I will take you down."

"Promises. Promises." Cage shakes his head, but there's a grin on his face.

I don't get what Mom says about siblings bickering. We're tighter than tight, never really argue about anything. Thick as thieves is the best descriptor. We keep each other's secrets. Have each other's backs. And we genuinely love one another. I know some siblings fight. It's just not something I understand.

THIRTY-FOUR

# Brody

After checking in with Grace and getting kicked out of the house by my mother, I spend the next several hours bumming around with my brothers. As the years pass, there are fewer opportunities for us to hang out, just the three of us, so I love when we can.

"You still running those ultra-marathon things?" Cage snaps a picture of the vines while I stand next to him. He's got an amazing eye and his photos are a testament to his skill. Featured in many national magazines, he travels the world on assignment for National Geographic and several other outdoor magazines.

"Still at it." I glance at the dirt road behind us. We're out in the field, almost at the exact same spot where I ran across Grace a week ago.

"Don't know how you do it." Cage shakes his head.

"It's a great way to meditate."

"Masturbate?"

"Meditate, asshole."

"Dude, there are better ways to *meditate* than run your body to exhaustion." Cage kneels on the dirt to snap a picture of the vines with the sky as a backdrop.

"I like it. It's just me, the road, and my thoughts."

Asher ambles up and down the long row of trellises inspecting the vines. Every now and then, he stops, lightly palms a bunch of grapes, and leans in for a close look. He signals for me to join him and I leave Cage to his photos.

"What's up?" I squint against the sun. It's a perfect day, clear-blue skies, puffy clouds overhead, and cool enough that we're not working up a sweat as we hike up and down the rows.

"See these irrigation lines?" Asher points to drip lines extending the length of each row.

"Yeah?" I shrug. "What about them?"

"They're not standard. Actually, they're rather ingenious. I installed them last year and we've seen a twenty percent increase in grape yield."

"So, this is good, right?"

"Except Atwood Estates has shown a steady decrease in yield over the past five years."

"What are you saying?"

"Only that Mark went on and on about them. How well they're doing."

"Okay?" I scratch my head, not getting what Asher's trying to say.

"He installed them five years ago. It's pricey."

"And?"

"The yield went down." Asher arches a brow. He gives a shake of his head when I return a flat stare. "Things aren't matching up."

"Looks like I need to do a deep dive into the books." I've done this, but it was general, looking for glaring errors and opportunities for improvement. This is more of a deep forensic dive, something I personally love.

"That's what I was thinking. Installment of this equipment would've required a major outlay of cash. I can make estimates of anticipated yield over the past five years, comparing them to what La Rouge produced and scaling down as appropriate. I have a feeling this place is going to come up short. It smells fishy."

My lips press together as I absorb what Asher tells me. "Where are the records for yield and production? I didn't see them in the materials I was given."

"You weren't?" Asher's shocked expression isn't a surprise.

"We do a top-level diagnostic when assessing new clients. If that checks out, we do a deeper dive. I started that with Grace, but it takes more than a day's worth of work. And that still doesn't get down into the nitty-gritty of counting pennies."

"Do you think…"

"If you're asking if I think Grace knows, or is knowingly withholding, she's not."

"I didn't mean her. Do you smell the same rat I'm smelling?" Asher glances down the row and shakes his head.

"I doubt it. Those two are really close, but to be honest, nothing surprises me. Let's keep this between ourselves. Don't say anything to Grace. She has enough going on right now with her mom."

"No problem. Let's take a look in the weeds." Asher calls out to Cage. "Hey, asshat, we're heading to processing."

"Almost done." Cage, who's flat on his back, has somehow managed to wiggle under the trellis. He gets in a few last shots, then squirms out like a worm. "Where're we going?"

"To look at vats and stuff." Asher walks over to Cage and gives him a hand up.

"I got some great shots." Cage glances at the screen on his camera, thumbing through the various shots. I glance over his shoulder and my brows lift. Don't know how the hell he got the pictures he did.

After Asher raises his concerns, I'm eager to snoop around. Today presents a unique opportunity because Mark is busy back at the house. A pang shoots through me because I feel like I should be with Grace, but I know it's better to give her the space she needs.

The three of us march through the fields and head to the processing warehouses. Asher stops every now and then to stare down the long rows of grapevines. He tugs at his chin and I see the winemaker in him crunching numbers.

Asher runs La Rouge Winery for us. I'm the CFO and work the books. Cage handles marketing. We each play to our strengths, but Asher is the one with the eye for the business of turning grapes into wine. To be honest, he's the best consultant money can't buy for this particular project.

Unlike Mark, who I'm starting to question, Asher commands my absolute faith. He won't steer me wrong.

A visit to the processing warehouses takes up the rest of the afternoon. I stay in close contact with Mom, checking in with her via text nearly every hour.

Grace and Mark remain by Lucy's side. The hospice nurse arrived a couple of hours ago to help as only they can. The bad news is the pancakes are all gone. Neither Asher, Cage, nor myself will have that pleasure today.

At the warehouses, Asher and I leave Cage alone to shoot the photos he needs to make this place sell.

"Mark's office is this way." Asher leads us to Mark's office, where I settle in on a worn leather couch while Asher fires up the office computer. Mark keeps his password on the blotter of his desk, which makes it easy to snoop.

"I suppose we want to compare projected yield with actual over the past five years?" I kick back and fire off another text to Mom.

"I was thinking the past ten years." Asher bends over the computer. "Do you know when the winery first started having problems?"

"Nothing particularly stood out, except it's been a steady drop over the past decade."

"Then I suggest we go further back. Things have changed some over the last decade, increases in yield across the board throughout the wine industry. We'll have to extrapolate and make educated guesses. But if we establish a firm baseline, I can use La Rouge data to make a fair estimate of what they should be producing."

"Are we a fair comparison?" La Rouge is easily ten times the size of Atwood Estates. It's one of the main reasons we haven't been swallowed up by the big corporate players in the area. "Frankly, I'm surprised Atwood Estates hasn't been bought out by now."

"No kidding." I sketch out numbers on a legal-sized pad of paper. "Hey, is cost still around 30K per acre?"

"Depends what you mean. Annual maintenance is about 5K an acre, but if starting from the ground up…"

"I meant what does the land cost?"

"Per acre?"

"Of course."

Asher scratches his head. "Napa ranges anywhere from 100K to a quarter of a million. Atwood Estates is prime real estate, flat land, pristine soil analysis. I'd peg it at the higher range."

"And yield?"

"Per acre?"

"Of course." I take notes as Asher tosses out numbers.

"We get about five- to five-and-a-half tons per acre."

"How much does that yield?"

"Two- to two-and-a-half thousand per ton. Five tons an acre, so 11 to 13 thousand an acre in revenue. Aren't you supposed to be the numbers guy?"

"Yeah, but I look that shit up. You live and breathe it. So, let's be conservative and say five tons to the acre, two thousand a ton, that leaves us with ten thousand in revenue per acre."

"Right, costs are about half that. So the expected net revenue, subtracting out costs and harvesting fees, and Atwood should be pulling in 5K an acre."

I go back to my doodling. From what I know from La Rouge, our profit margin is standard for local wineries at about fifty percent. Asher's right on the nose about that. A quick call to my assistant at the office and I get the files transferred to my phone.

It's a bit of a pain working on my phone, but I settle in while Asher digs around in Mark's computer.

My doodles turn into figures, costs, profit margins, yields. I do a quick check on the going rate, as well as historical rates for Cabernet Sauvignon varietal grapes, the predominant varietal grown at Atwood Estates.

"Got those yield numbers yet?"

"Yeah, Mark's filing system is messy. Want me to read it off?"

"Shoot."

Asher reads off the tonnage per acre produced each year for the past ten years. I scratch it all down and make a few quick calculations.

"Declining is right." I wave Asher over. "Come look at this."

I'm pretty handy with my phone and show him some graphs.

"Last season, they brought in four tons per acre, twenty percent less than predicted. Sales were down, but that's in direct correlation to the three years prior, if they're aging the Cabernet for three years."

"They are." Asher takes the pad of paper out of my hands. "Look at this, steady increase in yield as we would predict with better practices until six years ago. Then there's a plateau and steady decrease following that." He snaps the pad. "Can you say skimming?"

"Looks like, but why?"

"Any number of reasons. Let's say Mark decides he wants to take over. Grace goes away to college. Mrs. Atwood plans on Grace taking over. Maybe Mark's not on board with working for his niece, all he has to do is make the winery fail."

"So, what? He keeps production going, bankrupt the company, and sells out to the highest bidder. What did you say this land is worth?"

"Considering the state of the vines out there, mature, well-established, the soil reports are outstanding, add to that prime location in Napa, the cabernet varietal, most profitable grape around, and I'd say easily a quarter of a million per acre would be the starting price. They've got just a bit over forty acres, so a cool ten million? Considering supply and demand, I wouldn't be surprised if one of the corporations wouldn't eat the cost, take a loss in the short run for a chance to obtain the land for the future."

"Makes perfect sense. But how do you hide something like that?"

"Guess it depends how involved Lucy, and now Grace, are in the day to day operations."

"Surely, she'd know."

"Would you?"

"What do you mean?"

"Well, you're essentially Lucy and I'm Mark."

"You're the CEO, so you're more like Lucy than me."

"Not really. I'm the operations guy. You're the finance guy. I have a feeling they worked the same. She managed the books. He ran the land. It would be very easy to skim off the top."

"How? The harvest is the harvest. You can't hide grapes."

Asher draws at his chin. "Actually, it'd be really easy. All you'd have to do is divert a truck here and there. Look, the grapes are cut by hand, loaded into bins, placed in the trucks, and brought here for de-stemming, pressing, and fermentation. All he'd have to do is have one truck in ten divert elsewhere."

"Sneaky bastard. I'm itching to look into his finances. That kind of shit adds up. Maybe that's why he wants to buy Grace out."

"He does?"

"She mentioned it, but he offered two million—"

"Two million." Asher rubs his hand over his face. "That's outright theft when it's easily worth five times that. You gotta tell Grace."

"Not until I know more." I shift on the couch. "And it's easy to do this? Where would the grapes go?"

"To a central processing area. Most of the grapes grown around here are grown on vines that are leased on private land. The landowners aren't involved in any of it. Those grapes get harvested and taken to central processing facilities. He could be pocketing money on the side by collecting on delivery."

"Smart move. And there's no way Lucy would know."

"Unless she had some reason to suspect. She'd need to know how many trucks were filled and compare that to what's received. Honestly, with her illness and all the medical appointments, he could've pulled this off easily."

"I suppose, but this is all speculation."

"You're the numbers guy. Follow the money. Isn't that what you always say?"

"Right, but I need access to his records and personal statements. Until I have irrefutable proof, this stays between us."

Asher gestures toward the computer. "Right now, Mark's an open book."

"Hmm, not sure of the legality of that."

"Legality of what?" Cage saunters in, one eye on the screen of his camera and one on where he's going. He drops into the couch beside me and shows me a picture. "I've got a great idea for marketing."

"We've got bigger problems," Asher says.

"Problems?"

"Yeah." While I stew about options, Asher fills Cage in on our conversation.

"That's some shady shit." Cage pushes off the soft couch and wanders around to the desk. "You need snooping, I'm your guy. What're we looking for?"

"Technically, I can't be involved in any of this," I affirm my position.

"Why not? Isn't this like vital info for your company to know?" Cage spins around and opens the top drawer of a filing cabinet. He rifles through the folders before slamming the drawer shut and moving on to the next. His body tenses and interminable seconds pass. No need for words; I read my brother's body language perfectly because it's the same as mine.

"What did you find?"

Cage rips a folder out of the cabinet and scans a document. "I don't think there will be any need for Sterling Enterprise's CFO to go digging around in Mark's computer."

"Why's that?" I stand and stride over to my brother.

"Because…" He hands me a contract to sell Atwood Estates.

I flip through the legalese, searching for the important parts. "Twelve million?" My gut clenches.

"Let me see that." Asher yanks the contract out of my hand. He sits at the desk and pours over it. "Hey, Brody," he glances up, storm clouds brewing in his gaze, "it's signed."

"Signed?" I didn't get that far before Asher ripped it out of my hands. "How can that be? He doesn't own the rights."

"It's signed by both parties." Asher points at a signature page and looks up.

"That's not legally binding. Mark doesn't own the land. Lucy does."

"Are we sure about that?" Cage leans against the filing cabinet and crosses his arms.

"I'm pretty sure. Grace told me he's tried to buy her out." I search back through my conversations with Grace, wishing I paid better attention. "This is the worst time to be dealing with something like this." I turn to Asher. "Give me that."

"What are you going to do with it?" Asher tucks the contract back inside the folder and hands it over.

"I'm not sure yet." I don't know whether to start with Grace or go straight for Mark's jugular. "I need to get back to the house."

THIRTY-FIVE

# Grace

I sit vigil beside my mom, praying her next breath won't be her last, as if my will alone is powerful enough to tether her to this life. But I know Mom exists in a fog of pain, clinging to a life filled with agony, if only to spend one more day with me.

It's wrong to be this selfish, but I can't help it. Saying goodbye hurts too much.

The hospice nurse arrives. Abbie lets her in and the nurse comes to Mom's bedside to administer drugs to help my mother as she nears the end.

Mom appears more comfortable, struggling less to breathe.

I hate everything about this.

The medication takes mom from me long before she slips from this world. I'm beside her, holding her hand, as the last breath fills her lungs then stops.

Not really sure what I expect, mom's passing takes a moment to sink in. Her hand, which has been lax in mine all day, suddenly feels different.

Empty.

Vacant of life.

Both lighter and heavier.

I'm not sure how to describe it better than that.

But mom's gone.

Mark, who's been with me all day, and finally crashed in the rocker we pulled in from the porch a few hours ago, gives a start. His body twitches and he wakes up looking lost and confused.

"Is she…" He's not able to ask if she's dead, but he sees it in my tear-filled eyes.

I swipe at my cheeks and bow my head. "She just passed."

Mom and Uncle Mark were close. They've been with each other their whole lives, growing up together after Mom's mom, and Mark's dad, married and joined their families. When my grandparents passed, Mom was barely twenty-one. She had to step up, not only to run the business, but as Mark's guardian until he turned eighteen. After that, they ran this business together. I'm not surprised he wakes at the moment of her passing.

He comes to stand behind me and wraps his arms around my shoulders. Gently, he kisses the top of my head and holds me tight. "She's in a better place now. No more pain."

"Yes, no more pain."

A tsunami of sobs rises inside of me, demanding I lower the flood gates and let them loose, but I hold them back. There will be plenty of time for crying in the days to come. For now, I gaze upon my mother and sift through my memories, gathering all the love and light into one last goodbye.

"Goodbye, Mom." I lean over her bed.

As I kiss her on the cheek, the air in the room stirs. That's when I feel Brody's presence. He's back from whatever pulled him away with his brothers.

His large frame blocks the door and an agonized expression fills his face. That's all it takes to make my tears flow. A sob escapes me, but before I collapse from grief, Brody's there. His strong arms wrap around me, supporting me, loving me, letting me know I can get through this, and that I don't have to do it alone.

My cries release the floodgates and the tears tumble out in a mad rush while a piece inside of me rips apart and floats away. My sobs turn agonized and raw as I surrender to my grief.

Through it all, Brody is there, a pillar of strength I cling to as my entire life falls apart.

Not sure when, or really how, but we wind up on the porch, me cradled in his arms. Brody either carried me out here, or guided me out, while the delirium of my loss ran through me.

The tears slow. They stop. They fall again. Grief ebbs and flows within me as I struggle to process Mom's death.

*I'm all alone.*

*No, you've got Mark, and you've got Brody.*

The voices in my head soothe me but do little to ease the terrible ache of my loss.

Gentle fingers stroke through my hair. The soothing tug and soft draw on my hair quiet my mind. At some point, I realize it's Brody's presence that grants me comfort. He rocks me in his arms.

I swipe at my cheeks and sniffle. What a blubbering, snot-filled mess I make. My eyes open and my vision clears as I blink against the tears.

The first thing I notice is the birdbath outside my mother's window. A single white dove sits on the rim. It looks at me and blinks. We stare at each other, me and the bird, for the longest moment. Then it coos, a tiny trill, and shakes its feathers. One last look at me and the bird takes off.

It's a sign. I feel it.

Mom is going to be okay, and she wants me to know I will be as well. With a swipe of both cheeks, I push off Brody's masculine chest. His grip on me eases and he helps me off his lap to settle onto the bench beside him. Without saying a thing, he hands me a tissue and takes my hand in his.

We sit there, together, as I take several deep breaths, blowing out through my mouth. My nose is stopped up with tears. My eyes sting, swollen and raw from so many tears.

"I must look a mess." I dab at my eyes and blink against a fresh flood of tears. They refuse to stop. Once I think I'm done with the crying, my body says, *Not yet!* and sends a fresh rush of grief and agony rushing through me.

"You look absolutely beautiful." The low rumble of Brody's voice comforts me, like a warm blanket wrapped around me on a cold winter's night.

"Your definition of beautiful is sorely lacking." Wonder of wonders, I crack a smile. A small laugh escapes me.

Brody's squeezes my hand affectionately. "You don't see what I see."

"A sobbing mess?"

"A beautiful, resilient woman that I'm desperately in love with."

The ease with which he says those words sounds natural and truthful. So natural and so truthful, it takes a moment before what he said sinks in.

"Brody…" I sit a little straighter as the words turn in my head. "I don't know what to say." Something builds within my chest, a warming sensation that fills me nearly to bursting.

*He loves me.*

"You don't need to say anything right now." He reaches across and takes my other hand in his. "Right now, there are other things you need to deal with."

My attention shifts to the birdbath and then to the window of Mom's room. She used to spend hours watching the birds play in the water. That dove was her, telling me I'll be okay. I feel lighter, less overwhelmed.

"Mark's inside speaking with the hospice nurse. He asked me to bring you back inside when you were able. There are things…"

"I know." I pull my hands out of his grip and wipe away a sheen of fresh tears. The next step is dealing with the mortuary and her *body*. Another sob rips through me, but this time, I put myself together much faster than before. Another sniffle, a few more tissues, and I stand.

Brody's right there beside me. With me. He doesn't ask if I want him to come. He's simply there.

When I head inside, I pass by the still form of my mother's body. Mark pulled the covers up, tucking them around his sister. I pause at the foot of the bed.

"She looks so peaceful." I want to linger, but in my heart, I know that's no longer my mother. Her spirit's been freed. She's out there now, looking over me, and I know she'll be there for the rest of my life, guiding me and loving me.

Mark's in the living room speaking with the hospice nurse. When they see me, they break apart.

The nurse folds her hands in front of her. She bows her head. "I'm very sorry for your loss."

I sniff, unable to speak with the massive lump in my throat. The nurse waits me out, completely un-rushed. She's here to support Mark and me through the next steps.

After I swallow a few times, I find my voice. "What do we need to do now?"

"Not much. I'll take care of calling the mortuary. They'll send someone out when you're ready." *Someone to collect the body.* "I'll stay here until then if you want."

"Yes, that would be helpful." There's no way I'm getting through that *next step*.

Mark approaches and draws me into a hug. For some reason, Brody's entire body stiffens, but he steps to the side and gives Mark and I a moment to hold each other and grieve.

"Do you want to sit with her or wait out here?" He sweeps the hair off my face and gazes deep into my eyes. His are swollen and red, much like mine.

"I want to wash my face and sit outside, I think. I've said my goodbyes, and I honestly don't think I can handle dealing with the..."

I can't say it. Most definitely, I'll fall apart if I have to be there watching strangers carry out my mother's body.

"Do that." Mark gives a sharp nod of his head.

Movement in the kitchen draws my attention. Abbie is there, wiping her hands on her apron. Like the rest of us, her eyes are red and swollen. I step apart from Brody and go to Abbie.

"I'm so sorry, sweetie." The moment Abbie draws me into her arms, tears pour out of me, and I sob with overwhelming loss.

It's an ebb and flow. I studied up on grief and know how this is supposed to go, but knowing it is one thing. Living through it is a whole other monster.

"I made tea and sandwiches." Abbie leans back and gestures at the tray of food. "Brody, come and carry the tray out back. Let's sit in your mother's garden for a bit, why don't we?"

Nodding is the only form of communication I appear capable of at the moment. While Abbie draws me outside, Brody carries the platter stacked with food.

We settle down at an outdoor patio table in the middle of Mom's rose garden. The white dove is back at the birdbath and looks at me again. Brody places the tray on the table and sets a pitcher of iced tea beside it.

Mom's favorite finger sandwiches decorate the tray, reminding me I haven't eaten all day. My stomach rumbles and I can't help but smile.

Life goes on.

Funny the things I cling to, but the idea I can be hungry gives me hope. My life's not over, and while Mom won't be here to share in it, there will always be a piece of her in my heart.

"There's a smile." Abbie turns over three of the four cups and fills them with tea. "Let's get some food in you." Without waiting for me to ask, she places two of the finger sandwiches on a plate and sets it before me. Abbie then sits opposite me, while Brody sits beside me. "Tell me everything about last night." Her attention shifts to Brody. "That was the night of the event, right? I want to know how it went."

And just like that, Abbie takes my mind off my grief, if only for a moment. She encourages and keeps me talking, asking about every detail down to the color of the napkins to the fanciest dresses I saw. When my words trail off, Brody picks up, continuing our replay of last night.

It helps.

It helps because Abbie reminds me I have a purpose, one I'm growing to love. At first, taking on a vineyard seemed daunting. It wasn't anything I hoped I would be doing, but this is home, and it's all mine now. I'm excited for the future. Excited about what I can make of Atwood Estates.

And honestly, I believe Abbie is a worker of miracles because she makes me smile, and laugh, and not feel like I'm so alone. As for Brody, his words tumble in my head, and I can't help but hope we have a future together as well.

The worst day of my life isn't nearly as bad as I thought it would be. Sometime later, Mark joins us. I notice a hearse pull up outside the house and choose to ignore it. When it pulls away from the house, the four of us pause our conversation to watch it drive away.

"Your mother was an incredible woman, Grace." Abbie reaches across the table and takes my hand in hers. "I consider it an honor to have been her friend."

And there it is. We now speak of Mom in past-tense.

"Excuse me." I shoot to my feet and sprint toward the house. The kitchen door bangs as I run inside and race up to my room to sob.

The steady tread of boots sounds on the stairs beside me. My bedroom door squeaks as it's gently pushed open. The bed dips beside me as Brody sits, then I'm in his arms again, where I curl against his chest and cry until exhaustion pulls me down to a dreamless sleep.

# THIRTY-SIX

# Grace

———————

THE NIGHT IS FITFUL. I TOSS AND TURN, BUT EVERY TIME I WAKE, Brody is right there beside me. He doesn't push me to talk but gives me space to grieve as I struggle to make it through the first night without my mother.

He does the same in the week following Mom's death, even stepping in to help Mark finalize last-minute funeral arrangements when I find myself unable to stitch two coherent thoughts together. It's hard to think, let alone focus.

Thankfully, I have Mark. He's been amazing, keeping himself together much better than me. He steps in to help with all the things which must go on as we approach harvest season. If we fail to get these grapes off the vine, and processed into wine, it truly is the end.

Fortunately, Mom planned everything ahead of time, and there's not much to do. The day we bury Mom, the sun shines overhead, slanting a ray of sunshine on her grave. With misty eyes, I toss the first soil on top of her casket and choke back tears. Once again, Brody stands beside me, and the white dove returns. After everyone leaves, giving me time to say farewell to Mom for the last time, the dove lands beside her grave. It stares and me and coos, then flies away.

With no idea if it's the same dove from the day Mom passed, I choose to believe it is. I take it as a sign she's looking down on me, and some of the tightness in my chest eases. Not superstitious by nature, I do believe this is a sign, and I know I will be okay.

As for Brody, his entire family watches over me. Brody stays with me every night, holding me while we sleep. When he's forced to go into the city for work, Cage drops by.

He's rebranding Atwood Estates and makes me take him all over the property while he snaps photos of the most random things. He's easy-going, jokes a lot, and keeps me smiling until Brody returns.

The drive in and out of the city must be killing Brody. The one time I brought up how unnecessary it was for him to make the long commute, he growled like a feral animal and told me I was his to take care of now. I stopped asking after that, selfishly enjoying this new, protective side of Brody.

Abbie basically takes over my kitchen, making sure Mark and I have home-baked meals each night and every morning. At lunch, she brings Mark's lunch to his office and sits with me in the kitchen, where we talk about anything and everything.

And then there's Evie, a woman with whom I share far too much, although I didn't learn of this until after the funeral. We sit together in my kitchen, swapping stories about our families. Evie lost her family—mother, father, brother, and fiancé—in a tragic plane crash on the day of what was supposed to be her wedding. That tragedy eventually brought her out to California and wine country. In her grief, she turned inward, learning to take care of herself in the most basic of ways—she became a solo backpacker.

"I admire your strength." I take a sip of wine.

We've settled into a routine and start drinking once the hands of the clock pass noon. Lunchtime is quickly becoming a girls-only event.

Abbie chased Brody and his brothers out of my kitchen the day after the funeral, and it's just been the three of us since.

"I don't know about strength." Evie gives her empty glass a wiggle, signifying she needs a refill. Abbie tops off all our glasses and opens a second bottle of wine. "I faced some hard truths about who I was and who I wanted to be."

"But you literally left everything behind and set out across the country on a solo backpacking adventure. You reinvented yourself. I don't think I'd have the strength." I make a fist. "The grit to do what you did."

Yesterday, Evie told me how she met Asher and how that happened in the middle of a firestorm. I'm still gobsmacked by what she endured. My issues seem more surmountable, seeing how she turned her life around.

And she's happy. Gloriously happy.

With Asher.

That gives me hope.

There are still times I tear up out of the blue. It can be anything. The scent of Mom's favorite rose bush. Her meticulous handwriting on a pad of paper. The half-open bottle of orange juice in the fridge.

Each day is easier, but also more challenging.

"I did, and I wound up here." Evie places her hand over mine. "To be honest, you're stronger than you know. Life is nothing but a string of adversities tripping us up. You're smart. You know what you want, and one day you're going to wake up and realize it's okay to be happy again. You'll embrace life and find true joy. Most importantly, you won't feel guilty about it. And let's face it, Brody's hot. I should know, although I landed the sexiest triplet."

Abbie rolls her eyes.

"I beg to differ." My spine straightens, and the claws come out. "Brody is the sexiest triplet, and the things he can do with his…"

"Girls," Abbie pipes up, "remember you're sitting across from those insolent boys' mother. If you're going to discuss that kind of thing, give me a heads up, and I'll make myself scarce."

Evie and I laugh.

"Abbie," Evie says, "this might be a good time to leave."

"As if." Abbie huffs and rolls her shoulder's back. She's not going anywhere. She's feisty and fun, a true gift. I understand why she and Mom were such good friends.

"If you want," I say, "I can tell you what happened *after* that charity event." I don't know why, but I feel cheeky around Evie and Abbie —comfortable and confident.

We're drawn from the same cloth, the three of us. Some might say, thick as thieves, but there is some hesitation. I've not yet been drawn fully into the fold, but I will be. Brody loves me. Whatever it takes, I'll find my place in his world—and with his family.

Brody is mine.

"By the way Brody looks at you, I have a pretty good idea what happened Friday night." Abbie's cheeks turn red and she looks away. The moment I think I've won, Abbie turns back with a wicked grin. "I know about the ABCs, dear girl. I just don't need the particulars about my sons. That goes for you too, Evie. I *don't* need to know specifics."

"Speaking of men," Evie turns the tables on Abbie, "why don't you tell us all about your date with the judge?"

"Oh yes, the judge." I rub my palms together in anticipation, happy to have attention shifted from me to Abbie

"What I'm about to say is in the strictest confidence. Do not say a word to my boys." Abbie can't contain her excitement. "I need a solemn pinky swear on this." Her eyes pinch, and I realize she's serious.

"Pinky swear it is." We lock pinkies, and I'm sworn to secrecy.

Abbie's as eager for girl time as I am, and I'm learning all kinds of things about Abbie, my mom, and the friendship they shared. One of those things is how lonely Abbie's been since her husband passed, the year after Brody and his brothers graduated high school. It's one of many things I didn't know about the La Rouge family after Brody blew my life apart.

I spent so many years hating Brody that I missed the intense friendship my mother shared with his mother. I should be surprised, but I find myself excited to find out about these little kernels of my mother's life. It's a gift really, learning about her, not as a daughter, but as a fellow woman. I find myself falling in love with her all over again. It's a treasure and a blessing.

Somehow, through all of the tragedy surrounding their children, Abbie and Mom remained friends. It's something I never appreciated, let alone understood.

I broke off all ties to the La Rouge family and thought Mom had as well, but that was not the case. I'm happy she and Abbie maintained their friendship despite the conflict between their children, but I admit I'm a bit upset by the things Mom kept from me.

"I want to hear about this judge? Who is he?" I dig for information, thinking I'm all coy and shit like that, but Abbie sees right through me.

"*He* is no one, and if you tell Brody, I will cut you."

"Cut me?" I'm not sure if this is a threat, but Evie laughs. "I pinky swore…"

"Grace, she's messing with you." Evie cups her wine glass and breathes in the fragrant aroma. Her eyes close and a smile curves her lips. "This is my absolute favorite Atwood Estates' wine. As for Miss Abbie over here, she's been carrying on a torrid affair with one hot silver fox of a judge, and she's done it with the *Trips* none the wiser."

"Trips?" Abbie giggles. "It's been a long time since I've heard that. I see you girls have been talking behind my back."

"Not so much behind your back as trying to keep ahead of those hellions you raised." Evie lifts her glass in a toast. "To the men who drive women crazy. May we prevail against them all."

Lunch is quickly becoming my favorite time of day. Over the next hour, we gossip and down the second bottle of wine.

"Are you ready for tomorrow?" Abbie asks.

"I am." I tip my glass and finish the last of my wine. "Probate should be easy. Mom took care of everything before she passed." There isn't much with her will. Mom signed over her shares of Atwood Estates to me before her passing. I *bought* the house and land from her for a dollar over a year ago. There are only a few things left in her will, such as the transfer of financial assets in her bank account. But all the material things she gave to me before her death.

"So, you're happy here?" Abbie clears our glasses and washes them in the sink. "You're not thinking of selling this place?"

"I am, happy that is. Why?"

"Just something Brody mentioned."

"What was that?"

"That running a winery wasn't your plan."

"It wasn't. I mean, I knew it would pass to me eventually, but that *eventually* was supposed to be decades from now when Mom retired. Instead…"

"She was taken far too soon, but her dreams aren't your dreams." Abbie switches from friend to maternalistic figure with barely a blink.

"No, they aren't, but Atwood Estates is rubbing off on me."

For the first time, that statement rings true. I'm happier than I thought I could be.

"I'm happy to hear that. You might want to mention that to Brody."

"Why is that?"

"He thinks you've been saddled with this place rather than choosing it. Knowing my son, he's probably trying to *fix* that."

"Fix?" I give a shake of my head. "What is it with men always needing to fix things?"

"It's a genetic defect from missing out on that all-important second X-chromosome," Evie chimes in.

Abbie smiles as she dries the stemware. "And my boys worry. Not that I'm meddling or sticking my nose where it doesn't belong, but Brody's never talked to me about a girl before. The fact he's talking at all makes me listen harder for the things he doesn't say."

"What doesn't he say?"

"Only that he believes your dream is to work in the corporate world, and that's a threat."

"A threat? How?"

"Because my middle son is smitten by you. He doesn't have a clue what to do about it. If he lets you go, he loses you. If he keeps you, he denies your dream."

"If he's anything like Asher," Evie jumps into the conversation, "you're going to have to help him along."

"Evie, dear, Asher needed no help when it came to you. From the moment he pulled you out of the fire, that boy was completely infatuated with you. Now Brody, on the other hand, has never not been in control when it comes to women. He doesn't know what to do with a girl like Grace."

"And what about Cage?" Evie leans her elbows on the counter and cups her chin on her hand. "I've never seen him with a girl."

"He's worse than the other two, always proving himself, but Cage is a wild child. I don't think he'll ever settle down, but two out of three isn't too bad."

We chat over the next hour while Abbie makes dinner. She still refuses to let me do any of the cooking, telling me she's going to take care of Mark and me until our grief settles.

By three in the afternoon, we say our goodbyes, which leaves me alone in the house. I'd tell Abbie I'm good and can cook for myself, but as far as grief setting in, that doesn't appear to be anytime soon.

THIRTY-SEVEN

# Grace

I AVOID GOING INTO MOM'S ROOM, FOR OBVIOUS REASONS, BUT I need to go through her things. A few days after her death, the company we leased the hospital bed from came and reclaimed the bed, which leaves a gaping hole in the room. Each time I step foot beyond the threshold, that empty space rips away another piece of my heart, reminding me she's no longer here.

Today, I vow to tackle her room, and while my grief remains a sharp, stabbing, white-hot poker of pain, it no longer overwhelms me all the time—just now and then—and randomly for any number of different reasons.

And of course, when I enter her room.

For the next three hours, I go through her belongings, setting things into piles. One is for the women's shelter; clothing to help women who find themselves victims of unfortunate circumstances. Another pile is trash, things that I can't donate or give away. A third, much smaller pile, are keepsakes, treasures I'm unwilling to part with at this time.

The last items go into a box, which I tape and place into the closet. In a month, I'll come back and see if they're still things I wish to keep.

The front door rattles as I heft the large plastic bag of donations on my shoulder.

"Grace?" Brody's strong voice calls out.

"In here." I struggle beneath the unwieldy burden as it shifts across my back.

"Hey, beautiful." Brody takes one look at me and grabs the bag. "Let me."

"Thanks." I brush back the loose hairs that fall in front of my eyes and grab the much smaller, more manageable bag destined for the trash.

"You cleaned out your mom's room?" Concern edges his voice, but also warmth, support, and love.

"I figured it was time. I'm working through it."

"How do you feel?" Brody's been incredibly supportive and protective. I'll find my strength, eventually. Until then, I'm thankful for his concern.

Our timing is bad. Right after we connect, in a rather explosive evening of the best sex I've ever had, Mom dies and derails everything.

"Sad, but okay. It needed to be done, or at least worked on. I guess it was time." And it feels good. It feels good to let go of Mom's earthly chains. That's how I think about all this stuff. They're anchors weighing her spirit down.

"I'm happy to hear that." His fingers curl around a stray lock of my hair, twirling it in a spiral. He tucks it behind my ear and pulls me tight against his chest. "I love when you smile."

I love when he touches me. There's been far too little of that since Mom passed.

Breathing in his masculine scent, my pulse jumps. His fingers twitch, caressing and seeking contact. I miss the warmth of his touch. Brody hasn't left my side since Mom died, and he hasn't sought out intimate contact following her death. He's giving me space to grieve.

I don't know if I need that space. It concerns me because it feels as if we're drifting apart. Will I lose him as a result?

His fingers stretch, barely touching me, seeking the slightest contact. My lips part, and I intend to tell him I'm ready for more than a tender caress, but then my voice tangles around a lump forming in my throat. My mother is dead.

A wave of grief slams into me.

His fingers twitch against my nape, uncertain yet concerned. He notices the change overcome me. I know what he's doing. Brody's waiting for me to initiate. The man might be a dominate partner in bed, but that dominance means his control is iron tight. Protecting me governs his every action, even if that means putting the brakes on our physical relationship.

The wave of grief unbalances me, but I wrap my arms around Brody's thick chest and wait for it to pass. If I don't control this, and deal with it, even more distance will grow between us. That's not what I want after we finally found each other again.

"Come on." Brody takes the second bag from me and carries them both outside.

"The small one is trash." I wipe at my tears. "The other is for the shelter."

"Gotcha." He strides over to the trashcan and deposits the smaller bag inside of it. Then he puts the other bag in the trunk of his car. Brody extends a hand. "Come here."

I don't hesitate and run into his arms. He wraps one strong arm around my back. His hand goes to my head, where he draws his fingers through my hair. Damn, but I miss our intimacy. Maybe it's time to change that.

Am I ready?

My breathing slows as he strokes my hair. Each time he breathes in, I take a breath with him and curl against his much larger frame, snuggling into his arms.

"One day at a time. I promise it gets better." He walks me to the passenger side of his car and opens the door. "It's a great day for a drive."

He's right. We're coming into harvest season, which means the unrelenting summer heat slowly gives way to the cooler temperatures of fall. While I figure we're only going for a drive into Napa to drop off the donations, Brody surprises me, taking us on the back roads for an early evening drive. He lowers the top on his Porsche, and we drive with the wind whipping through my hair.

Whether from the sunlight dappling through the trees, or the clear, fresh air rushing over me, something lifts within me. A smile fills my face as I lean back and let the sun kiss my skin. The harrowing grief eases its hold, and I breathe.

We stop at the shelter and I stay in the car while Brody takes the donations inside. When he climbs back inside, he looks at me.

"Where to?"

It's Friday, and I have nowhere I need to be, but I know one man who needs me. "What about heading into the city?"

"Don't you need to be here?"

"Not really. Mark's got the crews working. He doesn't need me looking over his shoulder." Brody stiffens at the mention of Mark. "Something wrong?"

"No." He gives a sharp shake of his head. "Don't you want to check in on him and see what he's up to?"

"Not really. He's got his way of doing things and I don't want to mess with that by hovering."

"You're his boss." His voice hardens. "You should be familiar with all aspects of your business."

"I'm familiar enough. Besides, I trust Mark."

Brody's grip on the wheel tightens and the muscles of his jaw bunch. "I know you trust him; I was just thinking how new you are to the business. He might have a lot to teach you."

"True, and I will someday. I just don't want to step on his toes, or worse."

"What's worse?"

"Remind him that his niece is now his boss."

"How does that work, anyway?"

"What do you mean?"

"Why wasn't the winery split equally between him and your mom?"

"He was sixteen when my grandparents died. Mom was twenty-one. She became his guardian and took over sole-proprietorship of Atwood Estates. When he turned eighteen, she gave him forty-percent interest. It's what my grandparents wanted. Why?"

"It's only that splitting assets like that can create friction between siblings."

"Well, that's why I'm not interested in hovering over Mark. He's been at this for years. I don't want any friction now that I'm technically his boss, although we're more like partners."

"Mark mentioned he offered to buy you out."

"He did, and it was an incredibly generous offer."

"Was it?"

"Yeah, two million to sign everything over and walk away."

"Two million?" Brody grinds the words out. "And, why didn't you? I can't imagine owning a vineyard is what you imagined when you got your business degree."

"It wasn't. Not even close, but I have it now."

"And?"

"And what?"

"Are you thinking about selling?"

"Truthfully, I think about that a lot. If it didn't mean draining Mark's retirement, I'd take his offer. Now that we're working with your firm, it feels different."

"Is it different because of me? Because of us?"

"Not you, actually, and not us." I place my hand on his thigh and give it a little squeeze. "You're an unexpected… Well, unexpected everything, but the business is different."

"How?"

"Because it's a puzzle I get to work on, like a challenge. You know, taking Atwood Estates from the brink of bankruptcy to something sustainable and profitable? It's a challenge, but I can make it work."

"I'm glad you feel that way, and not because my company is investing in your success, but for more personal reasons."

"Personal reasons?" I squirm in my seat. I haven't forgotten he admitted he loved me, and I'm foolish enough, or hopeful enough, to believe the two of us have a chance of making things work. Abbie's words also whisper in my head.

He places his hand over mine and slowly moves it closer to his groin. "Yes, very personal reasons." Brody stops short and lifts my hand to his mouth. "I'm not interested in seeing you leave, but if that's what you need, or want, I support your dreams. I never want to be the one who stands in the way of you doing what you love."

"Why would you think I'd want to leave?"

"You're not the only one with doubts about us. Just when I find you, I worry you've been saddled with this tremendous burden. That it's stifling your dreams, and our business dealings are a part of that. Obviously, I don't want you to leave, which makes me incredibly selfish, but I love you enough to want you to be happy. I want you to pursue *your* dreams and not settle for the ones thrust upon you." His tone turns serious. "If you want out, say the word."

Want out? I don't want out. Exactly the opposite. I want in, deep inside Brody's life. If I give up Atwood Estates, how does that happen?

"Brody," my voice drops to a whisper, "is this your way of getting rid of me?"

There it is, my self-doubt. That voice in my head reminds me Brody is one of the most eligible bachelors in the country. Women fall over themselves trying to get to him.

"What?" The car swerves as he accidentally yanks the steering wheel to the right when his whole body turns toward me. A horn honks at us and he yanks us back into our lane. "That's not what I meant." He reaches across and places his hand on my leg, just above my knee. His fingers curl inward as his jaw clenches.

"Brody, you're hurting me."

"Shit." He releases my leg and runs a shaky hand through his hair. "I love you, Grace." His gaze darts to me, then shifts back to the crowded freeway. After that swerve, he slows down to seventy-five, and now all the cars whiz past us going eighty or more. "I want you to stay, and I've been thinking about nothing else since your mother's death, but I'm scared you don't want to stay. I'm terrified you'll leave me."

"You're scared I'll leave you?"

"Yes." He tucks his chin to his chest.

"The indomitable Brody La Rouge?"

"It's all I can think about."

"Is that why you've been hands-off?"

"I've been hands-off out of respect." His words rumble out of him in a growl. "Because I'm a gentleman who's worried sick about his girlfriend."

Girlfriend?

My heart skips a beat and a tiny thrill runs through me. I know what I want.

"I was thinking we could go out for dinner, spend the weekend doing silly tourist things, but I think you need to take me back to your place."

"And why's that?" His fingers curl over the steering wheel, tightening and releasing as his breaths deepen.

"Because…" Hesitation overcomes me.

Telling him what I need—what I want—places me in a delicate position, but really? Who am I kidding?

It's time to bring back the heat between us.

He brings up a lot of good points, talking about my dreams, my future, and the things I want. When I think about it, my heart steps in and reminds me to feel.

Brody loves me, and I'm pretty damn sure I love him too. Even when I hated him, my unrequited love simmered in the background. No way around it, I need Brody in my life. I need him just as much as I need air to breathe.

"Use your words, Grace." The change in his voice to that low throaty rumble turns my insides to mush and highjacks my senses, sending them on an adrenaline-fueled rush of wanton lust and heady desire. Somehow, he flicks a switch in my brain.

Immediately, I'm aware of him in a way I wasn't moments before. His body takes up more space. His muscles appear more pronounced, more powerful, more dominating. He's in control. The rasp of his breath proclaims he's all male.

An aroused, virile, male.

"What do you want?" He turns his steely gaze on me, and there's no sign of any gentleman in there. The atmosphere between us shifts, turning primal and heating up with every breath.

I need the Brody who makes my mind come to a stop. The man who flips the switch inside my head. I need the man who lets me ignore the rest of the world and allows me to do nothing other than feel.

Right now, I need to feel him.

He says nothing for a long moment, and the way he taps his finger on the steering wheel drives me insane. What is he thinking? Are we on the same page? Or is he still going to shelter and protect me, too concerned that my grief will overwhelm me and force him to be that gentleman?

But he seems to make a decision. Brody glances over at me, capturing my gaze. Fire burns in those amazing green eyes of his. Lust rolls outward with his desire to take and claim.

"What's your word, Grace?" He takes in a deep breath.

I bite my lower lip and drop my gaze. Folding my hands in his lap, I fiddle with my fingers, twisting them together as the entire atmosphere between us shifts to something heady and potent, sensual and sex-fueled. He intoxicates me.

"Look at me."

My gaze travels the long path to his face, lingering over the growing evidence of his arousal, which tents his pants. From there, my gaze climbs up his hardened physique, where I finally reach the determined set of his jaw. It's there where I land on the simmering heat of his gaze.

"What's your word?"

My entire body trembles, growing more excited by the second. I need this. I need to fall apart in his hands.

"Red. My word is red."

Until I say that word again, or until he's done with me, my fate lies in Brody's hands. I can't help but shift in my seat as a ripple of excitement shoots through me.

# THIRTY-EIGHT

# Brody

Dominance. Power. Control.

Submission. Respect. Trust.

Two sides of a coin.

I ask Grace for permission, and she puts herself into my hands. It's a tremendous gift. A terrible responsibility. It's a precious burden and everything I crave.

Since her mother died, I pulled back to give her space to grieve. Things have been hard on Grace, obviously, but it's been a struggle for me as well. Banking my desires to stand by her side, and be the support she needs, is necessary. It's what I signed up for, but that doesn't mean my desire for her is gone. It doesn't mean any of this is easy.

If anything, my desire grows with each passing day. I need Grace. I need to comfort her, to protect her—and hell, I need to fuck her.

I can't help it.

I'm not convinced intimacy is what she needs, but I'm happy she's thinking about something more than simply falling asleep in my arms. In all honesty, the best part of my day is when I get to curl around her tiny body and feel her ass press against my groin. It's silly, but I crave that physical, but non-sexual, intimacy. I don't care that it arouses me and leaves me aching. I simply enjoy the connection.

To be there for her is an overwhelming rush, and to know she seeks solace in my arms is mind-blowing. That depth of trust isn't something I've experienced before. It's sobering and shocking. I lock my arms around her and provide as much strength as I can. I only hope it's enough.

Her body twitches as the mood shifts between us, turning dark, sultry, and combustible. My body reacts, instinctually, when she responds to my demand.

*Red.*

She says *red*, which means I control what happens next, either until she says red again, or until I'm finished. What I want isn't sex, at least not immediately. She needs to know I'm here for her, no matter what, and whatever physical needs I have come second to her general well-being.

She peeks at me when she thinks I'm not looking. Her eyes pool with curiosity and round with anticipation. Her breathing kicks up a notch, becoming more shallow as she squirms in her seat. My girl is turned on.

Perhaps sex is exactly what she needs. Not soft and cozy, but hard and unrelenting.

I can do that.

But is this what she needs?

Breathing in her scent, I command my brain to focus on the road. The last thing we need is to get in a wreck because I'm fixated on how I'm going to fuck her first.

*My sweet and sexy, Grace, tonight I'm going to make you fly.*

Unfortunately, we're still some distance out. I thought to delay things, take her out to dinner and let the sexual tension between us build, but after a few minutes, Grace grows bold. She reaches across and places her hand on my thigh. I glance down and weigh the pros and cons of allowing this, but my little minx is two steps ahead of me. Her fingers brush against my groin, finding me hard and aroused.

She said *Red*.

Grace gave me control.

"Be careful." I huff out a laugh. "I'm driving."

"I know." Her fingers don't stop. They grow bolder, stroking along my shaft as my pants grow tighter by the second.

My hips jerk as the stimulation awakens my need. My fist captures her wrist with an unbending grip meant to grab her attention.

"Maybe I should be more direct with my commands." My grip tightens until a tiny yelp escapes her pert little mouth. "Safety first, my girl, and since you're so entranced with my cock, that's the first thing you'll take care of when we arrive." Her fingers lift away from my straining arousal, and I make a show of putting her hand back in her lap. "Hands to yourself. Remember, you're not the one in charge."

*I'm in charge, Grace Atwood. You gave me this power. You demanded I take it, and I'm relishing it.*

Redness creeps into her cheeks, and I swallow a low moan. This woman is going to be the death of me. All I can think about is thrusting into her silky, wet heat and losing my mind inside of her as I seek oblivion. But I know what she needs, the escape she craves, and that's exactly what she'll get.

There's the matter of my restraint because there won't be any when I finally get her alone. Which, considering her wandering hands, will work out to my advantage.

As I plan out our evening, we close in on my building. I pull into my spot in the parking garage and unbuckle. Turning toward Grace, I take in a deep breath. My next breath determines our future. Am I the man she needs?

"What's your word?"

This is a test.

"I already told you." She practically snorts.

"Excuse me?"

Her eyes roll, and I suppress a smile.

"Nevertheless, say it," I press for her consent, because that's what a man does. She's my responsibility. I don't take that lightly.

"There's no reason to say it." She commits, without committing, but I need a solid green light if we're to proceed. I demand this, as is my right.

Not my right.

It's my goddam responsibility. Nothing moves forward without her express consent. Her permission is what makes this work.

"Don't play games with me. Say it."

I love how her lashes flutter on her cheeks. It's intoxicating. That's the kind of power which makes this unsafe, but I'll never jeopardize Grace's safety. I'll make her uneasy, which is a part of the fantasy, but I'll never put her in the position of being unsafe.

"Just do it." She huffs with frustration.

"You sure about that? Because I'm not going to hold back."

"I know." She curls her lower lip between her teeth and coyly peeks up at me through her lashes.

"Then say it. Give me the goddamn green light." My molars grind together, demanding she commit.

"My mom's dead, and I'm drowning. Can you just get me out of my head?"

"Say it." This isn't something I'll force.

"You've got the green light. Can you please stop being so considerate and just take me out of my head?"

Not sure what overcomes me, but my pulse explodes. I leap out of the car and race around to her door, where I yank her out of her seat and press her forcibly against my car. She gives a yelp as my fists close around her tiny wrists, controlling her, dominating her, and turning her on. Leaning into her, I lay the full weight of my body against her, trapping her in place as I focus two-hundred plus pounds of male hunger on her body.

"Is this what you want?"

A whimper escapes her, which fuels my lust and sends heat shooting to my groin. Fully erect, I tamp down the irrational urge to spin her around and take her right here, but there are too many cameras and too many eyes in the parking garage. Instead, I lean in close and whisper in her ear.

"You're mine." I draw back enough to scan her expression, wondering if she fully understands that truth. I lean against her again, letting the full length of my erection jab at her from behind the prison of my pants. "Do you understand?"

Her head bobs, but I need words. I need her consent. A growl at the back of my throat gets her attention.

"Yes."

"You'll do as I say?"

"Y-yes."

"Promise me."

"I promise."

"And anytime you wish to stop…"

"I'll say my word."

"Good." My grip tightens until she gives a tiny mewl of discomfort. A thrill runs through me. "Follow me."

With those words, I drag her into the elevator. Keeping my hands off her hot body proves nearly impossible but, somehow, I manage. What happens next is for us, and us alone. I don't need some perverted security officer getting an eyeful of what I plan to do to my girl.

The moment we get through my door, all my restraint falls away. My hands are on her, ripping away her clothing, baring her creamy skin to my assault. I grab her, stroke her—hell, I practically maul her as I pin her against the wall.

Initially, my thoughts were to put her on her knees, to suck me off, payback for the stroking she attempted in the car, but that gives her too much control. If she wants to get out of her head for a bit, I know exactly what she needs.

I divest her of her clothing, and spin her to face the wall. She wants it hard, dominating, and rough. There's nothing like giving a woman what she wants. I reach down and free my cock.

Pinning her to the wall, I stab past her silky opening. All it takes is one thrust and I spear her to the hilt. She cries out in surprise, and I pause, checking to make sure I'm not too rough, but her pained gasp morphs into a moan of ecstasy.

A strangled groan sounds deep in the back of my throat as I embrace the ferocity she needs. Rocking against her, I thrust hard, burying myself as deeply as I can. Her body relaxes, and I pick up speed, ravaging and digging deeper, while grunting in her ear. This is what she wants, to see me unhinged, and I plan on giving Grace everything she wants and so much more.

I fuck her, driving myself in. Pulling out. My hands are everywhere, giving her no respite as I stroke and maul and ravage, all the while immobilizing her to give her the illusion of force. Although, this is the deepest expression of my love.

My strokes turn slippery as she grows wetter and wetter. I jerk out, slam forward, and build a damaging rhythm. She's right there with me, writhing before me, moving sensually as her need overwhelms her.

Fully engaged in this, both physically and emotionally, I fuck her with passion and let the fire between us build. Each time I slam forward, I imagine filling her with the force of my entire being, making her feel me from the inside out. My goal is to take over her body and delve deep into her core, where we'll latch onto one another and become one.

"Give me your mouth," I shout at her and twist her neck, forcing her to meet my mouth. Her taste floods my senses as my fevered tongue spears past her lips. With our mouths locked together, I pump harder, bury myself deeper, and nail her against the wall.

Suddenly, she cries out, her entire body shaking as pleasure rips through her.

Fucking incredible.

No way did I think she would come first, not when I'm unable to control myself. As her body pulses around my cock, I come unhinged. I lurch outward and ram back in as heat gathers in my groin and shoots out through my cock.

Only then do I realize my mistake.

"Holy shit. Fuck. Fuck." I try to stop, but it's too late. My hips thrust mercilessly until I groan with poisonous pleasure. "I'm sorry. I'm so fucking sorry." I bury my face in the crook of her neck as the full realization of what I did sinks in. "Christ, please tell me you're on the pill."

"I'm not." Her body stills as I pull out and handle her much more gently than moments before. Now that my fury is spent, there are other things to consider; the ramifications of my actions and how to salvage this situation.

"Any chance it's not the middle of your cycle?" My lips twist as I gently, softly, spin her around. I press my forehead against hers and admit my error. "No condom."

"Oh." She nibbles on her lower lip. "I—uh… Maybe we'll be okay? I'm clean, just had my annual physical a month ago."

"I always use condoms and test once a year. I'm not worried about STDs, Grace. I'm worried about…"

"Something that may or may not happen." Worry tugs at the corners of her mouth and pinches in her expression. I guess we were both too caught up in the moment to think about our actions. Although ultimately, this is my fault. I pull her to my chest and wrap my arms around her, holding her tight.

"Not that it matters."

"Why do you say that?" Her body stiffens and I realize my mistake.

"Only that if we happened to make a kid just now, it doesn't matter. I'm never leaving you. You're my forever."

"What does that mean?"

"I'm putting a ring on your finger."

"Because you may, or may not, have put a baby in me?" She draws back. "That's not a good enough reason for marriage."

"That's not the only reason. Baby, no baby, it doesn't matter. I love you, and I'm making you mine. Fight me all you want, but that's the way it's going to be. Forever means marriage and children. I want both, with you."

"Brody?" Her eyes well up with tears.

"Yes?"

"If that's a marriage proposal, it's the absolute worst one in history."

"Probably, but what do you say? Wanna get hitched?"

She slaps me playfully and squirms out of my grip. "I'm not answering that until you're down on one knee."

"Hunny, the only person who's going to be on their knees tonight is you."

Her eyes round and flare with desire. "Promises, promises."

# THIRTY-NINE

## Grace

———————

Brody follows through on his promises, all right. After that crazy, intense, wild, and insane fuck against the wall, he turns his attention to me, drowning me in so much pleasure I'm positive I won't survive the night. He lays me on the bed and sends me flying with the magic of his tongue. If he has neighbors, they're either calling the cops from all my screaming or giving Brody high-fives.

After the toe-curling orgasm, Brody turns me over and subjects me to his abject adoration as he treats me to a full body massage. Skilled fingers dig and knead at tight muscles until I'm limp as a noodle and drifting in a fog of pleasure. Hard turns to soft as his fingers dance along my skin making goose bumps pop up wherever they go. When I nod off, the heat of his mouth replaces the fingers, and I find myself shaking and shivering as he makes tender love to me.

We order in food when our stomachs growl and take a break to watch a sappy movie while demolishing pizza and wings. When I think we're finally headed to bed, Brody turns deliciously dominant again and orders me to my knees—as previously promised—where it's my turn to make him come unglued. With hands and mouth, I make his toes curl and body shake as I draw out his pleasure.

In the shower, he takes the soap from me, controlling the situation there as well. With sudsy bubbles, hot water, and tons of steam, he fingers me to another earth-shattering orgasm, then cradles me in his lap as the water pours down on us.

We talk about everything and nothing, enjoying the connection blossoming between us. The past comes up, and I wrap my arms around him, forgiving him for mistakes made when we were far too young.

Snuggling in his embrace, my eyes close as the steady *thump, thump, thump* of his heart sounds beneath my ear. That's what I think of when I think of him, rock steady. My fingers splay across his chest, enjoying tracing out the cuts and grooves of his defined musculature. He's the epitome of masculine beauty, and I take advantage of every second I'm with him.

"This feels good." There's no rush to do anything or be anywhere. It's as if the world doesn't exist outside this moment.

"I love you, Grace Atwood, and you will be my wife." His cocky demeanor returns, bringing a smile to my face.

"I will, will I?"

"Yes, and we'll have kids; if not as a result of tonight, then later. I want everything with you."

"And what about Atwood Estates?"

"What do you mean?"

"There's no way you're going to commute into the city each day. Where will we live?"

"I assumed it would be at your place. If that's not what you want, I can get a bigger place here. What about the vineyard? What are the chances you'll sell it?"

I curl my lower lip. "I don't really know."

A frown creases his forehead. He looks away, staring into the corner of the shower, and takes in a deep breath.

"What's wrong?" It's an odd shift in mood for him, especially since I'm naked and sitting in his lap.

"It's not important right now."

"Not as important as this?" I give a little wiggle and laugh at the way he responds, growing hard and stiff for me once again.

He holds back a groan as I roll my hips in a sensuous grind, no longer pretending I'm trying to get into a more comfortable position. Really, I'm messing with him, literally trying to get a rise out of him.

He lifts me up, freeing his rigid length, then slowly lowers me down the hard shaft. "God, that feels good. Warm and tight." His low, throaty moan makes my skin burn and tighten.

Answering heat simmers in my blood as my nerve endings sizzle and my body shakes. He kisses me and lets his hands roam. Every lick, every touch, burns through me. My entire body shakes as our bodies connect. Brody makes me believe in forever, showing me he's changed and that he wants me.

Forever.

I keep waiting to get smacked back into reality, where I realize he's only been playing me to get something he wants, but I can't deny our connection. He's not lying about how he feels about me.

And the man definitely knows how to make love to a woman. All heat and masculine virility, his stamina is impressive, not to mention daunting. Yet when he flips to dominant mode, plundering and claiming with his fury unleashed, he becomes undeniably sexy and powerful, and—Oh my God—euphoric.

Heat coils within me, tightening and tightening, until it releases in a rapturous wave. My head tips back as another strangled scream escapes me. Brody thrusts up with his hips as I lose control, taking me swiftly over the edge where I fall apart in his arms.

He follows shortly after, driving upwards like a piston until his release overtakes him. We sit there for a few moments, breathing each other in, touching, exploring, melding our souls.

A yawn escapes me, and I cover my mouth.

"Sorry."

"Don't be. Do you have any idea what time it is?"

"None at all."

"It's three in the morning, luv. How about we get some sleep and pick up where we left off in the morning?"

"Sounds fabulous." Another yawn escapes me, and then another.

Sedate, and well-fucked, I'm ready to fall asleep in his arms. It's the best part of my day. Well, next to waking up in his arms. That's pretty damn awesome too.

We snuggle in bed, giggling as we launch into a tickle fight. I lose. He wins. He fucks me again. Great night.

I wake to a gentle nudge on my shoulder.

"Hey, sweetie." His sleepy voice sounds like marbles rolling against each other.

"Ugh, go back to bed."

"Wish I could, but I've got to go into the office for a bit. Breakfast is on the counter, and I promise to be back by noon."

"Um, okay." I flop over to my belly and pull the pillow over my head.

"Grace…" He calls out to me, and I groan.

"Let me sleep."

"I will. When I get back, we need to talk."

"About the condom thing?" I roll to my side and peek up at him. "Fingers crossed."

"Which side are you leaning toward, baby or no baby? Because I'll take either one."

"Fingers crossed, I'm not preggers, but I guess it doesn't matter."

"No. I suppose it doesn't." The bed dips as he sits on the edge of the mattress. "I need to talk with you about Mark."

"Mark?"

"Yeah."

"Why?"

"We'll talk when I get back. Okay?"

"Okay."

"Now, go to sleep." He palms my head and gives it a playful shake.

"That's what I've been trying to do, but you keep talking to me."

"Fine. I'm leaving. Be back soon, beautiful."

"Yeah, yeah." I give a half-hearted flap of my hand and roll back to my belly.

Brody gathers his things and gives me a kiss goodbye as I snuggle into the covers and drift back to sleep.

A little after eleven, I finally drag myself from bed and take a shower to wake up. Brody's not back, which means I get to snoop. Not that I should. Snooping is bad, but when will I get a chance like this again? I want to see how he lives.

Mom used to say you could tell a lot about a person from the way they keep their home.

I pause and cock my head. That's the first time I thought about Mom without feeling an intense wave of grief. Wow, I just might see my way through this.

Mom would want me to be happy, and I'm going to try hard to honor her wish. She also used to say the only thing I needed to know about life are the three C's: choices, chances, and changes. *'You have to make a choice and take a chance to change your life.'*

*Well, Mom, I'm choosing to take a chance on Brody, and I hope that changes my life in a good way.* A thrill of excitement runs through me.

Eleven years ago, I never would've thought I'd wake up in Brody's bed after a night of intense sex, and I most certainly didn't think I'd be considering a future with him. My hand drifts to my belly, where I wonder about what the next nine months may, or may not, bring.

Honestly, I want children, but I'm not certain now is the best time. Although, I'm almost twenty-six and Brody's nearly thirty. If we want kids, sooner isn't such a bad idea.

I look through the drawers of Brody's dresser and put on one of his well-worn t-shirts. Nothing else. Then I meander around his apartment, curious as to how *normal* it seems. One of the country's most eligible bachelors, on track to becoming the next billionaire, his apartment is modest, reflecting nothing of his wealth.

It is on the top floor, but I wouldn't call it a penthouse, and it's only got two bedrooms. His place is spacious, however, taking up half of the top floor. The rest of the apartment is an open-flow design, with a gourmet kitchen, no skimping there, a smallish living room with a phenomenal view, a modest dining area, and there's a small alcove he obviously uses as a home office.

The decor is simple, clean lines, monochromatic gray with pops of blue to draw the eye. Steel, glass, and leather, it's utilitarian, masculine, and surprisingly cozy.

He's a neat freak. Either that or he has a maid. From what I know about Brody, I'm guessing he's the reason there's no dust on the hardwood floor, nothing under the couch, and not a speck in the corners. And yes, I checked.

I look everywhere. If I'm going to snoop, I'm going to do it right. Which brings me to the end of my tour of Brody's apartment, his office. It has a large desk, which is great to get fucked on. There's a man-sized leather chair with all kinds of gizmos for comfort. Sparsely decorated bookshelves with stunning photographs taken from all around the world sit on the far wall. I'm guessing those are from Cage.

His desk is clean, no piles of stuff scattered about. It's so clean, I wonder whether Brody suffers from a little closet OCD. If so, it wasn't enough to clean up after some vigorous sex last night. Thoughts of him bending me over this desk, and what ensued, sends licks of pleasure to my girly-bits. That man knows how to take a woman, but even better, he knows how to rut. Damn but I love when he comes completely unglued.

Scattered on the floor, opposite where he ravaged me, are several folders. Guilt gnaws at me for making the mess, and I decide tidying up isn't technically snooping. While I try not to peek at his personal things, one name jumps out at me.

Atwood Estates.

It doesn't occur to me not to look. I just do, and my eyes round as I scan the document, and my heart squeezes with pain.

How could he?

"Grace?"

I spin around. "What's this?" I don't care that I shouldn't have looked and go on the defensive, thrusting the folder toward him. "You're looking at selling Atwood Estates? Shopping for buyers? Is this the kind of business you run?"

I'm well aware of the terms of our contract with Sterling Enterprises. In a year's time, if they're not satisfied, written in the small print, Sterling Enterprises can exercise an option to sell the business to recoup their losses.

"Calm down." He holds up his hands. "We need to talk about this."

"Brody, there's not one goddam time in human history where the words *calm down* succeeded in calming anyone down." My fingers clench around the folder and crumple the contents inside. "You invest in companies, seeking weakness and opportunity, only to sell them later at a profit? Was this your game all along? Fuck me, literally and figuratively? Then discard me and move on?"

"Now, hold on." He takes a step forward, but my voice rises.

"Stay right where you are," I shout and point my finger at him. "We're done."

"No. We're not done." He says it with confidence and conviction. I almost believe him, but we're totally done.

"You were a player in high school, and you're still a goddamn player now. So, you were going to fuck with me for a year, watch me lose my business, then steal it out from under me?"

"Not me, but someone does want to steal it."

"If not you," I sneer, "then who?" Boiling hot, I rage at him. All I can think about is poking his eyes out, kicking him in the balls, or worse. There has to be something worse.

Cutting his dick off!

"Grace." His voice shifts to a lower register, the one that makes me weak in the knees and soft in the head, "I need you to listen."

I give a shake, unwilling to let him command me and somehow control this situation. My mind spins with what I'm going to do. How am I going to get home? Brody drove me, and Napa is way too far for a taxi.

"I'm done listening to you." I may not know how I'm getting home, but there's no way I'm staying here. Unfortunately, he's between me and my clothes, which are scattered all over his apartment. Collecting them is going to take time.

As far as storming out of here, that's a no-go, but I don't have to speak to him. In a huff, I hurl the folder with the purchase proposal at his face and duck around him. Only he's faster than me. Stronger than me. Brody grips my arms and backs me up against the wall.

"Goddamn it, Grace, I want you to listen." The muscles of his jaw bunch.

"Let me go."

"Not until you listen." His grip tightens as he makes his stand. He won't let up until I listen to whatever bullshit he has to say.

I stare into his eyes, where I see fear for the first time in my life, and I make my move. It's one word. One word to end everything.

He knows I'm going to say it before the word slips out of my mouth. Brody releases me like he's been shot. He takes a shuddering step backward and shakes his head.

"Don't. Don't do it, Grace."

But I do. My mind's made up, and I can't believe I fell for a man who used me once and only wants to steal from me now.

"Red."

"Grace—you don't mean that." All the color drains from his face as I shake my head.

"Either give me the keys to your car, or take me home."

His gaze drops to my midsection. With a shake of his head, he spins around and walks into the living room. "Get dressed. I'll take you home, but don't think for a second this is over."

"I said Red."

"I know exactly what you said, and I'll respect it. When you're ready, we're going to talk about what you think you saw."

Our gazes lock, but I meet the ferocity of his stare with incredible strength. No tears. No cracking. He blinks first, and I win.

In less than five minutes, I'm dressed and headed down to the garage with a very silent Brody beside me.

# FORTY

# Brody

---

THE DRUMMING OF MY FINGERS ANNOYS GRACE, BUT I DON'T STOP. For over two hours, we slog through heavier than usual traffic headed out of the city. It's the weekend rush and we're caught in the middle of it.

Grace gives another sniff, follows it with a huff, but doesn't say one damn word.

That's okay. She'll crack.

I'd fill the silence with words, words which explain what she thinks she saw, but she cut off any communication for the foreseeable future. *Red* means nothing outside of sex, but it's important enough that I honor it. Trust is an issue with Grace, and I won't do anything to weaken it further. Instead, I tap on the steering wheel because it bugs the shit out of her.

"Will you stop that?" She gives another huff and glares at the steering wheel.

"Will you speak to me?"

Grace shifts her attention back out the window while I control my frustration. This no speaking thing frustrates me, and I'm moving from frustration to full-on anger.

We pull off I-80 and head towards Napa. If anything, traffic gets worse. Now we're nearly at a standstill, crawling past vineyards and cow farms. My fingers curl around the steering wheel and tighten. Seconds from blowing my cool, I make a decision.

"We're talking about what you saw."

Her back stiffens; talk about being prickly.

"I have nothing to say to you."

"That's totally fine with me, you just need to listen."

She makes a show of rolling her eyes and shaking her head. "I said Red. That means we're done."

"We're far from over, and if you could pull your head out of your ass and listen for a second, you'll understand why."

"I don't want to talk about it."

"I get it, but I have something to say. Then we'll talk about what's happening now and why."

"What's happening now is we're breaking up. Why is because you're no different than you were in high school. This is just another way to fuck me over."

"We're not breaking up. I said you're mine, and you're mine."

"That means shit."

"As for why, I've changed, but I can see how difficult that can be for you to believe. Trust isn't our strong suit as a couple, but you can trust me. I've changed."

"Bullshit."

"The only bullshit going on is the shit deal your Uncle Mark is trying to make." Her mouth opens, but no words come out. I finally got her attention. "Cage found that folder the day your mother died. It was in your uncle's office. He knows what that land is worth. I believe he's been sabotaging your business for years, letting it slowly fail. Once it does, he's hoping you'll be desperate to sell and walk away. One of two things will happen then. Either Atwood Estates will make a miraculous comeback, or he'll walk away with a cool ten million. I have a feeling I know which is more likely to happen."

"That's not true."

"He's been systematically undermining your business, skimming off the top, and diverting your crop to force a sustained loss. He wants you to sell to him for pennies on the dollar."

"I don't believe you."

"Then talk to Asher. He's been looking into it."

"Why didn't you tell me sooner?"

"Because the day we found that, you lost your mother. It wasn't exactly a good time to bring up the fact that Mark's been embezzling from you and that he already has an offer for the land. I told you I wanted to talk with you about Mark. You finally seemed to be in a place where I could approach you with this. That proposal is what I wanted to discuss. I've hidden nothing from you. I've taken nothing from you."

"He wouldn't do that to me." Her voice gets small and meek.

"You sure about that? How else do you explain that offer? Asher says your yield is eighty percent what it should be based on what's hanging on the vine. I trust Asher with my life, and he knows what he's doing. Why do you think I asked you to check in on Mark? See what's going on with his side of the business. But more importantly, his offer, is he offering to buy you out of your share of the business, the land, or both?"

"Why does that matter?"

"Come on, Grace. You're smarter than this. That land is worth millions. Mark's trying to take advantage of you."

"It's not true."

"Then talk to Mark. Ask him. If he wants you to sell out your interest in the business, make a decision whether you want to keep Atwood Estates running, but tell him you're not selling the land. See what happens. Whether you believe me or not, doesn't matter. I'm right. Do what you need to do."

FORTY-ONE

# Grace

_______



Those words repeat over and over in my head. I need to believe them. The alternative sucks because Mark would never do anything like that to me. Not once in my life did Mom hint at conflict between them. Something else is going on.

But what if Brody's right?

I stare out the window, pointedly ignoring him. He continues tapping on the steering wheel—it's annoying as fuck—but I don't give him the satisfaction of letting him know it bugs me.

When he pulls up outside my house, I open the door before we come to a full stop. Brody reaches for the buckle of his seat belt, but I give a sharp shake of my head.

"You're not coming inside."

"Grace…" his jaw clamps shut, "we're not finished."

"I need space."

"You know I'm right."

"I don't know what's right, but I know what's wrong. You should've brought this to my attention the day you found out instead of keeping it to yourself for weeks."

"I…"

I hold up a hand. "I don't care why you did it or that you feel somehow justified because you felt I was too *overcome with grief* to deal with it. You don't get to decide that for me."

"And what about Mark? Are you going to talk with him?"

"I'm going to do whatever I feel is right. I know you're used to being in control and like to take charge of everything, but this is my business, not yours."

"It's very much my business. This is what people do when they're together. They watch out for the other person, protect them, shield them; they support them."

"Not like this."

"My intentions…"

"I don't care what your intentions are or aren't. You don't get to decide what I can and can't handle."

"I only meant to protect you."

"It doesn't feel like that."

"Then maybe you do need time. Think it through, and you'll see everything I've done was done to protect you."

"That may be, but I need to know I can count on you to be honest with me. That I can depend on you to tell me the truth, not because you decide whether I can handle it, but because it's the right thing to do. It's what couples do for each other. If I can't trust you…"

"I'm coming in."

"No. You're not. You're going to drive away and trust that I know how to handle my own life."

"And do what? You can't keep me away, not after last night. I meant every word." His green gaze blazes like fire, fueled by the intensity of his love. "You are mine, to protect, to cherish, and to love."

I see it. I hear it. And I should let all this go, but the truth is I don't trust that Brody won't hurt me again. My fears are rooted deep, and I don't know how to be free of them. I need time to sort it all out, especially after last night. But first, there's the issue of Mark.

"As for last night…" I take in a deep breath and let it out slowly. "I don't want to rush into something because I may, or may not, be pregnant. That's not a good enough reason."

"I love you. That's the best reason, and you said you loved me. You can't run from what's happening between us."

"No, but I can put it on pause. Don't call me. I'll call you. As for Sterling Enterprises, excuse yourself. Sign over our account to some junior executive who can use the experience. I can't work with you and remain objective."

The muscles tic in his jaw as he clamps his teeth tight together. "And how long is this *pause* going to last?" He's not happy. Tension coils in his entire body, and I sense he's a moment from losing control.

"I don't know."

"If you talk to Mark, you'll know what I've said is the truth."

"Whether it is, or isn't, there's still the matter of keeping this from me." I run my fingers through my hair to hide the way my hand shakes.

"I did it because I was concerned."

"Stop." I hold out my hand, palm facing him. "I told you I'm not in a good place where I can talk this out. Please, just drive away. Give me the space I need." I hate the way my voice shakes. Sending Brody away is perhaps the hardest thing I've ever done. It feels all kinds of wrong, but I need to be sure.

I need to not just see it or hear it. I need to feel his words are true, and I hate that I don't. The doubts swirling in my head are poisonous.

He curls his lower lip and stares out the front window. "My assistant will contact you on Monday with the name of the person who will be taking over your account."

"Thank you."

His green gaze cuts to me. "I'm not losing you over something like this. Not after…" His lips press together, and his Adam's apple bobs with a hard swallow.

"I'll call you when I'm ready." Those may be the hardest words I've had to say in a very long time. "I promise." Before he can say anything else, I spin around and head inside.

The car doesn't move for several long moments, but the crunching of tires over gravel finally signifies his departure. It takes a while before I stop shaking, then it's time to sit down and do some hard thinking.

Mom and Mark, half-siblings who ran a relatively successful business up until a few years ago, loved each other, or so I thought. The things Brody said might be true, but how do I confirm it without tipping my hand to Mark?

And that's the rub right there.

I believe Brody.

My faith should be in my uncle. Instead, Brody's truth is the one I believe.

But I do my own digging. That begins with a phone call to Asher, who confirms everything Brody mentioned. Somehow, Mark's been shuttling crop harvested from the fields and diverting it elsewhere.

But where?

For the rest of the afternoon, I look through the books, tracking every penny. With Asher's help, I uncover nearly a million in lost revenue going back over ten years.

Mark's been patient.

He's been stealing from the business for a decade and increasing what he takes each year.

Embezzlement.

It's a crime, one I'll have to deal with because I can't ignore it. Those millions are unreported income the IRS will be interested in. If I don't do the right thing, they'll come after me for tax fraud, not to mention I'll have to pay back taxes on that income and any associated fines. That's one sure way to bankrupt my company.

But I'm going to do my own investigation and make sure I've got my ducks in a row. There are people to call, advice I need, and I can't talk to Brody.

I'm not ready for that.

So, I reach out to a couple of my professors at Stanford who specialize in embezzlement cases. They connect me with the FBI. After a week, I've retained a lawyer, and we have a plan in place. As for Mark, I want to give him the benefit of the doubt.

He's not in his office, which gives me a chance to look around. I find invoices from two separate trucking companies. We're a small operation, which means we contract out a lot of things, like the trucks which haul our grapes from the field to the warehouses.

There's no reason to pay two separate companies.

Using my camera, I scan the documents and send them to my lawyer. A closer examination reveals exactly what Brody suspects. Last year, the first company hauled only three-fourths of our total yield. The other company carried the rest. Going back ten years, it was a single truckload that was diverted. Mark methodically stepped up how much he skimmed as the years went by.

A quick call to the second trucking company is the final nail in the coffin. Sure enough, Mark diverted our crop and sent it to a large aggregator. He's been pocketing the profits they gave him. That knowledge guts me and I stagger against the wall, refusing to believe it, but know it for the truth it is.

Am I strong enough to face him alone?

That answer is a resounding no, but I know someone who can help.

"Hey, sweetie." Abbie kisses me on the cheek and sweeps into my kitchen. "You ready for this?"

Abbie knows everything I'm up to. My assumption is she keeps Brody in the loop. Knowing him, he most likely pumps his mother for any information about me. He hasn't tried to contact me, giving me the space I desperately asked him for. With the passing of every day, I miss him more and more, regretting that I sent him away, but I need to do this alone.

"Thanks for coming." I greet her with a weak smile.

"My pleasure." Abbie makes herself at home in my kitchen. "You're nervous." She bustles about, and oddly her activity soothes me.

"I've been a nervous wreck for weeks."

It's been three weeks since I talked to Brody. Like I asked, he assigned our account to a junior executive at Sterling Enterprises. Not that I believe in fate or anything, but we received our first list of recommendations, all laid out into the three different tiers. It provides the perfect opportunity to sit with Mark and discuss where to go from here.

"I imagine you have, sweetie. Something like this is hard. I can't imagine how this must feel for you."

One of the things I love most about Abbie La Rouge is how she separates our friendship from her maternal instincts with her boys. She's well aware Brody and I aren't speaking and steers the conversation away from any maternal meddling in our affairs. I need that because she's right. This is hard to do without friends.

"Are you sure there wasn't a rift between Mom and Uncle Mark?" I ask.

"Those two have been tight since forever. It was hard when your grandparents passed. Lucy had to step up, taking over control of the business, and taking care of her brother."

I sat down with my lawyer going over Mom's will and all the assets surrounding the business. Uncle Mark owns a minority share in the business, forty percent. Mom's sixty-percent of Atwood Estates is now mine. The land is separate from the business and has been held by my family for generations, and this is the key.

My family.

Not Mark's.

Step-siblings, Mom and Mark aren't technically related. That land passed from my grandmother, to my mother, and then to me. It's an uninterrupted legacy going back well over a hundred years. I need to know what Mark intends to buy me out of; is it the business or the land?

"Hello!" Mark calls out as he opens the kitchen door. "It's a beautiful day outside. Grapes are looking good. Harvest is coming soon." His eyes light up as he rubs his palms together. "And it smells like heaven in here." He goes to Abbie first, pulling her into a hug and kissing her cheek. "You really don't have to keep spoiling us, although, I don't mind if you do."

"You know it's my pleasure."

Abbie doesn't come over as often as she did that first week, but she still does the majority of our cooking. The fridge is full of her amazing meals, and I'm not ready to ask her to stop. First off, I'm pretty sure this is her way to grieve. Second, her food is out of this world. Thirdly, she's my connection to Brody.

"Oh, I'm sure the pleasure is ours." Mark gives a long, exaggerated sniff of the air. His eyes close as he takes in a deep inhale. "What do I smell?"

"I'm making shrimp Alfredo." Abbie turns back to the stove to stir the sauce. Alfredo can be touchy, requiring near constant attention or it'll scald and burn.

"Fabulous."

"Hey, Mark." I greet him with a hug, a kiss, and a smile. All the while, I feel like I'm going to throw up. "We've got some time before lunch. Do you want to go over the suggestions now? Or wait until after lunch?"

"We can do it now. I don't have a ton of time, but when you said Abbie was cooking, I couldn't resist."

"Perfect." I wave him over to sit beside me on the opposite side of the massive kitchen island. Sterling Enterprises sent everything over electronically, a part of their zero-paperwork philosophy, but I printed everything out. My brain simply works better with real paper.

"I pulled out the important bits, but here's the full report if you want to look at it." Four stacks of paper sit in front of me. One is the full file. The other three are the different tier recommendations. "Do you want to start with Tier One or Tier Three?"

"Have you looked them over?" His warm gaze settles on me.

I can't tell if the worry lines are real or an act. I hate everything about this. Conflict is not my friend, and I'm not a suspicious person by nature. I rub my palms on my jeans, trying to scrub off the sudden sweat.

"You look worried." He takes the Tier One list of requirements and glances at them.

"I am." I gesture vaguely at the piles. "It's a lot to take in, and honestly, I don't know how we're going to meet all their requirements."

"Well, give me a moment to take a look." His attention turns to the papers while I share a look with Abbie.

She's been silent this whole time but is ready to support me as I need it.

"Hmm…" He scans the list. "This is a bit more than I anticipated."

"A bit?" With no idea whether Brody doctored the requirements or not, knowing this confrontation was coming, I agree with Mark. It's far more than I anticipated too, and those are Tier One requirements. We have no choice but to implement them. "It's way more than I thought it would be. Honestly, it's overwhelming."

He nods and continues scanning.

I pick up the Tier Two recommendations. "These aren't much better, but at least we can counter with some of these."

"I don't think their idea of a counter is the same as ours." He holds his hand out and I give him the Tier Two list.

Abbie busies herself with lunch preparation while I sit and wait. I can't push too hard. I'm not that good at deception. Finally, he lowers the papers and leans back.

"What's your gut say?"

"My gut?" I play up my nerves. Not that it's hard. I'm a nervous wreck. "My gut says, cut and run."

"You can't be serious?" His brow arches, but all I see is the eager gleam in his eyes. I'm suspicious of everything and hate it.

"You know I'd never walk away from Atwood Estates, but I'm nervous."

"Look, I know you feel like you owe it to your mother to keep this place afloat, but maybe that's not what you need to do."

"What do you mean?"

"Only that she wanted to give you something, and I don't think that was a sinking business." He points to the papers. "We can get all this done. Nothing is too far out there, but if you're not one-hundred percent positive this is what you want, there's always a way out."

"How?"

"My offer still stands. I can buy you out. You deserve to pursue your dreams, rather than keep your mother's afloat."

"I don't know." I squirm in my seat. "How would that work exactly?"

"A simple transfer."

"You'll keep the business going?"

"I'll definitely try."

"So, I hand over my interest in the business? What about Mom's home?" I want to know if he's after the land.

Businesses come and go. If Atwood Estates goes bankrupt, I can start something new. That's not what I want, but I have the education and skills to run any business; at least that's what my diploma from Stanford says.

"Well…" He rubs at the back of his neck. "We'd need to transfer everything."

"Everything?"

"The land and business."

And there it is, proof he wants my land.

"Oh, I just assumed that was part of it."

"Technically, it is, but we'd want to transfer all of it."

*Technically, Uncle Mark, they are two entirely different things.*

But I don't let on that I know he's trying to swindle me out of my family's legacy.

My legacy.

Not his.

For the first time, I no longer see Mark as part of my family.

"And you would do that for me?"

"I can get something drawn up by the end of the week." He glances at his cuticles and looks up, like he's doing me a favor.

*Crook!*

*Thief!*

"Wow." I shift in my seat and try to look as nervous as possible.

"Sweetie, you might want to sit on this for a bit." Abbie moves around the kitchen, pulling out dishes and flatware.

"Here, let me help you." I grab the plates from her as she whispers in my ear.

"You're doing great."

I smile. Such a little thing, her words smooth away my anger. All I really need is someone in my corner supporting me. I need Brody, and while I adore Abbie, I can't help but wish he was here backing me up. Pain stabs at my heart as I realize how much I miss him. Too blinded by anger, I pushed him away when I should've kept him close.

Especially now.

"It's a generous offer, but I can't abandon you." I need to hold Mark off.

"Don't worry about me. I'm much more familiar with how everything works around here." He lifts the papers with Sterling

Enterprise's recommendations on them. "Whether with these guys or through some of my contacts."

*Contacts that will offer you twelve million for the land you want me to hand over for two million. Not in this lifetime.*

"So, what about these?" I point to the papers. "You don't want to proceed with Sterling Enterprises?"

"I probably want to sit on it a bit." He glances at the food Abbie sets out and gives another long sniff. "Now that food smells amazing. I can't wait to dig in."

*And I can't wait to slam the hammer down on you.*

But the approach to dealing with Mark needs to be handled delicately. Even though I have people in play: my lawyer, law enforcement, the advice of my professors at Stanford, I feel like I'm missing the biggest gun in my arsenal.

Abbie carries the conversation while we eat, getting Mark to talk about meaningless things. She steers the conversation away from business to harvest festivals and the upcoming holiday season. Her bright and bubbly personality works on me as much as it does on Mark. By the end of lunch, that bundle of nerves is gone. I laugh and smile, almost like normal, but I'm far from feeling normal, not after Mark's betrayal.

As soon as he leaves, Abbie leaves me to clean the dishes. It's the only concession she gives me. After fighting over it one night, I put my foot down and told her, *She who cooks, does not clean.* Once all the dishes are put away, I clutch my phone to my chest and head out to the porch to make some calls.

When I open the door, I pull to a sudden stop.

"Brody…"

FORTY-TWO

# Brody

For the past half hour, the sound of Grace moving in the kitchen drives me crazy.

*Give me time. I need space.*

Her words rumble in my head, but each time they surface, I push them away. It's been three, horrifically long weeks without her in my life.

I lost count of the number of times I caught myself running past her place. Asher thinks I've lost my mind. Since the day I dropped Grace off, I've stayed at La Rouge. Each morning, I head out for a grueling twenty-mile run and pass by the lane leading to her home. It's there where I force myself to continue, punishing my body, as I give her the space she needs.

I didn't do that today. Mom told me Grace was confronting Mark, and I'll be damned if I won't be there for her. I know the truth, Grace knows it as well, but that doesn't mean this won't be devastating.

As far as work is concerned, I called Hawke and told him I'd be working from home for the foreseeable future. Hawke didn't bat an eye; the bastard isn't stupid. He knows exactly what's going on, putting two and two together when I insisted on taking the Atwood Estates account on personally.

Mom's been great. She updates me each evening when I sink with exhaustion into her couch and complain about giving Grace space. Mom listens, tells me to suck it up, and cooks dinner while imparting her wisdom on why it's important I let Grace handle things on her own. Each night, I run home, passing by Grace's place once again, where I stoically stay away and give her *space*.

Today, however, I made a decision. Grace may need space, but I can barely breathe. I can no longer stay away. One way, or another, we're fixing this. But when I get to her place, I stop at the top step of her porch and debate the wisdom of my decision.

The door swings open, surprising me. When Grace's soft voice says my name, my heart leaps for joy.

"Grace."

Her entire body trembles. She clutches her phone tight to her chest, turning the knuckles of that hand white. Her sun-kissed complexion is gone, and in its place, a sickly shade of loss and betrayal takes over.

"I'm here." I open my arms, and she rushes into my embrace. The way my arms wrap around her feels right. We simply fit together.

She leans against me and doesn't say a word. That's okay; we don't need words. I breathe her in as she settles against me. My need for her hums through my blood as my fingers float through her hair, stroking through the tangles. I touch her face and sweep my fingers along her cheek and over her lips. She lifts her hands, encircling my back, and snuggles in.

"I miss you," she says.

"I missed you more." God, I missed holding her in my arms. I miss the scent of her hair and the sound she makes when she gasps.

Easing back, I take a long look at her and wonder how I survived three weeks without her.

"Mark was here," she says.

"I know."

"And…"

"I know."

I've kept tabs on Grace, first through Asher, then through Mom. Jesus, I wish I'd been by her side, but I've had time to think about what she said. I cup her jaw and tip her face to look at me.

I lean down, and she lifts on her toes, closing the distance, offering herself, and silently pleading for a kiss. My gaze unerringly latches onto her beautiful, angelic face, creased with pain and tarnished by betrayal. I wish to take all her pain and carry it for her.

Her eyes simmer, heating with the undeniable pull we share for each other. Blistering heat sweeps through me, manipulating the flow of my blood, and sending it to awaken a desire I can't contain.

My balls tingle. My cock swells. I hold Grace in my arms, knowing this is exactly where I belong.

I'm desperately in love with Grace Atwood.

This thing between us is a potent force. Like gravity, it pulls us together. Electricity shoots along my nerves until every cell in my body is aware of her presence. Bound together by the irresistible force of a brutally flawed, but healing love, we're destined to be together.

"These last few weeks have been the worst of my life." She turns her face to mine, tilting it up, seeking to reestablish our connection.

"They've been the worst." It's a truth I'm ashamed to admit.

If Grace felt a tenth of what I endured these past few weeks when I turned my back on her all those years ago, I don't deserve her forgiveness. I definitely don't deserve her love, but I'm hopeful. "You captivate me."

"Brody…"

"I have something to say."

For a decade, I've avoided the trap of relationships because some small part of me knew what I lost when I walked away from this amazing woman.

"You don't have to…"

"It's taken a decade too long, but we're together now. Or, at least, I hope that's still the case. Mom always told us that love is nothing without action. Trust means nothing without proof. And being sorry is meaningless without change."

"You don't have to say anything. I'm glad you're here."

"I'm not done."

I may never be done telling this woman how much I love her, how resilient she is, how strong, how amazing, how incredibly wonderful, and… I could go on and on. She lays her head against my chest and takes in a deep breath.

"I'm sorry for pushing you away."

"I love you, and I'll show you every day for the rest of my days how very much I'm in love with you. It's my hope that I never cause you to doubt me, or lose faith in me, and I promise to never break your trust again. I'm sorry for all the pain I brought into your life. It's my hope you'll forgive me, and continue to forgive me, when I fuck things up. I'm not perfect, but I have changed. I changed for you, but more importantly, I changed for myself. Before you came back into my life, I was existing, but not really living. I was going through the motions, floundering to find happiness with empty, meaningless sex. I thought that meant I was in control, but it was really a hopeless spiral. A spiral you pulled me out of—the day I saw you in the vineyard, I knew. I knew what I lost, and I understood what was missing in my life. I want you. Forever and always. If you need more time and space, I'll be honest, I don't know if I can give it to you. Each minute I'm not with you, feels like a living death. I need you, and if that means I need to give you more time, more space, then I will, but I hope that's not the case. Not when you need someone in your corner, fighting for you, or simply holding a towel and offering a sip of water while you fight your own battles."

Her eyes fill with tears and threaten to fall. I place the pads of my thumbs to her lower lids where I catch her pain, just like I'll be there to catch her when she falls, support her when she's weak, and stand beside her as she conquers the world.

"You're my everything." The truth of those words sink deep inside where it matters most. Grace is a part of me. She's the missing piece of my soul. "You make me whole."

"I don't know what to say." She sniffs, and the tears stream down her cheeks. Unable to stop them with my thumbs, I lean in and kiss her tears away.

"Tell me you love me, too."

"I love you."

"Tell me I can stay."

"You can stay."

"I'm going to be with you every step of the way, fighting with you, or for you." I gesture toward the front door. "How about we make some calls and bring Mark down?"

Her lower lip curls inward, and her tears dry up. She gives a curt nod. "I'd like that very much."

We head inside, and she makes the calls that seal Mark's fate. He doesn't know he picked the wrong woman to steal from. Once Grace is done with him, he'll have me on his ass, and I'll make the bastard pay.

My eyes track Grace as she puts everything in play. She's tenacious and fierce, methodical and insanely intelligent. For the first time, I see the power she would bring to the boardroom and reaffirm my vow to make all her dreams come true. I see a merger in our future, a way to save Atwood Estates without Sterling Enterprises stepping in, and if I can manage a billion-dollar company and be the CFO of a winery, there's no reason she can't do the same. I'll need to have a conversation with Asher about expanding operations.

Grace finishes her last call and places her phone down on the counter.

"Is it done?" I go to her. Like always, when I'm close to her, my insides heat and tighten. For the first time, I want more from a woman than a few hours of pleasure.

"The FBI will investigate. My lawyer is on board. The IRS won't be a problem for me, but Mark will have a lot on his plate." Her gentle smile makes my heart race. "And thank you for being here. I'm sorry I pushed you away. You were only looking out for me."

"I'm sorry I hurt you."

FORTY-THREE

## Grace

_______

"Are you ready?" Brody holds out his hand and helps me out of the car. His steady gaze lends strength, support, and love.

My love for him increases with each passing day. My desire visceral and my need unquenchable. I wake like this each and every day, but my craving is no longer soured by fear. By his actions, Brody proves his commitment to me—to us—each and every day. We've come a long way over the past two months and found our new center.

The intoxicating taste of him lingers on my lips from the kisses he wakes me with to the carnal sex that follows. Morning sex is quickly becoming one of my favorite times of the day.

He hovers over me, and the way his scent reaches out for me, coiling around me, my brain is hit by the comforting sense, not of familiarity, but rather solid, unwavering love.

"I wish I didn't have to be here." My hand goes to my stomach in a failed attempt to quiet the butterflies churning around inside of it.

It's been two months since I made the call. Two months since the FBI invaded Atwood Estates and arrested my uncle for embezzlement. He's been out on bail, but I haven't seen him since that day. I'll never forget the shock and anger when he realized what was happening.

Mark said nothing, not that he would with Brody and his brothers standing by my side, but he communicated his thoughts in the righteousness blazing in his eyes and by the twisted grimace on his face.

"I'll be right by your side." Brody stands beside me and loops an arm around my shoulders. "And you don't have to be here. It's just his arraignment. We can leave."

Nervousness piles on top of itself within my chest and my belly. I can't help it, but I'm a bundle of nerves. Terrified to see Mark in person again, I wish I could put this off.

"I know, but I feel like I have to be here."

My reasons aren't I can rationally explain. It has to do with a certain white dove who seems to have become a frequent visitor of late. I sense my mother's spirit at work and she's sending a message I can no longer ignore. It's time to live up to my name and practice the grace of forgiveness.

Mark took from me. He took from her. And, while I don't understand his motives, I feel like I need to see this through. I need to understand why he did what he did.

Two months of a forensic accounting team digging through our books, and countless inquiries from multiple state and federal agencies, it feels as if my entire life has been turned inside out and scoured clean. Two million is the finally tally. Two million in lost revenue skimmed off our profits over the span of a decade, most of that in the past three years.

Today is only the first of many steps. Mark's arraignment is where the charges against him will be officially read. He'll either plead guilty, or not guilty. That plea determines my next step. All I want is for him to give back what he took, but even failing to do that, I want to know why.

While hurt, I'm not out for blood. Mark's the only family I have left and I wish for some sort of resolution. That may, or may not, be possible, but I'm willing to forgive if he's willing to make things right.

If it wasn't for Asher, who stepped up to help me run Atwood Estates, and the new marketing campaign launched by Cage's brilliant mind, I would be bankrupt. Restitution wouldn't matter. As it is, I'm limping along. Brody recused himself from my account with Sterling Enterprises and assigned a junior member of their team to see us through this process, but he watches over the entire process like a hawk.

Even now, knowing what Mark did, I still think of Atwood Estates as ours. Brody recommended a lawsuit demanding a judicial dissolution of Atwood Estates, formally kicking Mark out of the company. He's adamant I seek full compensation for the lost profits.

Expensive, and time consuming, it will be some time before that bit of nastiness finishes. Part of me hopes Mark will just sign over his interest in Atwood Estates and make this a clean break, but he hasn't shown any inclination he'll do that.

Instead, he's been out of communication. Only our lawyers speak to one another. I should hate him for what he did, but the truth is far different. I miss my uncle and the loving relationship I thought we had. Brody thinks I'm too soft. I feel differently about the whole thing.

"I'm nervous about seeing him again." I can, at least, admit that.

I rub my hands up and down my arms. Brody doesn't understand why I'm not going for the jugular with Mark, but I've spent too many years with hatred infesting my heart; not for Mark, but rather for Brody.

If I've learned anything it's that I'm not willing to live my life like that. Forgiveness is a much more powerful, active, and freeing emotion. The proof of it stands beside me right now. If I can forgive Brody, then I owe it to Mark to be open and receptive as well.

"There's nothing he can do to hurt you." Brody kisses the top of my head as he snugs me tight against him.

"I don't think he's going to hurt me." *At least not more than he already has.*

Brody's been by my side the entire time, a stalwart buffer against Mark's plan to steal not only Atwood Estates, but the land passed down for generations from mother to daughter as well. He intended to take all of it and I've yet to really wrap my head around that.

I reach for Brody's hand. He's a big man, who towers over me, and I can't help but snuggle up against him.

In moments like this, sometimes I wonder what it would be like to expand our bedroom dynamic, but I'm in no rush. We've got our entire lives ahead of us to sort that out.

"He saw an opportunity to take something that didn't belong to him. He's done far more than hurt you." Brody tells me what I already know, but it's hard.

I don't want to be bitter as a result of this. He presses his lips to the top of my head, kissing me with gentle reassurance that he is there to support me, fight for me, or stand by my side while I battle my enemies on my own.

"Somedays, I wake up and think all of this will go away." I've given a lot of thought to what I should do about Mark. In this, Brody and I are at odds with each other.

"I know you were close to him, but you need to stop excusing what he did."

"I know." Forgiving is not the same as excusing, but I'm not up for arguing the distinction.

"Come on," Brody pulls me up the steps of the courthouse. "Let's get this over with. The sooner this is done, the sooner we can get home."

Home.

I love hearing that word on Brody's lips. For us, home is an amalgamation of Atwood Estates, La Rouge Vineyards, and Brody's apartment in the city. We rotate between all three, settling into a very strange routine.

He's right. There's no reason for me to be present at the arraignment, but I feel like I need to be here. I need to give Mark the chance to apologize.

To make amends?

I suppose I'm hopeful he wants me to stay in his life as much as I want him in mine. I can't help it. We're family.

Or maybe, I'm just too soft-hearted? Brody thinks I should cut all ties and walk away, but Mark is my only family as I am his.

Brody and I enter the courthouse and make our way through security. Brody asks for directions, then leads me down a maze of passageways to a very modest courtroom.

Instead of a bench, there's an overly large mahogany desk facing the room. Two smaller desks face it. Bannisters sit behind each of the smaller desks where five rows of bench seats fill up the room. The prosecution is present. Dara Rose sits in her seat with a briefcase open on the desk and manila folders arrayed out in front of her.

We approach and Brody speaks first. "Good morning, Dara."

She spins around and flashes a sweet smile. A gorgeous woman, she tones down her natural beauty with a severe bun which pulls her golden hair tight against her head.

"Nice to see you again." She stands and presses out the wrinkles of her pencil skirt. Dara shakes with Brody, then turns her attention to me. "How are you doing, Grace?"

"Nervous." We shake and her attention lands on my engagement ring. Unlike most other women, envy is absent in the way she responds to the ring.

I'm still figuring out how Dara knows Brody. I'm too nervous to ask, in case it looks like I'm digging for information.

"How are your brothers?" Dara turns her attention back to Brody.

"Cage is back in town."

"That's nice." Dara keeps her voice a monotone, but I detect something in her indifference.

"You should come out and visit. We're having a cookout tonight. Celebrating the end of the wine harvest."

"I wouldn't want to bother you."

"It's no bother."

My attention shifts between the two of them, not understanding why Brody pushes for Dara to join us. Tonight is supposed to be a family thing.

"I'll think about it."

Commotion at the back of the room draws our attention. The defense attorney walks in with Mark right beside him. Dara points to the seats behind her.

"Have a seat. I don't anticipate this taking long. It's mostly a formality."

Brody takes me to one of those seats before Mark gets too close. He stands protectively over me as Mark and his defense attorney pass us by.

Mark's gaze shifts to mine for a millisecond, then turns down as he stares at the space in front of him. He and his attorney take their seats and their heads bow close together as they exchange a hushed conversation.

Mark's attorney nods after something Mark says and he unbuttons his dark jacket for comfort. Mark doesn't wear a jacket, but he's dressed in business casual with khaki pants and a button-down shirt. No tie. Mark abhorrs ties.

There's no one else in the courtroom and an oppressive silence settles over the room while we wait for the judge.

A few minutes later, the judge enters. We rise and then take our seats again. Mark and his attorney remain standing as the judge begins the proceedings.

This will be the first time the formal charges against Mark will be read. His crime reaches felony status which carries the risk of jail time, significant fines, and restitution.

I don't want Mark to go to prison. I grip Brody's hand and squeeze tight. Dara explained all of this to me previously. In California, embezzlement greater than $950 is considered grand theft with the potential of two to three years state prison time. Brody wants them to throw the book at Mark.

I just wish we never made it here in the first place. Why did Mark do this to me? To us?

The judge reads of the formal charges as Mark stands beside his defense attorney. Finally, the judge reaches the end and asks that fateful question.

"Mark Atwood, how do you plea?"

Before answering, Mark bows his head. I don't know if he's praying, delaying, or what. His lawyer bends close and they have another short conversation. From the way Mark bristles, I sense he's not happy with whatever it is his attorney says.

Mark looks up, stares at the judge, then he surprises me and spins around. Rather than directing his response to the judge, he looks directly at me.

"I plead…"

I take in a breath and it feels as if my insides twist into a knot. If he pleads 'not-guilty' we have a long, arduous, legal battle ahead of us. Years worth of depositions and trials, headaches and heartaches.

I tense beside Brody. He places his arm around my shoulder and tugs me close. Mark's gaze shifts to Brody and he swallows thickly. I watch his Adam's apple bob and fall. I don't know what the two of them exchange in that heated glare, except Mark's gaze softens when he swings his focus back on me.

"I plead guilty, your Honor."

Mark's attorney glances at the floor and his shoulders slump. Dara looks surprised. Her gaze darts between me and Mark.

Despite all the evidence stacked against Mark, there was still a chance he could have the entire case dismissed. In some ways, I'm surprised as well. I don't know why he's not fighting it.

Does he want to go to jail?

I get it. We were ready for a long drawn out process, but not once did I expect a plea of guilty. That carries mandatory jail time. The fines will be exorbitant, and I'm sure the judge will order some amount of restitution.

"What the hell?" Brody's molars grind together and his entire body goes rigid.

"Why…?" The rest of what I was going to ask is lost when Mark mouths I'm sorry. I don't know if anyone sees it but me, but I find comfort in his silent apology.

The judge appears as confused at the rest of the room, but he quickly wraps things up, concluding Mark's arraignment. We stand as the judge departs then another awkward silence descends on the room.

"What the hell is he thinking?" Brody grinds his teeth. He shifts, but I place a hand on his thigh.

"Let me."

I could hate Mark. I could rake him over the coals and ruin the rest of his life. I could've done that and more with Brody, but I didn't with Brody and I won't with Mark. Edging around Brody, I make my way to the aisle.

While Mark's attorney puts his things together, Mark makes his way to me. There's pain in his gaze, a haunted expression, remorse lies there as well. That's all I need.

We don't speak, but I open my arms for him. Mark breaks down, choking on a sob, and buries himself in my embrace.

I don't know what the future holds for us, for him, but we'll face it together.

Like a family that fights and laughs, loves and argues, Mark and I will find our way through this.

Brody says nothing, but he stands close, arm's length away and ready to jump in and defend me, if the need arises.

Mark and I part. I swipe a tear from the corner of my eye and he does the same. We stare at each other, and then a smile lifts my lips and my spirit as well. I bet there's a white dove out there taking flight, and I know my mother has a hand in this.

I place my hand on Mark's chest and look up at him again. Things aren't settled between us, but the healing's begun.

"I'll see you later, cupcake." His attention shifts to Brody and he takes a step back.

"I'd like that." I take a step back as well and come up solidly against Brody's imposing presence.

Brody wraps an arm around my midsection and draws me back another step, and that's it.

Mark pivots and exits the courtroom. His lawyer hands something to Dara, then follows on Mark's heels, rushing out of the courtroom.

Dara packs up her briefcase and joins us in the aisle. "Well, that was unexpected."

"What happens next?" Brody clears his throat.

She blows out a breath. "I'll speak with the judge. There will be a sentencing hearing, but likely not for several months. White collar crime is not a priority with the way the courts are backed up, but I'll see what can be done. And then, there's this." She hands me the folder Mark's lawyer gave her.

"What's this?"

"Mr. Atwood has signed over his interest in Atwood Estates and will be making restitution for what he took."

"He did what?" My mouth gapes. I look at the folder, but I'm too surprised to read anything right now. "Does this mean he won't be going to prison?" I place my hand over my belly and notice all the butterflies are gone.

"It's possible, but hard to say. That will be left to the judge during sentencing, but this will weigh in your uncle's favor." Dara gives a shrug. "I guess we'll see what happens."

## FORTY-FOUR

## Brody

GRACE TAKES MY BREATH AWAY. THE CAPACITY OF THIS WOMAN TO forgive boggles the mind.

First me and now her uncle?

I can't say I'm happy about that last part. I want to cut off the man's balls and shove them down his throat. To take advantage of another person is despicable. To take advantage of someone in your family is not only deplorable but deserves the most severe censure and condemnation. I want to string him up and show the dishonorable asshole what it means to suffer.

He's repugnant. His actions are inexcusable, indefensible, and unworthy of forgiveness. I don't want him anywhere near Grace, but that's not my call to make.

Actually, when I think about all of that, those are words which could equally be used to describe me.

Abandoning Grace to the jackals at school, leaving her to endure their ridicule alone, was morally reprehensible on my part. To think I was cocky and arrogant enough to step into the role of her *protector*, in our eagerness to explore concepts we were too immature to understand, was an even more egregious sin.

I understand now how colossal that failure was. Back then, I was an arrogant, self-absorbed asshole who put my needs above those of the girl I promised to protect at all costs. Instead of protecting her, I used her to build my reputation.

I was such a goddamn putz.

And yet, I stand by her side today, protecting her, and find myself forgiven of all my sins.

Grace is a far better person than I am. I can only hope to be more like her, but as I stare at Mark's retreating backside, it's an effort to tamp down my instincts to tear into him for hurting my girl.

Grace and I make our way to the car and settle in for the long drive back to Napa. Tonight, I plan on staying at Atwood Estates, rather than La Rouge, despite what I said to Dara Rose. She wouldn't come out anyway, which is a shame. Cage needs a woman like her in his life.

And he had her, until he fucked up.

I laugh with the memory.

"What's so funny?" Grace glances over at me.

"Nothing much. Just thinking about Cage." I reach over and take her hand in mine. Lifting her hand to my lips I gently kiss the back of her knuckles. Beneath my thumb, her pulse accelerates.

"Does that have anything to do with inviting that lawyer over for dinner tonight?"

"Dara won't show."

"Why?"

"Cage and I share similar pasts."

"Considering the whole triplet thing, you need to be a bit more specific."

"Let's just say he was just as much, or more, of an asshole than I was."

"That really doesn't narrow anything down."

"I made my mistakes in high school. He fucked up in college."

"With Dara?"

"With Dara."

"Oh, tell me more."

"That's a long and involved story. Let's save it for later."

"That's no fun." She crosses her arms over her chest, which pushes her tits up.

I lick my lower lip and hold back a groan. No matter how many times I slip into her wet heat, it'll never be enough.

"Let talk about something else."

"Like what?"

"Like how do you feel? That's the first time you saw Mark in months. What do you think about his plea?"

"I think he feels bad about what he did."

"I don't know how you do it."

"Do what?"

"Forgive the assholes in your life." I trace the pad of my finger along her jawline and wish I wasn't driving right now.

"I think it's something my mother would want."

"I hope that's true."

"Why?"

"As the biggest asshole in your life, I'd like to think I'd have her forgiveness, not to mention her blessing as well."

Grace leans back and closes her eyes. She breathes out a long sigh and rolls her head until she's looking at me. Something in her expression puts me on alert.

"I think she would have. I learned everything I know about love and forgiveness from her." She reaches for my hand.

With an eye on the road, I split my attention between the traffic and the way Grace's light touch outlines each of my fingers before turning my hand palm up. She traces the lines on my palm and then threads her fingers with mine.

"Brody?"

"Yeah?"

"It's been a really long and emotionally draining day. I need…"

"What do you need?"

She turns her eyes on me. "I need to get out of my head."

"You do?"

"I very much do, and I know one sure way to do that."

"How's that?"

"Ask me what my word is."

The energy between us suddenly shifts. My girl needs a different kind of loving, the kind only I can provide.

"What's your word?"

"My word is *red*…"

Red. It's the word that defines us. The beginning and the end.

That word means everything.

We're on the cusp of what comes next, where she gives me permission to take her away. It's a tremendous gift and a terrible responsibility, but it's everything I crave.

And this time, I won't let her down.

As far as driving all the way to Napa, I take the next exit and circle back around to my—our apartment.

I'm going to take her to bed and show her how desperately and madly in love I am with her.

"Grace Atwood, you are my forever."

Her smile is sweet, but not nearly as sweet as the screams I'll soon be pulling from her throat, or the smile on her face when I go to one knee in the morning and show her exactly how *mine* she will be.

Grace Atwood means everything to me. I need her in my life and I intend to make her my wife.

But first, I intend to make love to the woman with the grace to forgive my sins and I make a solemn promise to never hurt her again. I can't wait for our forever to begin.

***

If you enjoyed reading about Brody and Garce, you'll also enjoy reading Richard and Rowan's story.

Check it out!<br>
Get your copy of Richard: Billionaire Boys Club!

**Would you give up a year of your life? What if the price was right? What if he's a prince?**

When Prince Richard's latest sexual faux pas results in another royal scandal, it's something the Crown will no longer tolerate. Fortunately, Richard stumbles across a company called Infidelity, which provides their exclusive clientele discretion and ironclad nondisclosure agreements. Powerful men take what they want, or buy it outright, and it looks like Prince Richard might have found the perfect solution to exploring his darker cravings. While paying for an intimate companion isn't his style, it makes sense. What better way to ensure his sex life will become front-page news?

Turns out companionship is cheap, but happiness?

At the end of his year-long agreement, will he be left with the tattered remains of what could have been?

Not if he has any say, but with the pressure of the Crown, privilege becomes a burden, and he may have no choice but to walk away.

**GRAB YOUR COPY OF THIS STEAMY, MODERN-DAY FAIRYTALE romance. Will Prince Richard be able to keep his modern-day Cinderella? Or will he lose it all? Click now to find out!**

**Richard**

# ELLZ BELLZ

## ELLIE'S FACEBOOK READER GROUP

If you are interested in joining the **ELLZ BELLZ**, Ellie's Facebook reader group, we'd love to have you.

Join Ellie's **ELLZ BELLZ**.
The **ELLZ BELLZ** Facebook Reader Group

Sign up for Ellie's Newsletter.
Elliemasters.com/newslettersignup

# Also by Ellie Masters

The LIGHTER SIDE

Ellie Masters is the lighter side of the Jet & Ellie Masters writing duo! You will find Contemporary Romance, Military Romance, Romantic Suspense, Billionaire Romance, and Rock Star Romance in Ellie's Works.

***YOU CAN FIND ELLIE'S BOOKS HERE:***

***ELLIEMASTERS.COM/BOOKS***

***Military Romance***

***Guardian Hostage Rescue Specialists***

*Rescuing Melissa*

*(*Get a FREE copy of Rescuing Melissa

when you join Ellie's Newsletter*)*

***Alpha Team***

*Rescuing Zoe*

*Rescuing Moira*

*Rescuing Eve*

*Rescuing Lily*

*Rescuing Jinx*

*Rescuing Maria*

***Bravo Team***

*Rescuing Angie*

*Rescuing Isabelle*

*Rescuing Carmen*

*Rescuing Rosalie*

*Rescuing Kaye*

*Cara's Protector*

*Rescuing Barbi*

### Charlie Team

*Rescuing Rebel*

*Rescuing Stitch*

### Military Romance
### Guardian Personal Protection Specialists

*Sybil's Protector*

*Lyra's Protector*

### The One I Want Series
### (Small Town, Military Heroes)
### By Jet & Ellie Masters

EACH BOOK IN THIS SERIES CAN BE READ AS A STANDALONE AND IS ABOUT A DIFFERENT COUPLE WITH AN HEA.

*Saving Abby*

*Saving Ariel*

*Saving Brie*

*Saving Cate*

*Saving Dani*

*Saving Jen*

### Rockstar Romance
### The Angel Fire Rock Romance Series

EACH BOOK IN THIS SERIES CAN BE READ AS A STANDALONE AND IS ABOUT A DIFFERENT COUPLE WITH AN HEA. IT IS RECOMMENDED THEY ARE READ IN ORDER.

*Ashes to New (prequel)*

*Heart's Insanity (book 1)*

*Heart's Desire (book 2)*

*Heart's Collide (book 3)*

*Hearts Divided (book 4)*

*Hearts Entwined (book5)*

*Forest's FALL (book 6)*

*Hearts The Last Beat (book7)*

### *The LaRouge Triplets*

*Asher*

*Brody*

*Cage*

### *Billionaire Romance*

### *Billionaire Boys Club*

*Hawke*

*Richard*

### *Contemporary Romance*

*Cocky Captain*

### *Romantic Suspense*

EACH BOOK IS A STANDALONE NOVEL.

*The Starling*

*~AND~*

### Science Fiction

*Ellie Masters writing as L.A. Warren*

*Vendel Rising: a Science Fiction Serialized Novel*

# About the Author

ELLIE MASTERS is a multi-genre and Amazon Top 100 best-selling author, writing the stories she loves to read. These are dark erotic tales. Or maybe, sweet contemporary stories. How about a romantic thriller to whet your appetite? Ellie writes it all. Want to read passionate poems and sensual secrets? She does that, too. Dip into the eclectic mind of Ellie Masters, spend time exploring the sensual realm where she breathes life into her characters and brings them from her mind to the page and into the heart of her readers every day.

Ellie Masters has been exploring the worlds of romance, dark erotica, science fiction, and fantasy by writing the stories she wants to read. When not writing, Ellie can be found outside, where her passion for all things outdoor reigns supreme: off-roading, riding ATVs, scuba diving, hiking, and breathing fresh air are top on her list.

She has lived all over the United States—east, west, north, south and central—but grew up under the Hawaiian sun. She's also been privileged to have lived overseas, experiencing other cultures and making lifelong friends. Now, Ellie is proud to call herself a Southern transplant, learning to say y'all and "bless her heart" with the best of them. She lives with her beloved husband, two children who refuse to flee the nest, and four fur-babies; three cats who rule the household, and a dog who wants nothing other than for the cats to be his best friends. The cats have a different opinion regarding this matter.

Ellie's favorite way to spend an evening is curled up on a couch, laptop in place, watching a fire, drinking a good wine, and bringing forth all the characters from her mind to the page and hopefully into the hearts of her readers.

*FOR MORE INFORMATION*
elliemasters.com

facebook.com/elliemastersromance
x.com/Ellie__Masters
instagram.com/ellie_masters
bookbub.com/authors/ellie-masters
goodreads.com/Ellie_Masters

# Connect with Ellie Masters

Website:
elliemasters.com
Amazon Author Page:
elliemasters.com/amazon
Facebook:
elliemasters.com/Facebook
Goodreads:
elliemasters.com/Goodreads
Instagram:
elliemasters.com/Instagram

# Final Thoughts

I hope you enjoyed this book as much as I enjoyed writing it. If you enjoyed reading this story, please consider leaving a review on Amazon and Goodreads, and please let other people know. A sentence is all it takes. Friend recommendations are the strongest catalyst for readers' purchase decisions! And I'd love to be able to continue bringing the characters and stories from My-Mind-to-the-Page.

Second, call or e-mail a friend and tell them about this book. If you really want them to read it, gift it to them. If you prefer digital friends, please use the "Recommend" feature of Goodreads to spread the word.

Or visit my blog https://elliemasters.com, where you can find out more about my writing process and personal life.

Come visit The EDGE: Dark Discussions where we'll have a chance to talk about my works, their creation, and maybe what the future has in store for my writing.

Facebook Reader Group: Ellz Bellz

Thank you so much for your support!

Love,

Ellie

# THE END

www.ingramcontent.com/pod-product-compliance
Lightning Source LLC
Chambersburg PA
CBHW021229190726
48289CB00005B/1245